# WITHOUT ARMOR

# WITHOUT ARMOR

## BY JAMES HILTON

NEW YORK
WILLIAM MORROW & COMPANY
MCMXXXV

PRINTED IN THE U. S. A. BY
QUINN & BODEN COMPANY, INC.
RAHWAY, N. J.

JAMES HILTON IS AN INTERESTING
phenomenon in the world of Youth.  It is a banality to say
that today Youth is radical.  The testimony of the colleges,
above all, the rôle that Youth has played in all the revolutions
of the last fifteen years, bear the statement out.  Youth, con-
fronting contemporary society, rejects it, and being young
presses toward a new goal.  In all countries today youth leans
toward a radical solution of the social problem; inclines toward greater social—therefore state—control; is impatient of
the past and skeptical of history; is less and less concerned
with the adventure of the individual soul and more and more
caught up in the corporate adventure.

This influences the whole of the new literature. Among the
young, today, it is almost a prerequisite of any kind of writing
to state, at the outset, one's social standpoint.  The "important" novelist must be, in a measure, a pamphleteer and the
literature of the young is the literature of revolt.  It is false
to believe that no real art can be produced in this atmosphere.
The tensions of the present world produce their own themes
and their own passions; and passion is one essential element
of a work of art.  Clifford Odets' "Waiting for Lefty" is not
a bad play because it is written by a radical who uses the
theater, his natural medium, to express the passion of his belief.  On the contrary, the vigor and passion which make Mr.
Odets a radical also, as it happens, make him a good play-
wright.  Whether he would be as good a one should the dream
become reality is another question.

Now, the youthful author of this book stands out amongst
his contemporaries by reason of his conservatism.  But it is—

if this is not a paradox—a conservatism with a difference. It is almost completely in the realm of the spirit. James Hilton is acutely conscious of the world about him, delicately sensitive to it. He is aware of seismic change and utterly without revolt against it, feeling, as he does, its inevitability. He even, in the flesh, participates in it; he has not buried himself in any external ivory tower. But his passion is elsewhere. Passionately he loves certain qualities of the English mind and soul; and these qualities he believes to be as eternal, or as worth immortalizing, as anything in this revolutionary world. These qualities are disinterestedness, tolerance, fair play, and forbearance. Mr. Hilton believes in and admires—he actually does—gentleness. No more lovely tribute to gentleness has been written in our time than *Good-bye, Mr. Chips,* with perhaps a touch of allegory in the "Good-bye." *Lost Horizon,* again, is a fantastic picture of a last refuge in the world where gentle souls may dwell. And *Without Armor,* his latest novel to be published in America, sounds the same note.

Laid in Russia—the Russia of the revolutionary wars, of the battles between Whites and Reds, and ranging throughout the length and breadth of that titanic country—this novel is not a novel about Russia. It is a novel about a gentle Englishman. For a young novelist the theme is big, perhaps too big. The earthquake and the fire—and the still, small voice. Mr. Hilton's hero is the still, small voice.

It is the novel, of course, of a romantic. Mr. Hilton is at home in this world, because like all romantics he craves experience, accepts everything, even pain, and is able to transmute it into something rich and strange. All that he writes has a touch of romantic nostalgia. The best of what he writes has a curious—I might call it angelic—quality. Because certainly in the battle between angels and earthly creatures—Mr. Hilton believes in this eternal battle—he is on the side of the angels.

DOROTHY THOMPSON

*Barnard, Vermont.*
*August 1st, 1935.*

*Without Armor* WAS PUBLISHED in America six months after *Lost Horizon,* yet before *Lost Horizon* began to win popularity; thus it missed the wider appeal it might otherwise have had; and hence this new edition, which I am chiefly glad of because I have a personal fondness for the book itself.

It is curious, this fondness an author has for certain of his own books. He remembers when and where he wrote them, what private affairs were going on at the time, whether he wrote easily or with difficulty, whether there were interruptions, and how he got through the cold spell that so often comes in the middle of the job, when he is apt to wonder with horrible detachment whether his life is worth living and (that being grudgingly admitted) whether it would not have been more fun to breed pedigreed Alsatians.

In all these respects the writing of *Without Armor* left me pleasant memories; the first snag came later, when an English publisher to whom the manuscript was originally offered turned it down because he thought there were not enough people interested in Russia. I didn't think he was right, and the book's moderate success, even when it first appeared, made me sure that he wasn't. Anyhow, not being interested in Russia seems to me rather like not being interested in traffic-signals. It may be magnificent, but that is all.

Of course it is possible to be interested in a subject without wanting to read a novel about it. I meet people nowadays who say that they never read novels, that the novel as an art-form is on its last legs, and so on; and I half sympathize with them whenever I read a really dull novel or a really interesting biography. I say "dull" and "interesting" rather than "bad" and "good," because they are more personal and therefore safer words. I know what interests me, whereas I only *think* I know what is good. And because it interests me more, I confess I have a weakness for a novel that tells a story. It can do lots of other things besides, and its scenes can be laid in Tennessee or Timbuctoo or Tibet; but a story, please, a story.

Which tempts me to suggest that if the novel really is on its last legs, this may be because its essential story-foundation has been neglected amidst the various experiments through which it is now passing—or, as some would say, passing out. I believe that people like stories, and I believe that romantic and adventurous stories will hold their popularity because, with all its drawbacks, the romantic and adventurous view of life is the most sensible. Whatever things are false, these at least are true—the fervor of youth, the sadness of age, the thrill of danger, the splendor of achievement. That these things are backgrounded by the crazy litter of so much that nowadays passes for civilization does not dispossess them of their inherent virtue; it rather outlines them for our wonder. For the wonder certainly is that in a world like ours we still have them.

*Without Armor,* then, is primarily a story, an adventure-story if you like. It does not pretend or attempt to propagate anything—this being timely information in a foreword to any novel about Russia. I have my political opinions, but they are a mixed lot, on the whole, and I would not spoil a novel with them. My sympathies are certainly neither Red nor White enough to make me passionate over sun-bronzed citizens of the Soviet worshiping their new tractors, or over exiled princesses pawning their last jewels. I just felt, before and while I was at work on the book (and I think so still), that Russia during the first quarter of the century was probably the biggest anvil on which world-history was being hammered out; and therefore, *ipso facto,* it must be grand territory for the novelist. So I wrote *Without Armor,* and I enjoyed writing it.

James Hilton

*London, August, 1935.*

PART ONE

PROLOGUE

"THERE DIED ON THE 12TH inst. at Roone's Hotel, Carrigole, Co. Cork, where he had been staying for some time, Mr. Ainsley Jergwin Fothergill, in his forty-ninth year. Mr. Fothergill was the youngest son of the Reverend Wilson Fothergill, of Timperleigh, Leicestershire. Educated at Barrowhurst and at St. John's College, Cambridge, he was for a time a journalist in London before seeking his fortune abroad. Since 1920 he had been closely associated with the plantation rubber industry, and was the author of a standard work upon that subject."

So proclaimed the obituary column of the *Times* on the morning of October 19, 1929. But the *Times* gets to Roone's a day and a half late, and Fothergill was already beneath the soil of Carrigole churchyard by then. There had been some slight commotion over the burial; an English priest had wired at the last moment that the man was a Catholic. This seemed strange, for he had never been noticed to go to Mass; but still, there was the telegram, and since most Carrigole folk were buried as Catholics anyway, the matter was not difficult to arrange.

There was also an inquest. Fothergill had apparently died in his sleep; one of the maids took up his cup of tea in the morning and actually left it on his bedside table without knowing he was dead. She told the district coroner she had said, "Here's your tea, sir," and that she thought he had smiled in answer. Nobody found out the truth till nearly noon. Then a doctor who happened to be staying at the hotel saw the body and said it must have been lifeless for at least ten hours.

Just in time for the inquest a London doctor arrived to testify that Fothergill had consulted him some two months before about a heart complaint. It was the sort of thing that might finish off anyone quite suddenly, so of course all was clear, on the evidence, and the verdict "Death from natural causes" came in with record speed.

The whole affair provided an acute though temporary sensation at Roone's Hotel, which, though the season was almost over, chanced to be fairly full at the time owing to a cruiser in harbor. Roone himself was rather peeved; he was just beginning to work up his place after the many years of "trouble," and it certainly did him no good to have guests dying on him in such a way. He was especially annoyed because it had all got into the Dublin and London papers—that, of course, being due to Halloran, Carrigole's too ambitious journalist, who would (Roone said) sell his best friend's reputation for half a guinea.

As for the dead man, Roone could only shrug his shoulders. Rather crossly he told the occupants of his crowded private bar how little he knew about the fellow. Never set eyes on him till the September, when he had arrived from Killarney one evening with a small suitcase. Evidently hadn't meant to stop long, and at the end of a week had sent to London for more luggage. Very quiet sort, civil and all that, but somehow not the kind of chap a fellow would naturally take to. . . . Yes, practically teetotal, too—nearly as bad for business as the Cook's

2

people who came loaded with coupons for all they took and drank nothing but water. "Although, by the way," Roone added, "he did come in here for a nightcap the evening before—I remember serving him."

"Yes, I remember too," put in a plus-foured youth. "I made some casual remark to him about something or other—just to be polite, that was all—but he hardly answered me. Rather surly, I thought at the time."

At which Mrs. Roone intervened, tartly: "Of course it was easy to see what he was stopping on here for, and more shame to him, I say."

Everyone in the bar nodded, for everyone had been waiting for that matter to be mentioned. There had been an American girl staying at the hotel with her mother; the two had been the only guests with whom the dead man had struck up any sort of acquaintance. He had gone for drives and picnics with them; he had taken his meals at their table; he had sometimes danced with the girl in the evenings. He was after her, Mrs. Roone said, bluntly, and as he had plenty of money the artful old mother was trying to hook him.

"Oh, so he had money, then?" enquired the youth in plus-fours.

"Money? Why do you suppose that London doctor came all the way here to give evidence at the inquest if it wasn't for a fine fat fee? As a matter of fact, there were some people here a few weeks ago who said for sober truth they knew he was worth half a million—all made out of rubber, so they said." Mrs. Roone's voice rose to a shriek as she added: "Half a million indeed, and old enough to be the girl's father, as well as liable to drop dead at any minute! Disgraceful, I say!"

"D'you think the girl was after him too?"

3

"Maybe she was. Girls will do anything for money these days."

Here a youthful red-cheeked naval lieutenant interposed. "Personally, Mrs. Roone, I think I'd give her the benefit of the doubt—the girl, I mean. I spoke to her once or twice—danced with her once, too—and she seemed to me a very quiet, innocent sort of kid."

He spoke rather shyly, and a colleague, who had drunk quite enough, shouted: "Innocent? Too damned innocent for you, eh, Willie?"

"Anyhow," answered Mrs. Roone, with final truculence, "the way they both cleared off was quite enough for me. The very afternoon that we were all fussed and bothered about finding the man dead, up comes the old woman to have her bill made out in a hurry—must get away—catching the boat at Queenstown, or something or other. Disappointed, I suppose, because her trick hadn't worked in time. I didn't see the girl before they left."

"Well, well, she's had a narrow escape," said Roone, drinking, "though maybe not the narrowest she ever will have if she's going to go about dancing with young naval lieutenants, eh?"

They all laughed. Just then the *Times* arrived, and somebody in the bar, opening the paper casually, discovered Fothergill's obituary. They all crowded round and read it through with growing exasperation—it told so little that they would have liked to know. The son of a country parson, a public school neither good nor quite bad, Cambridge, journalism, rubber. What could anyone make of it? The youth in plus-fours fully expressed the general opinion when he commented: "Doesn't sound a particularly exciting career, does it?"

4

"And it says nothing about a wife," said Roone, "so I suppose he never married."

That was doubtfully accepted as a probable conclusion.

"Well, well," added Roone, pouring more whisky into his soda, "he wasn't *my* kind of chap, and I don't care who hears me say so. Neither a good Catholic nor a good Protestant nor a good anything else, I should say."

Which seemed the end of a rather unpleasant matter.

PART TWO

AINSLEY JERGWIN FOTHERGILL

was born in 1880.  He had five brothers and four sisters, and his father's living yielded seven hundred a year.  His mother died in 1881, having never quite got over her most recent contribution to the family, and the Reverend Wilson, left to keep house with ten children, wandered helplessly about his parish as if he were the last person on earth responsible for his own situation.  He was a large heavily-built man with fat hands and a bald head; he did his job in a dull, conscientious way, and thrashed his elder children irregularly and without relish.  He was an Evangelical and a Gladstonian Liberal; he disliked Dissent, had hated the Oxford Movement, and had a superstitious horror of Rome.  It was his habit to preach hour-long sermons explaining the exact meaning of Greek and Hebrew words to a congregation largely composed of farmlaborers.

A widowed sister came to keep house for him in due course; her husband had been an army officer accidentally killed in India in an age when few officers of either service ever died of anything more exciting than cirrhosis of the liver.  Aunt Nellie never tired of boasting of her unique bereavement, and it was she who had principal charge of Ainsley.  She had been a school teacher in earlier life, and along with two of his sisters the boy obtained from her a fairly complete grounding in reading, writing, simple arithmetic, and the sort of geography that consists of knowing what belongs to England. Barbara and Emily, fifteen months and two and a half years older than their brother respectively, had no aptitude for learning anything of any kind; Ainsley, even by the age of five, had far outstripped them. He was, indeed, a bright, fairly good-looking child—dark-eyed, dark-haired, well-molded, but perhaps (Aunt Nellie thought, doubtfully) "a little foreign-looking."

Timperleigh was a dull village in the midst of passable hunting country, and the Reverend Wilson, despite his small income, managed to hunt once a week during the season. It meant that the elder children could not be sent to a good school, but that did not trouble him. He hunted in the same joyless, downright manner as he preached and thrashed. Sometimes the hunt would meet in the rectory drive and the children would run about among the horses and dogs and have their heads patted by high-up, gruff-voiced men in scarlet coats. Ainsley liked this, but not quite so much as he enjoyed having tea in the kitchen with Cook. She was called Cook, but she was really only a good-natured person of middle age who, being also mentally deficient, had been willing for years to do all the rough work of the household in return for a miserably poor wage. Ainsley was fond of her, and the look of the large rectory kitchen, with the window-panes slowly changing from gray to black and the firelight flickering on all the pots and dish-covers, gave him a comfortable feeling that he was certain only Cook could share. And her talk seemed far more thrilling than any fairy-story; she had been born in Whitechapel, and she made Whitechapel seem a real place, full of real people and real if horrible happenings; whereas Capernaum, which his father talked about in Sunday sermons, and Gibraltar, which Aunt Nellie insisted belonged to England, were vague, shadowy, and impossible to believe in.

When Ainsley was seven, his father was killed in a hunting mishap. Aunt Nellie, behind a seemly grief, was again rather thrilled; next to being trampled to death on an Indian polo-ground, to die on the hunting-field was perhaps the most socially eligible of all earthly exits. The boy, quite frankly, felt no grief at all; he had had hardly anything to do with his father, having not yet attained the age of chastisement. Nor was he old enough to realize the problem presented by the existence of himself and his nine brothers and sisters. There was practically no money, not even insurance; the family, in terms of hard cash, was scarcely better off than that of a deceased farm-laborer. Fortunately, the Reverend Wilson had been one of as large a family as his own, and communication was soon and inevitably opened up with uncles and aunts, many far distant and some almost mythical. After long and peevish negotiations the family was divided somehow or other amongst such relatives, until only the two youngest remained. Then, in sheer desperation, a letter was written to Sir Henry Jergwin, whose wife had been Aunt Helen, and after whom the youngest Fothergill had been hopefully, but so far fruitlessly, named. Could Sir Henry do anything for Barbara, aged eight, and for Ainsley Jergwin, aged seven? The great man commanded the children to visit him at his London house; they were taken there by Aunt Nellie and solemnly exhibited. After a week he decided; he would have the boy, but not the girl. So Barbara, after further struggles, was pushed on to one of the other uncles, while Ainsley came to live at a big Victorian house in Bloomsbury already inhabited by his uncle, a secretary, a butler, a cook, a coachman, three maids, and a gardener.

Sir Henry, in fact, was tolerably rich. He had always cultivated influential friendships in the City, and he was also editor and proprietor of the *Pioneer,* a weekly paper of Liberal views. Sixty-three years of age, with a vigorous body, an alert mind, a mellow, booming voice, and an impressively long and snow-white beard, he was almost as well-known as he wished to be. He entertained; he was invited to speak at public dinners; he knew everybody; Garibaldi had stayed a night at his house; Gladstone had knighted him. Besides all this, his reputation as a man of letters stood high—and curiously high, for he had written nothing that could be considered really first-rate. Only, all along, he had had the knack of making the most of everything he did; even a very mediocre poem he had once composed had managed an entry into most of the anthologies. Somehow, too, he had got himself accepted as an authority on Elizabethan literature; he had edited the Hathaway edition of Shakespeare, and thousands of school children had fumbled over his glossaries. Surmounting and in addition to all else, the man was a character; should any big controversy arise in the press, he was always asked for his opinion, and always, without fail, gave it. His views, though unexciting, stood for something that still existed in far greater proportions than the brilliant youngsters realized—a certain slow and measured solemnity that flowed in the bloodstream of every Englishman who had more than a thousand pounds in Consols.

Sir Henry had begotten no children; he took Ainsley in the spirit of a martyr bearing his cross, and in the same spirit engaged a German governess. This capable person added history and music to the list of things the boy was supposed to have been taught; later on a beginning was made with French and German. The great Sir Henry rarely saw either him or her; sometimes, however, Ainsley was conducted into the library "to see the books" and to be called "my little man" and smiled at. "These," explained Sir Henry, on more than one such occasion, sweeping his arm towards the rows of shelves, "are my best friends, and some day you will find them your best friends, also." Ainsley was never quite certain whether this was a promise or a threat.

When he was twelve, Sir Henry sent him to Barrowhurst.

Barrowhurst was not a very old foundation; Liberal and Evangelical in tendency, it had several times entertained Sir Henry as its Speech Day guest of honor. Situated in wild moorland country, it provided a vast change from the atmosphere of governesses and Bloomsbury gardens. At first Ainsley reveled in the freedom suddenly offered him; for the first time in his life he could walk about on his own, read books of his own choosing, and make friends without the frosty surveillance of grownups. He did not, however, make many friends. He was rather shy and reserved in manner; amongst the school in general he was for a long time hardly known, and the masters did not care for him because he soon displayed that worst sin of the schoolboy—an indisposition to fit in to one or other of the accepted classifications. He was not exactly troublesome, and his work was always satisfactory; only, somehow or other, he was difficult to get on with; he was apt to ask questions which, though hardly impertinent, were awkwardly unanswerable; he wouldn't respond, either, to the usual opening gambits of schoolmasterly approach. For some reason he hated games, yet he wasn't by any means the too brainy, bookish youngster; on the contrary, he was physically strong and sturdily built, and soon became actually the best swimmer and gymnast the school had known for years.

There was another Fothergill at the school of a different family, and Ainsley, to avoid mistakes, always signed his papers with a very large and distinguishable "A.J." This became such a characteristic that he began to be called "A.J." by his friends, and the initials finally became an accepted nickname.

In his third year he suddenly startled everybody by leading a minor rebellion. There was a master at the school named Smalljohn who had a system of discipline for which A.J. had gradually conceived an overmastering hatred. The system was this: Smalljohn stood in front of the class, gold watch in hand, and said: "If the boy who did so-and-so does not declare himself within twenty-five seconds I shall give the whole form an hour's detention." One day, after confessing himself, under such threat of vicarious doom, the author of some trivial misdeed, A.J. calmly informed his fellows that it was the last time he ever intended to do such a thing. Couldn't they see that the system was not only unfair but perfectly easy to break down if only they all tackled it the right way? And the right way was for no one ever to confess; let them put up with a few detentions—Smalljohn would soon get tired of it when he found his system no longer worked. There are a few Barrowhurst men who will still remember the quiet-voiced boy arguing his case with an emphasis all the more astonishing because it was the first case he had ever been known to argue.

He carried the others with him enthusiastically and the

next day came the test. He was whispering to a neighbor; Smalljohn heard and asked who it was. Silence. Then: "If the person who whispered does not confess within twenty-five seconds the whole form will be detained for an hour." Silence. "Fifteen seconds more. . . . Ten seconds. . . . Five. . . . Very well, gentlemen, I will meet the form at half-past one in this room."

After that afternoon's detention Smalljohn announced: "I am sorry indeed that thirty-three of your number have had to suffer on behalf of a certain thirty-fourth person whose identity, I may say, I very strongly suspect. I can assure him that I do not intend to let a coward escape, and I am, therefore, grieved to say that until he owns up I shall be compelled to repeat this detention every day."

It was nearing the time of house-matches and detentions were more than usually tiresome. A.J. soon found his enemies active and even his friends inclined to be cool. After the third detention he was, in fact, rather disgracefully bullied, and after the fourth he gave in and confessed. He had expected Smalljohn to be very stern and was far more terrified to find him good-humored. "Pangs of conscience, eh, Fothergill?" he queried, and A.J. replied: "No, sir."

"No? That sounds rather defiant, doesn't it?"

A.J. did not answer, and Smalljohn, instead of getting into a temper, positively beamed. "My dear Fothergill, I quite understand. You think my system's unfair, don't you?—I have heard mysterious rumors to that effect, anyhow. Well, my boy, I dare say you're right. It *is* unfair. It makes you see how impossible it is for you to be a sneak and a coward—it brings out your better self—that better self which, for some perverse reason, you were endeavoring to stifle. To a boy who is really not half the bad fel-

12

low he tries to make out, my system is perhaps the unfairest thing in the world. . . . Well, you have been punished, I doubt not—for apart from the still small voice, your comrades, I understand, have somewhat cogently expressed their disapproval. In the circumstances, then, I shall not punish you any further. And now stay and have some cocoa with me."

"If you don't mind, sir," answered A.J. not very coherently, "I'm afraid I must go. I've got a letter to finish—"

"Oh, very well, then—some other evening. Goodnight."

And the next morning Smalljohn, whose worst crime was that he thought he understood boys, recounted in the common-room how magnanimity had melted young Fothergill almost to tears—how with shaking voice the boy had declined the cocoa invitation and had asked to be allowed to go.

It had been A.J.'s first fight, and he fully realized that he had lost. What troubled him most was not Smalljohn's victory but the attitude of his fellows; if they had only stood with him Smalljohn could have been defeated. Yet they called him a coward because in Rugby football, which he was compelled to play although he disliked it, he sometimes showed that he didn't consider it worth while to get hurt. At the end of his third year the headmaster's report summed him up, not too unreasonably, as: "A thoughtful boy, with many good qualities, but apt to be obstinate and self-opinionated. Is hardly getting out of Barrowhurst all he should."

A.J. had two adventures at Barrowhurst altogether; the first was the Smalljohn affair, which was no more than a nine days' wonder and certainly did not add to his popularity; but the second was in a different class; it established his fame on a suddenly Olympian basis, and passed, indeed, into the very stuff of Barrowhurst tradition. Two miles away from the school is the tunnel that carries the Scotch expresses under the Pennines. It is over three miles long, boring under the ridge from one watershed to another. A.J. walked through it one school half-holiday. Platelayers met him staggering out, half-deafened and half-suffocated, with eyes inflamed, soot-blackened face, and hands bleeding where he had groped his way along the tunnel wall. He was taken to the school in a cab, and had to spend a week in bed; after which he was thrashed by the headmaster. He gave no explanation of his escapade beyond the fact that he had wanted to discover what it would be like. He agreed that the experience had been thoroughly unpleasant.

A.J.'s fourth year was less troubled. He was in the sixth form by then, preparing for Cambridge, and was left to do pretty much as he liked. The tunnel affair had given him prestige of an intangible kind both with boys and masters, and he spent much of his time reading odd books on all kinds of subjects that form no part of a public school curriculum. He cycled miles about the moorland countryside picking up fossils and making rubbings of old brasses in churches; he also (and somehow quite incidentally) achieved an official Barrowhurst record by a long jump of twenty feet. His sixth form status carried prefecture with it, and rather to everyone's surprise he made an excellent prefect—straightforward, firm, and tolerant.

He went to Cambridge in the autumn of 1898; his rooms at St. Jude's overlooked the river and the Backs, being among the best situated in the University. Sir

Henry made him a fairly generous allowance and began to hope that the boy might prove some good after all, despite the tepid reports from Barrowhurst. A.J. liked Cambridge, of course. He didn't have to play games, there were no schoolmasters with their irritating systems, he could read his queer books, listen to string quartets, and wield a geologist's hammer to his heart's content. The only thing he seemed definitely disinclined for was the sort of work that would earn him a decent degree. Sir Henry encouraged him to join the Union, and he did so, though he never spoke. He made one or two close friends, and was well liked by those who knew him at all. (He was still called "A.J."—the nickname had followed him to Cambridge through the agency of Barrowhurst men.) Most of the vacations he spent in Bloomsbury; of late years he had seen less and less of his brothers and sisters, several of whom had emigrated. He also traveled abroad a little—just to the usual places in France, Germany, and Switzerland.

He had no particular adventures in Cambridge, and left no mark on university history unless it were by the foundation of a short-lived fencing club. He had picked up a certain skill with the foils in Germany; it was a typically odd sort of thing to capture his enthusiasm.

He took a mediocre pass degree in his third year and then wondered what on earth came next. Sir Henry was disappointed and made it very clear that he did not intend to support him any longer. A.J. fully agreed; he did not want to be supported; he would certainly find something to do of some kind or other, but he was completely vague about it, and there were so many jobs which, for one reason or another, were impossible. He did not care for the services; he had no vocation for the church; his degree was not good enough for schoolmastering or for diplomacy or for the law. Clearly, then, very little remained, and when, in the summer of 1901, he left Cambridge for good, it was understood that he was to become a journalist and that Sir Henry would "find him something." In August he went abroad for a month, and it was while he was doing the conventional Rhine tour that he received a typewritten letter signed "Philippa Warren" and conveying the information that Sir Henry's former secretary, a Mr. Watts, had died of pneumonia and that she had been appointed in his place. He thought little of it, or of her, except to reflect that Sir Henry's choice of a female secretary would probably be based on dignity rather than elegance. At the beginning of September he returned to London and found there was to be a big dinner-party on his first evening, which annoyed him slightly, as it meant he had to unpack everything in a hurry so as to dress. Sir Henry's sister, a Mrs. Holdron, was hostess; she said—"Oh, Ainsley, will you take in Miss Warren?"—and he smiled agreement and tried vaguely to associate the name with any particular one of the dozen or so strangers to whom he had been perfunctorily and indistinctly introduced. He had completely forgotten the Philippa Warren who had written to him.

The reception room was on the first floor, overlooking the square, and all its windows were wide open and unshuttered to admit the soft breeze of a September night. He felt an arm slipped into his and guiding him rather than being guided through the plush-curtained archway into the long and rather gloomy corridor that led to the dining-room. Almost simultaneously they both made the same banal remark about the weather, whereupon she

16

laughed and added, with a sort of crystal mockery: *"I said it first, Mr. Fothergill."* He laughed back, but could not think of an answer.

In the dining-room that looked on to the typical brick-walled oblong garden of London houses, he glanced at her curiously. She was young, and full of a vitality that interested him. Her dark, roving eyes gave poise, and even beauty, to a face that might not otherwise have seemed noteworthy. Her nose was long and well-shaped, but her lips were perhaps too small and thin, just as her forehead looked too high. She certainly was not pretty. Not till half-way through the meal did he realize that she must be Sir Henry's new secretary.

It was a distinguished gathering, in a small way—professors and professors' wives, a Harley Street surgeon, a titled lawyer, journalists, a few M.P.'s—all, of course, dominated by the patriarchal figure of Sir Henry himself. He was now seventy-seven, broad-shouldered, straight-backed, with leonine head and flashing eye—a truly eminent Victorian who had survived, wonderfully preserved, into the new reign. He had long ago reached the age when people said that he "still" did things. He still owned the *Pioneer,* which, after a stormy career in the 'sixties and 'seventies, had settled down, like Sir Henry himself, to an old age of ever-slightly-increasing respectability and ever-slightly-diminishing circulation.

The odd part of it (to A.J.) was the way Philippa Warren had suddenly fitted herself into Sir Henry's scheme of things. She seemed already to take both him and his views equally for granted; she was at once casual and proprietary, like a guide displaying a museum piece; she realized quite simply that Sir Henry had become an institution and that visitors liked to hear him gossip in an in-

17

timate way about great names that were already in the history books. She would give him conversational cues such as—"That's rather what Matthew Arnold used to tell you, isn't it, Sir Henry?"—or—"Sir Henry, I'm sure Mr. So-and-So would like to hear about your meeting with Thackeray." She rarely expressed opinions of her own, but she knew exactly, like a well-learned lesson, the precise attitude of Sir Henry towards every topic of the day. It was almost uncanny, and from the beginning A.J. found himself queerly fascinated. She had a clear, icy mind; she could compress her ideas into an epigram where others might have needed to employ a speech. On hearing about the Barrowhurst and Cambridge nickname she immediately called him "A.J." and expected him to call her "Philippa"; he was certain, from the first half-hour of the dinner-party, that they were destined for the most intimate of friendships.

After a week he was less positive, and after a month he was frankly puzzled and doubtful. He seemed so early to have reached an unsurmountable barrier; she would talk about anything and everything with the utterest frankness, yet somehow, after it all, he felt that it had no connection with getting to know her. Sir Henry, of course, never ceased to sing her praises. She was the model secretary; how he had ever managed so many years with that fellow Watts, he could hardly think. The scene in the library every morning at ten o'clock when Philippa arrived to begin work was almost touching. Sir Henry, stirred to a gallantry that had never been his in earlier days, would greet her with a benign smile, pat her shoulder and ask after her health, and, if he imagined or chose to imagine that she looked tired, would ring for a glass of sherry. And she on her side grudgingly yet somehow gratefully permitted time to be wasted on such courtesies.

A.J. agreed that she was marvelous. Her merely physical effect on the old man was remarkable; there came a sparkle into his eyes and a springiness into his walk that had not been seen since the first Jubilee. A.J. judged, too, that she did other things; Sir Henry's occasional articles in the press (writing was one of those things he "still" did) became more frequent, more varied, and—if that were possible—more characteristic of him than ever. Once A.J. glanced over her shoulder when she was working; she was preparing notes, she said, for some centenary article on Elizabethan literature that Sir Henry had promised to write. In neat, verbless phrases she had selected just the material he would need—"Marlowe in his worst moments grandiloquent and turgid"—"*Faërie Queene* a monument of literary atavism"—"*Titus Andronicus* probably not Shakespeare's"—and so on. Sir Henry did the rest, and how well he did it, too, and with what a sublime flavor of personality. A.J. kept the article when it appeared, underlining such sentences as—"I do not think it can be denied that in his less happy moments Marlowe was occasionally guilty of a certain grandiloquence of phraseology—almost, I might say, turgidity even."—"I cannot but think that the *Faërie Queene,* regarded from a strictly literary view-point, is in some sense atavistic."—and—"I have yet to discover any arguments that would lead me to suppose that *Titus Andronicus* was, in its entirety, a work by the master-hand that penned *Lear* and *Othello.*"

A.J. was kept fairly busy during the years that followed. Sir Henry got him reviewing jobs on the *Comet* and other papers, besides which he wrote occasionally for the *Pio-*

*neer* and was also understood to be at work upon a novel. But the plain truth soon became apparent that he was no good at all as a journalist. He was too conscientious, if anything; he read too carefully before he reviewed, and he gave his opinions too downrightly—he had none of Sir Henry's skill in praising with faint damns. Nor had he the necessary journalistic flair for manufacturing an attitude at a moment's notice; he would say, "I don't know" or "I have no opinion" far oftener than was permissible in Fleet Street. He even, after several years, gave up his projected novel for the excellent but ignominious reason that he could not make up his mind what it was to be about. But for the fact that Sir Henry was behind him, his journalistic career would hardly have lasted very long. Aitchison, the *Comet* editor, could never use more than a fraction of the stuff he sent in, though personally he liked the youth well enough and was sorry to see him slaving away at tasks for which he had so little aptitude.

Meanwhile at the Bloomsbury house, A.J.'s friendship with Philippa continued and perhaps progressed a little. Gradually, and at first imperceptibly, a warmer feeling grew on his side, but there was nothing tumultuous in it; indeed, he chaffed himself in secret for indulging something so mild and purposeless. He had certainly nothing to hope for; apart from his own lack of prospects, she had so often, in the course of their talks, conveyed how little she cared for men and for the conventional woman's career of marriage and home life. Nor, for that matter, had A.J. any particularly domestic dreams. In a way, that was why she attracted him so much; she was so unlike the usual type of girl who fussed and expected to be fussed over.

Then suddenly something quite astonishing happened.

20

It was rather like the Smalljohn episode at Barrowhurst;
it occurred so sharply and unexpectedly, and to the most
complete surprise of those who thought that A.J. was, if
anything, too sober a fellow. Philippa, he discovered, was
an ardent supporter of the woman's suffrage movement,
though, in deference to Sir Henry's views on the matter,
she kept her ardors out of the house. She was not a mili-
tant; but Sir Henry made no distinctions of such a kind;
he was genuinely and comprehensively indignant over the
burnings, picture-slashings, and other outrages of which
the newspapers were full. Philippa realized how hopeless it was to convert him, while, as for A.J., she probably
did not consider his support even worth the trouble of
securing. Yet, without effort, it was secured. A.J., in
fact, dashed into the movement with an enthusiasm
which even his greatest friends considered rather fatuous;
there was no stopping him; he went to meetings, walked
in processions, and wasted hours of his time writing prop-
agandist articles which Aitchison turned down with ever-
increasing acerbity. He really was caught up in a whirl
of passionate indignation, and neither Sir Henry's anger
nor Philippa's indifference could check the surge of that
emotion.

The whole thing ended in a quite ridiculous fiasco: he
got himself arrested for attacking a policeman who was
trying to arrest a suffragette who had just thrown a can
of paint into a cabinet minister's motor-car. The magis-
trate seemed glad to have a man to be severe with; he
gave A.J. seven days without the option of a fine, and,
of course, the case was prominently reported in all the
papers.

At Brixton jail A.J. thought at first he would hunger-
strike, but he soon perceived that hunger-striking during

a seven days' sentence could not be very effective; the authorities would merely let him do it. He therefore took the prison food and spent most of his time in rather miserable perplexity. He had, he began to realize, made a complete ass of himself.

When he was discharged at the end of the week he hoped and rather expected that Philippa, at any rate, would have some word of sympathy for him. Instead of that, she greeted him very frigidly. "What an extraordinary thing to do!" was all she commented. Sir Henry was far from frigid; he was as furious as a man of eighty dared permit himself to be. He had A.J. in the library for over an hour telling him what he thought. A.J. must clear out—that was the general gist of the discourse; Sir Henry would no longer permit their names to be connected in any way. If A.J. chose to emigrate (which seemed the best solution of the problem), Sir Henry would give him a hundred pounds as a final expression of regard—but it was to be definitely final—no pathetic letters begging for more. A.J. said: "You needn't fear that, anyhow." In the midst of the rather unpleasant discussion, Philippa entered the library, fresh and charming as usual, whereupon Sir Henry, his mood changing in an instant, remarked: "Perhaps, my dear, we had better tell Ainsley our piece of news."

She barely nodded and Sir Henry went on, more severely as he turned to A.J.—"Philippa has done me the honor of promising to be my wife."

A.J. stared speechlessly at them both. He saw the green-shaded desk-lamp spinning round before his eyes and the expanse of bookshelves dissolving into a multi-colored haze. Then he felt himself going hot, shamefully hot; he managed to stammer: "I—I must—congratulate you—both."

Philippa was not looking at him.

His eyes kept wandering from one to the other of them; she was so beautiful, he perceived now, and Sir Henry, with all his sprightliness, was so monstrously old. He had never noticed before how hideous were those rolls of fat between his chin and his neck, and how he very slightly slobbered over his sibilants.

"Yes, I congratulate you," he repeated.

He went out for lunch, paced up and down in Regent's Park during the afternoon, and spent the evening at a restaurant and a music-hall. Towards midnight he went to the *Comet* office and asked to see Aitchison. Aitchison, a hard-bitten Scotsman of sixty, smiled rather cynically when A.J. suggested being sent abroad as a foreign correspondent; he guessed the reason and personally thought it not at all a bad idea that A.J. should live down his notoriety abroad. There was, of course, no moral stigma attached to a seven days' sentence for trying to rescue a suffragette, but the boy had made a fool of himself and one can be laughed out of a profession as well as drummed out. The foreign correspondent notion, however, was hopeless; A.J. would be as useless, journalistically, abroad as at home. Aitchison knew all this well enough, and when A.J. further went on to suggest being sent out to the Far East to report the Russo-Japanese War which had just begun, he laughed outright. It was impossible, he answered; jobs like that required experience, and A.J. possessed none; reporting a war wasn't like writing a highbrow article about the stained-glass at Chartres. Besides, it would all be far too expensive; the *Comet* wasn't a wealthy paper and probably wouldn't have a

23

correspondent of its own at all. To which A.J. replied that, as for money, he had a little himself and was so anxious to try his luck that he would willingly spend it in traveling out East if the *Comet* would give him credentials as its correspondent and take anything he sent that was acceptable. Aitchison thought this over and quickly reached the conclusion that it was an ideal arrangement—for the *Comet*. It was, to begin with, a way of getting rid of A.J. and it was also a way by which the *Comet* could obtain all the kudos of having a war-correspondent without the disagreeable necessity of footing the bill for his expenses—though, of course, if A.J. did send them anything good, the *Comet* would be delighted to pay for it. And in haste lest A.J. should see any flaw in this most admirable scheme, Aitchison accepted, adding: "Naturally you'll bear in mind the policy of this paper—we don't much care for the Russians, you know. Know what I mean, eh? Not much use you sending us stuff we can't print, especially when it'll cost you God knows how much a word to cable."

A.J. left for Siberia at the beginning of April. Sir Henry declined either to approve or to disapprove of the arrangement; all he made clear was that A.J. could not expect any more chances, and that, if he wanted the hundred pounds, he must go abroad as one of the prime conditions. Siberia was undoubtedly abroad; its prospects for the emigrant were A.J.'s affair entirely. During the last week of hectic preparation that preceded the departure A.J. saw rather little of the old man, and the final goodbys both with him and with Philippa were very formal.

No one saw him off at Charing Cross, and he felt positive relief when, a couple of hours later, the boat swung out of Dover Harbor and he saw England fading into the mist of a spring morning. Two days afterwards he was in Berlin; and two days after that in Moscow. There he caught the Trans-Siberian express and began the ten days' train journey to Irkutsk.

The train was comfortable but crowded, and most of the way he studied a Russian grammar and phrase-book. Every mile that increased his distance from London added to a certain bitter zest that he felt; whatever was to happen, success or failure, was sure to be preferable to book-reviewing in Bloomsbury. His trouble had always been to know what to write about, and surely a war must solve such a problem for him. It was an adventure, any-way, to be rolling eastward over the Siberian plains. He met no fellow-countryman till he reached Irkutsk, where several other newspaper correspondents were waiting to cross Lake Baikal. They were all much older men than he was, and most of them spoke Russian fluently. They seemed surprised and somewhat amused that such a youngster had been sent out by the *Comet,* and A.J., scenting the attitude of superiority, preferred the compan-ionship of a young Italian who represented a Milan news agency. The two conversed together in bad French al-most throughout the crossing of the lake in the ice-breaker. It was an impressive journey; the mountains loomed up on all sides like steel-gray phantoms, and the clear atmosphere was full of a queer other-world melan-choly. Barellini, the Italian, gave A.J. his full life-history, which included a passionate love-affair with a wealthy Russian woman in Rome. A.J. listened tranquilly, watch-ing the ice spurt from the bow of the ship and shiver into glittering fragments; the sun was going down; already there was an Arctic chill in the air. Barellini then talked of Russian women in general, and of that touch of the

East which mingled with their western blood and made them, he said, beyond doubt the most fascinating women in the world. He quoted Shakespeare—"Other women cloy the appetites they feed, but she makes hungry where she most satisfies"—Cleopatra, that was—Shakespeare could never have said such a thing about any western woman. "But I suppose you prefer your English women?" he queried, with an inquisitiveness far too childlike to be resented. A.J. answered that his acquaintance with the sex was far too small for him to attempt comparisons. "Perhaps, then, you do not care for any women very much?" persisted Barellini, and quoted Anatole France—"*De toutes les aberrations sexuelles, la plus singulière, c'est la chasteté.*" "For thousands of years," he added, "people have been trying to say the really brilliant and final thing about sex—and there it is!"

Barellini was very useful when they reached the train at the further side of the lake. There was a curious and rather likable spontaneity about him that enabled him to do things without a thought of personal dignity (which, in fact, he neither needed nor possessed), and when he found the train already full of a shouting and screaming mob, he merely flung himself into the midst of it, shouted and screamed like the rest, and managed in the end to secure two seats in a third-class coach. He had no concealments and no embarrassments; his excitableness, his determination, his inquisitiveness, his everlasting talk about women, were all purified, somehow, by the essential naturalness that lay behind them all. The train was full of soldiers, with whom he soon became friendly, playing cards with them sometimes and telling stories, probably very gross, that convulsed them with laughter. The soldiers were very polite and gave up the best places to A.J. and the Italian; they also made tea for them and brought them food from the station buffets. When A.J. saw the English correspondents bawling from first-class compartments to station officials who took little notice of them, he realized how much more fortunate he had been himself. The hours slipped by very pleasantly; as he sat silent in his corner seat listening to continual chatter which he did not understand and watching the strange monotonous landscape through the window, he began to feel a patient and rather comfortable resignation such as a grown-up feels with a party of children. The soldiers laughed and were noisy in just the sharp, instant way that children have; they had also the child's unwavering heart-lessness. One of them in the next coach fell on to the line as he was larking about, and all his companions roared with laughter, even though they could see he was badly injured.

Harbin was reached after a week's slow traveling from Irkutsk. At first sight it seemed the unpleasantest town in the world; its streets were deep in mud; its best hotel (in which Barellini obtained accommodation) was both villainous and expensive; and its inhabitants seemed to consist of all the worst ruffians of China and Siberia. Many of them were, in fact, ex-convicts. A.J. was glad to set out the next day for Mukden, in which he expected to have to make his headquarters for some time. The thirty-six hours' journey involved another scrimmage for places on the train, but he was getting used to such things now, and Barellini's company continued to make all things easy. He was beginning to like the talkative Italian, despite the too-frequently amorous themes of his conversation, and when he suggested that they should join

27

forces in whatever adventures were available, A.J. gladly agreed.

A.J. had no romantic illusions about warfare, and was fully prepared for horrors. He was hardly, however, prepared for the extraordinary confusion and futility of large-scale campaigning between modern armies. Nobody at Mukden seemed to have definite information about anything that was happening; the town was full of preposterous rumors, and most of the inhabitants were rapidly growing rich out of the war business. All the foreign correspondents were quartered in a Chinese inn, forming a little international club with a preponderance of English-speaking members. A.J. found the other Englishmen less stand-offish when he got to know them better; several became quite friendly and gave him valuable tips about cabling his news, and so on. The trouble was that there was so little news to cable.

The ancient Chinese city wore an air of decay that contrasted queerly with the sudden mushroom vitality infused by the war. A.J. had plenty of time for wandering about among the picturesque sights of the place; indeed, after a week, he knew Mukden very much better than he knew Paris or Berlin. Then came the sudden though long-awaited permission for war-correspondents to move towards the actual battle-front. Barellini and A.J. were both attached to a Cossack brigade, and after a tiresome journey of some sixty miles found themselves courteously but frigidly welcomed by General Kranazoff and his staff. The general spoke French perfectly, as also did most of his officers. He obviously did not like the English, but he talked about English literature to A.J. with much learning and considerable shrewdness.

During that first week with the Cossacks nothing hap-

pened, though from time to time there came sounds of
gun-fire in the distance. Then one morning, about five
o'clock, a servant who had been detailed to attend him
woke A.J. to announce that a battle was beginning about
four miles away and that if he climbed a near-by hill he
might perhaps see something of it. While he was hastily
dressing, Barellini, who had been similarly wakened,
joined him, and soon the two were trudging over the
dusty plain in the fast-warming sunlight.

They climbed the low hill and lay down amongst the
scrub. For several hours nothing was to be seen; then
suddenly, about nine o'clock, a violent cannonade began
over the next range of hills and little puffs of white smoke
a couple of miles away showed where shells were bursting. A staff officer approached them and explained the
position; the Russians were over here, the Japanese over
there, and so on. It was all very confusing and not at
all what A.J. had imagined. The sun rose higher and the
cannonade grew in intensity; Russian batteries were replying. Barellini talked, as usual, about women; A.J. actually dozed a little until another staff officer ran to tell
them to move off, as the Russian line was beginning to
retreat. They obeyed, descending the hill and walking
a mile or so to the rear. By this time they were dog-tired
and thirsty. A Chinese trader on the road offered them
some Shanghai beer at an extortionate figure; Barellini
beat him down to half his price and bought four bottles,
which they drank there and then with great relish.

And that, by pure mischance, was all that A.J. saw of
the actual Russo-Japanese War, for the beer had been
mixed with foul water, and that same evening, after sending a long cable to the *Comet,* he fell violently ill and
had to be taken to the base hospital. There his case was

29

at first neglected, for it was hardly to be expected that the doctors, in the after-battle rush of work, should pay much attention to a foreign war-correspondent with no visible ailment. Later, however, when his temperature was a hundred and four and he was in the most obvious agony, they changed their attitude and gave him good nursing and careful attention. For a fortnight his life was in danger; then he began to recover. The hospital was clean and well-managed, though there was a shortage of drugs and bandages. Barellini, on whom the bad beer had had no ill effects at all, visited him from time to time, as also did some of the other correspondents. It was universally agreed that he had met with the most atrocious luck. Afterwards, however, he looked back upon his period in hospital as the time when he really began to know Russia and the Russians. To begin with, he made great progress with the language. None of the nurses or patients could speak anything but Russian, and after his third week in hospital he found himself beginning to converse with them fairly easily. What struck him most was the universal eagerness to help him; he could not imagine a foreigner in a London hospital being so treated. Both men next to him were badly wounded (one in the stomach and the other with both legs amputated), yet both took a keen delight in teaching him new words. They were middle-aged, with wives and families thousands of miles west; they accepted their fate with a fatalism that was bewildered rather than stoic. One of them always screamed when his wounds were being dressed, and always apologized to A.J. afterwards for having disturbed him. Neither could read or write, yet when A.J. read to them, very haltingly and with very bad pronunciation, from a book by Gogol, they listened enthralled.

They were devoutly religious and also very superstitious. They had not the slightest idea why their country was fighting Japan, but they assumed it must be God's will. The one with the amputations did not seem to worry very much; his attitude seemed chiefly one of puzzlement. It had all happened so quickly, almost as soon as he had gone into battle; he had had no time to fight any of the enemy; indeed, it was as if he had traveled seven thousand miles merely to have his legs blown off. He could not get rid of a dim feeling that the Japanese must have been personally angry with him to have done such a thing. He felt no vindictiveness, however. There was a badly wounded Japanese in the ward; the men treated him very courteously and often spoke sympathetically to one another about him. As they did not know a word of his language nor he a word of theirs, it was all that could be done.

Both A.J.'s neighbors told him all about themselves and showed the frankest curiosity about his own life. They thought it very strange that people in England were so interested in the war that they would send out men especially to describe it for them, and they were amazed when A.J. told them how much his journey had cost, the price of his cables to the *Comet,* and so on. They listened with great interest to anything he told them about English life, English politics, and so on, though such matters were difficult to compress within the confines of his still limited Russian. They always showed their appreciation with the most child-like directness, often giving him articles of food which he really did not want, but which he could not refuse without risk of hurting their feelings.

The effect of his weeks in hospital was to give him an

extraordinarily real and deep affection for these simple-hearted men, as well as a bitter indignation against the scheme of things that had driven them from their homes to be maimed and shattered in a quarrel they did not even understand. The fact that they did not complain themselves made him all the more inclined to complain for them, and the constant ingress of fresh wounded to take the place of men who died had a poignantly cumulative effect upon his emotions. He had already cabled Aitchison about his illness, promising to resume his job as soon as he could; now he began to feel that his real message might be sent as appropriately from a bed in hospital as from a position near the lines. After all, it was the tragic cost of war that people needed to realize; they were in no danger of forgetting its excitements and occasional glories. In such a mood he began to compose cables which a friendly nurse despatched for him from the local telegraph-office. He described the pathos and heroism of the Russian wounded, their child-like patience and utter lack of hatred for the enemy, their willingness to endure what they could not understand. After his third cable on such lines a reply came from Aitchison—"Cannot use your stuff advise you return immediately sending out Ferguson." So there it was; he was cashiered, sacked; they were sending out Ferguson, the well-known traveler and war-correspondent who had made his name in South Africa. A.J. was acidly disappointed, of course, and also (when he came to think about it) rather worried about the future. There was nothing for it but to pack up and return to Europe as soon as he was fit to leave hospital—to Europe, but not to England. The thought of London, of the London streets, and of Fleet Street especially, appalled him in a way he could not ex-

32

actly analyze. He had a little money still left and began to think of living in France or Germany as long as it held out, and as the most obvious economy he would travel back third-class. He left hospital at the beginning of August and caught the first train west. The discomfort of sleeping night after night on a plank bed without undressing did not prevent him from enjoying the journey; the train itself was spacious and the halts at stations were long and frequent enough to give ample opportunity for rest and exercise. His companions were nearly all soldiers, most of them returning to their homes after sickness or wounds, and their company provided a constant pageant of interest and excitement. The long pauses at places he felt he would almost certainly never visit again and whose names he would almost certainly never remember, gave an atmosphere of epic endlessness to the journey; and there was the same atmosphere in his talks to fellow-travelers, with some of whom he became very intimate. Sometimes, especially when sunset fell upon the strange, empty plains, a queer feeling of tranquillity overspread him; he felt that he wanted never to go back to London at all; the thought of any life in the future like his old Fleet Street life filled his mind with inquietude. And then the train would swing into the dreaming rhythm of the night, and the soldiers in the compartment would light their candles and stick them into bottles on the window-ledges, and begin to sing, or to laugh, or to chatter. Siberia surprised him by being quite hot, and sometimes the night passed in a cloud of perfume, wafted from fields of flowers by the railside. Then, early in the morning, there would be a halt at some little sun-scorched station, where the soldiers would fetch hot water to make tea and where A.J. could get down

33

and stretch his legs while the train-crew loaded wood into the tender. Often they waited for hours in sidings, until troop trains passed them going east, and for this reason the return journey took much longer than the eastward one.

At a station a few hundred miles from the European frontier A.J. got into conversation with a well-dressed civilian whom he found himself next to in the refreshment-room. The man was obviously well-educated, and discussed the war and other topics in a way that might have been that of any other cultured European. He made the usual enquiries as to what A.J. was doing and who he was; then he congratulated him on his Russian, which he said was surprisingly good for one who had had to learn so quickly. The two got on excellently until the departure time of the train; then they had to separate, since the Russian was traveling first-class.

At the next halt three hours later they met again in a similar way and the Russian expressed surprise that A.J. should be traveling so humbly. A.J. answered, with a frankness he saw no reason to check, that he was doing things as cheaply as possible because he had so little money. This led to further questions and explanations, after which the Russian formally presented his card, which showed him to be a certain Doctor Hamarin, of Rostov-on-Don. He was, he said, the headmaster of a school there; his pupils came from the best families in the district. If A.J. wished to earn a little money and was not in any great hurry to return to England (for so much he had gathered), why not consider taking a temporary post in Russia? And there and then he offered him the job of English master in his school. A.J. thanked him and said he would think it over; he thought it over, and at the next station jumped eagerly to the platform, met Hamarin as before, and said he would accept.

So he settled down at Rostov. It was a pleasantly prosperous city, with a climate cold and invigorating in winter and mild as the French Riviera in summer; it was also very much more cosmopolitan than most places of its size, for, as the business capital of the Don Cossack country, it contained many Jews, Armenians, Greeks, and even small colonies of English, French, and Germans. Picturesquely built, with many fine churches, it was interesting to live in, though A.J. had no initial intention of staying in it for long. He did, in fact, stay there for two years, which was about four times his estimate. His work was simple—merely to teach English to the sons and daughters of Rostov's plutocratic rather than aristocratic families. He made a successful teacher, which is to say that he did not need to work very hard; he had plenty of leisure, and during holidays was able to take trips into the Caucasus, the Crimea, and several times to Moscow and St. Petersburg. With a natural aptitude for languages, he came to talk Russian without a trace of foreign accent, besides picking up a working knowledge of Tartar, Armenian, and various local dialects. He was moderately happy and only bored now and again. A physical change became noticeable in him; he lost, rather suddenly, the boyish undergraduate air that had surprised the other war-correspondents when they had first seen him. He was liked by his pupils and respected by their parents; he moved a little on the fringe of the better-class town society, which was as high as a schoolmaster could well expect. He soon found that his profession carried with it little dignity of its own. During his first week at school the daughter of one of Rostov's wealthiest families, in sending up a very bad English translation exercise, enclosed a ten-rouble note between the pages, clearly assuming that it would ensure high marks.

At the close of his first year he saw in a literary paper that Sir Henry Jergwin, the celebrated English critic, editor, and man of letters, had died suddenly in London whilst replying to a toast at the annual dinner of a literary society.

Hamarin pressed him to stay another year at Rostov, and he did so chiefly because he could not think of anything else to do or anywhere else to go. It was during this second year that he began to gain insight into the close network of revolutionary activity that was spread throughout the entire country. Even bourgeois Rostov had its secret clubs and government spies, and there seemed to be an ever-widening gulf between the wealthier classes and the working people. When occasionally he went into better-class houses to give private English lessons he was often amazed at the way servants were bullied by everyone, from the master of the house even down to the five-year-old baby who had already learned whom he might kick and scratch with impunity. One youth, the son of a wealthy mill-owner, went out of his way to explain. "You see, they're all thieves and rogues. We know it, and they know we know it. They steal everything they can—they have no loyalty—they lie to us a dozen times a day as a matter of course. Why should we treat them any better than the scum that they are? It's their fault as much as ours."

A.J. became quite friendly with this youth, who had traveled in Germany and France, and looked at affairs from a somewhat wider standpoint than the usual Rostov citizen. His name was Sergius Willenski, and he was destined for the army. He had no illusions about the country or its people. "You simply have to treat them like that," he often said. "It's the only basis on which life becomes at all possible."

"And yet," A.J. answered, "I have met some of the most charming folk among the common people—ignorant soldiers whom I would certainly have trusted with my life."

"A good job you didn't. They may have been charming—quite likely—but they were rogues, I'll wager, and would probably have killed you for a small bribe. Our people have no morals—only a sort of good humor that impresses foreigners."

A.J. went to the Willenskis' twice a week to teach English to the two girls, aged fifteen and seventeen respectively. Neither learned anything, except in the dullest and least intelligent way; neither considered that life held any possible future except a successful marriage. The elder girl would have flirted with him if he had been inclined for the diversion. The younger girl was the prettier, but had a ferocious temper. She boasted that she had once maimed for life a man who had come to the house to polish the floors. It was his custom to take off one of his shoes and tie a polishing cloth round his stockinged foot so that he could polish without stooping. The girl, then aged eleven, had flown into a temper because he had accidentally disturbed some toy of hers; she had seized a heavy silver samovar and dropped it on to his foot, breaking several bones. "And it wasn't at all a bad thing for him," she told A.J., "because father pays him something every now and then and he doesn't have to polish the floors for it."

A.J. sometimes went to parties at the Willenskis' house;

monsieur and madame (as they liked to be called) were hospitable and refrained from treating him as they would have done a native teacher. Once he met Willenski's brother, who was a publisher in St. Petersburg. Anton Willenski, well-known to all the Russian reading public, took considerable interest in the young Englishman and, after an hour's conversation, offered him a post in his own St. Petersburg office. "You are far too good a scholar to be teaching in a little place like Rostov," he said. The post offered was that of English translator and proof-reader, and the salary double that which Hamarin paid. A.J. mentioned his contract at the school, but Willenski said: "Oh, never mind that—I'll deal with Hamarin," and he did, though A.J. could only guess how.

So A.J. left Rostov and went to St. Petersburg. That was in 1907, when he was twenty-seven. The change from the provincial atmosphere to the liveliness and culture of the capital was immeasurably welcome to him. The gayety of the theaters and cafés, the fine shops on the Nevsky, the splendor of the Cathedral and of the Winter Palace, all pleased the eye of the impressionable youth whose job left him leisure for thinking and observing. He had been to St. Petersburg before, but to see it as a visitor had been vastly different from living in it. His rooms were across the river in the Viborg district; from his windows he could see, at sunset, the Gulf of Finland bathed in saffron splendor, and there was something of everlasting melancholy in that sky and water pageant ushering in the silver northern night. Before he had been long in St. Petersburg he received other impressions—the glitter of Cossack bayonets and scarlet imperial uniforms, and in the darker background, the huge scowling mass of misery and corruption through which revolutionary currents ran like threads of doom. It was fascinating to watch those ever-changing scenes of barbaric magnificence and sordid degradation—to cheer the imperial sleigh as it swept over the snow-bound boulevards, to gaze on the weekly batches of manacled prisoners marching to the Nikolai Station *en route* for the Ural prison mines, to see the crowds of wild-eyed strikers surging around the mills of the new industrialism. His work at Willenski's office was easy; he had to superintend the translation of English works into Russian and to give them final proofreading. It was also expected that he should make suggestions for new translations, and it was over this branch of his work that, after a successful and enjoyable year, he came to sudden grief. At his recommendation a certain English novel had been translated, printed, published, and sent to the shops; it was selling quite well when all at once the police authorities detected or pretended to detect in it some thinly veiled allusions to the private life of the Emperor. Willenski was thus put in a most awkward position, since he supplied text-books to the government schools and had a strictly orthodox reputation to keep up; his only chance of escaping business ruin and perhaps personal imprisonment was by laying the entire blame on his subordinate. As he told A.J. quite frankly: "It just can't be helped. They won't do anything to you, as you're English. If you were Russian they'd probably send you to Siberia—as it is, they can only cancel your passport. I shall have to dismiss you, of course."

So Willenski made a great show of dismissing with ignominy a subordinate who had disgracefully let him down, and managed, by such strategy, to escape with a severe warning so far as he himself was concerned. As for A.J., he received a polite note from police headquarters informing him that he must leave Russia within a week.

He felt this as a rather considerable blow, for in the first place he was sorry to have brought so much trouble on Willenski, whom he had grown to like; and besides, he had his own problems to solve. He did not wish to return to England. He had no idea of anything that he could do if he did return; he had no special qualifications except a knowledge of Russian, which would be hardly as useful in London as was a knowledge of English in St. Petersburg. Journalism was hopeless; he could realize now, over the perspective of several years, what a complete failure he had been in Fleet Street. Teaching, of which he had had some experience, would be impossible in any good English school owing to his poor degree, while as for the other professions, he neither inclined towards them nor had any hope that they would incline towards him.

Beyond even this he had grown to like St. Petersburg. He had lived in it now for over a year, had seen it in all its climatic moods; and now it was April again and the sledge-roads on the frozen Neva would soon be closing for the thaw. The prospect of summer had been alluring him more than he had realized; he had been looking forward to many a swim at Peterhof and many an excursion into the flower-decked woods that fringed the city on so many sides.

His permitted week expired on Easter Tuesday and on Easter Eve he strolled rather sadly along the Nevsky and watched the quaint and fascinating ceremonial. Thousands of poor work-people had brought their Easter suppers to be blest, and the priests were walking quickly amongst the crowds, sprinkling the holy water out of large buckets. The food was set out on glistening white napkins on which stood also lighted tapers, and there was a fairy-like charm in that panorama of flickering lights, vestmented priests, and rapt, upturned faces. A.J. had seen it all the previous year, but it held additional poignancy now that it seemed almost the last impression he would have of the city. He was observing it with rather more than a sight-seer's interest when a well-dressed man in expensive furs, who happened to be pushed against him by the pressure of the crowd, made some polite remark about the beauty of the scene. A.J. answered appropriately and conversation followed. The man was middle-aged and from his speech a person of culture. He was not, A. J. judged, an Orthodox believer, but he showed a keen sympathy and understanding of the religious motive, and was obviously as fascinated by the spectacle as A.J. himself. The two, indeed, soon found that they had a great many common ideas and interests, and talked for perhaps a quarter of an hour before the stranger said: "Excuse my curiosity, but I'm just wondering if you're Russian. It isn't the accent that betrays you—don't think that—merely a way of looking at things that one doesn't often find in this country. At a venture I should guess you French."

"You'd be wrong," answered A.J., smiling. "I'm English."

"Are you, by Jove?" responded the other, dropping the Russian language with sudden fervor. "That's odd, because so am I. My name's Stanfield."

"Mine's Fothergill."

They talked now with even greater relish, and though Stanfield did not say who he was, A.J. surmised that he had some connection with the British Embassy. They discussed all kinds of things during the whole four-mile

41

walk down the Nevsky and back, after which Stanfield said: "Did you ever go to midnight Mass at St. Isaac's?" A.J. shook his head, and the other continued: "You ought to—it's really worth seeing. If you've nothing else on this evening we might go together."

They did, and the experience was one that A.J. was sure he would never forget. They arrived at the Church about eleven, when the building was already thronged and in almost total darkness. Under the dome stood a catafalque on which lay an open coffin containing a painted representation of the dead Christ. Thousands of unlighted candles marked the form of the vast interior, and Stanfield explained that they were all linked with threads of gun-cotton. There was no light anywhere save from a few tall candles round the bier. Soon the members of the diplomatic corps arrived, gorgeously uniformed and decorated, and took up their allotted positions, while black-robed priests began the mournful singing of the Office for the Dead. Then followed an elaborate ritual in which the priests pretended to search in vain for the Body. Despite its touch of theatricalism the miming was deeply impressive. Then sharply, on the first stroke of midnight, the marvelous climax arrived; the chief priest cried loudly—"Christ is risen!" while the gun-cotton, being fired, touched into gradual flame the thousands of candles. Simultaneously cannon crashed out from the neighboring fortress, and the choir, led by the clergy (no longer in black but in their richest cloth of gold), broke out into the triumphant cadences of the Easter hymn. The sudden transference from gloom to dazzling brilliance and from silence to deafening jubilation stirred emotions that were almost breath-taking.

Afterwards, amidst the chorus of Easter salutations, the

two men sauntered by the banks of the river. A.J. said how glad he was to have seen such a spectacle, and Stanfield answered: "Yes, it's one of the things I never miss if I happen to be here. I've seen it now at least a dozen times, yet it's always fresh, and never fails to give me a thrill."

Something then impelled A.J. to say: "I'm particularly glad to have seen it, because I don't suppose I'll ever have the chance again."

"Oh, indeed? You're only on a visit? You spoke Russian so well I imagined you lived here."

"I do—or rather I have done for some time—but—I'm going away—very soon, I'm afraid—for good."

"Really?"

A.J. was not a person to confide easily, but the difficulty of his problem combined with Stanfield's sympathetic attitude and the emotional mood in which the Cathedral ceremony had left them both, made it easy for him to hint that the circumstances of his leaving St. Petersburg were not of the happiest. Stanfield was immediately interested, and within half an hour (it was by that time nearly two in the morning) most of A.J.'s position had been explained and explored. Once the process began it was difficult to stop, and in the end A.J. found himself confessing even the ridiculous suffragette episode which had been the immediate cause of his departure from England four years before. Stanfield was amused at that. "So I gather," he summarized at last, "that you're in the rather awkward position of having to leave this country and of having no other country that you particularly want to go to?"

"That's it."

"You definitely don't want to return to England?"

"I'd rather go anywhere else."

"But you must have friends there—a few, at any rate. Four years isn't such a tremendous interval."

"I know. That's why I'd rather go anywhere else."

"Don't you think you're taking the suffragette affair rather too seriously? After all, most people will have forgotten it by now, and in any case it wasn't anything particularly disgraceful."

"Yes, but—there are other reasons—much more important ones. I—I don't want to go back to England." He gave Stanfield a glance which decided the latter against any further questioning in that direction. "Besides, even if I *were* to go back there, what could I do?"

"I don't know, do I? What *are* your accomplishments?"

A.J. smiled. "Very few, and all of them extremely unmarketable. I can speak Russian, that's about all. Oh, yes, and I can swim and fence, and I'm a bit of a geologist in my spare time. It doesn't really sound the sort of thing to impress an employment agency, does it?"

"Do you fancy an outdoor life?"

"I don't mind, provided it isn't just merely physical work. It may sound conceited, but I rather want something where I have to use a small amount of brains. Yet I wouldn't care for a job at a desk all the time. I'm afraid I'm talking as though I were likely to be given any choice in the matter."

"What about danger—personal danger? Would that be a disadvantage?"

"I'd hate the army, if that's what you mean."

"No, that isn't what I meant. I meant some kind of job where you had occasionally to take risks—pretty big

44

risks, in their way—playing for high stakes—*that* sort of thing."

"I'm afraid your description doesn't help me to imagine such a job, but as a guess I should say it would suit me very well."

Stanfield laughed. "I can't be more explicit. How about the money?"

"Oh, well, I'd like enough to live on and a little bit more. But isn't it rather absurd to be talking in this way, since I shall be very lucky to get any sort of job at all?"

"On the contrary, it's just possible—yes, it *is* just possible that I might be able to put you in the way of the kind of job you say you would like. And here in St. Petersburg, too."

"You forget that I have to leave. My passport expires on Tuesday."

"No, I don't forget that at all. I am remembering it most carefully."

"I don't follow."

"Let me explain. But first, I must pledge you to the strictest secrecy. Whether or not you and I can come to terms, you must give me that assurance."

"I do, of course."

"Good. Then listen."

Briefly, Stanfield's suggestion was that A.J. should become attached to the British Secret Service. That sounded simple enough, but an examination of all that it implied revealed a network of complication and detail. Stanfield, relying on A.J.'s promise of secrecy, was as frank as he needed to be, but no more so. British diplomacy, he explained, had its own reasons for wishing to know the precise strength and significance of the revolu-

45

tionary movement in Russia. It was impossible to obtain reliable information from official channels, whether British or Russian; the only sources were devious and underground. "Supposing, for instance, you decided to help us, you would have to join one of the revolutionary societies, identify yourself with the cause, gain the confidence of its leaders, and judge for yourself how much the whole thing counts. I think you'll agree with me that such a job calls for brains and might well involve considerable personal risks."

"I should be a spy, in fact?"

"In a way, yes, but you would not be betraying anybody. You would merely make your confidential reports to our headquarters—you would not be working either for or against the revolutionaries themselves. We take no sides, of course—we merely want to know what is really happening."

"I see. And the danger would be that the revolutionaries would find me out and think I was betraying them to the Russian police?"

"The danger, my friend, would be two-fold, and I'm not going to try to minimize it in the least. There would be, of course, the danger you mention, but there would be the even greater danger that the Russian police would take you for a genuine revolutionary and deal with you accordingly. And you know what accordingly means."

"But in that case I suppose I should have to tell them the real truth?"

"Not at all—that is just what you would *not* have to do. You would have to keep up your pretense and accept whatever punishment they gave you. If you *did* tell them the truth, the British authorities would merely arch their eyebrows with great loftiness and disown you.

I want you to be quite clear about that. We should, in the beginning, provide you with passport and papers proving you to be a Russian subject, and after that, if anything ever went wrong, you would have to become that Russian subject—completely. Do you see? We could not risk trouble with the Russian Government by having anything to do with you."

"It seems a rather one-sided arrangement."

"It is, as I can say from experience, having worked under it for the best part of my life. On the other hand, it has certain advantages which probably appeal to people like you and me rather more than to most others. It is interesting, it is adventurous, and it is quite well-paid. It is also emphatically a job for the Cat That Walks by Itself—you remember Kipling's story?—and I should imagine both of us are that type of animal."

"Maybe."

"Mind you, I don't want to persuade you at all—and I do want you to have time to think the whole thing over very carefully before coming to a decision. Unless, of course, you feel that you may as well say 'No' straightway?"

A.J. shook his head. "I'll think it over, as you suggest."

"Then we'd better meet again tomorrow." He gave A.J. an address, and the arrangement was made. A.J. did not sleep well that night. When he tried to look at the future quite coolly, when he asked himself whether his ambition really was to be a Secret Service spy in a Russian revolutionary club, the answer was neither yes or no, but a mere gasp of incredulity. It was almost impossible to realize that such an extraordinary doorway had suddenly opened into his life. It was not impossible, however, to grasp the fact that if he did not accept Stanfield's

47

offer he would have to leave Russia in two days' time with very poor and uncertain prospects.

He called in the morning at the address Stanfield had given him—a well-furnished apartment in one of the better-class districts. Stanfield was there, together with another man, introduced as Forrester. "Well," began Stanfield, "have you made up your mind?"

A.J. answered, with a wry smile: "I don't feel in the least like jumping at the job, but I'm aware that I must either take it or leave Russia."

"And you're as keen as all that on not leaving Russia?"

"I rather think I am."

"That means you'll take on the job."

"I suppose it does."

Here Forrester intervened with: "I suppose Stanfield gave you details of what you'd have to do?"

"More or less—yes."

"You'd have to be the young intellectual type—your accent and manner would pass well enough, I dare say. But what about enthusiasm for the cause—can you act?" He added, slyly: "Or perhaps you would not need to act very much, eh?"

"As an Englishman in Russia," answered A.J. cautiously, "I have always felt that I ought to avoid taking sides in Russian politics. You can judge from that, then, how much I should have to act."

Forrester nodded. "Good, my friend—a wise and admirable reply. I should think he would do, wouldn't you, Stanfield?"

The latter said: "I thought so all along. Still, we mustn't persuade him. It's risky work and he knows some of the more unpleasant possibilities. It's emphatically a game of heads somebody else wins and tails he loses."

"Oh, yes," Forrester agreed. "Most decidedly so. The pay, by the way, works out at about fifty pounds a month, besides expenses and an occasional bonus."

"That sounds attractive," said A.J.

"Attractive, eh?" Forrester turned again to Stanfield. "Did you hear that? He says the pay's attractive! You know, Stanfield, it's the money that most people go for in this job, yet I really do believe our friend here is an exception! He only admits that the money's attractive!" With a smile he swung round to A.J. "I'm rather curious to know what it is that weighs most with you in this business. Is it adventure?"

"I don't know," answered A.J. "I really don't know at all."

So they had to leave that engrossing problem and get down to definite talk about details. That definite talk lasted several hours, after which A.J. was offered lunch. Then, during the afternoon, the talk was resumed. It was all rather complicated. He was to be given a Russian passport (forged, of course, though the ugly word was not emphasized) establishing him to be one Peter Vasilevitch Ouranov, a student. He must secure rooms under that name in a part of the city where he was not known; he must pose as a young man of small private means occupied in literary work of some kind. To assist the disguise he must cultivate a short beard and mustache. Then he must frequent a certain bookshop (its address would be given him) where revolutionaries were known to foregather, and must cautiously make known his sympathies so that he would be invited to join a society. Once in the society, it would be his task to get to know

49

all he could concerning its aims, personnel, and the sources from which it obtained funds; such information he would transmit at intervals to an agent in St. Petersburg, whose constantly changing address would be given him from time to time. It would not be expected, nor would it even be desirable, that he should take any prominent or active part in the revolutionary movement; he must avoid, therefore, being elected to any position of authority. "We don't want you chosen to throw bombs at the Emperor," said Forrester, "but supposing anyone else throws them, then we do want to know who he is, who's behind him, and all that sort of thing. Get the idea?"

A.J. got the idea, and left the two men towards evening, after Stanfield had taken his photograph with an ordinary pocket-camera. That night and much of the next day he spent in packing. He had told the porter and the woman who looked after his room that he might be leaving very soon, so they were not surprised by his preparations for departure. In the evening, following instructions, he gave the two of them handsome tips, said good-by, and drove to the Warsaw station. There he left his bags in the luggage office, giving his proper name (which was, in fact, on all the luggage labels as well). After sauntering about the station for a short time he left it and walked to Stanfield's address. There he handed over to Forrester his English passport and luggage tickets. He rather expected to see Forrester burn the passport, but the latter merely put it in his pocket and soon afterwards left the house. Stanfield smiled. "Forrester's a thorough fellow," he commented. "He doesn't intend to have the Russian police wondering what's happened to you. Tonight, my friend, though it may startle you to know it, Mr. A. J.

Fothergill will leave Russia. He will collect his luggage at the Warsaw station, he will board the night express for Germany, his passport will be stamped in the usual way at Wierjbolovo and Eydkuhnen, but in Berlin, curiously enough if anyone bothered to make enquiries, all trace of him would be lost. How fortunate that your height and features are reasonably normal and that passport photographs are always so dreadfully bad!"

After an hour or so Forrester returned and informed A.J. that he was to stay with them in their apartment for a fortnight at least, and that during that time he must consider himself a prisoner. The rather amusing object of the interval was to give time for his beard and mustache to grow. A.J. rather enjoyed the fortnight, for both Forrester and Stanfield were excellent company and there was a large library of books for him to dip into. The two men came in and went out at all kinds of odd hours, and had their needs attended to by a queer-looking man-servant who was evidently trustworthy, since they spoke freely enough in front of him.

At the end of the fortnight, by which time A.J.'s face had begun to have a remarkably different appearance, Forrester again photographed him, and a few days later handed him his new passport and papers of identity. It gave him a shock, at first, to see himself so confidently described as "Peter Vasilevitch Ouranov," born at such and such a place and on such and such a date. "You must get used to thinking of yourself by that name," Forrester told him. "And you must also make it your business to know something about your own past life. Your parents, of course, are both dead. You have just a little money of your own—enough to save you from having to work for a living—you are a studious, well-educated person, at present engaged in writing a book about—what shall we say?—something, perhaps, with a slightly subversive flavor—political economy, perhaps, or moral philosophy. Oh, by the way, you may permit yourself to know a little French and German—as much, in fact, as you *do* know. But not a word of English. Remember that most of all."

The next morning A.J. was made to change into a completely different outfit of clothes. He was also given three hundred roubles in cash, a small trunk-key, and a luggage ticket issued at the Siberia station. After breakfast he said good-by to Forrester and Stanfield, walked from their apartment to the station, presented his ticket, received in exchange a large portmanteau, and drove in a cab to an address Forrester had given him. It was a block of middle-class apartments on the southern fringe of the city. There chanced (or was it chance?) to be an apartment vacant; he interviewed the porter, came to terms, produced his papers for registration, and took up his abode in a comfortable set of rooms on the third floor. There he unlocked the portmanteau, and found it contained clothes, a few Russian books, a brass samovar, and several boxes of a popular brand of Russian cigarettes. These miscellaneous and well-chosen contents rather amused him.

Thus he began life under the new name. He was startled, after a few days, to find how easy it was to assume a fresh identity; he conscientiously tried to forget all about Ainsley Jergwin Fothergill and to remember only Peter Vasilevitch Ouranov, and soon the transference came to require surprisingly little effort. Forrester had cautioned him not to be in any great hurry to begin his real work, so at first he merely made small purchases

52

at the bookshop, whose address he had been given, without attempting to get to know anyone. Gradually, however, the youthful studious-looking fellow who bought text-books on economic history (that was the subject finally fixed on) attracted the attention of the bookseller, a small, swarthy Jew of considerable charm and culture. His name was Axelstein. A.J. had all along decided that, if possible, he would allow the first move to be made by the other side, and he was pleased when, one afternoon during the slack hours of business, Axelstein began a conversation with him. Both men were exceedingly cautious and only after a longish talk permitted it to be surmised that they were neither of them passionate supporters of the Government. Subsequent talks made the matter less vague, and in the end it all happened much as Forrester had foreshadowed—A.J. was introduced to several other frequenters of the shop, and it was tacitly assumed that he was a most promising recruit to the movement.

A few days later he was admitted to a club to which Axelstein and many of his customers belonged. It met in an underground beer-hall near the Finland station. Over a hundred men and women crowded themselves into the small, unventilated room, whose atmosphere was soon thick with the mingled fumes of beer, makhorka tobacco, and human bodies. Some of the men were factory-workers with hands and clothes still greasy from the machines. Others belonged to the bourgeois and semi-intelligentsia—clerks in government offices, school teachers, bookkeepers, and so on. A few others were university students. Of the women, some were factory-workers, some stenographers, but most were just the wives of the men. A few were probably prostitutes.

A.J. allowed himself to make several friends in that

underground beer-hall, and the reality of its companion-ship together with the secrecy and danger of the meetings made a considerable impression on him. Often news was received that one or another member had been arrested and imprisoned without trial. Police spies were every-where; there was even the possibility, known to all, that some of the members might themselves be spies or agents provocateurs. Caution was the universal and necessary watchword, and at any moment during their sessions members were ready to transform themselves into a hap-hazard and harmless group of beer-drinking and card-playing roisterers.

It was only by degrees that A.J. came to realize the im-mensity of the tide that was flowing towards revolution. That club was only one of hundreds in St. Petersburg alone, and St. Petersburg was only one of scores of Rus-sian cities in which such clubs existed. The movement was like a great subterranean octopus stirring ever more restlessly beneath the foundations of imperial govern-ment. An arm cut off here or there had absolutely no effect; if a hundred men were deported to Siberia a hundred others were ready to step instantly into the va-cant places. Everything was carefully and skillfully or-ganized, and there seemed to be no lack of money. The Government always declared that it came from the Japa-nese, but Axelstein hinted that most of it derived from big Jewish banking and industrial interests.

A.J. became rather friendly with an eighteen-year-old university student named Maronin. He was fair-haired, large-eyed, and delicate-looking, with thin artistic hands (he was a fine pianist) and slender nostrils; his father had been a lawyer in Kieff. The boy did no real work at the university and had no particular profession in view; he lived every moment for the revolution he believed to be coming. A.J. found that this intense and passionate attitude occasioned no surprise amongst the others, though, of course, it was hardly typical.

Young Alexis Maronin interested A.J. a great deal. He was such a kindly, jolly, amusing boy—in England A.J. could have imagined him a popular member of the sixth form. In Russia, however, he was already a man, and with more than an average man's responsibilities, since he had volunteered for any task, however dangerous, that the revolutionary organizers would allot him. Axelstein explained that this probably meant that he would be chosen for the next "decisive action," whenever that should take place. "He is just the type," Axelstein explained, calmly. "Throwing a bomb accurately when you know that the next moment you will be torn to pieces requires a certain quality of nerve which, as a rule, only youngsters possess."

Regularly every week A.J. transmitted his secret reports and received his regular payments by a routine so complicated and devious that it seemed to preclude all possibility of discovery. He found his work extremely interesting, and his new companions so friendly and agreeable, on the whole, that he was especially glad that his spying activities were not directed against them. He was well-satisfied to remain personally impartial, observing with increasing interest both sides of the situation, which steadily became worse.

One afternoon he was walking with Maronin through a factory district during a lock-out; crowds of factory-workers—men, women, and girls—were strolling or loitering about quite peaceably. Suddenly, with loud shouts and the clatter of hoofs, a troop of Cossacks swept round the street-corner, their lithe bodies swaying rhythmically from side to side as they laid about them with their short, leaden-tipped whips. The crowd screamed and stampeded for safety, but most were hemmed in between the Cossacks and the closed factory-gates. A.J. and Maronin pressed themselves against the wall and trusted to luck; several horsemen flashed past; whips cracked and there were terrifying screams; then all was over, almost as sharply as it had begun. A girl standing next to Maronin had been struck; the whip had laid open her cheek from lip to ear. A.J. and Maronin helped to carry her into a neighboring shop, which was already full of bleeding victims. Maronin said: "My mother was blinded like that—by a Cossack whip,"—and A.J. suddenly felt as he had done years before when he had decided to fight Smalljohn's system at Barrowhurst, and when he had seen the policeman in Trafalgar Square twisting the suffragette's arm—only a thousand times more intensely.

Throughout the summer he went on making his reports, attending meetings, arguing with Axelstein, and cultivating friendship with the boy, Alexis. There was something very pure and winsome about the latter—the power of his single, burning ideal gave him an air of other-worldliness, even in his most natural and boyish moments. His hatred of the entire governmental system was terrible in its sheer simplicity; it was the system he was pledged against; mere individuals, so far as they were obeying orders, roused in him only friendliness and pity. The Cossack guards who had slashed the crowd with their whips were to him as much victims as the crowd itself, and even the Emperor, he was ready to admit, was probably a quite harmless and decent fellow personally. The real enemy was the framework of society from top to bottom, and, in attacking that enemy, it might and probably would happen that the innocent would have to suffer. Thus he justified assassinations of prominent officials; as human beings they were guiltless and to be pitied, but as cogs in the detested machine there could be no mercy for them.

About midnight one October evening A.J. was reading in his sitting-room and thinking of going to bed when the porter tapped at his door with the message that a young man wished to see him. Such late visits were against police regulations, but the chance of a good tip had doubtless weighed more powerfully in the balance. A.J. nodded, and the porter immediately ushered in Maronin, who had been standing behind him in the shadow of the landing.

As soon as the door had closed and the two were alone together A.J. could see that something was wrong. The boy's face was milky pale and his eyes stared fixedly; he was also holding his hand against his chest in a rather peculiar way. "What on earth's the matter?" A.J. enquired, and for answer Alexis could do nothing but remove his hand and allow a sudden stream of blood to spurt out and stain the carpet.

A.J., in astonished alarm, helped him into the bedroom and laid him on the bed, discovering then that he had been shot in the chest and was still bleeding profusely. The boy did not speak at first; he seemed to have no strength to do anything but smile. When, however, A.J. had tended him a little and had given him brandy, he began to stammer out what had happened. He had, it seemed, fulfilled a secret task given him by revolutionary headquarters. He had shot Daniloff, Minister of the Interior. He had done it by seeking an interview and firing

57

point-blank across the minister's own study-table. Daniloff, however, had been quick enough to draw a revolver and fire back at his assailant as the latter escaped through a window. A ladder had been placed in readiness by an accomplice, and Alexis had been descending by it when Daniloff's bullet had struck him in the chest. He had hurried down, unheeding, and had mingled—successfully, he believed—with the crowds leaving a theater. He had been in great pain by then, and knew that he dare not let himself be taken to a hospital because in such a place his wound would instantly betray him. The only plan he had been able to think of had been a flight to his friend's apartment, and though that was over a mile from Daniloff's house, he had walked there, despite his agony, and even in the porter's office had managed to make his request without seeming to arouse suspicion. Now, in his friend's bedroom, he could only gasp out his story and plead not to be turned away.

There was no question of that, A.J. assured him; no question of that. "You shall stay here, Alexis, till you are well again, but I must go out and find a doctor—I have done all I can myself, I'm afraid."

The boy shook his head. "No, no, you can't get a doctor—he'll ask questions—it's impossible. But I have a friend—a medical student—I will give you his address—tomorrow you shall fetch him to me—he will take out the bullet—and say nothing. . . ."

"Tell me where he lives and I will fetch him now."

"No, no—the police would stop you—they will be all everywhere tonight—because of Daniloff." He added: "I am sorry to be such a bother to you—I wish I could have thought of some other way. If only I had taken better aim I might have killed him instantly."

58

"Don't talk," A.J. commanded, huskily. "Try to be quiet—then in the morning I will fetch your friend."

"Yes. I shall be all right when the bullet is taken out."

"Yes—yes. Don't talk any more."

He held the boy in his arms, that boy with the face of an angel, that boy who had just shot a government minister in cold blood; he held him in his arms until past one in the morning, and then, very quietly and apparently with a gradual diminution of pain, the end came.

Till that moment, A.J. had felt nothing but pity for his friend; but afterwards he began to realize that he was himself in an extraordinarily difficult and dangerous situation. How could he explain the death of the boy that night in his apartment? What story could he invent that would not connect himself with the attack on Daniloff? The deep red stain in the midst of his sitting-room carpet faced him as a dreadful reminder of his problems. He had no time to solve them, even tentatively, for less than a quarter of an hour after the boy's death he heard a loud commotion in the street outside and a few seconds later a vehement banging on the door of the porter's office. Next came heavy footsteps up the stairs and a sudden pummeling on his own door. He went to open it and saw a group of police officers standing outside, with the porter in custody.

"We understand that a young man visited you a short time ago," began one of the officers, with curt precision.

"Yes," answered A.J.

"Is he here now?"

"Yes."

"We must have a word with him."

"I am afraid that will be impossible. He is dead."

"Ah—then, if you will permit us to see the body—"

"Certainly. In there."

He pointed to the bedroom, but did not follow them. One of the officers stayed behind in the sitting-room. After a few moments the others returned and their leader resumed his questioning. "Now, sir," he said, facing A.J. rather sternly, "perhaps you will be good enough to explain all this."

A.J. replied, as calmly as he could: "I will explain all I can, which I am afraid isn't very much. I was sitting here just over an hour ago, about to go to bed, when the young man was brought up to see me—"

"The porter brought him up?"

"Yes."

"Continue."

"I invited him to come in, and as he looked ill, I asked him what was the matter. Besides, of course, it was peculiar his wanting to see me at such a late hour."

"Very peculiar indeed. You must have been a very intimate friend of his."

"Hardly that, as a matter of fact. He used to drop in and see me now and again, that was all."

"Continue with the story."

"Well, as I was saying, I asked him what was the matter, but he didn't answer. He was holding his hand to his chest—like this." A.J. imitated the position. "Then he suddenly took his hand away and the result was— that." He pointed to the stain on the carpet. "Then he collapsed and I took him into my bedroom. I discovered that he had been shot, but I could not get him to explain anything at all about how it had happened. I made him as comfortable as I could and was just about to send for a doctor when he died. That's all, I'm afraid."

"You say he told you nothing of what had happened to him?"

"Nothing at all."

"And you could make no guess?"

"Absolutely none—it seemed a complete mystery to me during the very short time I had for thinking about it."

"You know who the young man is?"

"I know his name. He is Alexis Maronin."

"And your name?"

"Peter Vasilevitch Ouranov."

"How did you come to know Maronin?"

"We met in connection with some work I am engaged upon. I am writing a book of history and Maronin was interested in the same period. We used to meet occasionally for an exchange of ideas."

"What was he by profession?"

"A student, I rather imagined. He was always very reserved about himself and his affairs."

"Were you surprised to see him an hour ago when he came here?"

"I certainly was."

"You know it is against police rules for strangers to be admitted at that hour?"

"Yes."

"Had the porter ever admitted visitors to your apartment at such a time before?"

A.J., from the porter's woebegone appearance, guessed that he had already made the fullest and most abject confession, so he replied: "Yes, he had—but not very often."

"Had he ever admitted Maronin before at such a late hour?"

"I believe so—once."

"Why, then, were you surprised to see him when he came tonight?"

A.J. answered, with an effort of casualness: "Because on that last occasion when he paid me a call after permitted hours I gave the boy such a scolding for breaking rules and leading me into possible trouble, that I felt quite sure he had learned a lesson and would not do so again."

"I see. . . . And you still say that you have not the slightest idea how Maronin met with his injury?"

"Not the slightest."

"May we examine your passport?"

"Certainly."

He produced it and handed it over. While it was being closely inspected two police officers carried the boy's body to a waiting ambulance below. Finally the leading officer handed the passport back to A.J. with the words: "That will be all for the present, but we may wish to question you again." The police then departed, but A.J. was under no illusion that danger had departed with them. When he looked out of his sitting-room window he could both see and hear the march of a patient watcher on the pavement below.

He drank some brandy to steady his nerves and spent the rest of the night in his easiest armchair. He did not care to enter the bedroom. Now that the police had left him, personal apprehensions were again overshadowed by grief.

He had fallen into a troubled doze when he was awakened by the sound of scuffling on the landing outside, punctuated by shrill screams from the woman who usually came in the mornings to clear up his room and prepare breakfast. She was evidently being compelled to give up her keys, and a moment later the door was unlocked and two police guards strode into the room. They were of a very different type from those of the previous visit. Huge, shaggy fellows, blustering in manner and brutal in method, A.J. recognized their class from so many stories he had heard in that underground beer-hall. "You are to come with us immediately," one of them ordered, gruffly. "Take any extra clothes and personal articles that you can put into a small parcel." A.J. felt a sharp stab of panic; the routine was dreadfully familiar. "By whose orders?" he asked, feeling that a show of truculence might have some effect with men who were obviously uneducated, but the only reply was a surly: "You'll find that out in good time."

The men were armed with big revolvers, apart from which they were of such physique that resistance was out of the question. A.J. gathered together a few possessions and accompanied his two escorts to a two-horse van waiting at the curb. This they bade him enter, one of them getting inside with him while the other took the reins. The inside was almost pitch dark. After a noisy rattling drive of over half an hour the doors were opened and A.J. was ushered quickly into a building whose exterior he had no time to recognize. The two guards led him into a large bleak room unfurnished except for a desk and a few chairs. A heavily built and dissipated-looking man sat at the desk twirling his mustache. When A.J. was brought in the man put on a pair of steel-rimmed spectacles and stared fiercely. "You are Peter Vasilevitch Ouranov?" he queried; and to A.J.'s affirmative merely replied: "Take him away."

The guards continued their journey with him along many corridors and across several courtyards. He knew that he was in a prison, though which one out of the

63

many in St. Petersburg he had no idea. At last one of
the guards unlocked and opened a door and pushed him
into a room already occupied by what at first seemed a
large crowd. But that was because, in the dim light admitted by a small and heavily barred window, it was difficult to distinguish the inhabitants from their bundles
of clothing.

They had seemed asleep when A.J. entered, but as soon
as the guards retired and the door was relocked they all
burst into sudden chatter. A.J., dazed and astonished,
found himself surrounded by gesticulating men and
youths, all eager to know who he was, why he had been
sent there, and so on. He told them his name, but
thought it wiser to say that no charge had been made
against him so far. They said: "Ah, that is how it very
often happens. They do not tell you anything." They
even laughed when he asked the name of the prison; it
amused them to have to supply such information. It was
the Gontcharnaya, they said.

Altogether there were a score or more inhabitants of
that room. About half were youths of between seventeen and twenty-one. One of them told A.J. he had already been imprisoned for two months without knowing
any charge against him, and there was a steady hopelessness in his voice as he said so. "These people are not all
politicals," he went on, whispering quietly amidst the
surrounding chatter. "Some are criminals—some probably government agents sent to spy on us—who knows?—
there is always that sort of thing going on. A fortnight
ago two fellows were taken away—we don't know where,
of course—nothing has happened since then until you
came."

Considering their plight the majority of the prisoners

64

were cheerful; they laughed, played with cards and dice, sang songs, and exchanged anecdotes. One of them, a Jew, had an extensive repertoire of obscenity, and whenever the time fell heavily somebody would shout: "Tell us another story, Jewboy." Another prisoner spent most of his time crouched in a corner, silent and almost motionless; he was ill, though nobody could say exactly what was the matter with him. He could not take the prison food, and so had practically to starve. The food was nauseating enough to anyone in good health, since apart from black bread it consisted of nothing but a pailful of fish soup twice a day, to be shared amongst all the occupants. A.J. could not stomach it till his third day, and even then it made him heave; it smelt and tasted vilely and looked disgusting when it was brought in with fishheads floating about on its greasy surface. It was nourishing, however, and to avoid it altogether would have been unwise. There were no spoons or drinking vessels; each man dipped his own personal mug or basin into the pail and took what he wanted, and the same mugs, unwashed, served for the tea which the men were allowed to make for themselves.

At night they slept on planks ranged round the wall about a foot from the floor. The cracks in the planks were full of bugs. Most of the men were extremely verminous; indeed, it was impossible not to be so after a few days in such surroundings. A smell of dirty clothes and general unwholesomeness was always in the air, mixed with the stale fish smell from the soup-pail and other smells arising from the crude sanitary methods of the place.

The warders were mostly quite friendly and could be bribed to supply small quantities of such things as tea,

65

sugar, and tobacco (to be chewed, not smoked). The entire prison routine was an affair of curious contrasts—it was slack almost to the point of being good-humored, yet, beyond it all, there was a sense of complete and utter hopelessness. One felt the power of authority as a shapeless and rather muddled monster, not too stern to be sometimes easy-going, but quite careless enough to forget the existence of any individual victim. Most hopeless of all was perhaps the way in which some of the victims accepted the situation; they did not complain, they did not show anger, indignation, or even (it seemed) much anxiety. When the warders unlocked the door twice a day their eyes lifted up, with neither hope nor fear, but with just a sort of slow, smoldering fever. And when the man in the corner grew obviously very ill, they did what they could for him, shrugged their shoulders, went on with their card-playing, and let him die. After all, what else was possible? Only in the manner and glances of a few of the youngsters did there appear any sign of fiercer emotions.

One of the prisoners, a political, had a passion for acquiring information on every possible subject. Most of the others disliked him, and A.J., to whom he attached himself as often as he could, found him a great bore. "I am always anxious to improve my small knowledge of the world," he would say, as a preface to a battery of questions. "You are a person of education, I can see—can you tell me whether Hong Kong is a British possession?" Something stirred remotely in A.J.'s memory; he said, Yes, he believed it was. "And is Australia the largest island in the world?" Yes, again; he believed so. "Then, sir, if you could further oblige me—what is the smallest island?" A.J. could never quite decide whether

66

the man were an eccentric or a half-wit. He afterwards learned that he had aimed a bomb at a chief of police in Courland.

All this time A.J. was immensely worried about his own position, which, from conversation with other prisoners, he gathered might be very serious. There were, apparently, few limits to the power of the police; they might keep arrested persons in prison without trial for any length of time, or, at any moment, if they so desired, they might send them into exile anywhere in that vast region between the Urals and the Far East.

For five weeks nothing happened; no one either left or joined the prisoners. Then, on the thirty-eighth day (A.J. had kept count) one of the warders, during his morning visit, singled out A.J. and another prisoner to accompany him. From the fact that the two were ordered to carry their bundles with them, the rest of the prisoners drew the likeliest conclusion, and there were many sentimental farewells between friends. The jailer obligingly waited till all this was finished; he did not mind; time was of little concern to him or to anyone else at the Gontcharnaya. Then, with a good-humored shrug of the shoulders, he relocked the door and led the two prisoners across courtyards and along corridors into the room that A.J. had visited on first entering the prison. The same man was there behind the desk, twirling his mustache upwards almost to meet the bluish pouches under his eyes.

He dealt first with the other prisoner, verifying the man's name and then declaring, with official emphasis: "You are found guilty of treason against the Government and are sentenced to exile. That is all." The man began to speak, but a police guard who was in the room dragged him roughly away. When the shouts of both had died down in the distance, the man behind the desk turned to A.J. "You are Peter Vasilevitch Ouranov? You too are found guilty of treason. Your sentence is exile—"

"But what is the charge? Of what am I accused? Surely—"

"Silence! Take him away!"

A police guard seized him by the arms and dragged him towards the door and out into the corridor. A.J. did not shout or struggle; he was suddenly dumbfounded, and into the vacuum of bewilderment came slowly, like pain, the clutchings of a dreadful panic. Although he had had exile in mind for weeks, it had been a blow to hear the word actually pronounced over him.

Outside in the corridor the rough manners of the police guard changed abruptly to a mood of almost fatherly solicitude. "I wouldn't worry so much if I were you," he remarked, soothingly. "Personally I should much prefer exile to being herded in jail with criminals and such like. I always think it is a great scandal to mix up decent fellows like yourself with that scum." He went on to give A.J. some practical advice. "As an exile you are entitled to a fair amount of luggage, though the authorities will try to do you out of your privileges if they can. I suggest that you make out a list of anything you want to take with you, and I will see that the things are collected from where you have been living."

A.J. was too tired and depressed at that moment to consider the matter with any zest, and the guard continued, with a curious mixture of friendliness and officialdom: "Ah, I see—you are upset—perhaps, then, you will be so good as to tell me and *I* will make out the list. Oh, yes, I can write—I am a man of education like yourself. Come now, there is no time to lose. You will want heavy winter clothes, the usual cooking utensils, blankets, and things like that. Oh, yes, and books—you are permitted by the regulations to take a few with you. You are a reader, of course? Ah, education is a wonderful thing, is it not? Perhaps you would like me to have your books packed up and sent with the other things?"

"There are too many of them," A.J. answered, dully. "Far too many to carry."

"But you would be allowed to take a dozen or so. Do you mean that you have more than a dozen books? You are perhaps a professor, then, eh? Ah, well, I will ask them to send on a dozen for you, anyhow."

And in due course the pertinacious fellow, whose name was Savanrog, compiled his list and the bureaucratic machine, with numerous clankings and rumblings, got to work upon it. Savanrog was delighted when, a few days later, the complete assortment of articles arrived. By that time A.J. had grown more resigned to his fate, a few days of solitary confinement in a comparatively clean and comfortable cell having helped considerably towards such a state. "You see," Savanrog exclaimed, taking both A.J.'s hands in his and shaking them, "I have managed it all for you! Oh, yes, I do not let anything slip past me. It is the turn of fortune that has brought us together, Peter Vasilevitch—I have done my duty—and as for our acquaintance, it has been a thing of delight. I have always counted it a privilege to make myself known to eminent politicals like yourself."

"But surely I am not an eminent political?" A.J. answered, half-smiling.

"Ah, you are too modest. Were you not the friend of Maronin, who killed Daniloff, Minister of the Interior?"

A.J. let the question pass. It was the first intimation

he had had that his offense was reckoned as "friendship" with the boy-assassin. He had sometimes feared that he would be ranked as an accessory to the crime itself, in which case, of course, his status would have been that of a criminal, not a political. Savanrog's chatter was in its way reassuring.

At last the morning came when he was ordered to prepare for the journey. Savanrog, at the final moment, shook hands with him, kissed him on both cheeks, and gave him a black cigar. "It will be a breach of regulations to smoke it until you are across the Urals," he told him, with a last spasm of official correctitude. Then, leading A.J. into the corridor, he marched him into a courtyard in which a hundred or so other prisoners were already on parade, and with a great show of blustering brutality, pushed him into line. A.J. did not recognize any of the faces near him. He was ordered to separate his luggage into two bundles, a personal one to carry on his back, and a larger one consisting of things he would not require until the end of the journey, wherever and whenever that might be. The larger bundles of all the prisoners were then collected into a van and carried away. Afterwards the men themselves were divided up into two detachments, and here came the final welcome proof that A.J. was a political; he was not put into the group of those who had to wait for the blacksmith to manacle their wrists together. Finally the whole melancholy procession was led out through the prison-gate into the street. It was only a very short distance to the railway station, and the throngs on the pavements stared with just that helpless, half-compassionate, half-casual curiosity which A.J. had observed on so many previous occasions when he had himself formed part of them.

70

After marching into a goods yard beyond the station and halting beside a train, the manacled prisoners were pushed into cattle-trucks, but the politicals were allowed to choose their own places in ordinary third-class rolling-stock, passably clean and comfortable. A.J. found himself cordially welcomed by the men of his compartment. There were five of them, with one exception all young like himself. The exception was a very ancient fellow with a huge head and a sweeping beard. Even before the train moved off A.J. was told a good deal about his fellow-passengers. The old man's name was Trigorin—just Trigorin—he seemed to possess no other. His offense had been the preaching of roadside sermons in which had occurred certain remarks capable of seditious interpretation. He had been exiled once before for a similar offense. "I am an old man," he said, "and nothing very dreadful can happen to me now. But of course it is different for you youngsters."

The journey to Moscow took two days, and then there was considerable delay while the prison-train was shunted round the city and linked up with other coaches from different parts of the country. Finally the complete train, by this time very long, set out at a slow pace on its tremendous eastern journey. To many of the prisoners there was something ominous in the fact that they were now actually on the track of the Trans-Siberian, and spirits were low during the first few hours. A.J., however, did not share the general gloom; he remembered Siberia from his previous visit, and the name did not strike any particular terror into his mind. When some of the young men spoke with dismay of the possible fate in store for them, he felt strongly tempted to tell them that parts of Siberia, at any rate, were no worse than many parts of

Europe. Trigorin, however, saved him from any temptation to recount his own experiences. Trigorin described how conditions had improved since the opening of the railway; during his first exile, he said, he had had actually to walk three thousand miles from railhead at Perm, and much of the way through blinding rain and snow. He gave lurid and graphic descriptions of the horrors of the old forwarding prisons at Tiumen and Tomsk, and of the convict barges on the rivers, and of the great Siberian highway along which so many thousands of exiles had been driven to misery and death. "Things are much better now," he said, with sadly twinkling eyes. "We politicals are pampered—no floggings, hospitals if we fall ill— what more can we expect, after all? You youngsters, whose knowledge of Siberia comes from Dostoievski's book and a few lurid novelettes, can't realize what a good time politicals have nowadays. We die, of course, but only of loneliness, and a man may die of that in bed in his own home, may he not?"

A mood of curious fatalism sank upon A.J. during those days and nights of travel. The journey was not too arduous; the food was coarse, but sufficient in quantity and fairly nourishing; the military guards were easygoing fellows, especially after all the politicals had given parole that they would not attempt to escape during the train-journey. The future, of course, loomed grim enough, but A.J. did not seem to feel it; his mind had already attuned itself to grimness. He kept remembering his interviews with Stanfield and Forrester, and their repeated assurances that the game was one of "heads somebody else wins and tails you lose." Well, he had lost, and he could not complain that he had not been amply warned of the possibility. He felt, however, that he had had distinctly bad luck; it had been pure misfortune, and not any personal carelessness or stupidity of his own, that had led to his present position. But for his friendship with Maronin all would have still been well. But he did not regret that friendship. It was, on the contrary, one of the few things in his life that he prized in memory.

He remembered one of Stanfield's remarks: "If anything goes wrong, you will have to become a Russian subject completely." That seemed of peculiar significance now that things *had* gone wrong, and it was true, too, that whether he willed it so or not, he was becoming Peter Vasilevitch Ouranov in a way he had certainly never been before. He wondered frequently whether by this time the Secret Service people knew all about his trouble. Most probably information had reached them, by their own secret channels, within a few hours of his arrest. He could picture their attitude—a shrug of the shoulders, a vaguely pitying look, and then—forgetfulness. Perhaps Stanfield might have commented to Forrester or Forrester to Stanfield: "Well, *he* didn't last long, eh? Still, we warned him. Wonder if he'll play the fool by trying to make out he's English?"

A.J. had no intention of so playing the fool. It was not merely that he had given his word, but that his common sense informed him how utterly useless it would be. Apart from his knowledge of the English language, there was nothing at all he could advance in support of any claim he might make to be other than the Peter Vasilevitch Ouranov set out with authentic-looking detail on his passport and papers of identity. And even supposing he managed to persuade the authorities to inquire into his case, the result could only mean a communication to

73

the British Embassy, with what result he had been warned. "The British authorities would merely arch their eyebrows with great loftiness and disown you," had been Stanfield's way of putting it. No; there was nothing to be gained by attempting the impossible; the only course was simple endurance for the time being, and later, if he could manage it, escape. Henceforward he was doomed to be Peter Vasilevitch Ouranov without qualification, and, rather curiously, he now began to feel what he had hardly felt before—a certain pride in his new identity. He *was* Peter Vasilevitch Ouranov, exiled to Siberia for a political offense; and he felt that same quiet, unending antagonism towards the imperial authorities that the other exiles felt; he began to understand it, to understand them, to understand why they were so calm, why they so rarely roused the sleeping fury in their souls. They were saving it, as themselves also, for some vaguely future day.

He began, too, to breathe with comfort and comprehension the vast easy-going laziness of the country; he perceived why no one ever hurried, why trains were always late, why the word *sichass* (presently) was so popular and universal; after all, if people were merely waiting for something to happen, there could be no especial urgency about things done in the meantime. And they *were* waiting for something to happen—the exiles, the soldier-guards, the criminals in their chains, the railway-workers, the prison officials—a calm, passionless anticipation gleamed in their eyes when one caught them sometimes unawares. As the train rumbled eastwards this sense of anticipation and timelessness deepened immeasurably; life was just sunrise and sunsetting; food, drink, talk; the train would pull up in a siding; when would

74

it move out again?—*Sichass,* of course; that might be in an hour or two, or perhaps the next day; nobody knew—nobody very much cared. When the train stopped the prisoners sometimes climbed out and walked about the country near the track, or else lay down in the long grass with the midday sun on their faces. The nights were cold, but no snow had fallen yet. At Omsk, Krasnoiarsk, and other places, some of the men left the train in charge of Cossack guards. Trigorin explained that they were the milder cases—men who had not definitely committed any crime, but were merely suspected of being "dangerous" or of having "dangerous opinions." "It is clear," he declared, comfortingly, "that something much more serious is in store for all of us. We shall know when we reach Irkutsk."

They reached the Siberian capital three weeks after leaving Moscow; the busy city, magnificently situated at the confluence of two rivers, gleamed brightly in the late autumnal sun. The exiles were marched from the station to the central forwarding prison and there split up into several groups. Trigorin was sent off almost immediately; he was bound for Chita, near the Manchurian frontier, and was to travel there with a contingent of local criminals. The other politicals were immensely indignant about this; it was against all the rules to put a political along with criminals, and much as they hated the penal code, such a breach of it stirred them to punctilious anger. The prison governor apologized; he was very sorry, but he could not help it; Trigorin must go with the criminals, but he would be given a separate railway coach. "Besides," he explained, reassuringly, "they are only local murderers—not bad fellows, some of them." Trigorin himself did not object at all, and actu-

ally rebuked his friends for their uncharitable champion-
ship. "Let us not forget," he said, "that the only persons
to whom Christ definitely promised paradise were two
criminals. He, the greatest of all political prisoners, was
actually crucified between them."

A.J.'s other fellow-passengers were also sent away, but
whither, he could not discover. He himself was kept at
Irkutsk. It was a better-managed prison than the Gontcharnaya at St. Petersburg, but after the easy-going train-
journey the return to routine of any kind was irksome.
A.J. found most of his fellow-prisoners in a state of depression and melancholy that soon began to affect him
also, especially when the freezing up of the river and the
first big snowstorm of the season marked the onset of
Siberian winter.

The prison-governor was a good-tempered, jovial fellow who liked to make the days pass by as pleasantly as
possible for himself and mankind in general. Every
morning he would tour the prison and greet the men
with a bluff, companionable "Good morning, boys—how
goes it?" He was always particular about their food and
the warmth of their rooms, and he would sometimes pay
a surprise visit to the kitchens to sample the soup that was
being prepared for them. He seemed a little in awe of
some of the politicals, but he was on friendly terms with
most of the criminals and enjoyed hearing them give
their own accounts of their various crimes. The more
bloodthirsty and exciting these were, the better he liked
them; he would sometimes, at the end of a particularly
thrilling recital, clap a man on the back and exclaim:
"Well, you *are* a fellow, and no mistake! To think of
you actually doing all that!" Naturally the criminals invented all kinds of incredibilities to please him.

A.J. soon found that the only way to keep his mind from descending into the bitterest and most soul-destroying gloom was to think of the only inspiring possibility open to a prisoner—that of escape. Together with another political he began to plan some method of getting away, not immediately, but as soon as the spring weather should make the open country habitable. This task, with all its complications, helped the winter days to pass with moderate rapidity. Unfortunately a fellow-prisoner who was a government spy (there were many of these, sometimes unknown even to the prison authorities) gave the plan away, and A.J. and his co-conspirator were summoned before the governor. His attitude was rather that of a pained and reproachful guardian whose fatherly consideration has been basely rewarded. "Really, you know," he told them, "that was a very foolish thing to do. Your attempt to escape has already been reported to Petersburg, and it will only make your eventual punishment more severe. The original idea was to exile you to Yakutsk as soon as the season permitted, but now heaven knows where you will be sent." And he added, almost pathetically: "Whatever made you act so unreasonably?"

So the position seemed rather more hopeless than ever. Soon, too, the easy-going governor was sent away to another prison; the St. Petersburg authorities transferred him to Omsk, and in his place was sent a different type of man altogether—a small, dapper, bristling-mustached martinet whom everyone—prisoners and prison-officials alike—detested with venomous intensity. It was he who, the following May, sent for A.J. and barked at him in staccato tones: "Ouranov, your case has been reconsidered by the authorities in view of your recent attempt to escape. Your revised sentence is that of banishment for

77

ten years to Russkoe Yansk. You will go first to Yakutsk, and then wait for the winter season. You will need special kit, which you will be allowed to purchase, and I am instructed to pay you the customary exile's allowance dated back to the time of your entry into Siberia. Perhaps you will sign this receipt."

A fortnight later the journey commenced. A.J. had spent part of the interval in making purchases in the Irkutsk shops; the two Cossack guards who were to accompany him to his place of exile advised him what to buy and how much to pay for it. They were big, simple-hearted, illiterate fellows and could give him few details about Russkoe Yansk, except that the journey there would take many months. A.J. suspected that with the usual Siberian attitude towards time, they were merely estimating vaguely; he could not believe that even the remotest exile station could be quite so inaccessible. The first stage was by road and water to Yakutsk. Along with hundreds of other exiles, including a few women, the trek was begun across the still frost-bound country to Katchugo, near the source of the Lena. This part of the journey was made in twenty-mile stages and lasted over a week. The nights were spent in large barn-like sheds, horribly verminous, and well-guarded by sentries on all sides.

At Katchugo the entire detachment was transferred to barges, and resigned itself to a two months' meandering down the river to Yakutsk, which was reached towards the end of July. The horrors of that journey, under a sky that never, during the short summer, darkened to more than twilight, engraved still more deeply the mood of fatalism that had already descended on most of the prisoners. A.J. was no exception. He did not find himself worrying much, and he was not nearly so low-spirited as he had been amidst the comparatively comfortable surroundings of the Irkutsk prison. He felt scarcely more than a growing numbness, as if a part of his brain and personality were losing actual existence.

Yakutsk was almost pleasant after the barges, and the remaining weeks of the summer passed without incident. Prison regulations, owing to the remoteness of the settlement, were lax enough, and A.J. made several acquaintances. One of them, an educated exile who had been allowed to set up as a boot-repairer, had even heard of Russkoe Yansk. It was on the Indigirka River, he thought, well beyond the Arctic Circle. It could only be a very small settlement and it was years since he had heard of anyone being sent there. "Perhaps they have made a mistake," he hazarded, with dispassionate cheerfulness. "Or perhaps the place does not exist at all and they will have to bring you back. That *has* happened, you know. There was a man sent to one place last year and the Cossacks themselves couldn't find it. They looked for it all winter and then had to hurry back before the thaw began." He laughed heartily. "Ho, ho, I'm not inventing the story, I assure you. Some of those Petersburg officials don't know their own country—they just stare at a map and say—'Oh, we'll send him here—or there'—and maybe the map is wrong all the time!"

Early in September, the Lena, miles wide, began to freeze over, and soon the whole visible world became transfixed in the cold, darkening glare of winter. The two guards who had left Irkutsk in charge of A.J. and who had spent the summer amusing themselves as well as the amenities of Yakutsk permitted, now indicated that the time for the resumption of the journey had arrived.

From now onwards it became a much more personal and solitary affair—almost, in fact, a polar expedition, but without the spur of hope and ambition to mitigate hardship. The three men, heavily furred, set out by reindeer sledge into the long grayness of the sub-Arctic winter. Two of them carried arms, yet the third man, defenseless, was given the place of honor on all occasions—at nighttime in the wayside huts, usually uninhabited, and during the day whenever a halt was made for rest and food. The temperature sank lower and lower and the sky darkened with every mile; they crossed a range of bleak mountains and descended into a land of frozen whiteness unbroken anywhere save by stunted willows. For food there were birds which the guards shot or snared, and unlimited fish could be obtained by breaking through the thick ice in the streams. The fish froze stiff on being taken out of the water; it had to be cut into slices and eaten raw between hunks of bread. A.J.'s palate had by this time grown much less fastidious, and he found such food not at all unpleasant when he was hungry enough. The cold air and the harsh activity of the daily travel bred also in him a sense of physical fitness which, at any other time, he would have relished; as it was, however, he felt nothing but a grim and ever-deepening insensitiveness to all outward impressions. He imagined vaguely the vast distance he had already traveled, but it did not terrify him; it was merely a memory of emptiness and boredom, and though he knew that the end of the journey would mean the end of even the last vestige of changefulness, he yet longed for it because, for the moment, it seemed a change in itself.

One evening, thirteen weeks after leaving Yakutsk, the three men were crossing a plain of snow under the light of the full moon. At the last settlement, ten days previously, they had exchanged their reindeer transport for dogs, and since then had been traversing this same white and empty plain. There seemed, indeed, no obvious reason why the plain and the journey might not go on forever. The temperature was fifty below zero. A.J. had noticed that for some hours the guards had been muttering to each other, which was unusual, for in such cold air it was painful to speak. Suddenly, out of the silver gloom, appeared the hazy shapes of a few snow-covered roofs; the guards gave a cry; the dogs barked; a few answering cries came from the dimness ahead. They had reached Russkoe Yansk.

It was smaller and more desolate than he had imagined. There were only four Russians in exile there, none of them educated men; the rest of the population consisted of a score or more of natives of very low intelligence. The native men, under the direction of the guards, began to dig an entry through the snow into an unoccupied timber hut that was to belong to the new exile; there were several of these deserted huts, for the settlement had formerly been larger. The natives looked on in amazement when A.J. began to unpack the bundle that he had not been allowed to touch since leaving St. Petersburg; they had never before seen such things as books, writing-paper, or a kerosene-lamp. The Russians looked on also with a curiosity scarcely less child-like; they had seen no strange face for years, and their eagerness bordered on almost maniacal excitement. A.J. addressed them with a few cordial words and they were all around him in a moment, shaking his hands and picking up one after another of his belongings; they had evidently been half afraid of him at first. One of them said:

"This shows that the Government has not forgotten us—they know we are still here, or they would not have sent you."

A fire was made, and the two Cossack guards stayed the night in the hut. The next morning they hitched up their dog teams, shook hands cordially enough, and began the long return journey. A.J. watched them till the distance swallowed up their sledge and the hoarse barking of the animals. Then he set to work to make his habitation more comfortable.

Russkoe Yansk was close to, but not actually on, the Arctic Ocean; the nearest settlements, not much larger, were four hundred and four hundred and fifty miles to west and east respectively. There was no communication of any regular kind with the civilized world; sometimes a fur-trapper would take a message and pass it on to someone else who might be going to Yakutsk, but even in most favorable circumstances an answer could scarcely arrive in less than twenty months. The nearest railway and telegraph stations were over four thousand miles away.

The year was composed of day and night; the day lasted from June to September only. In winter the temperature sometimes fell to seventy below zero, and there were week-long blizzards in which no living human being could stir a yard out of his hut. During the short summer the climate became mild and moist; the river thawed and overflowed, causing vast swamps and floodings that cut off the settlement from the world outside even more effectively than did the winter cold and darkness.

A.J. had brought a fair supply of tea and tobacco, and with small gifts of these he could secure the manual services of as many natives as he wanted, apart from the four Russians, who would have lived their whole lives as personal slaves in his hut if he had wished it. He did not feel particularly sad, but he did begin to feel a strange Robinson-Crusoe kind of majesty that was rather like an ache gnawing at him all the time. He was the only person in Russkoe Yansk who could read, write, work a simple sum, or understand a rough map. The most intelligent of the Russians had no more than the mind of a peasant, with all its abysmal ignorance and with only a touch of its shrewdness. The others were less than half-witted, perhaps as a result of their long exile. They remembered the names of the villages from which they had been banished, but they had no proper idea where those villages were, how long their banishment had lasted, or what it had been for. Yet compared with the native Yakuts, even such men were intelligent higher beings. The Yakuts, with their women and families, reached to depths of ugliness, filth, and stupidity that A.J. had hardly believed possible for being classifiable as mankind. Their total vocabulary did not comprise more than a hundred or so sounds, hardly to be called words. In addition to physical unpleasantness (many were afflicted with a loathsome combination of syphilis and leprosy), they were abominable thieves and liars; indeed, their only approach to virtue was a species of dog-like attachment to anyone who had established himself as their master. With a little of the most elementary organization they could have murdered all the exiles and plundered the huts, but they lacked both the initiative and the virility. Life to them was but an unending struggle of short summers and long winters, of snow and ice, blizzard and thaw, of fishing in the icy pools and trapping small animals for flesh and fur, of lust, disease, and occasional gluttony. They had never seen a tree, and knew timber only as material providentially floated down to them on the spring-time floods. Even when he had picked up their rudimentary language, A.J. could not interest them by any talk of the outer world; they were incapable of imagination, and the only thing that stirred them to limited excitement was the kerosene-lamp, which, after some experimenting, he made to burn with certain kinds of fish-oil.

Now especially he had cause to be grateful to Savanrog, the enterprising and sympathetic prison-guard at the Gontcharnaya. For the luggage, packed according to the latter's instructions, included all kinds of things that A.J. would never have thought of for himself, but which now were found to be especially useful. With them, and with the miscellaneous articles he had purchased in Irkutsk, he was not badly equipped. He had his twelve books, chosen apparently at random from his shelves in St. Petersburg; the only one he would have thought of selecting himself was a translation of "Don Quixote," but the others soon grew to be odd, but no less faithful companions. One was a school text-book in algebra, another an out-of-date year-book; another was Dickens's "Great Expectations"— of course in Russian. Mr. Pumblechook and Joe Gargery became the friends of all his waking and sleeping dreams, and before them alone he could relax and smile.

Besides his few books his luggage contained several other things never seen in Russkoe Yansk before. He had a watch and a clinical thermometer, a few bottles and jars of simple medicines, and a pair of scissors; he had also (he was sure) the only boot-trees north of the Arctic Circle. The police in St. Petersburg, with typical inconsequence, had packed them inside a pair of field-boots.

Oddly, perhaps, the time did not seem to pass very slowly. There was always so much to be done—the mere toil of getting food, of repairing and improving the hut, of keeping himself well clothed to withstand the almost inconceivable cold. He did a little amateur doctoring whenever he found anything he fancied he could cure amidst that nightmare of disease and degradation. He made notes, without enthusiasm, yet somehow because he felt he must, about the customs and language of the natives. He even tried to teach the least stupid of the Russians to learn the Russian alphabet. And whenever, during the long winter, or while day after day of blizzard kept him a prisoner in the hut, he felt pangs of loneliness or disappointment piercing to his soul, he would slip into a coma of insensibility and wait. The waiting was not often for long. When, after the gray night of winter, the sunlight showed again over the frozen earth, at first so very timidly, he welcomed it with a smile that no one saw. Sometimes at midsummer he sailed down the swollen river in a small boat; once, with a couple of natives, he reached the open Arctic and made a rough sketch-map of fifty miles of coast-line. He hardly knew why he did such things—certainly not from any idea of ultimate escape. There was nothing at all to prevent his making such an attempt except the knowledge of its utter hopelessness. His stern jailers were the swamps in summer and the icy waste in winter; and even if, by some miracle, he could pass them by, there was no place of safety to be reached. It would have been more hopeful to make for the North Pole than for the semi-civilized places in Siberia.

His first winter at Russkoe Yansk was that of 1909/10.

PART THREE

IN THE LATE SPRING OF 1917
a small party of Cossacks set out from Yakutsk by reindeer and dog sledge. They were seven in number and
traveled swiftly, visiting each one in turn of the remoter
settlements. Russkoe Yansk was almost the last.

They reached it in the twilight of a May noontide, and
at the sound of their arrival the entire native population—
some dozen Yakut families—turned out of their huts to
meet them, surrounding the dog-teams and chattering
excitedly.

At length a tall figure, clad in heavy furs, approached
the throng; and even in that dim northern light there
was no mistaking leadership of such a kind. One of the
soldiers made a slight obeisance and said in Russian:
"Your honor, we are from Yakutsk."

A quiet, rather slow voice answered: "You are most
welcome, then. You are the first to visit us for three
years. Come into my hut. My name is Ouranov."

He led them a little distance over the frozen snow to
a hut rather larger than the rest. They were surprised
when they entered, for it was so much better furnished
than any other they had seen. The walls were hung with
clean skins, and the stove did not smoke badly, and there
were even such things as tables, chairs, a shelf of books,
a lamp, and a raised bed. Ouranov motioned the men to
make themselves comfortable. There was something in

86

his quiet, impersonal demeanor that made them feel shy, shy even of conveying the news that they had brought with them. They stood round, unwilling to sit in those astonishing chairs; most of them in the end squatted on the timber floor.

Ouranov was busying himself with the samovar. Meanwhile the soldiers could only stare at one another, while the still shouting and chattering Yakuts waited outside the hut in a tempest of curiosity. At last the spokesman of the party began: "Brother, we are the bearers of good news. Don't be too startled when you hear it, though it certainly is enough to send any man such as yourself out of his wits for joy. At Kolymsk that did actually happen to one poor fellow, so you will understand, brother, why we are taking such a long time to tell you."

Then Ouranov turned from the samovar and smiled. It was a curious smile, for though it lit up his face it seemed to light up even more the grimness that was there. "Whatever news it is," he said, "you may be sure I shall not be affected in that way."

"Then, brother, it is this. You are a free man. All exiles everywhere are now released and may return to their homes, by order of the new revolutionary government. Think of it—there has been a revolution in Petrograd—the Emperor has been deposed—" And as if a hidden spring had suddenly been touched the soldiers all began to talk, to explain, to shout out the good news, with all its details, to this man who knew nothing. They had told the same story at each one of the settlements, and every time of telling had made it more marvelous to them. Their eyes blazed with joy and pity, and pride at having the privilege of conveying the first blessings of revolution to those who stood most in need of them. But if only Ouranov had been a little more excited, they would have been happier. He handed them tea so quietly, and after they had all finished talking he merely said: "Yes, it is good news. I will pack my things."

The soldiers again stared at one another, a little awed, perhaps even a little chilled; they had enjoyed such orgies of hysteria at the other settlements, but this man seemed different—as if the Arctic had entered his soul.

He said, rather perceiving their disappointment: "It is very kind of you to have come so far to tell me. As I said before, there has been no news for three years. There were four other exiles here then, but that same winter three died of typhus, and another was drowned the following summer."

"So for over a year you have been altogether alone?" said one of the soldiers.

"Oh, no. There have been the Yakuts." And once more that grim smile.

They fell to talking again of the revolution and its manifold blessings, and after a little time they noticed that Ouranov seemed hardly to be listening; he was already taking his books from the shelf and making them into a neat pile.

Two days later eight men set out for the south. There was need to hurry, as the warmer season was approaching and the streams would soon melt and overflow.

As they covered mile after mile it was as if the earth warmed and blossomed to meet them; each day was longer and brighter than the one before; the stunted willows became taller, and at last there were trees with green buds on them; the sun shone higher in the sky, melting the snows and releasing every stream into bursting, bubbling life, till the ice in the rivers gave a thunderous shiver from bank to bank; and the soldiers threw off their fur jackets and shouted for joy and sang songs all the day long. At Verkhoiansk there was a junction with other parties of released exiles, and later on, when they had crossed the mountains, more exiles met them from Ust Viliusk, Kolymsk, and places that even the map ignores.

Yakutsk, which was reached at the end of July, was already full of soldiers and exiles, as well as knee-deep in thick black mud and riddled with pestilence. Every day the exiles waited on the banks of the Lena for the boat that was to take them further south, and every hour fresh groups arrived from the north and north-east. Food and money were scarce; sick men and women staggered into the settlement with stories of others who had died during the journey; a few were mad and walked about moaning and laughing; every night the soldiers drank themselves into quarrelsomeness and careered about firing shots into the air and falling off the timbered paths into the thick mud; every morning dead bodies were pushed quietly into the Lena and sent northwards on their icy journey. Yet beyond all the misery and famine and pestilence, Yakutsk was a city of hope.

Ouranov had little money, but he did not go hungry. The seven soldiers of his escort had taken a curious fancy to him. They called him their captain, and saw to it that he always had food and shelter. There was much in him that they did not understand, but also something that attracted them peculiarly. During the first part of the southward expedition he had naturally taken command, for he knew the land far better than they, and was in less danger of losing the track. After that it had seemed natural that he should go on telling them when and where to halt, where to stay for the nights, and so on. They let him do that, in spite of (or perhaps because of) the fact that they thought him a little mad. They had a nickname for him which meant "The man who has forgotten how to talk." It was an obvious exaggeration, since he did talk whenever there was need for it; yet even on such occasions, it was as if he were thinking out the words, and as if each word cost him effort. They told one another that this was because he had been exiled by himself and had been left alone so long. By the time of reaching Yakutsk the legend had grown; Ouranov, they were saying, had been such a dangerous revolutionary that, by the ex-Emperor's personal order, he had been sent to the remotest and most terrible spot in all Siberia. And after a week of gossip in Yakutsk it was easy to say and believe that he had been ten years utterly alone in Russkoe Yansk, and that he had not spoken a word during the whole of that time. So now, when the soldiers saw him reading a book or making pencil notes on paper, they said he must be learning language over again.

At last came the long-awaited steamer, an old paddle-boat, built in Glasgow in the 'seventies, towing behind it a couple of odorous and verminous convict-barges. Fifteen hundred persons crammed themselves into the boat and another thousand into the barges. There was nowhere to sleep except on the bare boards of the deck, or in the foul and pestilential holds; men and women sickened, died, and were dropped overboard during that month of weary chug-chugging upstream through a forlorn land.

By August the exiles were in Irkutsk. The city was in chaos; its population had been increased three-fold; it was the neck of the channel through which Siberia was

emptying herself of the accumulated suffering of genera-
tions. From all directions poured in an unceasing flood
of returning exiles and refugees—not only from Yakutsk
and the Arctic, but from Chita and the Manchurian bor-
der, from the Baikal mines and the mountain-prisons of
the Yablonoi. In addition, there were German, Austrian,
and Hungarian war-prisoners, drifting slowly westward
as the watch upon them dissolved under the distant rays
of the Petrograd revolution; and nomad traders from the
Gobi, scraping profit out of the pains and desires of so
many strangers; and Buriat farmers, rich after years of
war-profiteering; and Cossack officers, still secretly loyal
to the old régime; Irkutsk was a magnet drawing together the whole assortment, and drawing also influenza
and dysentery, scurvy and typhus, so that the hospitals
were choked with sick, and bodies were thrown, uncof-
fined and by scores, into huge open graves dug by patient
Chinese.

On a warm August afternoon A.J. wandered about the
Irkutsk railway depot, threading his way amongst the
refugees and listening for a few odd moments to various
political speeches that were being made by soldiers. He
was dressed in a nondescript, vaguely military uniform
which he had acquired at Yakutsk as soon as the cold
weather had begun to recede; he might have been taken
for a Russian soldier, though not, at a second glance, for
a very ordinary one. His fine teeth, spare figure, and
close-cropped hair and beard, would all have marked him
from a majority. His features, lined and rugged, were
not without a look of gentleness and pity; but as he
wandered about the station and freight yards he seemed
really to have no more than the shadow of any quality;

all was obscured by a look of uncomprehendingness that did not quite amount to bewilderment.

The seven Cossacks who had been with him for so many weeks were also on the platform, very dejected because they had been ordered east, while he, of course, must take the first train in the other direction. He joined them for a final meal of tea and black bread before their train arrived. "You must go to Petrograd," one of them told him, earnestly. "All the exiles are going there to work for the new government—Kerensky will find you a job—perhaps he will make you an inspector of taxes."

"No, no," interrupted another. "Our brother is surely fitted to be something better than an inspector of taxes. He has books—he must be a great scholar. I should think Kerensky might make him a postmaster, for a postmaster, after all, has to know how to read and write."

They argued thus until the train arrived, and A.J. stayed with them, smiling at their remarks occasionally, but saying very little. There was a great rush for seats on the train, and when at last the seven soldiers had all crowded into a coach they leaned out of the open window and kissed him—their captain, their legend, the man whom they would remember and wonder at until the end of their lives. And he, when their train had gone, strolled away still half-smiling.

He lay at night, like thousands of others, in any sheltered corner he could find, with a little bundle of all his possessions for a pillow. After three more days a train came in from the east; it was grotesquely full already, but he managed to find a place in a cattle-truck.

The train was very long, and between the first coach next to the engine and the last cattle-truck at the rear, the whole world lay in mad microcosm. For the first coach was a dining-car, smooth-running and luxurious; you could look through the windows and see military officers, spattered with gold braid, picking their teeth after fried chicken and champagne, while attendants in evening-dress hovered about them obsequiously. Next came the first-class coach in which these magnates lived when they were not eating and drinking; and next the second-class coaches, containing those who were not fortunate enough to be high military officers; they were not allowed to use the dining-car, but the attendants would sometimes, at an extortionate price, supply them with food and drink. After that came the third-class coaches, crammed with soldiers of the revolution who bought or commandeered food at wayside stations; and last, comprising two-thirds of the whole train, were the cattle-trucks, packed from floor to roof with refugees and peasants and returning exiles—folk who had spent their last paper rouble on a railway ticket, or else had smuggled themselves on board with no ticket at all; and who had nothing to eat except the food they could bargain for, or the ghastly tit-bits they could rake out of rubbish-bins behind the station refresh-ment-rooms.

A.J. spent hours in his corner of the truck, watching through the slats the constant procession of miles. He was half-oblivious of those about him, of babies who screamed and were sick, of women who moaned with hunger, of men who chattered or quarreled or were noisily companionable. In a similar way he half-noticed the changes that had taken place since he had last moved over the scene—the extraordinary evidences of a new Si-beria that had sprung up ribbon-like along the thin line of the railway, the new factories and freight yards, the trams in the streets of Omsk, the steel bridges that had replaced wooden ones.

The journey was tiring, but worse for others than for himself, for his body, like his mind, seemed only capable of half-sensations. For years he had been unaware of this, but now, in a world of men and women, he perceived and was puzzled by it; he found himself doing things in a curious dream-like way, as if part of him were asleep and were obeying the other part automatically. Even when he talked, he heard his own voice as if it were another person speaking; and when he felt tiredness, or hunger, or a physical ache, the sensation came to him slowly, incompletely, almost at second-hand.

A near-by fellow-exile tried to converse with him, but received little encouragement. The man was an ex-university professor named Tribourov—fat, pompous, and tremendously eager to reach Petrograd because he knew many people in the Government and felt sure of a good appointment. He was also extremely annoyed that he had not been able to find a place for himself and his wife in the second- or first-class coaches. "Really, the Government ought to arrange things better," he complained continually.

Madame Tribourov, a thin and rather delicate-looking woman who had shared the professor's exile for five years, was suffering acutely from illness and hunger; she could not eat any of the rough food that was the only kind obtainable at wayside stations, and every day she grew weaker and nearer to collapse. Tribourov himself, dreaming bureaucratic dreams, paid little attention to her beyond an occasional word of perfunctory encouragement; she would be all right, he kept saying, as soon as they reached the end of the journey.

94

One morning the train stopped to load fuel in the midst of forest country, far from any station or settlement, and some of the men, glad of the chance to stretch their legs, climbed out of the trucks and walked about. A.J. and Tribourov were together, and Tribourov, as usual, talked about himself and his future importance and the iniquity of his having to travel in a cattle-truck. His complaining increased when they had strolled along the track as far as the dining-car and could see its occupants talking, laughing, and guzzling over an excellent lunch. Seen through the window from the track-level, the dining-car presented a vista of large, munching jaws, glittering epaulettes, and the necks of wine-bottles. One man was gnawing the leg of a fowl, another was lifting champagne to his lips, another was puffing at a cigar in full-stomached contentment. At the far end of the car was the little kitchen-compartment where the food was cooked and stored; the window was open and on the shelves could be seen rows of bottles as well as canned foods, cheeses, and boxes of biscuits. "All that stuff comes from Japan and America," Tribourov explained. "They load it on board at Vladivostok and it lasts all the way to Moscow and back. Excellently organized, but the scandal is—" And he resumed his usual complaint and continued until the engine-whistle warned them to hasten back to their truck.

That night, when it was almost pitch-dark and his fellow-travelers were mostly asleep or half-asleep, A.J. climbed out on to the footboard and began to feel his way cautiously along the length of the train. His hands and mind were functioning automatically; half of him was asking—"What on earth are you doing?"—and the other half was answering—"I am going to the dining-car to steal some food for Madame Tribourov." He did not know why he was doing so; he cared nothing at all for Madame Tribourov; it was no feeling of chivalry, or of compassion, or of indignation. It was rather a chance idea that had entered his half-mind—just an idea that loomed unwontedly large in a void where there were no other ideas.

The train was traveling at a moderate speed—not more than twenty miles an hour; the night was cloudy and the fringe of swamps to the side of the track was only to be dimly perceived. Little could be done by eye as he made his way from truck to truck; his hands groped for the slats and his feet for the buffers between one truck and the next. It was not a particularly dangerous progress, provided one kept one's nerve, and A.J. kept his easily enough; or rather, in another sense, he had no nerves at all—he was simply unaware of fear, terror, joy, triumph, and all other excitations. His hands and feet did what was required of them, while his brain looked on with mild incredulity.

Soon he reached the second-class coaches, in which candles were glimmering in bottle-necks; and he could see the occupants asleep—wealthy traders, bound on this business or that—well-dressed women, wives or mistresses of high officials—a few military officers of lower rank. He passed them all and then swung himself over the buffer-boards to the first-class coach, which rolled along less noisily on well-greased trucks. Here the compartments were well-upholstered, lit by electricity, and provided with window-blinds. Many of the latter were not drawn, however, and A.J. could see officers of high rank, partially undressed, lying on the cushions with their mouths gaping in obvious snores. The coach was not crowded;

no compartment held more than two occupants, and some only one. An especially luxurious coupé with a large red star pasted on the windows contained a small table and a comfortable couch on which a man sprawled in sleep. A military tunic hung on a hook above his head, and in the far corner of the coupé there was a compact lavatory-basin and water-tank. Such details fastened themselves with curious intensity on A.J.'s mind as he made that slow hand-over-hand journey from window to window. At last he passed on, over the last set of buffers, to the object of his pilgrimage—the dining-car. It was a long heavy vehicle belonging to the international company, and at three in the morning it was naturally deserted, with only a glimmer of light showing from the further end where the attendants slept in their bunks. A.J. continued his way along, but this final stage was more difficult, because of the increasing volley of sparks from the engine-chimney. When he reached the tiny kitchen compartment he was quite prepared for a climb through the window, with all the risk it involved of waking the attendants; but fate, at that last moment, was unexpectedly kind. The window was still open, and rolls of white bread, tins of American pork and beans, and wine-bottles lay so accessibly that he could reach them merely by putting in a hand. He did so as quickly as he could, filling his pockets, and then beginning the backward crawl by the same route. It had taken him, he reckoned, twenty minutes to reach the dining-car from the truck at the far end of the train, but he could not hope to accomplish the return journey so quickly, for his hands were a little numbed and his swollen pockets impeded movement.

He reached the first-class coach and swung himself on

to it, but the effort, employing a different set of muscles, made him wince; and when he reached the footboard in safety he paused to regain strength. Suddenly he realized that he was standing opposite the window of the coupé and that the occupant of the couch was sitting up and staring at him. He began to move on hurriedly, but before he could reach the next compartment the door of the coupé was flung open and strong hands seized his wrists. It was impossible to struggle; the slightest attempt to do so would have meant his falling backwards to the track, and his arms, too, were aching after those successive swings from coach to coach. At first he thought the man was trying to push him off the train, but soon he realized that the intention was to drag him inside the coupé. As he could not free himself and as to be dragged inside was better than to be flung off, he yielded and the next minute found himself sprawling on the couch with the door closed and the man above him flourishing a revolver. He was a tall man with a trim beard and mustache and an exceedingly good set of teeth; just now he was snarling with them and punctuating his words with waves of the revolver. "So?" he cried, venomously. "You try to assassinate me, eh? You creep along by the windows and shoot while I am asleep, perhaps, eh? Your friends in Omsk have heard of my promotion and they send you to execute revenge, no doubt? But instead, it is I who turn the tables, my friend! Now let me relieve you of your weapons." He felt in A.J.'s bulging pockets and pulled out, not the revolver he had expected, but a bottle of wine. "So?" he snarled, flinging it aside. "A little celebration after the deed, eh? How disappointed your friends will be! And especially when they hear you have been shot, also. For, mistake not, my friend, I will have you shot at the next station. Assassin! Do you hear that?" He rapidly went through A.J.'s other pockets, pulling out, to his increasing surprise, nothing but long rolls of white bread, pieces of cheese, and tins of food.

All this time A.J. had not spoken a word, but now he judged it expedient to confess nothing less than the simple truth. "You see I am not armed," he began. "I am not an assassin, and I had no intention of making any attack on you. I have no friends at Omsk, and I did not even know you were traveling on this train. I am an exile, returning to Russia, and all I wanted was food. I took these things from the dining-car and was on my way back with them to the truck in which I have been traveling from Irkutsk."

The other seemed scarcely mollified by this explanation. He obviously believed it, but the revelation that he had been made to suffer such shock and inconvenience by a mere petty pilferer angered him, if anything, more than the idea of being assassinated. "A thief, indeed?" he cried, harshly. "You are only a thief, do you say? And you were only crawling along in the middle of the night to steal food from the dining-car? Do you know that the food is all required for high officers of the Government? You do, no doubt; but that did not deter you. Very well, you will find that the penalty for thieving is just the same. We behave with fine impartiality, you will find—thief or assassin—it does not matter—all face the firing-squad."

"Some of the refugees in the trucks are starving," said A.J. slowly.

"Are they, indeed? Then let them starve. Why do they all want to come crowding on the trains at a time like this? Let them starve—the scum—the country could well manage with a few millions less of them. And as for these things—after your dirty hands have touched them they are clearly no use at all." And with childish rage he began to pick them up and throw them out of the window—first the bottle of wine, then the rolls, then the cheese, and lastly the tins.

Something jerked forward in A.J.'s mind at that moment. As the other stooped to pick up the last tin, he suddenly hurled himself at the sneering face and flashing teeth, while his right hand caught hold of the revolver by the barrel and twisted it back. A.J. was still in a dream, but it was a different dream, a rising, billowing nightmare. He saw and heard the revolver slip to the floor, and then he felt both his hands move to the red, mottled neck in front of him; he saw the eyes bulge in terror and the snarl of the teeth transfix into something glittering and rigid.

A moment later he stood by the side of the couch looking down upon its curious occupant. There was no life now in the staring eyes and in the twisted limbs.

All at once it occurred to him; he had killed the fellow. He had not intended to—or *had* he? Yet no—there was hardly such a thing as intention in him. It had just happened; the sight of the food disappearing through the window had set up some unwonted electrical contact between mind and body—something, in fact, had fused.

He tried to think what to do next, and his mind worked with icy clearness, as in a vacuum. The dead man had clearly been a person of importance, and that meant certain death for his slayer. Assuming, of course, that the latter were discovered. But need he be? Was there a chance of escape? No one had seen him so far; the blinds of the windows next to the corridor were drawn and the corridor-door was fastened on the inside. He must, of course, hasten back to the cattle-truck and feign sleep; his absence might or might not have been particularly noticed, but perhaps he would be safe if he could return unobtrusively. At the next station, he knew, there would be a huge commotion, with probably the most minute examinations and cross-questionings of everybody in the train.

He was just about to open the door of the coupé and begin a swift return journey along the footboards when he heard a tap at the corridor-door. "Tarkarovsk in fifteen minutes' time, sir," came the voice of the train-attendant. After a pause the message was repeated, and then A.J. managed to stammer out, "All right." He heard the attendant move away and tap at other doors along the corridor with the same message—"Tarkarovsk in fifteen minutes' time, sir."

And that, unfortunately, settled it. He could not return to the truck; it had taken him twenty minutes to make the forward journey, and it was impossible to think of doubling his rate on the way back. Besides, the train attendant's warning would waken the passengers in the compartments; they would be sitting up and yawning, and would certainly see him if he passed their windows. The only alternative seemed to be a risky jump off the train and an escape across country, though his position would be desperate enough even then. Tarkarovsk was dangerously near; the body would be discovered quite soon; within an hour the surrounding country would be swarming with armed searchers. Nor, among those open, desolate swamps, could a fugitive hope to elude pursuers for long.

Then suddenly his mind alighted on a third possibility

—fantastic, almost incredible, yet not, in such circumstances, to be rejected too scornfully. After all, one way, and perhaps the best way, in which a culprit might avoid discovery was by contriving that his crime should not be discovered either. A.J. looked at the dead man, then at the tunic hanging above him; and all at once his mind began arranging the future with astonishing precision. Yet there was no astonishment in the way he accepted every detail of an amazing scheme. He was cool, almost slow, in his movements. First he stripped the body of the dead man. Next he undressed himself and put on the dead man's clothes. After that he dressed the body in his own discarded garments. Then, opening the door of the coupé, he hurled the clothed body as far away from the track as he could. With luck it might sink into a swamp and never be discovered at all, but even without luck, it was hardly likely to attract much attention in such circumstances as he would arrange. Refugees and peasants often fell out of trains; several bodies had been noticed on the way from Irkutsk, but no one had thought of stopping to identify or examine them.

After reclosing the door of the coupé he washed in the lavatory-basin and completed his toilet. The other man's uniform fitted him very well indeed, as did also the military top-boots. The brakes were already grinding on the wheels as he pulled down the window-blinds, half lay down on the couch, took up a magazine that was on the table, and closed his eyes. If anyone opened the door from the platform it would appear that he had fallen asleep whilst reading.

The rest of his scheme was comparatively simple, if only he could escape attention at Tarkarovsk. Between Tarkarovsk and the next station there was almost sure to be some suitable spot where, before dawn, he could jump from the train and slip away across country. The disappearance of a high officer would create a stir, but only eventually; it would be more natural first of all to assume that any one of a dozen minor mischances could account for it.

The train jerked and jangled to a standstill—Tarkarovsk—Tarkarovsk. A sound of shouting reached him from outside and then the scurry of footsteps running along the platform as the train halted. He did not think Tarkarovsk was a very large place, but of course even the smallest stations were crowded with refugees. Suddenly sharper cries pierced the general din, and the door of the coupé opened violently to admit an intruder very different from any A.J. had anticipated. He was of small stature and corpulent, was dressed in a black frock coat and trousers, and carried a rather shabby top hat. "Welcome, sir!" he cried, making a profound bow. "As chairman of the local council of Khalinsk, I bring you the town's most gracious felicitations." A.J. rose in astonishment, whereupon the other, smiling and still bowing, took hold of his hand and gave it a tremendous shaking. The dream in which A.J. had been living for so long turned a corner now and swept into the infinite corridors of another dream. Somehow or other he found himself stepping out of the train; porters immediately entered it and began lifting out quantities of luggage. Other men in frock coats and top hats were presented to him, and he heard the little man saying sweetly: "The cars are waiting outside, sir, if you are ready." He walked across the platform and out into the courtyard where a huge Benz was waiting. He got in; several frock coats followed him; the luggage was packed into a second car behind.

Then the two cars lurched forward along a dusty uneven road. He did not speak, but his companions, evidently thinking he was very sleepy, commiserated with him on the inconvenience of arriving at a country railway station at half past three in the morning. Soon the road widened into the typically Siberian town of Tarkarovsk. The cars pulled up outside the small hotel, and A.J. was informed that a room had been engaged for him and that he could take a rest, if he chose, until breakfast, after which the journey to Khalinsk would be resumed. He gave rather vague thanks and said the arrangement would suit him very well. The frock coats conducted him upstairs to his room with obsequious gestures and then went down again, he guessed, to have many drinks and much gossip about himself.

*About himself*—that was the question. Who was he? Who was he supposed to be? Why was he being taken to Khalinsk? And why the finery of a frock-coated railway-station reception at such an hour? Then, alone in the rather dingy bedroom as the first light of dawn paled against the edges of the window-blinds, it occurred to him that the contents of his pockets might afford a clew. He examined them; he found a thick wallet containing a large sum in paper money and several official documents. One was a letter from Petrograd addressed to a Colonel Nikolai Andreyeff, of Krasnoiarsk, appointing him Commissar of the town and district of Khalinsk, Western Siberia. And another was from the local council of Khalinsk, tendering their best respects and expressing sincere appreciation of the privilege conferred on them by the Petrograd Government. A.J. read them through, put them back in the wallet, and then sat on the edge of the bed with his head in his hands. He was still in his dark dream, and he dared not try to waken. There was no help for it; from the moment the frock coat had entered the train at Tarkarovsk, a third identity had descended on him like a sealed doom.

So he became Nikolai Andreyeff, Commissar of Khalinsk, and he began to wonder whether he would be fortunate enough to arrange an escape before he was found out. As it chanced, it became increasingly impossible to arrange an escape; but then, on the other hand, he was not found out. Both time and place were, in fact, especially favorable to the impersonation; Khalinsk was a small town, well away from the main avenues of Siberian communication, and too remote at first even to be affected seriously by the Revolution itself. Most of its inhabitants, some ten thousand or so in number, were quietly and prosperously bourgeois; the surrounding district provided abundant food, and though the usual exchange of exports and imports with European Russia had been impeded, that had meant to the folk of Khalinsk no greater privations than a shortage of cotton-thread and Ford motor parts, and the necessity to use their best butter as axle-grease for warm-wagons. Khalinsk, indeed, was a little island of normality in the midst of a rising sea of chaos, and its new Commissar fitted in to its peaceful scheme of things without much difficulty. Everyone agreed that he was a "queer" man with "queer" ways, but most were glad, in their bourgeois hearts, that Petrograd had not sent them a fire-eater. About a week after his arrival news came that his wife and child had died of typhus in Vladivostok, and Khalinsk people felt much sympathy for the quiet, rarely-speaking man who had to sit in his office signing travel-passes while his family were buried at the other end of a continent. When someone ventured to express that sympathy all he received was a patient "Thank you—it is most kind of you"—courteously given, but somehow not an encouragement to continue.

Once a visitor to Khalinsk who had known of Colonel Andreyeff in Krasnoiarsk commented that he would hardly have recognized him for the same man. "He was a wild fellow in those days—always ready to crack a joke —or another man's head, for that matter. And now look at him!"

Khalinsk looked at him quite often, for the commissary office was in the center of the town, adjoining the courthouse and the prison, and the Commissar walked between his office and his hotel four times a day. In the hotel he had rooms of his own and took all his meals in private. But Khalinsk people could see him in their streets, and behind his desk whenever they had business with him; he presided, too, in the local court-house, and paid official visits to the prison. His justice was firm, and the town's young bloods soon learned that they could play no tricks with the new ruler; yet it was noticed and commented upon that in court he always looked as if he were only half attending and didn't really care what happened.

His subordinates respected him, with the possible exception of Kashvin, the Assistant Commissar. Kashvin, a local youth of considerable intelligence, felt that the Petrograd authorities had needlessly superseded him in bringing Andreyeff from Krasnoiarsk, and he was the more antagonistic to his superior because he could not, with all his shrewdness, understand him. The two men, indeed, were complete opposites. Kashvin was cordial, unscrupulous, an astute observer of politics, and an impassioned orator. Probably, too, he was clever enough to foresee that power at Petrograd would eventually pass into the hands of extremists. During the autumn the normally easy-going life of Khalinsk did very rapidly deteriorate; a garrison of soldiers arrived from Europe with new and wilder doctrines; they were hardly willing to obey their own officers, much less a local commissar. Great excitement, also, had been caused by the establishment, in custody, of the ex-Emperor and his family at Tobolsk, a few hundred miles away. Throughout October conditions grew more and more turbulent, and it was clear that the situation in Petrograd was already slipping out of the hands of the moderates. Then in November came news of the Bolshevik revolution, and an immediate acceleration in Khalinsk and all such places of the trend already in progress.

Even Kashvin found it increasingly difficult to keep his balance on the political tight-rope. Following a custom beginning to be prevalent, the soldiers had got rid of their officers and had elected others from their own ranks; unfortunately, however, they obeyed their elected superiors no better than anyone else. Kashvin's loudest oratory could not persuade them to cease their plundering raids into the town shops. Andreyeff did not try the oratorical method; he collected a few personal supporters and made arrests. Sternness succeeded for a while, until, quite suddenly, the blow was struck. While the Commissar was sitting at the court-house one morning in January, the building was surrounded by soldiers and a spokesman entered to deliver an ultimatum. The soldiers, he announced, wished to choose their own commissar as well as their own officers; they had been in communication with Petrograd and had received official support; so would, therefore, the Commissar kindly consent to consider himself no longer a commissar until a vote had been taken? Most observers expected Andreyeff to give a sharp answer, but to general surprise he merely smiled (which he so rarely did) and replied: "Certainly—with pleasure." The vote was taken there and then, and Kashvin was elected commissar, with Andreyeff as his civilian assistant. Again it was expected that the latter would indignantly refuse to serve under his recent subordinate, but Andreyeff continued to give surprise by his easy acceptance of the situation. And, indeed, the reversal of position made more difference in theory than in fact. Kashvin, though nominally in authority, was completely at the mercy of his military supporters, while Andreyeff, exactly as before, continued his patient work of issuing ration-cards, arranging for the distribution of food and fuel, and making out travel-passes.

During the early months of the new year the position at Khalinsk was still becoming worse. The nearness of Tobolsk, with its illustrious prisoners, brought to the district a heavy influx of revolutionary and counter-revolutionary spies, German and Allied secret agents, and free-lance adventurers of all kinds. Tobolsk was their goal, but Khalinsk was a safer place for plotting. Half the peddlers and market-dealers were in the service of one or other organization, and every day brought new and more startling rumors. In March a regiment of the new Red Army arrived from Ekaterinburg to relieve the older men who had already served through most of the Siberian winter. Many were criminals freshly released from European prisons; the best of them were miners and factory-workers lured into the army by generous pay and rations. They were all completely undisciplined and changed their officers with monotonous regularity.

Towards the end of March the long succession of rumors did at length culminate in something actual. Late one night the telephone-bell rang in the commissary office; Andreyeff, who was there working, answered it; the call came from a post-house halfway between Khalinsk and the railway. The message reported that there were rumors that the Trans-Siberian line had been cut by White guards, assisted by Czecho-Slovak prisoners-of-war.

A.J., tired after a long day of wrestling with the complications of a new rationing system, took no particular notice, since such scare messages arrived almost regularly two or three nights a week. But a quarter of an hour later another message came—this time from Tarkarovsk; no train, it said, had arrived from the east since noon, and there were rumors that counter-revolution had broken out at Omsk. A.J. rang through to the garrison but could get no answer; Kashvin, he guessed, would be in bed and asleep; he walked, therefore, a mile or so over the hard snow to the soldiers' barracks. He found the place in a state of utter chaos and pandemonium, with all the officers more or less drunk and incapable. Most of the men were in a similar condition; it was a saint's day, and by way of celebration they had looted several wine-cellars in the town. A.J. tried to make known the dangerous possibilities of the situation, and while he was actually in the officers' room there came a further telephone message from Pokroevensk, ten miles away, conveying the brief information that counter-revolutionary bands had occupied and plundered a neighboring village. At this a few of the officers struggled to rouse themselves, and men were hastily sent to the armory for rifles and ammunition. Meanwhile, orders were given for a general turn-out, but out of nearly a thousand men only two hundred could be equipped for whatever emergency might arise. Hundreds were so drunk that they could not stir from the floors on which they had collapsed; many also were sleeping with women in the town and could not be reached at all.

A.J. himself took a rifle and a belt of cartridges, and soon after midnight the detachment, in charge of an officer, set out along the gleaming snow-bound road. The cold air soon cleared the drink-sodden heads of the men, and they stepped out at a good pace in the direction of Pokroevensk. Ruffians though most of them were, A.J. found them almost pathetically companionable and full of amazement that he, a civilian commissar, should be accompanying them. Surely, as a government official, it was his privilege—his perquisite, as it were—to keep out of all serious danger? He smiled and answered that he had come because he knew the district very well—the roads, directions, and so on. It would not matter his temporarily deserting the office-desk; there was Kashvin in charge. And at this the men laughed. Though they loved to let themselves be stirred by Kashvin's eloquence, a moment such as this brought out their secret contempt for the man whose tongue is so much mightier than his sword.

During the first hour the men sang songs—not spirited marching songs but dragging, rather melancholy refrains that seemed to be known by all. One was "Far Away and over the Marshes"—a weird recitative about exile; another favorite was "A Soldier Lays Down His Life." Into these slow crooning tunes the men somehow contrived to insert a strange ghost of rhythm, hardly noticeable to the listener, yet sufficient to keep them in rough, plodding step. After the first few miles, however, A.J. suggested that they had better march in silence, since voices carried far in that still, cold atmosphere. The men obeyed him, not instantly, as from a military order, but with a gradual trail of voices from high melody to the faintest murmur amongst themselves. The officer who should have had the wit to give the order was staggering along still very drunk. The men said tranquilly that it was because he was not satisfied to get drunk like other men; he dosed himself with a sort of yeast-paste which produced more permanent effects.

The remaining events of that night might serve as a model for much that was happening and that was yet to happen throughout the vast territory between the Pacific and the Vistula. All the typical ingredients were present —confusion, rumor, inconsequence, surprise. To begin with, at Pokroevensk, which was reached about three in the morning, the officer in charge suddenly collapsed and died. A.J. telephoned the news to Khalinsk and gathered that the town was in the wildest panic; rumors of an overwhelming White advance along the line of the Trans-Siberian were being received, and the garrison was already preparing to evacuate the town. This seemed to A.J. the sheerest absurdity as well as cowardice, but he could not argue the matter over the wire with a person who, from the sound of his voice, was still half-drunk. He determined, if the soldiers were willing (for of course he had no real authority over them), to march on to the railway and tear up a few lengths of line—the usual and most effective way of delaying an advance. The men agreed to this plan, and were just about to leave Pokroevensk when a mortifying discovery was made. The ammunition that they carried would not fit the rifles, the former being of French pattern, while the latter were

Japanese. Similar mistakes, the men said, had often been made during the war against the Germans. It meant, of course, that the detachment was practically unarmed, and A.J. could see nothing for it but to return to Khalinsk as quickly as possible. But then something else happened. In the grim light of dawn a band of White guards swept suddenly into the village along the frozen road from the west; there were several hundred of them, all fully armed and all in a mood to wreak terrible havoc upon a small village. They were not, however, prepared for Andreyeff and his couple of hundred men. Still less was Andreyeff prepared for them. He realized that a fight would be hopeless, and rather than have all his followers shot to pieces he would prefer to surrender; he had none of the more spectacular heroic virtues and conceived that a soldier's aim should be to preserve his own life at least as much as to destroy his enemy's. As it chanced, however, the White captain thought similarly and was, moreover, a little quicker in action. He surrendered to Andreyeff a few seconds before the latter could possibly have reversed the compliment. It was amusing, in a way, to see four or five hundred well-armed Whites surrendering to less than half as many Reds who could not, if they had tried, have fired a shot. The White captain explained that he was not really a very convinced White; he had always, in fact, inclined to be a little pink. Some of the White soldiers raised cheers for the Soviets. Andreyeff nodded gravely; the procedure was very familiar.

More important than the White soldiers was a party of civilians whom they had been escorting. These were various personages, more or less illustrious, who had escaped from European Russia and were hoping to cross Siberia and reach America. They had traveled disguised as far as Tarkarovsk and had there given themselves into the hands of a White detachment which, in return for an enormous bribe, had undertaken to get them through to Omsk.

A.J. was in no doubt as to his proper course of action. Such a distinguished party must be conveyed to Khalinsk and held as hostages. He arranged this promptly, after arming his men with the rifles taken from the White soldiers. Khalinsk was reached by noon, and by that time the atmosphere was completely changed; the Whites had everywhere been defeated, and Red reënforcements were already arriving from Ekaterinburg. A.J.'s prisoners were examined and locked away in the town jail, with the exception of most of the soldiers, who were permitted to join the Red army. In the reaction that followed the excitements of the whole episode A.J. felt a certain bewildered helplessness; all was such confusion, incoherence, chaos—a game played in the dark with fate as a blind umpire. The chapter of accidents found itself interpreted as a miracle of intrepid organization, with A.J. as the hero of the hour. Even Kashvin congratulated him. "I would have accompanied you myself," he explained, "but as Commissar, it would have been improper for me to leave the town. Now tell me, Andreyeff, do you think it would be better to ask for Japanese ammunition to fit the rifles or for French rifles to fit the ammunition?" He then showed A.J. a few reports he had drafted and which were to be telegraphed away immediately. They were all circumstantially detailed accounts of atrocities committed by White guards—women raped, babies speared on the ends of bayonets, wounded men tortured to death, and so on. Kashvin seemed extremely proud of the collection. "But surely," A.J. said, "you

113

can't have received proof of all this in so short a time?"
Kashvin replied cheerfully: "Oh, no—they are my own
invention entirely—don't you think they read very well?
After all, since we have no rifles and ammunition for the
present, we must do what we can with moral weapons."

And, as it further chanced, the Whites *had* committed
atrocities, though less ingeniously than Kashvin had imagined. The Reds, too, were not without a natural lust
for vengeance. Hundreds of prosperous local inhabitants
were thrown into prisons on charges of having been in
sympathy with the White insurrectionists; wholesale raids
and arrests were made, and the Khalinsk prison was soon
quite full. Meanwhile in the town itself all semblance
of civilian authority vanished. A strongly Red local soviet was appointed by the soldiers; Kashvin, despite prodi-
gies of oratory and private maneuver, was deposed from
office and a Jewish agitator named Baumberg took his
place. A.J. was allowed to remain as Assistant Commissar because he was personally popular and because nobody
else either wanted or was capable of performing his various jobs. These jobs now vastly increased, especially as
food grew less plentiful and disease broke out in the
overcrowded prison and barracks. Baumberg was a loud-
voiced, heavy-featured Pole whose ferocity in public was
only rivaled by an uncanny mildness in private life. His
ruthlessness gratified the soldiers, and his speeches, sin-
cerer if no more extreme than those of Kashvin, were
constant incitements to violence. Yet he was a pleasant
person compared with the military commandant, an ex-
railwayman named Vronstein. Vronstein was a psycho-
pathological curiosity; he had been long in exile, and
its results had been an astounding assortment of perver-
sions. Even his sadism was perverted; when prisoners

114

were punished or shot he would never watch the scene himself, but would insist that a full and detailed report, complete with every horror, was submitted to him in writing. Over such reports he would savagely and secretly gloat for hours. Baumberg openly despised him, but there was a sinister power about the fellow which gave him considerable hold over the soldiers.

Among the commissary duties was that of visiting the prison and prison hospital, which were now under the control of the local soviet. Both were small and crammed with White prisoners, most of whom were sullenly resigned to whatever fate might be in store for them. A few were defiant, exulting in the still-expected breakdown of the revolution. Almost every day fresh arrivals were brought in by Red guards, and—as it were to make room for them—others were removed by Baumberg's orders, taken to the military camp, and shot. Baumberg never explained on what system he selected his victims; perhaps, indeed, he had no system at all. His ferocity was coldly impersonal; when he had done his day's duty, including perhaps the ordering of half a dozen shootings for the morrow, he would go home to his daughter, who kept house for him, and play noisy, capering games with his fatherless grandchildren.

The White prisoners included a score or more women, who were lodged separately in a large, overcrowded room. This was a thoroughly unsatisfactory arrangement, since the room was badly needed as a supplementary hospital ward for the male prisoners, many of whom were sick and wounded. Baumberg, though he would have scorned any idea of sex-distinction, did not in fact have any of the women shot, and was willing enough to allow the majority of them to be transferred to Omsk, where the prison was larger. His only stipulated exceptions were the two most distinguished captives, whom he wished to keep at Khalinsk, and who, after the departure of the rest, were transferred to separate cells. Both had been captured by A.J.'s men in the affair at Pokroevensk. The Countess Vandaroff was one, and A.J., who had the job of visiting her from time to time, soon recommended her transference to hospital, since she was clearly going out of her mind. The other woman prisoner was the Countess Marie Alexandra Adraxine. She was of a different type; calm, exquisitely dignified, she accepted favors and humiliations alike with slightly mocking nonchalance. When A.J. first visited her she said: "Ah, Commissar, we have met before, I think? That morning at Pokroevensk—I dare say you remember?"

He said: "I have come to ask if you have any particular complaints—is your food satisfactory, and so on?"

"Oh, fairly so, in the circumstances. My chief wish is that there were fewer bugs in my mattress."

"I will try to see that you have a fresh one, though, of course, I cannot promise that it will be perfectly clean."

"Oh, I'm not fastidious—don't think that." She went to the narrow mattress by the wall of the cell and gave it a blow with her clenched fist. After a second or so a slowly spurting red cascade issued from every rent and seam. "You see?" she said. "It's the trivial things that really bother one most, isn't it?"

The second time he paid her cell an official visit she thanked him for having replaced the mattress by a comparatively unverminous one. Then she said: "Have you any idea what is going to happen to me, Commissar?"

He shook his head. "It is altogether a matter for others to decide."

"You think I shall be shot?"

"No women have been shot as yet."

"Nevertheless, it is possible?"

"Oh, perfectly."

"Would you approve?"

"I should not be asked either to approve or to disapprove."

She seemed amused by his attitude. After that he did not again visit her alone, for he did not care to be asked questions which he could not answer.

As spring advanced it could be foreseen that events in the district were hastening to a further crisis. Along the whole length of the Trans-Siberian the Czecho-Slovak prisoners-of-war, whom the Petrograd Government had promised a safe journey to Vladivostok, had seized trains and station depots. This comparatively small body of men, stretched out in tenuous formation for four thousand miles, was practically in possession of Siberia, and there was talk that the Allies, instead of letting them proceed across the Pacific, intended to use them to break the Soviets and re-form the eastern front against Germany. Simultaneously the forces of counter-revolution were again massing for an attack. In April the Reds began to send important political prisoners away from the endangered districts; the ex-Emperor was removed from Tobolsk for an unknown destination. From Khalinsk there would doubtless have been a big exodus but for a dispute between the district commissars of Tobolsk and Ekaterinburg as to who held authority over the town. Baumberg favored Ekaterinburg; Vronstein preferred Siberian rule. A hot quarrel arose between the two officials, broken only by intermittent shootings that both could agree upon.

At last came news that Omsk itself had been taken by

the counter-revolutionaries. Khalinsk was then caught up in another sudden scurry of panic; military and civilian authority both made preparations to evacuate the town; stores and ammunition were packed and sent away west; and Baumberg's speeches grew more and more tumultuous. Kashvin's invented atrocity stories now began to trickle back with many elaborations; they drove the Red garrison to the highest pitch of fury, and this, in the absence of any convenient battlefield enemy, was vented upon the White captives in the prison.

One night the quarreling between Baumberg and Vronstein came to a head. Difficulties had arisen over the provision of transport for sending certain of the prisoners to safer places—safer, that was, from White capture. Rather than run the risk of any being rescued by their friends, Vronstein was for a wholesale massacre; but this was too much for Baumberg. The two stormed and threatened each other, Vronstein declaring in the end that he would march at the head of his soldiers and take the prison by storm. As soon as he had left the commissary office, Baumberg turned to A.J. in his suddenly normal and placid way and said: "I do believe the fellow means it. He'll have them all murdered before the night's out. Andreyeff, I think you ought to go to the prison and get out the two women. Petrograd will be furious if they are slaughtered by those drunken hogs." He added, a little pompously: "The women are both very important links in the chain of evidence against the enemies of the revolution, and I have already received strict orders that they are to be taken care of. When the counter-revolution has been crushed, they are to be put on trial in Petrograd—I tell you that in confidence, of course."

It was almost midnight when A.J. reached the prison.

Even so soon there was in the atmosphere a queer feeling of impending terror; the prison-guards were nervous and inclined to question his authority. It was obvious that most of them, if only to save their own skins, would join with the soldiers in whatever bloodthirsty orgy was to ensue. A.J. sought Countess Vandaroff first; she was kept in an outlying part of the prison under semi-hospital conditions. As soon as the warder unlocked her door she sprang screaming out of bed and crouched in the furthest corner of the cell. A.J. began: "Do not alarm yourself, Countess, but get ready to move away at once. You are to be taken elsewhere." Then, as he saw the warder's eyes upon him, he knew that he had blundered. In the hurry of the moment he had called her "Countess." Commissars had been degraded and private soldiers shot, he knew, for less than that. Perturbed by the possible results of his slip, he went on to the other woman's cell. She was asleep and had to be wakened. He gave her the same message, but with careful omission of the forbidden word.

Waiting in the prison-hall for the two women to present themselves, he could hear the sound of shouting and rifle-fire from the barracks not far away. Intense nervousness had by this time communicated itself to warders and prisoners alike; all were wide awake and chattering, and A.J. wondered what might be in store for them during the next few hours. He knew Vronstein and had no illusions about him.

Countess Adraxine appeared first; she had put over her shoulders a light traveling cloak that still retained a trace of its original fashionableness, and she carried a few personal belongings in a small bundle. In the presence of the guards he did not speak to her; they waited for a moment in silence, and then he despatched one of the guards to fetch Countess Vandaroff. A little later the guard returned with the astonishing news that the woman was dead. A.J. rushed to her cell; it was true. Mad with terror at the thought that she was to be taken away and shot, the woman had killed herself by a desperate and rather difficult method; she had stabbed herself repeatedly in the throat with an ordinary safety-pin and had died from shock and loss of blood.

A.J. was a little paler when he rejoined the other prisoner. There was no time to be lost, and accompanied by guards the two hurried out of the prison and across the town-square to the commissary office. Baumberg was waiting; he had heard of the suicide by telephone and was in a fine fury. The Petrograd authorities would hold him responsible; how was it that the woman had been allowed to have in her possession such a dangerous weapon as a safety-pin; and much else that was extreme and absurd. Then, with one of those sudden returns to mildness that were such an odd trait in his character, he handed his assistant a sheaf of papers. "You are to take the remaining prisoner to Moscow, Andreyeff; there you will hand her over to the authorities. Two guards will go with you. Here are all the necessary papers; you will board the first train west from Tarkarovsk. The horses are waiting outside—you must set out instantly, for the latest news is that the Whites are advancing quickly along the line from Omsk."

In the courtyard of the office building stood a couple of tarantasses—the ordinary Siberian conveyance which, badly sprung and yoked to relays of horses, would sometimes accomplish the journey to Tarkarovsk in five or six hours. There was a small moon shining, and a sky of starlight. The roads, after the grip of winter, were on the point of thawing; in a few days they would be choked with mud. A.J., clad in a heavy soldier's great-coat and fur cap, superintended the stowing away of the luggage into the first vehicle which, driven by one of the guards, pulled out into the deserted street and clattered away south towards one o'clock in the morning. A few minutes later the second tarantass followed; A.J. and the woman sat together in the back of the swaying, rickety vehicle, while the other guard drove.

In the commissary yard A.J. had spoken a few words to his prisoner—formal courtesies and so on, but as soon as the journey began he relapsed into silence. He was, to begin with, physically tired; he had been working at more than normal pressure for weeks, and now reaction was on him. Apart from that, the stir of Countess Van-daroff's death and the sudden unfolding of a new future gave him a certain weariness of mind; he felt too men-tally fatigued to realize what was happening. Fortu-nately, fatigue drove away anxiety; he felt again as if he were living in the midst of some vague and curious dream, full of happenings over which he had no control and with which, in any major sense, he was completely unconcerned. He was, he supposed, bound for Moscow, yet how and even whether he would ever get there did not seem in the least important. He had a pocketful of documents stamped with all the official seals and signa-tures Baumberg had been able to commandeer, but he had no confidence that they were worth more than the paper they were written on. The ex-Emperor, it was ru-mored, had been seized by the local soviet at Ekaterin-burg in defiance of official orders; things like that were constantly happening; anything, indeed, might happen. The only course was to drift onwards, somehow or other, inside this busy dream, always ready, in an emergency, to grope into a wakefulness that was but another dream of another kind.

Steadily through the night the horses galloped over the softening earth. Only once was anything said, and that was at Pokroevensk, where the horses were changed and rumors were shared with the local telegraph official. The latest report was that Tarkarovsk had already fallen to the Whites. A.J., with better knowledge of distances, did not credit this, but it was futile to argue. As the journey was resumed the woman said: "So you are going on to Tarkarovsk, Commissar?"

"Yes."

"But if the Whites hold the place, that means we shall be running into them?"

"Yes. Only I don't believe they do hold it."

"What would happen if they did?"

"You would be freed and I should be shot, most probably."

"Whereas, if all goes well, and we get to Moscow safely, it is *I* who will be shot?"

"Possibly."

"You strike the Napoleonic attitude rather well, Commissar."

"Pardon me, I am not striking any attitude at all. I am merely very tired—really too tired to talk."

After that she said nothing.

He was right; Tarkarovsk was still Red, though the town and district were being rapidly prepared for evacuation. The two jolting vehicles drove up to the railway station towards dawn, after a journey of nightmare weariness. Hour after hour the Commissar and his prisoner had been bumped along over the interminable Siberian plain, and now, at the station, with limbs sore and aching, they had to begin the next and perhaps more arduous task of finding seats on the train. The station was swarming with refugees from the surrounding country, most of them in a pitiable condition, and all frantically anxious to be out of the way when the White troops should enter. There had been no trains since the previous evening, though several were rumored to be on their way. The station master bowed respectfully when A.J. presented his papers; yes, he should certainly be given a compartment in the next train, but would there be any next train?—that was the real question. "I cannot, you see, invent a train, Commissar—not being God, that is to say." A.J. detected a slight impertinence behind the man's outward obsequiousness. Of course the Whites were coming and the Reds were leaving; the fellow was adroitly trimming his sails to catch the new wind.

Throughout the hardships of the journey and now amidst the throng and scurry of the railway platform, the woman prisoner preserved a calm that had in it still that same slight touch of mockery. Of course it was not her place to worry about the train or the White advance; if the latter arrived before the former, the advantage would all be hers. She could afford to watch with equanimity and even exultation the growing congestion of the station precincts and the increasing anxiety on the faces of the two Red guards. Yet for all that, her attitude was no more than calm; it was as if she were neither hoping nor fearing anything at all. She sat on her bundle of possessions and watched the frantic pageant around her with a sleepy, almost mystical detachment. Even when, at three in the afternoon, the station master came shouting the news that the train was arriving after all, she did not move or betray by a murmur that the matter concerned her; and this attitude, because it so queerly accorded with his own, stirred in A.J. a slight and puzzled attention.

The train arrived at half-past four, already full, with Red soldiers and refugees crouching between and on the roofs of the coaches. The two guards, doubtfully assisted by the station master, opened the door of a second-class compartment (there was no first-class on the train) and drove its occupants on to the platform at the point of the revolver. They were refugees from Omsk, and pity for them was tempered with indignation at the horrible state in which they had left the compartment. They had ripped up the cushioned seats to make puttees to wind round their legs; they had scattered filth of every description all over the floor; and they (or some previous occupants) had also stripped the compartment of every detachable object. The two guards worked for half an hour to make the place habitable, and even then its interior atmosphere was still unpleasant.

The train left Tarkarovsk about dusk and crawled slowly westward. A.J., his prisoner, and the guards made a frugal breakfast of coffee and black bread. Both guards were huge fellows—one of a typical peasant type, and the other of superior intelligence but less likable. As for the prisoner her attitude remained exactly the same. At the first station west of Tarkarovsk news came that the Whites were on the point of entering that town; the train had apparently escaped by only the narrowest of margins. Yet the woman betrayed no suspicion of disappointment. She obeyed all A.J.'s requests with unassuming calmness; she sat where he told her to sit, ate when he told her to eat, and so on. He had now time to notice her appearance. She was perhaps under thirty years of age, though her type was that whose years are difficult to guess. Her hair was smooth and jet-black, framing a face of considerable beauty. Her lips had the clean, accurate curving of the thoroughbred, and her eyes, when they were in repose, held a rather sleepy, mystical look. And she was not only calm; she was calming.

Towards evening the train reached Ekaterinburg. The Ural Mountain city, noted for its extreme brand of revolutionary sentiment, was in a state of wild excitement, and for two reasons—the White advance along the railway, and the murder of the ex-Emperor that had taken place a few nights before. The station was packed with Red soldiers, and from their looks as the train sailed past their faces to a standstill, A.J. did not anticipate pleasant encounters. The first thing that happened was the invasion of the compartment by a dozen or so of them, extravagantly armed and more than half drunk. The two guards wisely made no attempt to resist, but A.J. said, authoritatively: "I am a Commissar on my way to Moscow on important government business. This compartment is reserved for me." His manner of speaking was one which usually impressed, and most of the invaders, despite their ruffianism, would probably have retired but for one of them, a swaggering little Jew about five feet high, who cried shrilly: "Not at all—nothing is reserved, except by order of the Ekaterinburg Soviet. Besides, how do we know you are what you say? And who is this woman with you?" A.J. pulled out his wallet of documents and displayed them hopefully. They were so magnificently sealed and stamped that most of the men, who could not read, seemed willing enough to accept their validity. But again the Jew was truculent. He read through everything very carefully and critically examined the seals. Then he stared insolently at the woman. "So you are taking her to Moscow?" he remarked at length. "Well, I'm afraid you can't. Khalinsk has no authority over Ekaterinburg and we refuse you permission to pass. I must see Patroslav about this. Meanwhile, you fellows, stand here on guard till I come back."

He jumped down to the platform and disappeared amidst the throng. The soldiers remained in the compartment, talking among themselves and getting into conversation with the two Khalinsk guards. One of the latter talked rather indiscreetly but A.J. did not think it wise to interfere.

After a few moments the little Jew returned, accompanied by another obvious Jew, taller and rather finelooking. Without preamble he addressed himself to A.J.

"You are the Assistant Commissar at Khalinsk?"

"Yes."

"And this woman was formerly the Countess Marie Alexandra Adraxine?"

"Yes."

"Then we cannot permit you to pass—either of you. In fact, you are both arrested."

A.J. argued with sudden and rather startling vehemence; the central government wanted this woman; she was to supply evidence which would be wanted at a fulldress trial of all the counter-revolutionary ring-leaders; there would be a tremendous row if some local soviet were to interfere with such intentions. A.J. ended by an astute appeal to the men personally—"You two are doubtless ambitious—you would perhaps like to see yourselves in higher positions than a local soviet? Do you think it will help you to countermand the orders of the central government? Whereas if, on the other hand—" It was pretty bluff, but he played it well, and the two Jews were reluctantly impressed. At last the man called Patroslav said something to his colleague in a language A.J. did not understand, and a lively and evidently acrimonious argument developed between them. Then Patroslav swung round on his heel and went off. The other Jew turned to A.J. "You are to be allowed to proceed with your prisoner," he announced, with sullen insolence. "But your guards must return to Khalinsk—we will replace them by two others. And your prisoner will travel in a third-class compartment with the guards—we do not allow privileges of any kind to enemies of the revolution. You, yourself, being a government official, may remain here."

"On the contrary, I shall go wherever the prisoner goes, since I am still in charge and responsible."

"As you prefer."

It was all, A.J. perceived, a scheme of petty annoyance, and on the whole he was glad to be escaping from Ekaterinburg with nothing worse. During the whole of the delay, the woman had not spoken a word, but as they walked down the platform to change their compartment she said: "I am sorry, Commissar, to be inconveniencing you so much. If I give my parole not to escape, would you not prefer to stay in comfort where you were?"

"There is little difference in comfort between one place and another," he answered.

But there was, for the third-class coaches were filthy and verminous, and there was neither time nor opportunity to make even the most perfunctory turn-out.

The night had a brilliant moon, and the hills, seen through the windows of the train, upreared like heaving seas of silver. There was no light in the compartment save that of a candle-stump fixed in the neck of a bottle. The heavy bearded faces of the guards shone fiercely in the flickering light. They were Ukrainians and sometimes exchanged a few husky words in their local dialect. A.J. had a slight understanding of this, but the men talked so quietly that he could not catch more than a few words here and there.

Suddenly the train came to an abrupt standstill, and after some delay a train official walked along the track with the information that a bridge had been blown up just ahead and that all passengers must walk on several miles to the next station, where another train would be waiting. A.J., his prisoner, and the two guards climbed down to the track, which ran in a wide curve through densely wooded country. One of the guards declared that he knew the spot quite well, and that there was an easy short-cut to the station across country. A.J. doubtfully agreed and they set off along a wide pathway that met the railway at a tangent. They all walked in silence for a few minutes, with the voices of the other passengers still within hearing; but soon they were amongst tall pine-trees, and A.J. imagined, though he could not be certain, that the path was veering too far to the north. He said to the guards: "Are you quite sure that this is the way?"—and one of them answered: "Oh, yes—you can hear the engine-whistle in the distance." A.J. listened and could certainly hear it, but it sounded very remote.

They all walked on a little further, with the two guards chattering softly together in Ukrainian. A.J.'s acute sense of direction again warned him, and a somewhat similar feeling of apprehension must have seized on his prisoner, for she said: "Don't you think we should have done better to keep to the railway line?"

128

At last even the guards seemed to be undecided; they had been walking a little ahead and now stopped and began arguing together in excited undertones.

"*Don't* you think it would have been better?" she repeated.

"Possibly," he answered, in a whisper. "It was certainly foolish to let them lead us into this forest."

"You think they have lost the way?"

"Maybe—or maybe not."

"Ah," she answered. "So you too are wondering?"

"Wondering what?"

"What they are chatting about so quietly."

He said quickly: "I have a revolver. I am keeping a look out."

He was, in fact, beginning not to like the look of things at all. Had the two guards led them deliberately astray, and if so, with what intention? In the train he had heard them chattering together, but they could hardly have been plotting this particular piece of strategy, since the blown-up railway-bridge could not have been foreseen. Perhaps, however, the idea had come to one of them as a quick impromptu, a variant upon some less immediate scheme that they had had in mind.

One of the guards approached him with a measured deliberation which, in the moonlight, seemed peculiarly sinister. "If you will both wait here with me," he began, "friend says he will find out where we are and will come back to tell us."

At first it seemed an innocent and reasonable suggestion, involving the somewhat lessened danger of being left alone with one possible enemy instead of two. But then A.J. recollected an ancient ruse that bandits sometimes played on their victims in Siberian forests; they said they were going away, but they did not really do so; they crept back and sprang on their enemies from behind. "No," he answered, with sudden decision. "It doesn't matter—we'll go back to where we began and then walk along the track. I think I can remember the way."

He began to walk in the reverse direction with the woman at his side and the two guards following him at a little distance. They seemed rather disconcerted by his decision and continued to exchange remarks in whispers.

After a few moments A.J. said quietly to his companion: "I want you to be on your guard. I don't trust those fellows."

"Neither do I. What do you think their game is?"

"Robbery. Perhaps murder. This going back to the railway has upset their plans—I can gather that from the way they're talking."

"What can we do?"

"Nothing—except keep our heads. Have you good nerves?"

"Yes, I think so."

"Then take this revolver and use it if necessary, but not otherwise." He handed it to her quickly as they passed into the shadow of dark trees.

For the next few moments there came no sound except the crunch of four pairs of footsteps over the fir-cones. Neither A.J. nor the woman spoke, and the two guards also had ceased their whispered conversation.

A.J.'s eyes were searching ahead for any sign of the railway as well as preparing for any lightning emergency in the rear. The silence and darkness of the forest were both uncanny, and though he listened acutely for any repetition of that distant engine-whistle, he heard nothing. After walking for some ten minutes, by which time he estimated that the railway ought to have come into view, the track narrowed and began to twist uphill. He whispered suddenly: "I've lost my way."

"What does that mean?"

"It means we may have to spend the rest of the night in the forest with these ruffians." A moment later he added: "They're talking again—they're guessing we're lost, and I'm afraid it suits them only too well. I think I'd rather have it out with them than go on like this."

He stopped abruptly, facing the guards so quickly that they had not time to conceal the revolvers in their hands. "Gentlemen," he said calmly, "I think you must find it a burden to carry those weapons as well as our luggage. Suppose you hand them over to me—I can guard the party if we are attacked."

The very unexpectedness of the request might have succeeded with one of the men, had not the other, with a snarl of rage, flung himself all at once upon A.J. The other then went to his companion's assistance, and the three men were soon engaged in a desperate struggle in which darkness seemed an extra enemy of them all. One powerful pair of arms gripped A.J. round the neck, while another seized his right arm and sought to wrest away the revolver. Both assailants were exceedingly strong, and though A.J. was strong also, he could not have held out for long against such odds. Suddenly one of the guards managed to wrench his own revolver free and aimed it full in A.J.'s face; and simultaneously a second revolver swung on to the scene and glinted in a shaft of moonlight. The two triggers were pressed almost together, but there was only one report. The guard's weapon misfired, and a second later its owner collapsed to the ground.

A.J. turned to deal with the second guard, but with a sharp movement the latter drew back and plunged wildly into the undergrowth and away.

A.J. was left, revolver in hand, peering down at a huddled body. The woman stood close to him, also holding a weapon, but hers was smoking.

He stooped and said, after a pause: "He's dead."

"Is he? I did it."

"Probably saving your own life as well as mine."

"Yes, I dare say. But what has to be done now?"

"This—before anything else."

He dragged the body to one side of the path and pushed it into the midst of thick undergrowth.

"Was the other fellow hurt?" she then asked.

"No—only terrified. He'll soon find his way to the nearest village and tell everybody. There'll be a pretty big fuss."

"But we were being attacked—it was self-defense, surely?"

"In a way, yes, but he's hardly likely to say so, and nobody's likely to take our word for it against his. Probably he'll say we're counter-revolutionary spies and that we seized the chance of a train hold-up to lure our two guards into the forest and attack them."

"But you have your papers to prove who we are?"

"You saw for yourself how doubtfully they were accepted in Ekaterinburg. After the stories that fellow will spread about us, they'll count even less."

"Then it looks as if we'd better move on."

"Yes. Instantly."

"Do you know which way to go?"

"Away from the nearest village. That means, almost certainly, uphill."

Then they discovered that they were both quite breathless. All about them were the dark pillars of tree-trunks, with here and there a delicate pattern on the undergrowth where moonlight spilled through. He began to gather up the various bundles that the two guards had thrown down. Then they hurried away. They climbed in silence for some time, till at last she asked, in a very ordinary casual voice, what he was thinking about. He answered: "To be exact, about a packet of chocolate I left on the seat in the train."

She laughed softly. "Never mind. I have some. Shall we share it?"

"Not yet. Better get on further."

They went on climbing amongst the trees, stopping only now and then to listen for any distant sound. But none could be heard distinctly, though once, from the very edge of the world, it seemed, there came what might have been the wail of a train-whistle. As they climbed higher, the trees thinned out into the open, and suddenly they reached a high, curving summit outlined against the moonlight like a knife-edge. The air, after the cool forest depths, was warm, and they themselves were again breathless. "Keep in shadow," he ordered, and they took a few backward steps into a little hollow full of dead leaves. A squirrel scampered past them as they halted. "Now for your chocolate," he said.

They sat down on a leafy slope and shared the chocolate and also a hunk of black bread that he had brought from Tarkarovsk. There was nothing to drink, but he had a water-bottle and they could find a stream as soon as it grew daylight. They ate ravenously and were still hungry when they had finished. Then it was necessary to make plans, tentatively, at any rate, for the future.

133

A.J. was not disposed to minimize the seriousness of the situation. The story that the runaway guard would doubtless tell was just as credible as theirs—perhaps more so to those he would be addressing. A man supposed to be a Siberian Assistant Commissar, supposed also to be escorting to Moscow a dangerous female counter-revolutionary and member of the aristocracy; the doubts that the Ekaterinburg officials had had, and their precautionary escort of two Red guards; the shooting of one of these guards in the middle of a forest—such a story would not seem difficult either to believe or to interpret in a district notorious for its "redness." And as for the wallet-full of assorted stamps and seals, A.J. began to feel that their presence might be a danger quite as much as a safeguard.

If they could only make their way to another district, across country, say, to the northern railway at Perm, they could there continue their journey to Moscow incognito, as it were. A.J. was fairly sure that his story would be credited at headquarters, especially as the Moscow authorities had had so much trouble themselves with the turbulent Uralian provinces. Anyhow, all that remained in the less immediate future; the more pressing problem was to avoid detection by search-parties who might soon be scouring the forests.

Fortunately for their chances of escape, the surrounding country was full of wanderers, refugees driven from their homes by the press of war or famine, seeking friends or relatives in distant parts of the country, or else tramping vaguely from village to village in default of anything more definite to do. Even in the forest country there were folk of this kind to be met with, and A.J. could not think of any better diguise than for the two of them to appear to be such wanderers. His own attire was reason-

134

ably suitable as it stood, but he realized that it would take a certain amount of adjustment to make his prisoner look like anything but a former aristocrat. Her clothes, though old and shabby, were hardly such as a peasant would ever have possessed, and her shoes, even after repeated patchings, were still recognizably foreign. He dared not allow her to be seen until these incongruities were removed, and he explained the matter to her briefly. "We shall have to be particularly careful during the next twenty-four hours," he insisted. "As soon as it is daylight I will leave you in some arranged spot and try to get clothes for you. If there is a village anywhere within a few miles I ought to be able to manage it."

After their short rest he climbed the hill while she remained more prudently below. The moon was now fast sinking over a distant ridge, and while he crouched in the long grass trying to get his bearings he saw the first whiff of dawn creeping over the eastern horizon like a child's breath on a window-pane. Soon he could see the forests turning from black to green and the sky from gray to palest blue; then, very slowly, the mist unrolled along the floor of the valley. But there was no sign of any village. It was, he knew, a sparsely populated district, and, quite possibly, the nearest settlement might be a score or more miles away. If that were so, he and his prisoner must hide in the forest during the day and push on as fast as they could when night fell.

By the time he rejoined her it was quite light, and the clear, cloudless sky showed promise of a hot day. He took off his coat and then looked around for a stream from which to fill his water-bottle. Cautiously he descended the slope, skirting the hill in a wide curve, with the first rays of sunlight splitting joyously through the foliage. How lovely the world seemed, but for human beastliness, and how disgusting to wish that the birds were not singing so loudly, because they made it difficult to listen for anyone approaching in the distance. Yet behind a certain quiet rage and perturbation, excitement was on him, and when at last he found a stream, bubbling crystal-clear over pearl-gray rocks, he knelt to it and, dashing the icy water over his face and head, felt what was almost a new sensation—happiness.

After filling his water-bottle he looked up and saw something that gave him a sudden shock. It was a timbered roof half-hidden among the trees no more than a hundred yards away, yet even so close it would have been easy to miss it. Probably a woodman's cottage, he thought, and with still cautious steps approached a little nearer to find out. Then he saw a thin wisp of smoke curling up amidst the treetops that screened the tiny habitation. The loneliness of the place as well as its look of cozy comfortableness lured him to an even closer examination; he worked his way through the trees towards a side which no window overlooked. In another moment he was standing against the outside wall and listening carefully—but there were no sounds of voices or of movement from within. Then he turned the corner and, crouching near the window, slowly lifted his head and peered over the sill. It was the usual one-roomed habitation of the peasant, very dirty and untidy; two persons, man and woman, were sleeping on a heap of straw and rags in a corner, and from their attitude and state of attire, A.J. guessed it to be a sleep of drunkenness. With greater interest, however, he saw the heap of clothes on the floor which the couple had thrown off. That settled it; it seemed that fortune had given him a chance which it would be far bigger folly to miss than to take. With his revolver in one hand he lifted the door-latch with the other; as he had hoped and expected, the door was not locked. He simply walked in, picked up the litter of clothes, walked out, closed the door carefully behind him, and climbed the hill through the trees. Nothing could have been easier, and he was glad that, from their appearance, the couple would still have many hours to sleep.

His prisoner laughed when he threw down the heap of clothes in front of her. Then she took grateful gulps of water from the bottle he offered. "You are very kind, Commissar," she said. "But you had better not make a habit of leaving me alone as you did just then. I warn you that I shall escape at any suitable opportunity."

"Naturally," he answered, with a shade of irony. "But for the present remember that we are both escaping."

"Yes, that's queer, isn't it? You are taking me to Moscow, where I shall probably be put on trial and shot; but for the time being I haven't to think about that—I must only bother about preserving my life during the next twenty-four hours."

"Well?"

"I'm afraid it all strikes me as rather illogical. If I am to be killed anyhow, does it matter very much who does the job?"

"That, of course, is for you to decide. Personally, if I were in your place, I should rather think it *did* matter."

She suddenly put a hand on his sleeve. "Commissar, I can lose nothing, can I, by asking a question? Just this— must you really take me to Moscow and hand me over? Hasn't my own—our own—our rather unusual fate so far —given you a hint of anything else? To me it almost seems as if fate were asking you to give me a chance.

137

Briefly, Commissar, I have friends abroad—influential friends—who would make it considerably worth your while if you would take me somewhere else instead of Moscow. Odessa, shall we say—or Rostov? You would have earned the reward by your courtesy alone, and as for me, how can the Revolution suffer because one poor woman takes ship for a foreign country?"

He looked at her for a moment in absolute silence. Then he merely replied: "You are mistaken in me—I am not bribable. And also, by the way, you must remember in future not to call me 'Commissar.'"

"I see." And after a pause she added: "You are quite incorruptible, then?"

"Quite."

She smiled and shrugged her shoulders. "Well, anyhow, let's not quarrel about it. Perhaps, after all, you think I deserve to be shot?"

"No, I don't say that. I don't think anything at all about it. You are my prisoner and I am taking you to Moscow. That is all." He went on, more quickly: "Will you please put on these clothes without delay? We *must* get on—every minute increases the danger."

"Are they clean?"

"I don't know—I hadn't time to look. Probably not, but you must wear them, anyhow."

She laughed and their serious conversation ended by tacit agreement. She was amused at having to dress herself in a peasant's long skirt and coarse, colored blouse, and she was still further amused when he told her how he had obtained them. Her own clothes they buried in a hiding-place under a heap of dead leaves; it was safer, he decided, than trying to burn them. Then he shaved his beard and mustache, transforming his appearance to

an extent that caused her a good deal of additional amusement. Next their joint luggage was carefully sorted out
and all articles that might seem suspicious were also hidden away under the leaves. Finally he slit open the lining
of his coat and carefully hid away all his commissary papers and a few government banknotes of large denomina-
tion.

These preparations took some time, and it was after
eight o'clock when a fairly typical pair of peasant wanderers made their way down the hill to the valley on the
far side of it. The man was tall and well-built, with a
thin stubble of beard round his chin (he had not dared to
give himself a close shave because of the deep tan that
covered the rest of his face). The woman, slighter in
build and pale even in the sunlight, trudged along beside
him. They did not converse a great deal, but the man
exchanged cheerful greetings with fellow-peasants passing in the opposite direction.

Arrangements had been reached about other matters.
They had given each other names that were common
enough, yet not suspiciously so; he was Peter Petrovitch
Barenin, of the imaginary village of Nikolovsk, in the
province of Orenburg; she was his daughter Natasha
(called "Daly"). They were trying to reach Petrograd,
where he had a brother who had formerly been a workman in the Putilov factory. They were both poor people,
he a simple-minded peasant who could neither read nor
write, but his daughter, thank God, had had an education
and had spent some years as lady's maid in an aristocratic
family. (Hence her accent and soft hands.) But they
had both fallen lately on evil times—she, of course, had
lost her job, and he had had his cottage burned down by
White brigands. It was all just the sort of ordinary and

quite unexceptionally pathetic case of which there were probably some millions of examples at that time throughout the country.

The morning warmed and freshened as the couple wound their way along the valley road. They met few people, and none save humble travelers like themselves; from one of these peasant wayfarers A.J. bargained a loaf of bread. With this and a few wild strawberries gathered by the roadside they made a simple but satisfactory meal, washed down with icy mountain-water from a stream.

Throughout the day they did not see a solitary habitation or come within rumor of a village. All about them stretched the lonely forest-covered foothills of the Urals, dark with pine-trees and soaring into the hazy distance where a few of the peaks still kept their outlines hidden in mist. The air was full of aromatic scents, and by the wayside, as they trudged, high banks of wildflowers waved their softer perfumes.

Towards evening they met an old, bearded peasant of whom A.J. asked the distance to the nearest village. "Three versts," he answered. "But if you are travelers seeking a night's shelter, you had better not go there." A.J. asked why, and the man answered: "A band of soldiers have been raiding the place in search of someone supposed to have murdered a Red guard in the forests. The soldiers are still there, and if you were to arrive as a stranger they might arrest you on suspicion. You know what ruffians these fellows are when they are dealing with us simple folk." A.J. agreed and thanked the man; it was a fine night, he added, and it would do himself and his daughter no harm to rest in the forest. "Oh, but there is no need to do that," urged the other. "You can have shelter at my cottage—just away up yonder hill. I am a woodcutter—Dorenko by name—but I am not a ruffian like most woodcutters. As soon as I saw you and your daughter coming along the road I thought how tired she looked and I felt sorry for her. Yes, indeed, brother, you are fortunate—not many woodcutters are like me. I have a kind heart, having lost my wife last year. Perhaps I may marry again some day. I have a nice little cottage and it is clean and very comfortable, though the cockroaches are a nuisance. Come, brother, you and your girl will enjoy a good meal and a night's rest under a roof."

A.J., thinking chiefly of the soldiers in the neighboring village, accepted the invitation, and the three began to walk uphill, turning off the road after a short distance and entering again the steep and already darkening forest. A.J. told the old man the barest facts about himself, and was glad to note that they were accepted quite naturally and without the least curiosity. "I, too, had a daughter once," said Dorenko, "but she ran away and I never heard of her afterwards. She was not as good-looking as yours."

After a quarter of an hour's hard climb they came to another of those forest cottages, timber-built, and completely hidden from any distant view. The interior was not particularly clean and comfortable, despite Dorenko's contrary opinion, and though also, after his warning, they were prepared for cockroaches, they had hardly imagined such a plague of them as existed. They swarmed over everything; they were on walls and roof, and in every crack and corner; they had to be shaken off the bread and skimmed out of liquids; they crackled underfoot and fell in soft sizzling pats on to the smoldering hearth. "Yes," admitted Dorenko, tranquilly, "they are a nuisance, but I will say this for them—they never bite."

Dorenko was certainly hospitable. He made his guests an appetizing meal of soup and eggs; barring the cockroaches there would have been much to enjoy. He talked a good deal, especially about his late wife and his loneliness since she had died. "Yes, indeed, I may marry again some day. I am on the lookout for the right sort of person, as you may guess. And, of course, it would not be a bad match in these days for a girl to marry an honest woodcutter who has his own cottage and perhaps a little money hidden away too." He leered cunningly. "You see I am trusting you, Peter Petrovitch. I know you are not the kind that would rob an honest woodcutter. But it is a fact, I assure you—I have hundreds of roubles buried in the ground beneath this cottage. Think of it—and you are, without doubt, a poor man!"

"I am a poor man, it is true, but I certainly would not rob you."

"I know that, brother. As soon as I saw you coming along the road I thought—'Here comes an honest man.' And honest men are rare in these days—nearly as rare as roubles, eh? Or shall we say nearly as rare as a good-looking woman?"

A.J. conversed with him amiably for a time and then, as it was quite dark and Dorenko possessed no lamp, suggested settling down for the night. He was, in fact, dead tired, and he knew that Daly (as he had already begun to think of her) must be the same. He arranged for her to have the best place—near the fire and for that reason not so popular with the cockroaches; he and Dorenko shared the ground nearer the door. He was so sleepy that he felt almost afraid of going to sleep; he guessed that in any emergency he would be hard to awaken. However, Dorenko seemed trustworthy and there was always the revolver at hand. He lay down with it carefully concealed beneath the bundle of clothes that formed his pillow. Neither he nor Daly undressed at all, but Dorenko took off his outer clothes and performed the most intimate ritual of toilet quite frankly and shamelessly in the darkness. A decent honest fellow, no doubt.

A.J. went to sleep almost instantly and knew nothing thenceforward till he felt himself being energetically shaken. "What's the matter?" he cried, rubbing his eyes and groping for his revolver. It was still dark and all was perfectly silent except for the scurry of cockroaches disturbed by his sudden movement. "It's only me, brother—Dorenko, the woodcutter," came a hoarse whisper a few inches from his right ear. "I waited till your daughter was asleep so that we could have a little talk together in private."

"But I'm really far too sleepy to talk—"

"Ah, but listen, brother. You are a poor man, are you not?"

"Certainly, but does it matter at this time of night?"

"It matters a great deal when you have to tramp the roads with a poor, sick daughter. She looked so very tired and ill tonight, brother—it's plain she isn't used to walking the roads."

"Of course she isn't—as I told you, she's been used to a much more delicate life."

"In a fine house no doubt, eh, brother? Ah, that's it—it's a home she wants—a roof over her head—not to be tramping the roads all day long. And you—wouldn't you be able to get to Petrograd quicker without her? After all, a man can rough things, but it's different when he has a girl dragging along with him." He added in a fierce whisper: "Brother, haven't you ever thought of her getting married to some decent hard-working fellow who, maybe, has a comfortable house and a bit of money put away? I'm a good fellow, I assure you, though I am only a woodcutter, and to tell the truth, your daughter's just the kind of woman I've been looking out for ever since my poor wife died. And you shall have a hundred silver roubles for yourself, brother, if you give her to me."

A.J. was still too sleepy to be either amused or annoyed. He said merely: "Dorenko, it's quite out of the question. My daughter, I know, wouldn't consider it."

"But if, as her father, you ordered her to?"

"She wouldn't, even then."

"She would disobey you?"

"Undoubtedly."

"Ah, I sympathize. My own daughter was like that— disobedient to her own father. It is a dreadful thing to have children like that. All the same, brother, I will make it a hundred and fifty roubles for you if you could manage to persuade her."

"No, Dorenko, it's no use—it's impossible."

"Not because I am only a woodcutter?"

"Oh, no, by no means. Not in the least for that reason."

"Ah, Peter Petrovitch, you are a good fellow like myself, I can see. It is a pity we could not have come to some arrangement. However, perhaps it is God's will that I should look elsewhere. Good night—good night."

A.J. was soon asleep again and did not wake till the sunlight was pouring through the narrow window. Dorenko was already up and preparing a breakfast meal. He did not refer to the matter he had broached during the night, and after a homely meal the two travelers thanked him and set out to continue their journey. A.J. would have liked to offer him money, but that such generosity would not have suited the story of being poor.

Dorenko had given them directions before starting, telling them how they might travel so as to avoid the village which the soldiers had raided, and reach another less dangerous one by the end of the day. The route led them through the forest for several miles and then along a narrow, winding track amidst the hills. It was again very hot in the middle of the day. They slept for a time in the shade of the pines and then, towards evening, walked into a small town named Saratursk, whose market-place was full of Red soldiers, bedraggled and badly disciplined after long marches. It was hardly likely that they could be bothering about a casual forest murder, for much more serious events had happened during the past twenty-four hours. The Whites and the Czecho-Slovaks, acting together, had crossed the Urals and were reported in rapid invasion; the entire Revolution seemed in danger. All day long a steadily increasing stream of refugees had been entering Saratursk from the west; A.J. and Daly were but two out of thousands, and quite inconspicuous. They found it impossible to obtain any food except black bread at an extortionate price, and every room in the town was full of sleepers. Fortunately the night was warm, and it was not unpleasant to spread out one's bundle on the cobbled stones and breathe the mountain air. Sleep, however, was interrupted by the constant noise and shouting; fresh detachments of soldiers were entering the town from the west and south and reuniting with their comrades already in possession. They were a fierce-looking crowd, all of them, dressed in shabby, tattered, and nondescript uniforms—dirty, unkempt, heavy with fatigue. They had no obvious leaders, but throughout the night they held meetings in the market-square to elect new officers. There was much fervid oratory and cheering. The news of the White advance had put them in considerable consternation, for they themselves were badly armed—only one man in five or six possessing a rifle. The rest carried swords, knives, and even sticks. Some of them had been dragged out of hospitals too soon, and still wore dirty red-stained bandages. This curious, slatternly throng was, for the moment, all that stood between Moscow and counter-revolution.

All night long the hubbub proceeded, and soon after dawn something—but it was not clear exactly what—was decided upon. A few squads of men marched out of the town to the east; the rest, apparently, were to follow later. But shortly afterwards came a sharp outbreak of rifle-fire among the hills behind the town, and in less than an hour the original squads returned in a condition bordering on panic. The hills, they reported, were already in the hands of White outposts; Saratursk must be abandoned instantly. Whereupon soldiers, civilians, and refugees immediately gathered up as many of their personal possessions as they could and took part in a furious stampede to the west. The road was narrow—no more than a mere track—and military wagons jammed and collided into an immovable obstruction during the first quarter-mile. The wagons were full of ammunition and other military equipment, and after a vain attempt to disentangle the chaos the soldiers unloaded the stores and carried them forward on their backs. The sun rose blindingly on weary men staggering ahead with glazed and desperate eyes, straining the utmost nerve to put distance between themselves and a relentless enemy. Some of them, tired of scuffles in the roadway, took to the open fields and blundered on, with no guide to direction save the blaze of the sun on their backs. All through the morning came intermittent bursts of rifle-fire, each one rather nearer, it seemed; and there was a fresh outbreak of panic when a small child, fleeing with her parents, was struck and slightly injured by a spent bullet. Towards noon the rout was already becoming more than many could endure; refugees and even soldiers were collapsing by dozens along the roadside, throwing themselves face downwards in the dust and writhing convulsively. Some of them seemed to be dying, and there were rumors that White spies in Saratursk had put poison in the drinking-water from which many of the fugitives had filled their bottles.

A.J., hastening onwards, felt suddenly very ill himself. Severe internal pains gripped him, and at last he guessed that he was on the verge of collapse. He staggered and fell, tried to rise again, but could not; all the earth and the wide sky swam in circles before his eyes. He had to say: "I can't go on any further. I'm ill." And to himself he added that fate, after all, was giving her the chance she had been wishing for; she could escape now, quite easily, and he had no power to stop her.

He knew that she was raising his head and staring into his eyes. "Is there anything I can do?" she asked.

"Nothing at all for me. But for yourself—well, you have only to go back into Saratursk and meet your friends."

"They'll find me here if I stay."

"Yes, but in that case they'd find me, too, and I don't fancy being taken prisoner. Besides, there's bound to be

firing along this road. Take the papers out of my coat—
they'll prove who you are."

"And yourself?"

"I shall manage, I dare say, with luck."

"You want me to leave you here?"

"I think you ought to take the chance that offers itself.
If you stay, there'll only be greater danger to both of us.
So go now—and hurry. Don't forget the papers."

"You are letting me go, then?"

"Circumstances compel me, that's all."

"It—it is—good of you. I hope you manage yourself
all right."

"Most probably I shall if I'm not found with you. Take
the papers."

"Good-by."

"Yes, but the papers—the papers—in the lining of my
coat—"

He felt her hands searching him; he heard her say
something, but he could not gather what—he was fast
sinking into unconsciousness. Ages seemed to pass; at
intervals he opened his eyes and heard great commotion
proceeding all around and over him. Successive waves of
pain assaulted and left him gasping with weakness. It
was dark when he finally awoke. Pain was ebbing by
then, and his strength with it. Queer sounds still echoed
in his ears—murmurs as of distant shouting, distant rifle-
fire. The starlight shone a pale radiance over the earth;
he saw that he was lying in a sort of gully and that, a few
yards away, there was something that looked like another
man. He called "Hello!" but there was no answer. Perhaps the fellow was asleep. He was suddenly anxious to
meet somebody, to speak a word to somebody. There
had been a battle he guessed, and it would be interesting

to learn whether the Whites or the Reds had been victorious. It hardly seemed to matter very much, but, just out of curiosity, as it were, he would like to know. And Daly, his prisoner, had she by now been safely received and identified by her friends? . . . God, how thirsty he was—he would offer that man some money in return for a drink of anything but poisoned water. Slowly, and with greater difficulty than he had expected, he crawled along the gully towards the huddled figure. Then he perceived that the man was dead—killed by a smashing blow in the face. That, for all that he had seen so many dead bodies in his time, unnerved him a little; he stared round him a little vaguely, as if uncertain how to interpret the discovery. Then he rose unsteadily to his feet and began to stagger about. He climbed on to the roadway and up the sloping bank on to the pale stubble fields. He walked a little way—a few hundred yards—and then saw another dead man. Then another. A man with his head nearly blown off at close range. A man huddled in the final writhings of a bayonet-thrust through the stomach. A man covered with blood from a drained and severed artery. Most of the dead, from their uniforms, were Reds; a few only could have belonged to the other side. Sickly qualms overspread him as he wandered aimlessly among these huddled figures. Then he suddenly heard a cry. It seemed to come from a distance; he turned slightly and heard it again. "Brother!" it called. He walked towards it. "What is it?" he whispered, and the reply came: "Are you not wounded, brother?" "No," he answered, and the voice rejoined: "Neither am I. Come here."

He approached a prostrate form that proved to be a Red soldier whose face was ghastly with congealed blood.

Only, as the man explained with immediate cheerfulness, it was not his own blood. "Brother," he said, "I am an old soldier and I know from experience what war is like. It is all very fine if you are winning easily, but it is unpleasant when you are being attacked by a much stronger enemy. The best thing to do at such a time, in my opinion, is to fall down and pretend to be dead. Then, if you are lucky, the enemy doesn't bother about you. I have saved my life three times by this method—twice with the Germans and once again today. I suppose you too, brother, did the same?"

"No," answered A.J. "I fell ill in the morning and that's all I remember."

"Ah, yes, it happened to so many of our poor fellows. Some White spy poisoned the water in Saratursk—a disgusting way of carrying on war, I call it. Not that I'm tremendously against the Whites—I believe they give their soldiers very good pay. For myself, I have a great mind to go into Saratursk tomorrow and join them. Do you feel like coming with me, brother?"

"No, thanks."

"Mind you, I wouldn't do it if the Reds were as generous. I really *prefer* the Reds, really. But a soldier's job, after all, is to fight, and if he gets good food and pay, why should he bother what side he fights on? It isn't for him to pick and choose. That's how I feel about it. Would you like something to eat, brother?"

"I should indeed."

"Then sit here with me. I have some bread and a sausage. I'm afraid I was rather scared at first when I woke up and saw you walking about. I thought you were a ghost—they say there are ghosts that haunt battlefields, you know. Yes, it was a sharp little fight, but our men stood no chance at all—every man on the other side had a rifle and ammunition. It was ridiculous to make a stand."

"Where are the Whites now?"

"Still chasing our poor fellows, I expect. Whereas you and I, my friend, have had the sense to let them pass over us. We are all right. Two hours' walk and we shall be in the woods, and an army corps wouldn't find us there. Do you know this part of the country?"

"Not very well."

"Then after our little meal I will take you along. Perhaps, after all, I need not be in any hurry to enlist with the Whites. A few days' rest first of all, anyhow. We have three hours yet before dawn. If we hurry we shall reach the woods in good time."

They ate quickly but with enjoyment, and then began the walk over the stubble fields. During the first mile or so they passed many dead bodies, but after that the signs of battle grew less evident. They avoided the road, along which White military wagons were still tearing westward in the rear of the pursuing army. A.J. wondered if there were not some danger of their being found and taken prisoner, but his companion, whose name was Oblimov, seemed quite confident of being able to reach the hills in safety. He had thrown away his soldier's cap and the rest of his clothing was certainly so nondescript that it could convey little to any observer. "Besides," he said, "if anyone questions us, we can say we are White refugees returning to our homes."

They skirted Saratursk on the north side, working their way through orchards and private gardens, and passing within sight of several big houses in which lights were visible. In one of them the blinds had not been lowered, and they could see that a party of some kind was in progress. White officers were drinking and shouting, and there came also, tinkling over the night air, the sound of women's laughter. A.J. wondered if his former prisoner were there, or in some other such house, celebrating her freedom and rescue. Oblimov said: "They will soon drink away their victory." It certainly looked as if many of the White officers had preferred Saratursk to the continued pursuit of the enemy.

They reached the lower slopes of the hills just as the first tint of dawn appeared, and by the time the sun rose they were high amongst the woods. A.J. was by now beginning to feel very comfortable amongst the pine trees; he liked their clean, sharp tang, and the rustle of fir-cones under his feet. He was tired, however, after the climb, and also, beyond his relief, rather depressed. The world seemed a sadly vague and pointless kind of place, with its continual movement of armies and refugees, and its battles and tragedies and separations. He kept wondering how his prisoner had fared. He did not particularly regret her escape; he had done his best, but fate had out-maneuvered him. Nine-tenths of life seemed always to consist of letting things happen.

Oblimov was an excellent and resourceful companion. He made a fire and boiled tea, and while A.J. slept in the dappled sunshine he raided a woodman's cottage in the valley and came back with bread and meat. He also brought some coarse tobacco which he smoked joyously during the whole of the afternoon. He was a great talker and looked on life in a mood of pleasant fatalism. Soldiering was doubtless the worst job in the world, but what else was there for a man of his type? He had no home; he couldn't settle down. And soldiers did, in a sense, see the world. They met people, too—people they would never have met otherwise—"like yourself, brother. We came across each other on the battlefield, surrounded by dead men, and now we are yarning in a wood with our bellies full and the blue sky over us. To-morrow maybe, we shall say good-by and never see each other again. But is it not worth while? And will you ever forget me, or I you?"

He went on to tell of his many experiences; he had been fighting, he said, for years—ever since he had been a young man. He had fought for the Serbs in the first Balkan War, and against the Serbs in the second Balkan War, and in the Great War, of course, he had fought the Germans. But that war had not pleased him at all, and after a year of it he had allowed himself to be taken pris-oner. He admitted it quite frankly; his view of war was a strictly professional and trade-union one; if soldiers were not treated properly, why should they go on perform-ing their job? Two years in a German prison-camp had not been pleasant, but they had been preferable, he be-lieved, to what he might have had to endure otherwise. The return of the prisoners to Russia after the Treaty of Brest-Litovsk had brought him back again to normal life —that of ordinary, rational soldiering. "A soldier does not mind occasionally risking his life," he explained, "nor does he object to a battle now and again or a few tiring marches across country. But to stand in a frozen trench for weeks on end is another matter—it isn't fair to ask such a thing of any man." The warfare between Reds and Whites was much more to his taste—the localness of it, its sudden bursts of activity, its continual changes of scene, and its almost limitless chances of loot and per-sonal adventure—all agreed with him. He did not much care on which side he fought; he had already fought on both and would doubtless do so again. "But personally," he added, "I am a man of the people."

His completely detached attitude towards life and affairs prompted A.J. to confide in him more than it was his habit to confide in acquaintances. He told him briefly about the "daughter" with whom he had been wandering and from whom he had become separated during the excitements of the day before. What was really on his mind was whether she was likely to have been decently treated by the White soldiers before the proving of her identity. To Oblimov, of course, he merely expressed his anxieties as a father. Oblimov was sympathetic, but hardly reassuring. "What will happen to her depends on what sort of a girl she is," he declared, concisely. "If she is pretty and not pure she will have a very good time. If she is pure and not pretty she will be left alone. But if she is pretty and wishes to remain pure . . ." He left the sentence unfinished. "Women," he added, "are really not worth worrying about, anyway, and evidently you think so too, else you would be searching Saratursk for your daughter at this present moment instead of enjoying the sunshine." A.J. was a little startled by this acuteness. Oblimov laughed and went on: "Brother, you cannot deceive an old soldier. I believe she is not your daughter at all, but your wife or mistress, and you are more than half glad to be rid of her! Don't be offended —I know you think you are very fond of her and are worried about her safety. But I can see that deep down in your heart you do not care."

He went on talking about women in general, and A.J. went on listening until both occupations were suddenly interrupted by a sound that came to them very clearly

154

across the valley. It was the sharp rattle of machine-gun fire. Oblimov, all his professional instincts aroused, scented the air like a startled hound. "It looks as if the battle's moving back on the village," he said. "Let's go down a little and see if we can judge what's happening."

They picked their way amongst the trees till they reached a small clearing whence could be seen the whole of the valley. Machine-gun and rifle-fire was by that time intense, and a thin chain of white smoke ringed the town on the further side. Already a few cavalry wagons were leaving Saratursk by the mountain-road. By late afternoon the battle was over and its results were obvious; the Reds had retaken the town and the Whites were in full retreat to the east. "Now," advised Oblimov, "we had better move along ourselves. If the Whites are pursued too hard, some of them may hide in these woods, and it would be just as well for us not to be found with them." So they descended the hillside and walked boldly into Saratursk. There was no danger of their being noticed or questioned; the recaptured town was in far too much uproar and chaos. The earlier victory of the Whites had been due largely to the poisoning of the water that the Red soldiers had drunk; many more men had died of that than of battle-wounds, and the survivors were disposed to take revenge. The whole place, they said, was White in sympathy, and it was certainly true that the more prosperous shopkeepers and private citizens had loaded gifts upon White officers. Now they wished they had been more discreet. As the victorious Reds lurched into the town, drunk with that highly dangerous mixture of triumph and fatigue, the shopkeepers put up their shutters and made themselves as inconspicuous as possible. All the omens were for an exciting night.

Oblimov soon joined his soldier companions, but A.J. preferred to mingle with the crowd that surged up and down the main street. It was a hot, swaying, tempestuous, and increasingly bad-tempered multitude. The market-place, packed with wounded Reds for whom there was no hospital accommodation and hardly any but the most elementary medical treatment, acted as a perpetual incitement to already inflamed passions. Amidst this acre of misery the town doctor and a few helpers worked their way tirelessly, but there was little that could be done, since the retreating Whites had commandeered all medical supplies—even to bandages and surgical instruments. This was bad enough, but even worse to many was the fact that the Whites seemed also to have drunk the whole town dry. There was not a bottle of beer or a dram of vodka in any of the inns, and the litter of empty bottles in all the gutters told its own significant tale. The first "incident" was caused by this. A few soldiers, refusing to believe that there was absolutely no drink to be had at all, insisted on inspecting the cellar of one of the inns. There they found a couple of bottles of champagne. They drank without much enthusiasm, for they preferred stronger stuff, and then wrecked the inn-keeper's premises. The news of the affair soon spread and led to a systematic search, not only of inns, but of private houses. In many cases the terrified occupants handed over any liquor they possessed; where they did not, or had none to hand over, the soldiers usually went about smashing pictures and furniture amidst wild shouts and caperings. All this time the town was becoming more crowded; soldiers were still pouring in from the west, and these later arrivals, having endured more prolonged hardships, were in fiercer moods. Towards eight o'clock the rumor went round that a certain local lawyer had been responsible for the poisoning of the water-supply the day before. The man, who was hiding in his house, was dragged out into the middle of the street and clubbed to death. This only whetted appetites; between eight and midnight, perhaps a dozen citizens, mostly shopkeepers and professional men, were killed in various ways and places. Then the even more exciting rumor gained currency that a whole houseful of Whites, including highborn officers and ladies, were in hiding about a mile out of the town, their retreat having been cut off by the Reds' rapid advance. The village school master saved his life by giving details of this illustrious colony; it included, he said, no less a personage than the Countess Marie Alexandra Adraxine, well-known in pre-Revolution St. Petersburg society, and distantly connected with the family of the ex-Emperor. She had been passing as a peasant, continued the informative school master, and had caused a great sensation among the White officers by declaring and establishing her true identity. Many of them had known her in former times, and a great party had been held both in her honor and to celebrate the glorious White victory of Saratursk. And it was the effects of this and similar parties that had helped towards the equally glorious Red victory that had so immediately followed.

Some of the crowd were for marching on the house and storming it, but the Red leader, a shrewd and capable fellow, was impressed by the political importance of the prisoners and anxious to act with due circumspection. Let a few local shopkeepers be butchered by all means, but countesses and highly-placed White officers were too valuable to be wasted on the mob. Besides, being a person of good memory and methodical mind, he seemed to recollect that there had already been some bother about that particular countess; she had been captured in Siberia, hadn't she, and had been on her way to Moscow in charge of some local commissar when, somehow or other, the two had escaped from the train and had not been heard of since? The beautiful countess and the susceptible commissar—what a theme for a comic opera! General Polahkin, whose victory over the Whites had been due partly to military ability but chiefly to the sudden and almost miraculous repair of a couple of machine-guns, smiled to himself as he gave orders that the house should be surrounded, and that, if its occupants gave themselves up, they should be conducted unharmed to the town jail.

This operation was carried out without a hitch, and towards three o'clock in the morning the little procession entered the town. There were about a dozen White officers, whose resplendent uniforms and dejected faces contrasted piquantly with the shabby greatcoats and triumphant faces of their guards. There were five women also—dressed in a weird assortment of clothes, some of them walking painfully in ball-room slippers, and all rather pale and weary-looking. All except one gave occasional terrified glances at the jeering crowds that lined the streets to the prison-entrance. The exception was the woman whose name everyone now knew—the woman who (according to a story that was being improved on, saga-like, with every telling) had beguiled a commissar into escaping with her and had then, somehow or other, escaped from him! The crowd were not disposed to be too unfriendly towards such a magnificent adventuress, and if she had only played the actress well enough, they were quite drunk enough to have cheered her. But she did not act the right part, and her appearance, too, was disappointingly unromantic. She gazed ahead with calm and level eyes as if she were not caring either for them or for anything in the world.

When the captives were safely locked in the prison the crowd, suffering a kind of reaction, began a systematic looting of the shops. They were, in truth, disconcerted by the tameness of what had promised to be highly exciting, and now worked out their spleen as best they could. Polahkin did not object; loot was, after all, the perquisite of the poorly-paid soldier. By dawn the town presented a forlorn appearance; every window in the main street had been smashed and the gutters were full of broken glass and miscellaneous articles that had been stolen, broken, and then thrown away. Some of the local peasants, professing violently Red feelings, had taken part in the looting, and they, perhaps, had made most out of it, since they had homes in which they could store whatever they took. One small cottage attracted attention by having the end of a piano sticking out of the doorway; the acquirer could not play, but banged heavily with his fists to indicate his delight.

The following day was to some extent anti-climax; the revelers were tired and spent most of the time sleeping off the effects of the carousal. In the afternoon, however, fresh Red reënforcements arrived from the west—men of even more violent temperament than those already in possession, and accompanied, moreover, by several fluent and apparently professional orators who harangued the crowd in the market-place with unceasing eloquence. Polahkin, it soon appeared, was unpopular with these new arrivals; they doubted his "redness," and were particularly incensed because he had permitted the White captives to retain their lives.

A.J., mingling during the day with the crowds in the town and sleeping at nights on the bare boards of an inn-floor, could sense the keying of the atmosphere to higher and more dangerous levels. He did not feel any particular apprehension, still less any indignation; he had seen too many horrors for either. Every barbarism perpetrated by the Reds could be balanced by some other perpetrated by the Whites; the scales of bloodshed and cruelty balanced with almost exquisite exactness. There was also a point of experience beyond which even the imagination had no power to terrify, and A.J. had reached such a point. What he felt was rather, in its way, a sort of selfishness; out of all the chaos and wretchedness that surrounded him he felt inclined to seize hold of anything that mattered to him locally and personally in any way. And so little, when he came to think of it, *did* matter to him. Up to now he had been a blind automaton, letting fate push him whither it chose and calmly accepting any task that was nearest. He had not cared; at Khalinsk he had been kind and wise and hard-working, but he had not cared. Yet now for the first time he felt a curious uprise of personality, a sort of "you-be-damned-ness" entering his soul as he paced the streets and observed, still quite coldly, the wreckage of a world that cared as little for him as he for it.

Only very gradually did he perceive that he wanted the woman to escape. To any normally-minded person it would have seemed an absurd enough want, for the prison was strongly and carefully guarded. But A.J., just then, was not normally-minded. The more he tried to reconcile himself to the fact that his former prisoner would eventually be shot, like hundreds of other pleasant and possibly innocent persons, the more he felt committed to some kind of personal and intrepid intervention. But how, and when? He guessed that the revolutionary ardor of the soldiers would soon boil over and lead to the overthrow of Polahkin and the massacre of the White prisoners; he had seen that sort of thing happen too often not to recognize the familiar preliminary portents. Whatever was to be done must be done quickly —yet what *could* be done? He did not know in which part of the prison she was kept, nor even whether she were alone or with others. No doubt, wherever she was, she was being well guarded as one of the stars of some future entertainment.

At the prison entrance there was always a Red soldier on guard, and it was through these men alone that A.J. fancied he could accomplish anything. He spent many an hour furtively watching them and speculating which of them might be most likely to be useful for his purpose. At last he singled out a rough, fierce-looking fellow whom, about midnight, when the street was fairly quiet, he saw accept a small package from a passing stranger and transfer it guiltily to his own pocket. A.J. took the chance that thus offered itself.

"Good evening, comrade," he began, walking up to the man a moment later and looking him sternly between the eyes. "Do you usually do that sort of thing?"

It was a blind shot, but a lucky one. The guard, for all his fierce appearance, was a coward as soon as he thought himself discovered. He obviously took A.J. for an official spy who had been set deliberately to watch him, and A.J. did not disabuse him of the notion. He soon drove the fellow to an abject confession that he had been systematically smuggling tobacco into the prison for the benefit of the White officers. "Only tobacco, your honor," he insisted, and produced from his pocket the little packet he had just received. "You know, your honor, how hard it is for a poor soldier to make a living in these days, and the White officers, who are going to be shot very soon, promised me twenty roubles for this little packet. After all, your honor, I don't have the chances that some of our men get—I had to be here on duty all that night when they were looting the shops."

"That was unfortunate," said A.J. dryly. "All the same, you must be aware of the penalties for smuggling things into the prison?"

"Yes, your honor, but surely you wouldn't wish to get a poor man into serious trouble—"

And so on. After a quarter of an hour or so A.J. felt he had succeeded pretty well. He had learned all about the positions and arrangements of the prisoners, their daily habits, and the way in which they were guarded; and, most important of all, he had given the guard a note to be delivered secretly to the Countess. He wrote it in French; it merely said that he was on the spot and ready to help her to escape, and that she must be prepared to do her share in any way and at any time he should command. He told the guard it was merely a family message. "I am a Red," he added, "but I do not see what harm there can be in treating a woman prisoner with ordinary courtesy. No more harm, anyway, than in smuggling tobacco for the men." The guard agreed eagerly. "You are quite right, your honor—and I have said the same even to my comrades. Why not be more civil and polite to people before you shoot them? It is not the shooting that makes so much bad feeling but treating people like dogs."

The next time the guard was on duty A.J. received back

his note together with an answer. It was a verbal one—merely a conventional "Thank you" which, though not very enlightening, seemed, in the circumstances, sufficient. He felt, anyhow, that something was being accomplished. He knew that she was in a ground-floor cell overlooking a yard which was patrolled by sentries day and night. Any romantic escapade with ropes and ladders was thus out of the question. The tobacco-smuggling guard, whose name was Balkin, had stressed how carefully she was watched, and after much thought and the formation of many tentative plans, A.J. reached the conclusion that escape could only take place, if at all, during some general commotion that would temporarily upset the prison-routine. This, as days passed, seemed more likely to happen, for the clamor of the extremists increased and there were strong rumors that at any moment Polahkin's writ might cease to run. Then, no doubt, there would be a brief civil war culminating in a mob-attack on the prison and the massacre of its occupants.

A.J. argued thus: the attack on the prison would probably take place at night, if only because at such a time men's spirits were always most inflamed with speech-making and drink. The prison-guards might or might not attempt any resistance, but in either case it was unlikely that the regular routine of the sentry-patrol would remain unaffected. Most likely there would be either fighting or hilarious fraternization. In the darkness a good many of the invaders would not know where they were, or where to look for the prisoners; there would be confusion of all kinds. Most fortunately, as it happened, the Countess's cell was among the last that could be reached, being the end one in a long corridor. And let into the corridor wall close by was an ordinary unbarred window overlooking the yard. If only the prisoner were once outside her cell it would not be too difficult to climb out through that window. A.J. did not wish to rely too much on Balkin's assistance, for he did not seem a man of either trustworthiness or intelligence; the only promise to be exacted was that, as soon as there might be any hint of trouble, he should slip a small revolver through the bars of the cell. "You see, Balkin, you are a kind-hearted fellow, and I don't mind telling you the truth—the poor creature wishes to kill herself rather than fall into the hands of the soldiers. Personally, I sympathize with her in that, and you also, I am sure, will feel the same. Is it not enough that she should die, without being torn to pieces to amuse a crowd? Let her have a decent death— the sort that a soldier, if he could choose, would ask for." Balkin, greatly stirred, put his hand sentimentally on A.J.'s shoulder. "You are quite right, your honor. It is only fair that she should die properly. Why, I will shoot her myself rather than let her fall into the hands of those ruffians!"

"No, no—all you need do is to give her the revolver. She is no coward, and would rather do the job in her own way. It is more dignified—more seemly. Do you not understand?"

Balkin at length and with great melancholy admitted that he did understand; and he agreed also to take a further message to the woman. A.J. wrote it out and handed it over with the revolver.

That was in the morning; from all outward indications the crisis was likely to develop that night. Polahkin had already been openly insulted in the streets, and a brutal Lettish Jew named Aronstein had been haranguing the crowd all afternoon. The actual *coup d'état* took place about seven o'clock. Polahkin was arrested and Aronstein duly "elected" in his place. One by one all the official buildings in the town went over to the extremist party, and at last came the inevitable attack on the prison. Aronstein had promised the attackers that not a single counter-revolutionary life should be spared, and in such a mood of anticipated blood-lust the mob surged round the building. The guard at the entrance-gate offered no resistance, and within a few moments the invaders were pouring into the inner courtyard.

A.J., in a narrow lane behind the prison, waited with keen anxiety. At first it seemed that the whole affair was being conducted far too methodically, but soon the traditional chaos of all insurgency began to be evident. He could hear the shouts of the crowd; then he saw the sentries suddenly run from their posts in the prison-yard, from which the lane was separated only by tall iron railings. That was his signal for action. He walked along the railings quickly till he reached a certain spot; then he halted and listened. There was a loud commotion proceeding inside the prison—shoutings and screamings and revolver-shots; it was difficult to judge exactly the right moment. However, the lane looked quite deserted, and in the darkness it would be hard to see him in any case. He got hold of two of the iron railings and lifted them out of their sockets. He knew from previous observation that those particular railings were loose, for he had seen the sentries lift them out to admit women into the yard.

He waited for several minutes, refusing rather than unable to draw conclusions from what he could hear; he knew that noise could mean anything and everything; he knew also that Balkin was stupid and perhaps unreliable, that he might do the totally wrong thing, or else just nothing at all, either from error, slackness, or malice. He knew that the chance he had planned for was fantastically slender, that at a dozen points there were even odds of disaster. And he knew, too, that even if the miracle did happen, there were still further miracles to be accomplished in leaving the town and reaching comparative safety.

Then suddenly he saw a dim and shadowy figure rushing across the yard. He gave a loud cough; the figure stopped for a fraction of a second, changed its direction slightly, and came rushing towards him. He said softly: "Here—here—through here. Wait—I must put them back afterwards. Take this coat—I have another underneath. Quickly—but keep calm. Are you hurt at all?"

"No."

"You managed it all right?"

"Yes—I had to fire three times—it's surprising how little damage a bullet can do." She laughed quietly.

"Don't laugh. Don't talk either, now. Put your collar up. If we meet anybody we must be drunk. There are clothes hidden in a field for you."

The greatcoat was useful in making her look, at any considerable distance, like an ordinary Red soldier; at any nearer encounter the semblance of drunkenness would give them their best chance. A Red soldier, half-tipsy, taking a half-tipsy woman towards the outskirts of the town was not an unusual sight, and for the woman to be wearing a soldier's coat was common enough in days when currency depreciation was making payment in kind increasingly popular.

They passed several people on their way and the stratagem seemed to succeed. One of the passers-by, a soldier, called out to ask what was happening in the town; A.J. replied, with fuddled intonation, that he rather thought the prison was being attacked. "Ah," answered the other, laughing, "but I see you've evidently got something more important to do than join in, eh?" A.J. laughed, and the woman laughed too, and they passed on.

They reached the end of the town and climbed over the roadside into the fields. Hidden in a ditch were the clothes he had carefully obtained and carefully placed in position an hour before; it was a relief to find them, for there had always been the possibility of their being found and stolen in the interval. The clothes consisted of a more or less complete military outfit, including topboots and a shabby peaked cap such as soldier or civilian might equally be wearing.

"Well?" she whispered, as he showed them to her. "So I am to be your obedient prisoner once again?"

He did not answer, except to urge her to dress quickly. Her own clothes, as she discarded them, he rolled into a bundle—it would not be safe to leave them behind. She was very calm; that was a good thing, yet he wondered if she realized that difficulties were beginning rather than ending, and that in a short while hundreds of blood-drunken searchers would be scouring the district for the escaped White countess. One thing he was sure of—the peasant disguise would never work a second time near Saratursk. Everyone knew that she had escaped as a peasant before; everyone would be prepared for the same disguise again. There was only the slender chance that as two soldiers they might escape through the cordon into safer country.

"Please hurry," he said again. "And we had better not talk much."

"I'm ready now, except for the boots."

"Let me do them."

He knelt on one knee and laced them quickly.

She whispered, looking down at him in the darkness: "You are very, very kind."

"It will be safer not to talk just yet—your voice, you know. And when you do talk, you must call me 'Tovarish'—it's the word the soldiers use. We must be very careful, even in details."

"Yes, of course. I understand. Now I'm ready."

"Good. We must try to get a long way into the forests by daylight."

"Still *en route* for Moscow, I suppose?"

He answered, shouldering his bundle and helping her quickly over the uneven ground: "No. I have decided to accept your suggestion and will try to get you to the coast where you can take ship for abroad. Now don't answer me—don't talk at all—just save all your strength for the long journey."

PART FOUR

HE STOOD ON THE SUMMIT OF the first low ridge that lifted out of the long level of the plains. Dawn was creeping over the horizon; distant and below lay the clustered roofs of the town. He and his companion had stopped for but a moment, to share bread and water together; she was so tired that she was already half asleep on the springy turf.

He stared strangely upon that freshening August dawn, yet in his own mind, for some reason, he saw another picture—a frozen Arctic river under sunshine, all so still and stiff, and then suddenly the splitting shiver of the ice-crust and the surge of water over the quickening land. He felt as if something like that were happening within himself. "Come now," he said, picking up the bundles. She was asleep and he had to waken her. She smiled without a word and stumbled forward.

He dared not have allowed more than that moment's halt, for though they had had good fortune so far, there was still danger, and perhaps the greatest of all now that daylight had come. They plunged on and on as the glow in the eastern sky deepened and became glorified by sunrise over pine-covered ridges and down into a little lonely valley through swishing gullies of dead leaves and round curving slopes whence Saratursk, glimpsed between tree-trunks, seemed ever further away, yet ever dangerously near. By ten o'clock they had covered seven or eight miles, and were already deep in the foothill forests; but she was so tired that she could not take another step. There was nothing for it but to rest for at least a few moments. They sat on a fallen tree-trunk and she was asleep again instantly, with her head leaning forward into her hands.

He was tired himself and after a short time, being afraid of falling asleep also, he got up and moved about. Ten minutes—a quarter of an hour—might be enough to give her just the needful strength to scramble a few miles further. Even during those few minutes, he guessed, pursuers would be gaining on them. He had no illusions or false optimism; he knew that the escape must have been discovered within a few hours, at most, of its taking place, and that immense efforts would certainly be made to recapture such a fugitive. He had seen the whole routine carried through so often before—a price upon some prisoner dead or alive—a whole army setting out on perhaps the cruelest and therefore the most intoxicatingly thrilling game in the world—a man-hunt. And a woman-hunt would be even a degree better than that. Then suddenly, even while he was pondering over it, he heard, very faintly in the distance, a shrill whistle, and, a few seconds later, a still fainter whistle answering it. The hunt had begun already.

He touched the woman on the shoulder, but it was no use—he had to shake her thoroughly to get her awake. He said quietly: "We must hide for a time—I think searchers are somewhere in the woods."

She answered in a dazed way: "All right. I'm ready." He helped her to her feet and they moved away, he with eyes alert for a good hiding-place.

He was fortunate in finding one quite soon. A steep

valley ended in a large and desolate tract of undergrowth amidst whose tangle there seemed a good chance of escaping notice. Even if pursuers ever reached it they would not be likely to give every thicket the attention it deserved. He plunged eagerly into the bushes and for ten minutes, out of sight of the world around them, they both wriggled further and deeper into the dense undergrowth. At last the seemingly perfect spot revealed itself —a little hollow hidden behind thick brambles and knee-deep in litter of twigs and leaves. "Here," he cried, with sudden satisfaction. He stared thankfully about him at the protecting foliage, and then upwards at the blue sky just visible through the lacery of branches. Then he heard once again, but a little nearer, that shrill whistle and its answer.

He laid her gently on the ground and yet again she fell asleep instantly—so instantly that he smiled a rather rueful smile, for he had intended to give her some cautionary advice. No matter; it could probably wait. He did not think of wakening her. And then as the moments passed and he watched her sleeping, a queer feeling of tenderness came over him, like a slow warmth from another world, and he did something he had never done before in all his life—he put his arm round a woman and drew her gently towards him. She would sleep more comfortably so. He gazed on her with quiet, almost proprietary triumph; all the way from Khalinsk he had not ceased to guard her, through all manner of difficulty and peril, and here she was still, by miracle, under his protection. He was hungry and thirsty and tired and anxious, yet also, in a way he had never known before, he was satisfied.

The thicket was noisy with buzzing insects, but every

few moments over the distant air came the whistling—now quite distinctly nearer. His heart beat no faster for it; he felt: We are here, and here is our only chance; we must wait and take whatever comes. . . . The nearest of the pursuers, he judged, must be perhaps half a mile away; there were others, too, not far behind, and probably hundreds already combing the forests on the way from Saratursk. Soon the whistling became less intermittent and seemed to come from north and south as well as west; once, too, he thought he heard voices a long way off. Hunger and thirst were now beginning to be importunate, but he dared not satisfy them, since it might be night before he could risk leaving the thicket in quest of any fresh supplies.

Then he saw that her eyes were wide open—dark, sleepy eyes staring up at him. She whispered, half-smiling: "How uncomfortable you must be—with me leaning on you like this!"

"All the better," he answered, with a wry smile. "It helps me to keep awake."

"I think it is your turn to sleep now."

"No, no—you go on sleeping."

"But I *can't*." Her voice dropped agonizingly. "I've kept my nerve pretty well up to now, but I'm afraid—I'm beginning to be just—terrified."

"Terrified? Oh, no need for that."

"Those whistles that keep on sounding—we're being hunted—that's what they mean, don't they?"

"They're looking for us, of course. That was to be expected. But it doesn't follow that they're going to find us."

"Promise me—promise me one thing—that you'll kill me rather than let them get me again!"

"Yes, I promise."

"You mean it?"

"Absolutely."

A whistle suddenly shrilled quite close to them—perhaps two or three hundred yards away, on the edge of the undergrowth. Even he was startled, and he felt her trembling silently against him. He whispered: "Keep calm—they're a long way off yet—they might easily come within ten yards and not see us in a place like this. Don't worry."

All she could muster, amidst her fear, was: "You have your revolver? You remember?"

"Yes, of course."

His arm tightened upon her; he whispered: "Poor child, don't give up hope." Then they both waited in silence. It seemed an age until the next whistle—an answering one that appeared to come from about the same distance on the other side. What was happening was not very clear; perhaps the two searchers were passing along the edges of the undergrowth and did not intend to make any detailed search amongst it. He could imagine their condition—tired, hot, thirsty, and probably bad-tempered after the so far fruitless search. The prickly brambles would hardly tempt them. On the other hand, there was the big reward that had most likely been offered—men would do most things for a few hundred roubles.

After a short time it was evident that the searchers numbered far more than two; whistling proceeded from every direction, and sounded rather as if fresh searchers were coming up at every moment. Then came echoes of shouting and talking, but voices did not carry very well and he could not catch any words. He judged, however, that some sort of a consultation was in progress. Next followed a chorus of whistling and counter-whistling from both sides, the meaning of which was only too easy to guess.

"They're coming through!" she gasped.

He whispered: "I dare say they've got the sense to realize that this is a good place to hide. And so it is, too. There are so many of them there's bound to be overlapping and confusion. Keep calm. We've still a good chance." The approach of almighty danger gave him a feeling of exaltation as difficult to understand as to control. He went on a moment later: "Leaves—these leaves. A childish trick, but it might work. I want you to lie down in this hollow and let me cover you up."

"Yes, if you wish."

He placed her so that, with the leaves over her, there seemed no break in the level ground. The whistling by this time was very much nearer, and there could be heard also the tearing and breaking of twigs as some of the searchers broke through. He whispered: "Keep still— don't move or say a word. And whatever happens, trust me and don't be surprised. Whatever happens, mind." A moment afterwards the tousled head of a Red soldier, streaked with dirt and perspiration, pushed itself through the undergrowth a few yards away. A.J. did not wait to be accosted. Wiping his forehead with his sleeve and kicking up some of the litter of twigs, he shouted: "Hallo? Found anything yet? There's nothing here."

The man answered: "Nor here either, Tovarish. It's my belief she didn't go into the forest at all. And if she did, she wouldn't have got so far as this. It's a terrible job, searching through this sort of country on a hot day."

A.J. agreed sympathetically. "You're right, my friend

—it's the devil's own job. And I've lost my whistle too, confound it."

The other laughed. "Never mind, I'll whistle for you." He gave two mighty blasts. "That'll show we've done *our* duty, anyway. Have a drink with me, Tovarish, and let's get out of this muddle."

A.J. accepted the offer by no means ungratefully, for he wanted the drink badly enough. The soldier seemed a simple, good-natured fellow, with a childishness, however, that was quite capable of being dangerous. "You were with the other lot, I suppose?" he queried, and A.J. nodded. They struggled through the thickets and reached at last the open ground. There a few other soldiers were already gathered together, evidently satisfied that they had performed their share of the search. They were all rather disgruntled. It was a ticklish moment when A.J. joined them, but his highest hopes were realized; there had been a tremendous amount of confusion and no man expected to know his neighbor. The chief concern of all was the food and drink due to arrive from the forests below.

A.J. found them a friendly lot of men behind their temporary ill-humor; he soon learned that they had been promised a large reward for the discovery of the escaped Countess, and that the latter, if captured alive, was to be accorded a solemn full-dress execution in the market-place at Saratursk. "She will be hanged, not shot," said one of the men, rolling a cigarette between grimy fingers. And he added, contemplatively: "It is a pity, in some ways, to hang a woman, because their necks are made differently. I am a hangman by profession, and I can speak from knowledge."

Soon a few men came toiling up the valley with sacks

175

of bread and buckets of thin potato soup. The searchers greeted them boisterously, relieved them of their burdens, and began to eat and drink ravenously. A.J. and his tousled companion, whose name was Stephanov, managed to secure a loaf of black bread between them, as well as a large can of soup. Stephanov was not astonished that A.J. knew none of the men. "That is the worst of the army nowadays," he said. "They shift you about so quickly that you never get to know anybody. It was different in the old days when there were proper regiments." He went on chatting away in a manner most helpful to A.J. "I suppose all the others have got lost—that's what usually happens. I only know one of the fellows here by name. That's little Nikolai Roussilov over there. Do you see him? That man snoring against that tree-trunk." A.J. looked and observed. "I can tell you a secret, Tovarish, about that man—and though you'll hardly believe it, I assure you it's the heavenly truth and nothing less." He dropped his voice to a hoarse whisper. "That man was once kissed by the Emperor."

A.J. made some surprised and enquiring remark and Stephanov went on, pleased with his little sensation: "Ah, I guessed that would startle you! Well, you see, it all happened like this. Nikolai was doing sentry duty one night outside a railway train in which the Emperor was sleeping. The train was drawn up on a siding, and it was Easter Sunday morning—in the old days, of course. You know the custom—you kiss the first person you meet and give the Easter greeting. Well, Nikolai was the first person the Emperor met that morning when he stepped out of the train, so the Emperor kissed him. Isn't that remarkable? And you would hardly think it to look at him, would you?"

Many of the men had already fallen to dozing in the shade, but Stephanov's conversation showed no signs of early abatement. A.J. was not wholly sorry, for the man's garrulous chatter gave him much information that he guessed might be of value in the immediate future. At last, towards the late afternoon, an officer appeared on the edge of the scene and gave leisurely instruction to the half-sleeping men. They were to form themselves into detachments and march back to Saratursk. Evidently the search, for that day, at any rate, was being abandoned.

A.J.'s problem, of course, was to escape from the soldiers without attracting attention, and there were many ways in which he hoped to be able to do so. Having, however, been given such incredible good fortune so far, he was determined to take no unnecessary risks, and he saw no alternative to accompanying the men for some distance, at least, on their march back to the town. He and Stephanov walked together, or rather, Stephanov followed him with a species of dog-like attachment which threatened to be highly inconvenient in the circumstances. The retreat began about six o'clock and dusk fell as the stragglers were still threading their way amongst the pine-trees. From time to time as they descended, other parties of soldiers joined them—all tired and rather low-spirited. But for the too pertinacious Stephanov it would have been a simple matter to slip away in the twilit confusion of one or other of these encounters. At last, however, when the last tint of daylight had almost left the sky, an opportunity did come. Stephanov halted to take off his boot and beat in a protruding nail; A.J. said he would go ahead and see how far they had still to go. He went ahead, but he did not return, and he hoped that Stephanov would realize that in the darkness nothing was more likely than that two companions, once separated, should be unable to find each other again.

A.J. waited till the last faint sounds of the retreating men had died away in the distance; some were singing and could be heard for a long time. Then he took deep breaths of the cool pine-laden air and tried to induce in himself a calm and resourceful confidence. He took careful note of his bearings; the stars and the rising moon and the slope of the ground were all helpful guides. His Siberian experiences had made him uncannily expert at that sort of thing; with a night lasting for nine months it had been necessary to train the senses to work efficiently in the dark. Still, it was not going to be an easy task to locate the exact whereabouts of that valley wilderness. During the journey with Stephanov he had tried to memorize the ground passed over, and he had counted five successive ridges that they had crossed.

Cautiously he climbed to the summit of the first ridge. There moonlight helped him by showing a vague outline of the next one. He paused a moment to munch a little bread he had managed to save; there was still some left. At the next stream he filled his water-bottle to the brim. On the top of the second ridge he saw cigarette wrappings that had been thrown away by the soldiers, and that was heartening, for it showed that he was in the right direction. Twice after that he imagined he was lost, and the second time he had just decided to stay where he was until dawn, when he caught a distant glimpse of a pale clearing that seemed somehow familiar. He walked towards it, and there, glossy under the moonlight, lay that steep valley with the wilderness of thickets like a dark velvet patch at the upper end of it. He stumbled over the turf with tingling excitement in his blood, and all at once and surprisingly for the first time, the thought came to him that she might not be there. What if she were not? If she had grown tired or terrified of waiting—if she had wildly sought to escape on her own—if she had lost hope of his ever returning? He gave a low whistle across the empty valley, and at once a hundred voices answered, so that he shivered almost in fear himself. Then he smiled; they were only owls. He reached the edge of the thickets and plunged into them, not caring that the brambles tore at his clothes and face and hands. In a little while he dared to speak—he shouted softly: "I'm coming—don't be afraid—I'm coming. Tell me where you are." And a voice, very weary and remote, answered him.

When he came at last to that little hollow of dead leaves she sprang up and clung to him with both arms, sobbing and laughing at the same time. "Darling—Darling—" she whispered, hysterically, and he felt all the ice in his soul break suddenly into the flow of spring. "Were you thinking I wouldn't come?" he stammered, dazed with the glory of her welcome. She could not answer, but she was all at once calmed. Then he stooped and kissed her lips, and they were like the touch of sleep itself. "You must be so tired," she said, and he answered: "I am—yes, I am." There was a curious serenity about her that made him feel a child again—a child to whom most things are simple and marvelous.

They shared food and water and then lay down together on the bed of leaves until morning.

The chorus of birds awoke him at sunrise; he looked up and saw the blue sky between the branches and then looked down and saw her sleeping. He memorized her features as he might have done the contours of some

179

friendly, familiar land; he saw her wide, round eyelids, and her slender nose, and her lips a little parted as she slept. He wondered if she were really beautiful, as one may wonder if a loved scene is really beautiful; for to him, as she lay there, she meant so much more than beauty. He saw her as the center of a universe, and all else—those years of exile and loneliness and wandering—dissolved into background.

Then, as if aware that he was thinking about her so intensely, she wakened and smiled.

They finished what remained of the food and then talked over what was to be done next. Their immediate aim, of course, was to get as far away as possible from Saratursk, and for this the soldier disguise seemed the safest, though later it might be advisable to drop it. Even more pressing might soon be problems of food and shelter, since they could not expect to leave the forest for several days and the warm and dry weather had already lasted exceptionally.

As they set out under the trees that early morning they talked as they had never done before—about themselves. She told him of her family, of which, she believed, she might be the only survivor; her mother was dead; her father and two brothers had certainly been killed by the Reds; and among other relatives there were few whom she could be sure were still alive. They had all, of course, lost their money and possessions. Almost as an afterthought she told him that she had been married, and that her husband had been killed in Galicia fighting the Austrians. "Almost as soon as the war began, that was. We had been married four years, but we had no children. I am glad."

She continued: "I stayed on our estates as long as I

could—I never believed our old servants would turn against me, but they did, in the end. I suppose one can hardly blame them. To stay on the sinking ship may be brave, but it's also rather stupid."

"That's a very calm way of looking at it."

She smiled. "I've had time to become calm, you see. I soon gave up worrying about the loss of possessions— personal danger takes the edge off most inconveniences."

"Yes, that's true."

"You also are very calm about things."

He did not reply, and she went on, after a pause: "When you took me prisoner I was dreadfully disappointed at first, but presently a mood came on me in which nothing seemed to matter at all. Even when I tried to bribe you and you refused, I didn't find myself caring very much. But now—I'm just beginning to care again."

He was still silent. She waited a moment and resumed: "It hurts to have feelings again. It hurts even to want to live, after so long not caring. But I *do* want it now—I want it for us both. Oh, we *must* live through it all, mustn't we?"

"Yes," he replied, and the word, as he uttered it, seemed a keystone set upon his life. Then he began to tell her, quite simply and dispassionately, of his own years of exile, though not of anything previous to that. As it was, the accounting was like turning old keys in rusty locks; to no one before had he spoken of those bitter years that had frozen his soul with their silence just as hers had been numbed with grief. And there came upon them both, as they talked and compared experiences, a curious sense of the freakishness of their two personal fates, threading so far and so deviously from gilded salon and

Arctic hut, and joining here in the woods above Sara-tursk. They could not in their hearts believe that such a vast completion was no more than a single marking in a map of gigantic intricacy. Their own private world was limitless; they had discovered it for themselves, and the confused background of affairs seemed oddly irrelevant, at times almost invisible. "Don't be too anxious about me," she said suddenly, after that first interchange of confidences. "Remember that I'm happy. I *am,* whatever happens."

"I shall be happier myself when we're further from danger."

"Yes, I know. So shall I, but don't be too hard on danger. Don't forget it was danger that brought us together. In a safe world we couldn't possibly have met."

He did not know what to say to that. He was never articulate about his own emotions, and the fact that her mood awakened the deepest response in him made him even less so.

All morning they trudged from ridge to ridge, skirting Saratursk at a wide radius. He kept careful watch, for he thought it more than possible that the Reds would resume their search of the forests. Nobody, however, appeared within sight until mid-afternoon, when they saw, far off on a hillside, a man gathering small timber for fuel. They were so hungry by then that A.J. took the risk of walking up to him and, posing as a soldier who had lost his way, asking to buy food and drink. The man was quite cordial, and took A.J. to his tiny cottage half a mile away, where he lived with his wife and a large family amidst conditions of primitive savagery. It seemed a pity to take food from such people, but the man was glad to sell eggs, tea, and bread at the prices A.J. offered. It was hard, indeed, to escape from his good-natured friendliness, and especially from his offer to show the way in person for a few miles. At last, when A.J.'s desire to be unaccompanied had been made almost offensively clear, the man's puzzlement changed to a gust of amusement. "Ah, I begin to see how it is, comrade," he chuckled. "You have a woman waiting for you out there in the woods, eh? Oh, don't be afraid—I shan't say anything! You're not the first soldier who's deserted the Red army and taken to the hills with a woman. But I'll give you this bit of advice—if you do happen to meet anyone else at the same game, be careful—for they shoot at sight. They're wild as wolves, many of 'em."

A.J. thanked the fellow and was glad to walk away with an armful of food and nothing worse than a roar of laughter behind him. When he rejoined his companion they continued their walk for a mile or so and then sat down to eat, drink, and rest. It was already late afternoon and they had had nothing since the few crusts of bread at early morning. A.J. now gathered sticks for a small fire, on which he boiled eggs and made tea. The resulting meal lifted them both to an extraordinary pitch of happiness; as they sat near the smoking embers while the first mists of twilight dimmed the glades, a strange peacefulness fell upon them, and they both knew, even without speaking, that neither would have chosen to be anywhere else in the world. All around them lay enemies; tomorrow might see them captured, imprisoned, or dead; there might be horror in the future to balance all the horrors of the past; yet the tiny oasis of the present, with themselves at the core of it, was a sheer glow of perfection.

They were so tired that they did not move before darkness came, and then merely lay down on the brown leaves. The evening air was chilly, and they clung together for warmth with their two greatcoats huddled over them. All the small and friendly sounds of the forest wrapped them about; an owl hooted very far away; a mouse rustled through the near undergrowth; a twig broke suddenly aloft and fell with a tiny clatter to the ground. She kissed him with a grave, peaceful passion that seemed a living part of all the copious, cordial nature that surrounded them; they hardly spoke; to love seemed as simple and as speechless as to be hungry and thirsty and tired. That night he could almost have blessed the chaos that had brought them both, out of a whole world, together.

On the fifth day they fell in with a peasant who told them of a quick way into the plains. He was a bent and gnarled fellow of an age that looked to be anything between sixty and eighty, and with the manner of one to whom Bolshevism and revolution were merely the pranks of a young and foolish generation. He was full of chatter and told A.J. all his family affairs, besides pointing to a small timbered roof on a distant hillside that was his own. He had left a sick daughter alone in that hut with five small children; her husband was a soldier, fighting somewhere or other—or perhaps dead—no news had been received for many months. "Of course he will never come back—they never do. She has had no baby now for over two years—is it not dreadful? And she would make a good wife for any man when she is in good health—oh, yes, a very good wife."

A.J. made some sympathetic remark and the old man continued: "But what are young men nowadays? Mere adventurers pretending to want to see the world! What *is* the world, after all? When you have seen one forest, you have seen them all, and one field is very much like another. I myself am quite happy to have been no further than Vremarodar, seventy versts away." He chuckled amidst the odorous depths of a heavy matted beard and still continued: "I don't suppose you'd ever guess my age, either, brother. I'm a hundred and three, though people don't always believe me when I tell them. You see my youngest daughter's only twenty-five, and people say it's impossible." He chuckled again. "But it *isn't* impossible, I assure you—I'm not the sort of fellow to tell you a lie. Why, look at me now, still fit and hearty, as you can see, and if there was a pretty woman about, and my honor as a man depended on it, I don't know but what . . ." His chuckles boiled over into resonant laughter. "Mind you, I'm not what I used to be, by a long way, and I think it's a girl's duty to look after her father when he lives to be my age, don't you? She's not a bad girl, you know, but she's inclined to be lazy and I have to thrash her now and again. Not that I like doing it, but women—well, you know all about them, I dare say. Ah, well, there's your path—it leads out into a long valley and at the end of that there are the plains as far as you can see. Good day to you, brother, and to you too, madam."

The next day they reached the edge of the forests and saw the plains stretching illimitably into the hazy distance. But before descending, it was necessary to make certain arrangements. It was certain that they would meet many strangers once they left the hillsides, and with the prospect, too, of colder weather, they could no longer rely on sleeping out of doors. A soldier's disguise, for the woman especially, seemed therefore likely to be a source of danger, and A.J. decided that it would be better for them to resume their peasant rôles. In his own case the change was inconsiderable, since so many peasants wore army clothes whenever they could acquire them; and as for Daly, she had only to change into the female attire that she had been carrying with her all the way from Saratursk.

The change was made, and on the seventh day, very early in the morning, they left the forests. The sky was fine, but clouds were already massing on the horizon for a thunderstorm that would doubtless bring to an end the long spell of fine weather. It was still hard to make more than the sketchiest plan of campaign. Amidst those lonely Ural foothills there had been an atmosphere of being out of the world, removed from many of its bewilderments and troubled by nothing more complicated than the elemental problem of the hunted eluding the hunter. In the plains, however, all problems were subtler and more intricate—as intricate, at least, as the political and military situation of the country generally. At Saratursk, before the escape, A.J. had tried to visualize what was happening as a whole, and not merely locally, but it had been difficult owing to the wildness of the rumors that gained credence. Every morning there had come a fresh crop of them—that the German Kaiser had committed suicide, that Lenin had been shot in Moscow by a young girl, that a British army was invading from Archangel, that the Japanese were approaching from the east along the line of the Trans-Siberian—there had been no lack of such sensational news, much of which was always more likely to be false than true. It seemed, however, fairly probable that Czecho-Slovak detachments were by this time in full occupation of great lengths of the Trans-

Siberian, and it was also possible (as rumor alleged) that they had pushed up the Volga and captured Sembirsk and Kazan. The repulse of the Whites from Saratursk would appear, in that case, to have been a merely isolated and local affair—as local, in fact, as the Red Terror that had followed it. But then, all Russia was seething with such local affairs, and the history of the whole country could scarcely be more than the sum-total of them. A village here might be Red, or there White, and a stranger could hardly tell which until he took the risk of entering it. The Czechs, despite their imposing position on the map, held merely the thin line of the railway; a few versts on either side of the track their sway ended, and the brigandage of Red and White soldiery went on without interruption.

So much A.J. had in mind, though there was little he knew for certain. If there had been any fixed battle-line between Red and White, it would have been a straightforward task, despite the danger of it, to make for the nearest point of that line and cross over. As it was, however, there could be no advantage in joining up with some small and local White colony which, in a few days or weeks, might surrender to the Reds and be massacred.

The two of them talked the matter over during that early morning descent to the plains, and she said at length, putting it far more concisely than he would care to have done: "The whole question is really—am I to escape alone, or are you to come with me? You are to come with me, of course, and that means we must go right away—out of the whole area of these local wars." Then she looked at him and laughed rather queerly. "Oh, it all comes to this, I suppose, that what I want more than anything in the world is to be with you. Can't you believe me? In a way I'm enjoying every minute of all this—it's an adventure I don't want ever to end—but if it must end, then let anything end it rather than separation. Promise that wherever we go and whatever happens to us, it will be together!"

"That is all I hoped you would say," he answered. "We will make south for the railway, then, and take a train, if there are trains, towards Kazan. And there, if the situation remains the same, we can join the Czechs."

The hill country ended with disconcerting abruptness; by noon they were crossing land so level that it looked like a sea, with the horizon of hills as a coastline in the rearward distance. It was dizzily hot; the threatened storm had passed over with a few abortive thunderclaps. The earth was caked and splitting after weeks without rain; dust filled eyes and nostrils at the slightest breath of wind; the crops were withering in the unharvested fields.

As distance increased between themselves and the mountains, they found tracks widening into roads, and roads becoming more frequented. Every side-track yielded its stragglers, most of whom were peasants carrying all their worldly goods on their backs. Where they had come from and where they were bound for were problems that were no more soluble after, as often happened, they had unburdened their secrets to the passing stranger. But many were too ill and dejected even to give the usual greeting as they passed, and some showed all the outward signs of prolonged hardships and semi-starvation.

For every passer-by in the opposite direction there were at least a dozen bound, like themselves, for the railway twenty miles to the south. The chance of getting aboard a train did not, in such circumstances, seem very promising, and still less attractive was the prospect of camping out for days or weeks on the railway platforms, as thousands of refugees were doing. A.J. learned this from a youth with whom, along the road, he effected an exchange of a couple of eggs in return for a small quantity of butter made from sunflower-seeds. The boy—for he was scarcely more—seemed so knowledgeable and intelligent that A.J. was glad enough to agree when he suggested pooling resources for a small roadside meal. The stranger hardly got the better of the bargain, since his own provender included white bread (an almost incredible luxury) and part of a cooked chicken; but he only laughed when A.J. apologized. He was a merry, pink-cheeked youth, eager to treat A.J. with rouguish bonhomie and the woman with a touch of gallantry. He was eighteen, he said, and his life had been fairly adventurous. At sixteen he had been a cadet in an Imperial training-school for officers, but the revolution had happened just in time to fit in conveniently with his own reluctance to die in a trench fighting the Germans. He seemed also to have quarreled with his family, for he said he neither knew nor cared what had happened to them. He had joined the revolutionaries at the age of seventeen, doubtless to save his own skin, and in a single year had risen to be a military commissar. But even that, in the end, had become too tedious and exacting, for in his heart he had always pined for something more individually adventurous. Presently he had found it. He had become a train-bandit. He admitted this quite frankly, and with a joyous taking of risks in so doing. "It suits me," he explained, "because I'm a bad lot—I always was."

It appeared that he had been the leader of a group of bandits operating on the Cheliabinsk-Ufa line before the advance of the Czechs had put an end to such enterprise. His colleagues had since dispersed, and he himself was now at a loose end, but he rather thought there was a good chance of successful banditry on the Ekaterinburg-Sarapul line, which was still to a large extent in the hands of the Reds. All he needed were a few suitable companions; the rest would be easy. There was a steep incline not far away where westbound trains always slowed down. One man could jump into the engine-cab and make the driver pull up; the others would then go through the train, coach by coach and compartment by compartment. It was the usual and most always successful method. A.J. expressed surprise that the passengers, many of whom were doubtless well armed, did not put up a fight. The boy laughed. "You must remember that it's in the middle of the night, when most of them are asleep and none of them feel particularly brave. Besides, some of them *do* try their tricks, but we try ours first. If you shoot straight once you don't often have any trouble with the rest." He spoke quite calmly, and not without a certain half-humorous relish. "After all," he then went on, as if feeling instinctively some need to defend himself, "it's not a bad death—being shot. Better than starvation or typhus. A good many people in this country, I should reckon, have got to die pretty soon, and the lucky ones are those that get a bullet through the heart." Looked at in such a way, the situation undoubtedly showed him in the guise of a public benefactor. And he added: "I suppose you don't feel you're the sort of fellow to join forces with me?"

When A.J. smiled and shook his head, the boy smiled back quite amicably. "That's all right—only I thought I'd just put it to you. You look the sort of man I'd like to work with, that's all. Anyhow, I can help you with a bit of advice. There's not a thousand to one chance of your getting on board a train at Novochensk. The station's already cram-full. But if you go about three versts to the east you'll come to that incline I was talking about —where the trains all slow up. There you might manage it."

"I suppose the trains are full, too."

"Absolutely, but they'll make room for you and your lady if you shout that you've got food. Show them a loaf of bread and they'll pull you into the cars even if they murder you afterwards."

A.J. thanked him for the excellent-sounding advice, and after a little further conversation the eighteen-year-old bandit shouldered his bundle and departed. Following his suggestion, they reached the railway late that evening at a point a few miles east of the railway station. It was too dark to see exactly where they were, and they were just preparing to sleep on the parched ground until morning when, from the very far distance, came the sound of a train. It was a weird noise amidst the silence of the steppes—rather like the breathing of a very tired and aged animal. Once or twice, as the wind veered away, the sound disappeared altogether for a time, and they listened for it intermittently for nearly half an hour before they first saw the tiny sparkle of a headlight on the horizon. They perceived then that they were on the ridge of some low downs, which the train would have to surmount—that, presumably, being the incline they had been told about. And soon, to confirm this assumption, the breathing of the engine became a kind of hoarse pant as the rising gradient was encountered. More and more asthmatic grew the panting, until, with a sudden sigh, it ceased altogether, and a sharp jangle of brakes showed that the train was locked at a standstill.

"Let's walk down," A.J. said, rapidly gathering up the bundles. "They might take us on board—at any rate, we can try."

They walked along the track down the noticeable slope; evidently the builders of the line had been unable to afford the evening out of the gradient by means of cutting and embankment. The train, as they approached it, looked in some commotion, and to avoid being seen too clearly in the glare of the headlight they made a detour into the fields and returned to the track opposite the third vehicle. They could see now that the train was composed of some dozen box-cars of refugees and a single ordinary passenger-coach next to the engine.

Scores of heads peered at them through the slats of the cars, and several occupants, evidently taking A.J. for some wayside railway official, enquired why the train had stopped. A.J. said he thought it was because the engine could not manage the hill, and then, feeling that nothing was to be lost by broaching the matter immediately, added: "I have a little bread and some tea and sugar—could you make room for just the two of us?"

"We cannot," answered several, which did not sound unreasonable in view of the fact that men were even perched on the buffers between the cars. One or two voices, however, began to ask how much tea and sugar he had.

The whole colloquy was then sharply interrupted by the sound of shots proceeding from the passenger-coach. At once women began to shout and scream, and a few of the men standing on the buffers actually dropped to the ground and hid themselves beneath the cars. Other shots followed in rapid succession; then suddenly a group of men appeared out of the darkness, brandishing weapons and shouting. One carried a lantern and flashed it in A.J.'s face, exclaiming in bad Russian: "What are you doing here? Didn't you hear the order that no one was to get out?"

A.J. explained with an appropriate mixture of eloquence and simplicity that they hadn't got out, and that, on the contrary, they were a couple of poor peasants trying their best to get in.

Another man then joined in the argument; he was clearly for shooting the two of them out of hand, but the first man restrained him with some difficulty. "They are only peasants," he said, and turning to A.J., added: "You say you were only looking for a place on the train?"

A.J. assured him that this was so, and just as he had finished, a soft, rather plaintive voice from the car above them cried out: "Yes, he is speaking the truth, your honor —they were offering us tea and sugar if we would make room for them."

The man with the lantern grunted sharply. "Tea and sugar, eh? Come on—hand them over." Obedience seemed advisable in the circumstances, and A.J. yielded up his precious commodities; after which the men, with a few final shouts, hurried away into the darkness, leaving the couple standing there by the side of the train, unharmed, but bereft of their most potent bargaining power.

After a judicious interval the occupants of the train took courage and set up a chorus of loud and indignant protests. The engine-whistle began a continuously ear-piercing screech, while from the passenger-coach sprang half-a-dozen Red soldiers, armed with rifles and fixed bayonets. It soon became known that the bandits had run off with a large quantity of money and had also killed two Red guards on the train. The survivors, to excuse themselves, estimated the number of bandits at twenty, but A.J. did not think there could have been more than half that number.

Rather oddly the crowd of harassed and scared refugees were now inclined to show sympathy towards A.J. and his companion. "They were going to share their tea and sugar with us," said the man with the plaintive voice. And another man said: "It's all very well to kill the soldiers and steal the money, but to take away a poor man's food is something to be really ashamed of. Climb up, friends, and we'll make room for you somehow."

So A.J. and Daly got aboard the train after all. There was hardly a square foot of space, and they were huddled together against the dirtiest and most odorous fellow-travelers, but there they were, as they had dreamed of being for many days—on board a train that would take them a further stage on their journey.

It was dawn, however, before the train started. In despair of surmounting the hill from a standstill, the engine-driver reversed for a mile or so and tried to take the gradient by storm. The maneuver failed, and the train was again reversed. This time the order was given for all able-bodied men to get out and push the cars over the crest of the rise, and by this means, with many snortings and splutterings, the train did finally crawl over the summit. There was then a further long wait while the pushers regained their places, and it was not till an hour after sunrise that the train steamed into Novochensk station, less than three miles from the scene of the hold-up.

A first view of Novochensk proved to A.J. how fortunate, after all, had been the boy-bandit's advice. The station was packed from end to end of its large platform and freight yards, and the train, as it entered, seemed to push a way through the crowd like a vehicle threading through a fairground. There was much agitated shouting and gesticulation among the railway officials as the bodies of the dead soldiers were removed from the train. The remaining soldiers had already revised their earlier estimate of the number of attackers; it was now reckoned about a hundred.

Scarcely any of those waiting at Novochensk succeeded in getting a place on the train, and those already in occupation dared not moved for fear of losing their own places. The train left Novochensk shortly before midday, and amidst the drowsy torpidity of the afternoon A.J. had plenty of time and opportunity to observe his fellow-passengers.

Here and there, and from time to time, some isolated phenomenon detached itself from that jumble of rags, chatter, and drowsiness; a baby cried; a woman opened her blouse and exposed a drooping, shrunken breast; a man groaned heavily as he stirred in sleep; the train lurched over a bad patch of line and drew a sigh, a curse, or a muttered exclamation from every corner of that strange assembly. The sunlight, shining through the wooden slats, made a flickering febrile patchwork of the whole picture, showing up here a piece of gaudily colored cloth, there a greasy, dirt-stained face, and everywhere, like a veil drawn in front of reality, the smoke rising from the men's coarse tobacco and the myriad nodding particles of dust.

The speed of travel was very slow—never more than ten miles an hour, and oftener no more than five; nor could anything be seen outside save that vast, vacant expanse of brown earth, on which the horizon seemed to press like a brazen, livid rim. Miles passed without sight of a habitation, while nothing moved over the emptiness save swirls of dust and curlews scared by the train.

Actually Daly whispered to him as she leaned against the curve of his arm: "Oh, I'm happy—I'm happy. I'm beginning to have hope. When do you think we shall reach Kazan?"

"In two or three days, at this rate. Are you hungry?"

"Very, but I don't mind. We had a good meal yesterday."

"I'll try to get you some water to drink at the next stop."

"Yes, if you can. And for yourself too."

"Oh, I'm all right. Are you tired?"

"Just a little."

"Then go to sleep now, if you like. At night it may be chilly and you'll be kept awake."

She gave him a single quick glance that somehow expressed the utter simplicity of their relationship. Their lives had been knit together perfectly and completely; to have shared hunger and thirst and cold and tiredness, to have hidden in dark thickets from enemies, to have washed in mountain streams and slept under high trees —all had built up, during those few hurried weeks, a tradition of love as elemental as the earth on which they had lain together.

They talked for a time before she became drowsy. She was very cheerful and much heartened by their good fortune in getting aboard the train. She said, whispering: "We *are* lucky, aren't we?"

He hesitated before answering, and she added: "To

have known each other at all, I mean. These are our real lives that we're living, and nothing but a miracle could have given them to us. Don't you feel that?"

It was her constant theme, and he sometimes wondered at the satisfaction she drew from it. She was like a child in many ways; she loved to play over their situation with a wayward and mercurial subtlety. He imagined that her life before the days of war and revolution had been very brilliant, in profound contra-distinction to his own; perhaps it was true, as she said, that nothing but a nightmare miracle could have found for them a common ground. Yet on that ground had blossomed a flower that was almost a flame, and a flame blown to fierceness by the storm outside. Once, half whimsically, he had said: "What are you *really* like? After all, I've never seen you in a house, eating at a table, or sleeping in a bed!" And she had laughed and replied: "*You* know what I'm really like, and no one else ever knew or ever could have known."

He thought of that now as she fell asleep and as he stared at the slowly passing landscape until he was drowsy himself. He had a deep, primitive consciousness that she belonged to him, that they were melting into a single defensive unity against all that could ever happen, and that they both had reserves of personality that would, as time passed, similarly cohere. He was thinking thus when a little man next to him began to smile and make friendly remarks. Something in the little man's soft lilting voice sounded familiar, and soon A.J. realized that it was he who had shouted down to the bandits in confirmation of A.J.'s own account of himself. As this intervention had quite probably saved the situation, A.J. felt grateful to him, though his appearance was far from pleasant. He was dirty and very verminous, and had only one eye. He was full of melancholy indignation over the cowardice of the others in dealing with the bandits. "Nobody but me had the courage to say a word to them," he kept repeating, and it was undoubtedly true. "Just me—little Gregorovitch with the one eye—all the rest were afraid to speak." A man some distance away shouted to him to stop talking, and added, for A.J.'s benefit: "Don't listen to him, brother. He's only a half-wit. The other half came out with his eye." There was laughter at that, after which the little man fell into partial silence for a while, muttering only very quietly to himself. A.J. was inclined to believe the diagnosis correct; the man's remaining eye held all the hot, roving mania of the semi-insane.

Later the little man began to talk again. He seemed to have something on his mind, to be nourishing some vast and shadowy grievance against the world in general, and from time to time he would scan the horizon eagerly with his single eye. His talk was at first so idle and disjointed that A.J. had much difficulty in comprehending him; it was as if the man's brain, such as it might be, were working only fitfully. But by degrees it all worked itself out into something as understandable as it ever would be. He had been a soldier, conscripted to fight the Germans; after the revolution he had tried to get back home, but he had lost his papers, and apparently nothing could be done without papers. All he knew was his own name—Gregorovitch—and the name of his village—Krokol; and these two names, it appeared, hadn't been enough for the authorities. With rather wistful indignation he described his visit to a government office in Petrograd, whither he had drifted after the collapse of the battle-fronts. "I should be glad," he had said, "if you could tell me my full name and how I can get home. I am little Gregorovitch with the one eye, and I live at Krokol."

"Krokol?" the clerk had said. (The little man imitated the mincing educated tones of the bureaucrat with savage exaggeration.) "Krokol? Never heard of it. How do you spell it?"

"I don't spell it," Gregorovitch had replied.

"Don't spell it? And why not?"

"Because I don't spell anything. But I can describe it to you—it is a village with a wide street and a tiny, steepled church."

"I am afraid," the clerk had then answered, "we can do nothing for you. Good day."

The little man's eye burned with renewed fever as he recited this oft-told plaint. "Is it not scandalous," he asked, "that in a free country no one can tell you who you are or where you come from?"

That had taken place a year before, and since then Gregorovitch had been traveling vaguely about in search of Krokol. He had just got on trains anywhere, hoping that sometime he might reach a place where Krokol was known. Occasionally he left the trains and walked, and always he hoped that just over the horizon he would come across the little, steepled village.

A.J. was interested enough to question him minutely about Krokol, but it was soon obvious why the clerk at Petrograd had been so impatient. Gregorovitch could give nothing but the vaguest description that might have applied to a thousand or ten thousand villages throughout the length and breadth of the country. Even the name, without a spelling, was a poor clew, since local people often called their villages by names unidentifiable in maps or gazetteers. Nor had Gregorovitch a notion whether

Krokol was near or far from the sea, near or far from any big city, near or far from any railway or river. All he could supply was that repeated and useless mention of the wide street and the steepled church.

A.J. questioned him further about his family, but again his replies were valueless; he could only say that he had a brother named Paul and a sister named Anna. Of any family name he was completely ignorant, and was, indeed, completely convinced that it was unnecessary. "Is it not enough," he asked, "that I am little Gregorovitch with the one eye? Everyone in Krokol knows me."

He went on quietly protesting in this way until the train came to a slow standstill in the midst of the burning steppe. The halt was for no apparent reason save the whim of the engine-driver and fireman, who climbed down from their cab and lazed picturesquely on the shady side of the train. The air, motionless as the train itself, soon became hot and reeking inside the car, and those whose heads chanced to be in sunlight twitched and fidgeted under the glare. Movement, with its own particular discomforts, had somehow kept at bay the greater tortures of hunger and thirst; but now these two raged and stormed in a world to themselves. Water—bread— the words became symbols of all that a human being could live and die for. A scuffle suddenly arose at one end of the car; a man was drinking out of a bottle and his neighbor, unable to endure the sight, attacked him with instant and ungovernable fury. For a few seconds everyone was shouting at once, till at last the assailant was overborne, and was soon sobbing to himself, aware that he had behaved shamefully. And the others, beyond their anger, seemed not unwilling to be sorry for him. Then, with a sharp lurch, the train began to move again and the resulting breath of air took away the keener pangs for another interval. Towards evening they reached a small station called Minarsk, where they were shunted into a siding and given water, but no food. The satisfaction of thirst, however, put everyone in a good humor for a time; chatter became quite animated, and noisy fraternization went on between the occupants of the car and the swarming refugees from the station.

The train remained in the siding until dawn, by which time cheerfulness had sunk to zero again, for the night air had been bitterly cold. To most had come the realization that summer was practically over, and that to hunger and thirst would soon be added that more terrible enemy —winter. The transition between the seasons was always very short in that part of the country, so that when, soon after dawn, the sun did not appear and the cold wind still blew, it seemed as if winter had come in a single night.

Then the train moved out and resumed its slow jog-jog over the badly-laid track. Towards noon the weather, which till then had been merely cold and cloudy, turned to rain, which at first was greeted with joy, for it removed all fears of a water-shortage. It was, plainly, the end of the long drought, and such torrents were falling within an hour that the thirsty had only to hold their tin cups through the slats to have them, after a few moments, half-filled. But the removal of thirst served only to accentuate hunger, from which many, especially the women, were already suffering torments.

A.J. had slept intermittently during the night and had tried to shelter Daly with his greatcoat; she too had slept, but he was concerned by the way she had felt the cold. Throughout the morning the weather worsened in every way, and by late afternoon everyone was in the lowest depth of misery and depression. The roof of the car leaked water on the huddled occupants, and a slanting wind cut in like knives. It was sad to remember that twenty-four hours before men had been shielding their faces from the sun; for now the sun seemed a last good friend who had deserted them. No one could draw comfort from the gray and empty desolation of those plains that stretched mile beyond level mile until all was hazy in rainswept distance.

Again and again the train came to sudden jangling stops, till at last the occupants were too tired and dispirited to say anything, even to ask each other why; they just lay where they were, crouching away from the wind, and trying not to listen to the tattoo of rain on the roof. But after one particularly long wait the engine-driver and fireman came walking together along the track and to a few dismally enquiring faces announced that the train could proceed no further; a heavy storm just ahead had caused part of the line to subside. As for how long it would take to repair the damage, they could only shrug their shoulders and mutter "Nichevo." Where were they?—someone asked; and the same answer came—"Nichevo"—neither the driver nor the fireman had had any previous knowledge of that line. After which, cursing the rain that was drenching their thin clothes, they returned to the warmth and dryness of the engine-cab.

For the passengers in the box-cars, however, such consolations were not available. They were wet, cold, miserable, ravenous with hunger, and stranded in an unknown land. It was the little one-eyed man who, still dreaming of Krokol, gave them their first lift of hope when, for a few seconds, the rain slackened. During that interval he alone chanced to be searching the horizon with his single eye and saw the towers and roofs of a town in the far distance. It gave him no thrill, for the place was decidedly not Krokol, but the others, when he told them, were swept into a flurry of anticipation. A town—perhaps a large town—food—shelter—warmth—their cravings soared dizzily as they began in frantic haste to gather up their bundles and clamber out of the train. How even a large town could instantly supply the wants of a thousand starving and penniless refugees was a question that did not, in that first intoxicating moment, occur to them.

A.J. shared, though more soberly, the general jubilation, but he had the more reason to since money was in his pocket and he could buy if there were anything at all to be bought. Daly, tired and chilled, summoned all her strength for the effort, and they climbed out of the train with the others and began the dismal trek over the fields. To those already weak and feverish it was a perilous journey. The rain continued to fall in heavy slanting swaths, through which, from time to time, the distant town showed like a mocking mirage; and the dry brown dust of the steppes had been transformed to a jelly of squelching mud, into which the feet sank ankle-deep with every pace. After the first mile the procession had thinned out into a trail of weary, mud-smeared stragglers, floundering along at scarcely a mile an hour.

It was dark when A.J. and Daly reached the outskirts of the town, and he had had to lift her practically every step during that last half-mile. She was so obviously on the verge of collapse that when he saw a large barn not far away he made for it eagerly, anxious to reach any place where she could rest out of the rain. There were already several sheltered in the barn—women and children, mostly, to whom weariness had grown to mean more than hunger, cold, or any other feeling. He laid her gently on a heap of sodden straw; the others were too tired to speak, and so was she. "Wait here till I come back," he whispered, and she gave him a faint, answering smile.

Then, bracing himself for the renewed buffeting of rain and wind, he struggled on into the town. It seemed fairly large, but he looked vainly for shop-signs or public notices from which he might learn its name. The streets were deserted in the down-pour, but it was good, any-how, to leave the mud and reach the firm foothold of paved roads. And he had roubles in his pocket—that, in the circumstances, was the most cheering thing of all.

He walked so quickly that he arrived at the apparent center of the town well ahead of the others, many of whom had committed the tactical error of knocking at the first habitations they came to and begging for food. The cottagers, fearing invasion by a seemingly vast rabble, had replied by barricading their doors and refusing even to parley. A.J. had guessed that this would happen, and his own plan was based on it, though perhaps it was not much of a plan in any event. He passed the church and the town-hall, noticing that most of the shops were closed and shuttered and that even those whose windows were on view looked completely empty of goods. Soon he came to a district of small houses such as might belong to better-class artisans or factory-workers. He turned down a deserted street, passing house after house that looked as if it might be equally deserted, till at length he saw one whose chimney showed a thin curl of ascending smoke. He tapped quietly on the front door. After a pause it was opened very cautiously by an elderly, respectable-looking woman, but his hopes fell heavily as he observed her. The too vivid eyes and jutting cheek-bones told the tale he had feared most, and her first words, in answer to his question, confirmed it. The whole town, she told him quite simply, was half-starving. Factories had closed down; men scoured the countryside every day in quest of food which became ever scarcer and dearer; foodshops opened only twice a week, and there were long queues for even the scanty allowances permitted by the new rationing system.

A.J. mentioned that he had a little money and was prepared to pay generously for food and shelter for himself and his wife, but the woman shook her head. "We *have* no food," she said, "no matter what you were to offer us for it. We haven't had a meal since the day before yesterday, and as soon as the rain stops my daughters and myself are going to take turns in the bread-queue. The shop opens tomorrow morning, but to be in time for anything we shall have to wait all night."

He thanked her and went on to another house a little further along the street. There he was told a similar tale. He entered another street. In all he tried nearly a dozen houses before he found one whose occupants, very cautiously and grudgingly, offered a little bread and a promise of shelter in return for a quite fantastic sum of money. He gave them something on account, took a piece of the bread, and hastened back to the other side of the town. There he found rioting already going on between the invading refugees and the local inhabitants; several persons had been seriously hurt. He reached the barn where women were still sheltering, took Daly in his arms, helped her to her feet, and almost carried her across the town.  He dared not offer her the bread until they were well away from the others.

At last, at last, he had her safely under the roof of the cottage, and its occupants, under promise of more money, were lighting a fire.

They were curious people, and he could not at first place them.  There seemed to be a mother, two sons, and two daughters, all living in four small rooms; their name was Valimoff.  They had much better manners and cleaner habits than were usual amongst working people; they were secretive, too, about their personal affairs, though inquisitive enough about A.J.'s.  When, later in the evening, news reached them of the rioting at the other end of the town, Madame Valimoff asked A.J. if he were one of the refugees from the train.  He said yes, he was.  She replied, severely: "We should have had nothing to do with you if we had known that.  Why can't you wretched people stay in your own towns, the same as we have to stay in ours?"

But soon a small wood-fire was burning in the hearth and a scanty meal of black bread and thin soup was being prepared.  The two travelers ate, drank, and dried themselves as well as they could, but A.J.'s pleasure at such comparative good fortune was offset by anxiety about Daly.  She seemed to have taken a bad chill, and he promised a further bribe to one of the daughters of the house in return for the loan of dry clothes.  The daughter, a clean and neatly-dressed girl, helped him to prepare a bed near the fire, and Daly, by that time feverishly tired, was helped into it.  She was soon asleep.  He sat up for a time by the fire, and towards midnight the girl entered the room and brought him a small tumbler of vodka.  The gift was so unexpectedly welcome that he

was profuse in his thanks, and he was still more astonished when she went on: "You see, sir, I think I know
who you are. You are Count Adraxine."

"What?" he cried, and was about to make an indignant
denial; then he checked himself and added, more cautiously: "Why, whatever makes you think that?"

"I remember the Countess, sir. I used to be lady's maid
at Baron Morvenstein's house in Moscow, and I remember her quite distinctly."

He still stared in bewilderment, and she continued:
"You need not be afraid, sir—we are all very happy to
be of service to you and the Countess."

The revelation had been so sudden that, coming with
the vodka after all the hardships and adventures of the
day, it made him a little dizzy. Then, before his uncertain eyes, a curious pageant was enacted. The rest of the
household, which till then had been rather unfriendly
and had bargained greedily for every rouble, came into
the room and were solemnly and separately presented to
him by the girl, whose name was Annetta. They all
bowed or curtsied, and stared hard at the woman asleep
in bed. Then they said polite things, and he said (or
thought he said—he was too dazed to be sure of it)
polite things in return. And afterwards, which was more
to the point, Annetta brought him a second glass of
vodka.

She told him that they had all been servants in big
houses until the Revolution; the men had been footmen
and the girls lady's maids. Madame Valimoff had been
a housekeeper. They had all saved money, so that the
loss of their jobs had not meant instant poverty; besides,
their masters and mistresses had been generous with farewell gifts. But much more important than money, An-

netta confessed, was the fact that they had managed to hoard up supplies of food.

After she had gone, A.J. sat for another hour in front of the fire. The vodka had set the blood tingling in his veins; his mind was still bewildered. He partly undressed and lay down in the bed beside Daly; he went to sleep and awoke to find himself somehow in her arms. She was asleep then, and fever-hot; the fire in the hearth was smoldering; rain was still falling outside. How fortunate was their lot compared with that of the night before. . . . Then she awoke and he told her all that had happened. She was quietly astonished and confirmed the one fact confirmable—that she had, on several occasions before her marriage, visited Baron Morvenstein's house in Moscow. He listened to her, yet all the time he was thinking of something rather different; he was thinking how strange, yet how natural, that they should both be lying together, he and she, ex-Commissar and ex-Countess, there in a workman's cottage in a town whose name they did not yet know. (Which reminded him that he must ask Annetta in the morning.) He said: "Of course, they take me for the Count—which is funny, in a way."

She shivered with laughter. "Isn't it *all* funny? Isn't everything rather a bad joke? Everything except . . ." And she cast over him again the spell of her own dark and sleepy passion.

In the morning they both rose late, the household evidently preferring not to waken them. As soon, however, as they were up and dressed, Annetta appeared with a pot of steaming coffee, fresh rolls made of white flour, and cherry jam. It was miraculous, and they guzzled over it like children at a party.

Thus, for the time, they settled down with the Valimoffs in that once-prosperous town (whose name, by the way, was Novarodar). Daly, as A.J. had suspected, had caught a severe chill, and only very slowly recovered. But the Valimoffs did not appear to mind the delay; on the contrary, they showed every sign of wishing it to continue. Nor, now that they knew or thought they knew the identity of their guests, would they accept a single rouble in payment. A.J. was grateful, but he found it perplexingly difficult to like them for it all. Their obsequiousness got on his nerves, and he was a little disconcerted, at times, by the utter ruthlessness of their attitude towards their less fortunate neighbors. The cottage was certainly a treasure-trove; it contained sacks of white flour, dozens of tins of meat, fruit, and vegetables, and large quantities of wines and spirits. Knowing what servants were, A.J. was of the opinion that most of it had been systematically thieved during the decade preceding the Revolution. Anyhow, it was there, fortunately, in the house of the Valimoffs, stowed away carefully in wardrobes and cupboards, while the rest of the town raked for potato-peelings in rubbish-heaps. A.J. had ample evidence of this, for he took many walks about the streets. Sometimes, fresh from an almost luxurious meal, he would pass the bread-queue, stretching its unhappy length for nearly a quarter of a mile along the main street. He saw women who had been waiting for many hours faint and shriek hysterically when they were told that nothing was left for them. The Valimoffs were careful never to give any cause of suspicion to their neighbors; they took turns in the bread-queues themselves, and they banged the door relentlessly on every beggar—more relentlessly, indeed, than they need have done. They seemed quite confident that A.J. could be trusted with their secret; they had his secret in return, and doubtless felt it to be sufficient security. What puzzled him most was why they should trouble to be so generous; he hardly thought it could be because they hoped for future favors, for they probably knew how slender were the chances of the old aristocracy ever getting back their former possessions. He knew, too, that it could not be from any altruistic notion of helping a stranger, since before they had identified him they had been eager to drive the hardest of bargains. In the end he was forced to the conclusion that their motive was one of simple snobbery—they were just delighted to be in a position to help a Count and Countess. They had lived so comfortably (and perhaps thieved so comfortably, too) in a world of superiors and inferiors that now, when that world seemed completely capsized, they clung to any floating shred of it with a fervor born of secret panic. Perhaps, too, they envisaged a certain bitter prestige appertaining to them when all Novarodar should learn that they, the Valimoffs, had given shelter to two such illustrious persons as Count and Countess Adraxine.

Novarodar was Red, but not as Red as many other places; its geographical position had kept it so far out of the battle-area, and also, owing to its small importance as a railway center, it had escaped Czecho-Slovak occupation.

An event occurred in mid-September which made the overthrow of the Revolution more remote than ever. That was the capture of Kazan by the Bolsheviks. The new army, under Trotsky, drove out the Czechs after a two-day fight, thereby changing the entire military and political situation. With the Czechs in retreat down the Volga it was no longer likely that the pincers would close and the British troops from Archangel link up with the Czech drive from the south. The news of the fall of Kazan caused great commotion in Novarodar, for it was hoped that the Bolshevist victory would mean the release of quantities of food that had been hitherto held up. Its first effect, however, was disappointingly contrary. Hundreds of White refugees, many belonging to wealthy families, streamed into the town from Kazan, where they had been living for some time under Czech protection. The whole situation was further complicated by exceptionally heavy rainfall, which had flooded the surrounding country and made all the roads to the south of the town impassible. Many White refugees, caught between the floods and the Bolsheviks, preferred to remain in the town and come to terms with its inhabitants, whose redness did not preclude the acceptance of large bribes for temporary shelter. Thus Novarodar actually received more mouths for feeding instead of more food to feed them, and the plight of those who had little money became much worse than before.

To A.J., living through those strange days while Daly slowly recuperated, it seemed impossible to state any sort of case or draw any sort of moral from the chaos that was everywhere. It was as if the threads of innumerable events had got themselves tied up in knots that no historian would ever unravel. The starved townspeople, the wealthy refugees, the poverty-stricken refugees, the youths of seventeen and eighteen in civilian clothes who had obviously been Imperialist cadets, the streams of ragged, famished, diseased, and homeless wanderers who passed into the town as vaguely and with as little reason as they passed out of it—all presented a nightmare pageant of the inexplicable. Novarodar's small-town civilization had crumbled instantly beneath that combined onslaught of flood, famine, and invasion; all the niceties of metropolitan life—cafés, cinemas, electric light, shop-windows—had disappeared in quick succession, leaving the place more stark and dreary than the loneliest village of the steppes.

Daly grew gradually stronger, though the strain of recent weeks had been more considerable than either she or A.J. had supposed. A.J. was divided between two desires—to give her ample time to rest and recover, and to continue the journey. He did not like the way events were developing in Novarodar, especially when, towards the end of the month, came further news that the Bolshevik army had taken Sembirsk. At last, to his great relief, Daly seemed well enough again to face the risks of travel—so much the more formidable now that the cold weather had arrived. Their plans were of necessity altered owing to the Czech retreat; indeed, it had been a bitter disappointment to have to stay in Novarodar day after day and know that every hour put extra miles between themselves and safety. The nearest city now at which they could hope to link up with the Whites was Samara, some two hundred miles distant.

Meanwhile affairs at Novarodar became very rapidly worse. As the inflowing stream of refugees continued, the last skeleton organization of the town collapsed; bread-riots took the place of the bread-queues, and the main streets were the scenes of frequent clashes between Red police and bands of White fugitives. It looked, indeed, as if the latter were planning a *coup d'état;* so many had entered the town that they stood a good chance, if they were to try. The inhabitants, starved and dispirited, were hardly in a mood to care what happened, so long as, somehow or other, they received supplies of food.

Then came news that the Bolsheviks were moving down the Volga towards Samara. This sent a wave of panic amongst the White refugees, for, unless they got away quickly eastward, there was every possibility of their being trapped. Yet eastward lay the floods, still rising, that had turned vast areas into lakeland and swamps. Some took the risk of drowning and starvation and set out, but for most there began a period of anxious tension, with one eye on the floodwater and the other on the maps which showed the rapid Red advance. A shower of rain was enough to plunge the town in almost tangible gloom, and groups of White cadets, a little scared beyond their boyish laughter, climbed the church tower at all times of the day and scanned impatiently that horizon of inundated land. Even the local inhabitants were beginning to be apprehensive. Their position was a ticklish one, and the worried expression on the faces of local Soviet officials was wholly justified. Was it wise to have been so complacent with the White refugees? The latter were too numerous now to be intimidated, but at first, when they had begun to enter the town, would it not have been better to have been more severe? Troubled by these and similar misgivings, and with their eyes fixed feverishly on the war-map, the Novarodar Soviet, from being mildly pink, flushed to deep vermilion in almost record time.

A.J. and Daly, like the rest, were waiting for the floods to subside. They were both keen to get away, and even the hospitality of the Valimoffs, so unstintingly given, would not induce them to stay an hour longer than need be. The Valimoffs assured them that Novarodar was quite safe whatever happened, but A.J. did not think so. At last a day came when the floods showed signs of falling. He had made all preparations for departure, had accepted supplies of food from the still generous Valimoffs, had thanked them, and pressed them in vain to take some money in return for all their gifts and services; and then, just as he was tying up a final bundle, one of the young men rushed in from the street with the news that Samara had fallen.

All Novarodar was in instant uproar. With Samara in Bolshevik hands the last hope that the Czech retirement was only temporary disappeared. Worse still, the White line of retreat was cut off; Novarodar was now ringed round on three sides by Red troops, and the fourth and only line of escape was waterlogged. White refugees were gathering in little excited groups to discuss the matter; some set out across the swamps, and later on that very day a few stragglers came back, mudcaked from head to foot, to report catastrophes as horrible as any that were to be feared.

Once again A.J.'s plans suffered a blow. There seemed little hope now of ever catching up with the retreating Czechs. A.J. and Daly talked the whole question over with the Valimoffs; the latter, of course, thought that the best plan would be for them to stay, disguised as they were, in Novarodar. But A.J. was still all for movement; he felt instinctively that every moment in Novarodar was, as it were, a challenge flung to fate. He talked of making for the Don country, where White troops, under Denikin, had already driven a northward wedge to within a few score miles of Voronesk. His eagerness increased as he computed the chances of the plan, and it was an advantage, too, that the way towards Denikin was the way towards the Black Sea ports.

In the end it was agreed that the southward plan should be tried; it was, in fact, the only practical alternative to remaining in Novarodar. "We shall trust to our disguise," A.J. said, "and work our way, by trains, if we can find any, through Kuszneszk and Saratof." He agreed, however, in view of the change of plans, to postpone departure to the following morning.

The Valimoffs were keenly interested in the adventure, and, though discouraging at first, soon came to regard it with tempered enthusiasm. In particular the mention of Saratof roused them to a curious interchange of looks amongst one another which A.J. did not fail to notice. That evening, after the excellent dinner with which he and Daly were always provided, Madame Valimoff humbly presented herself and craved an interview. He treated her politely, as he always did, but with reserve. Daly was more cordial, and this cordiality, natural as it was in the circumstances, had often given him a feeling which he could only diagnose as petulance. The fact was that Madame Valimoff, behind her obsequious manners, was an exceedingly strong-willed person and had, he was sure, acquired a considerable influence over Daly, whether the latter was aware of it or not. He had no reason, of course, to believe that this influence was for the bad, yet somehow, though he could not explain it, he had misgivings.

Madame Valimoff, with many apologies for troubling them, soon came to the point. Before the Revolution, she said, she and two of her sons had been servants in Petrograd at the house of the Rosiankas. Prince and Princess Rosianka had been murdered by the Reds at Yaroslav;

there was a large family, all of whom had been massacred with their parents except the youngest—a girl of six. This child, the sole survivor of the family and inheritor of the title, had been hidden away by loyal servants and taken south. It had been intended to smuggle the child abroad, but owing to increased Bolshevist vigilance, it had not been possible to reach the Black Sea ports in time. The two servants, a former butler named Stapen and his wife, who had been a cook in the same household, were now living in Saratof, and the child was still with them there.

Madame Valimoff then produced a letter from this ex-butler, written some weeks previously and delivered by secret messenger. It conveyed the information that the child was in fairly good health, and that Stapen was constantly on the watch for some chance of sending her south, especially now that Denikin was advancing so rapidly. It was a risky business, however, and the person to be trusted with such a task could not be selected in a hurry. "You see," Madame Valimoff explained, after A.J. and Daly had both examined the letter, "the Bolshevists have photographs of all the persons they are looking out for, and the little princess is of course one of them. So many escapes have been made lately that the examination is now stricter than ever."

Briefly, Madame's suggestion was that he and Daly, when they reached Saratof, should call at Stapen's house and take the princess with them into safety. She was sure they were the right sort of people to carry through such a dangerous enterprise successfully. She gave them Stapen's address and also a little amber bead which, she said, would convince him of their bona-fides, even if he did not recognize them. "But he probably will," she added. "Butlers have a good memory for faces, and I'm sure you must sometime or other have visited the Rosiankas."

Daly admitted that she had.

After Madame Valimoff had gone, A.J. was inclined to be doubtful. Madame's dominant personality, the delivery of Stapen's letter by secret messenger, and various other significant details, had all made him gradually aware that Madame was a person of some importance in the sub-world of counter-revolutionary plotting. He did not himself wish to be drawn into White intrigue; his only aim was to get himself and Daly out of the country, and he had no desire to jeopardize their chances of success for the sake of a small child whom they had neither of them ever seen. "If the child is safe at Saratof," he argued, "why not let her stay there?"

All that Daly would say was that there could be no harm in promising the Valimoffs to do what they could. "Our plans," she said, "may have to be altered again, so that we may never go anywhere near Saratof. We can only give a conditional promise, but I think we might give that—we really owe them a great deal, you know."

It was true, beyond question, and later that evening A.J. assured Madame Valimoff that he would certainly call on Stapen if it were at all possible. Privately he meant the reservation to mean a great deal.

Very early next morning he bade farewell to his hosts, to whom he felt immensely grateful, even though he had not been able to like them as much as he felt he ought. He could not imagine how Daly and himself would have managed without them; they had provided food and shelter just when it had been most of all needed, and now they were prodigal to the last, making up bundles of well-packed and artfully disguised food supplies for them to take with them on their journey. A.J. thanked them sincerely, yet was never more relieved than when he turned the corner of the street.

Only a few moments afterwards a loud boom sounded from the distance, followed by a shattering explosion somewhere over the center of the town. The streets, which till then had been nearly empty, filled suddenly with scurrying inhabitants, all in panic to know what had happened, while a few youths, White cadets, rushed by in civilian clothes, hastily buckling on belts and accouterments as they ran. A.J. did not stop to make inquiries, but he gathered from overheard question and answer that the White refugees had organized a *coup d'état* during the night, had killed the Soviet guard, taken possession of all strategic points, and were now preparing to defend the town against the approaching Red army. The latter, however, had evidently learned of these events, and were bombarding the town (so the rumor ran) from an armored train some miles away.

A.J.'s first idea was to get as far from the danger-zone as possible, and with this intention he hurried Daly through the rapidly thronging streets. At intervals of a few minutes came the boom of the gun, but the shells were bursting a safe distance away. Daly was not nervous—only a little excited; and on himself, as always, the sound of gun-fire exercised a rather clarifying effect. He began to reckon the chances of getting well out of the town before the real battle began. There was irony in the fact that for weeks his aim had been to reach some place that was held by the Whites, and that now, being in such a place, his chief desire was to get out of it. It would be the most frantic folly, he perceived, to trust himself to this local and probably quite temporary White success, for his judgment of affairs led him to doubt whether the White occupation could last longer than a few days at most.

Disappointment faced him when he reached the outskirts of the town, where an iron bridge spanned the swollen river. White guards were holding up the crowd of fugitives who sought to cross, while other guards were hastily digging trenches on the further bank. They were all in an excitable, nerve-racked mood, aware of unwelcome possibilities, and prepared to act desperately and instantly. Not a single refugee, they ordered, must leave the town; this was to prevent spies from reporting to the Reds the preparations that were being made for the town's defense. The ban applied to women and children as well as to men, and was being enforced at every possible exit.

There was nothing to be gained by arguing the point, apart from which A.J. was anxious that both he and Daly should remain as inconspicuous as possible. He felt that their best chance of safety lay with the crowd of dirty, ailing, poverty-stricken wretches who, merely because nobody cared about them at all, were usually exempt from too close attention by either side. Most of them were squatting miserably in doorways along the road back to the town, nibbling precious fragments of food, or rebandaging their torn and blistered feet.

It was an anxious morning for Novarodar. Shells fell every ten minutes or so on the center of the town, but many did not burst, and even the others were of poor construction and caused little damage. Once one realized that the likelihood of being hurt by the long-range bombardment was considerably less than that of catching typhus from the town's water-supply, it was possible to ignore the intermittent booming and crashing. But such philosophic detachment was not possible to everyone, and towards midday there was evidence that many of the White defenders were themselves losing nerve. Already rifle-fire was being exchanged between the White trenches and advanced Red scouting-parties. During the afternoon the leaders of the local Soviet were dragged out of prison by White guards, lined up in the market-square, and ceremonially machine-gunned before a public for the most part too apprehensive of its own immediate future to be either repelled or elevated by such an entertainment.

During most of the morning A.J. and Daly sat patiently in a side-street with a crowd of other refugees. But in the afternoon, shortly after the shooting of the Soviet leaders, White guards toured the town in motor-cars and rounded up all who were out of doors. Those who had no homes were lodged in some of the big rooms of the town-hall.

Thus it happened that the refugees had a sort of grand-stand view of the entry of the Bolsheviks into Novarodar, which took place about five o'clock in the afternoon, after a sharp and bloody battle at the town outskirts. At some points the Whites had resisted to the last, but at others they had run away into the town and sought refuge in houses.

Mysteriously and marvelously there appeared a dazzling array of red flags to greet the invaders. The actual march into the town was an almost suspiciously quiet affair. Not a rifle-shot, nor a cheer, nor a lilt of a song disturbed the march of those squads of hard-faced, bearded veterans and grinning, wild-eyed boys, caked

220

with mud and blood, badly clothed, flushed with bitter triumph, helping their wounded along or carrying them in improvised stretchers made of greatcoats. The Red leader, a keen-looking youth of not more than twenty, halted his troops in the market-square and read a proclamation declaring the friendliest intentions of the invaders towards all who had not given assistance to the Whites.

From the large windows, mostly broken, of that first-floor room in the town-hall, history could be seen enacting itself at a prodigious rate. The first task after the reading of the proclamation was to deal with the White prisoners actually captured in the trenches outside the town. These men, battered and mud-stained as their captors, were lined up and machine-gunned from a roof on the opposite side of the square—not very copiously, however, for there seemed to be a shortage of ammunition. Their bodies, some still twitching, were then dragged away and piled in a heap in a side-street.

The Reds were quite convinced that the shot prisoners represented only a very small fraction of the Whites who had held the town, and as night approached, the rage of the invaders grew into a very positive determination to root out all Whites who might be in hiding. Then began a house-to-house search by groups of blood-maddened soldiery. The market-square was the scene of some of the worst incidents, for in it were the larger houses and shops in which Whites might be expected to have found sympathizers. Terrified wretches were dragged out of doorways and clubbed to death; several were flung out of high windows and left broken and dying on the pavements. Firing sounded from all over the town, with now and then the sharp patter of a machine-gun. Later on vengeance became more extended and took in the entire bourgeois element among the townspeople; shops were looted and better-class citizens seized in their houses, accused vaguely of having assisted the Whites, and butchered there and then on their own thresholds.

Some of the refugees screamed hysterically at the sights that were to be seen from the town-hall windows, and many covered their faces and refused to look. A few, however, of whom A.J. was one, gazed on the scene almost impassively, and this either because they were already satiated with horrors, or because their minds had reached that calm equilibrium, born of suffering, in which they saw that market-square at Novarodar as but a tiny and, on the whole, insignificant fragment of a world of steel and blood. To A.J. the latter reason applied with especial force; and more than ever, as the moments passed, his mind clung to what was all in his life that counted—the woman there at his side. The rest of the world was but a chaos of canceling wrongs, and to offer pity for it was as if one should pour a single drop of water on an infinite desert. He felt, as he gazed down upon all the slaughter, that it could not really matter, or it would not be happening.

He was pondering and feeling thus when a man near him, who had also been watching the scene quite calmly, began to talk to him. He was a thin, ascetic-looking man, middle-aged, with deep-set eyes and a lofty forehead. His voice and accent were educated.

"If I may read your thoughts," he said quietly, "you are wondering just how much and how little all this can mean."

A.J. was unwilling to betray himself by any too intelligent answer, so he merely half-nodded and let the other continue talking, which he was more than willing to do. He had been a professor of moral philosophy, he confided, and was now penniless and starving. Probably also (though he did not say so) he was a little mad. He expounded to A.J. a copious theory of the decadence of western civilization and the possible foundation of a new and cruder era based on elementals such as hunger, thirst, cruelty, and physical uncleanliness. "No man," he said, oracularly, "has really eaten until he has starved, or been clean until he has felt the lice nibbling at him, or has lived until he has felt death." He also praised civil war as against war between nations, because it was necessarily smaller and more personal. "It is better, my friend," he said, "that I should kill you for your wife, or for the contents of your pockets, than that we should stand in opposing trenches and kill each other anonymously because a few men in baroque armchairs a thousand miles away have ordered us to."

Conversation was several times interrupted by gusts of machine-gunning; once a spray of bullets shattered the already broken windows and several refugees were cut by falling glass.

About two in the morning there was a sudden commotion in the building below, and a Red officer, armed with two revolvers, rushed into the room with the brusque order that all refugees were to form up in the square outside for inspection, since it was believed that many White guards and bourgeois sympathizers were hiding in disguise amongst them.

The whole company, numbering between five and six hundred, were marshaled in long lines facing the town-hall front, where other groups of refugees were already drawn up. The procedure had a certain ghastly simplicity. Red officers, carrying lanterns, peered into the face of each person, searching for any evidences of refinement such as might cast suspicion on the genuineness of identity. Hands were also carefully inspected. When A.J. observed these details he felt apprehensive, not on his own account, but on Daly's. The examining officers, shouting furiously to those who from weakness or panic could not stand upright, were certainly not in a mood to give the benefit of any doubts. Those whose faces were not seared deeply from winds and rains, or whose hands were not coarse and calloused, stood little chance of passing that ferocious scrutiny. Slowly the group of suspects increased; the ex-professor of philosophy was among the first to be sent to join it. The officer who was examining those near A.J. was a cool-headed, trim young fellow much less given to bullying his victims than the rest, but also, A.J. could judge, much less likely to be put off by a plausible tale. He did not linger more than a few seconds over A.J.—that grim, lined face, and those hands hardened by Arctic winters were their own best argument. At Daly, however, he paused with rather keener interest. A.J. interposed with the story he had prepared for the occasion—that she was his daughter, a semi-invalid, and that he was taking her to some distant friends by whom she might be better looked after. The officer nodded but said: "Let her speak for herself." Then he asked her for her name, age, and place of birth— all of which had been agreed upon between A.J. and herself for any such emergency. She answered in a quiet voice and did not seem particularly nervous. That clearly surprised the questioner, for he asked her next if she were not afraid. She answered: "No, but—as my father has just said—I am ill and would like to be allowed to finish my journey as soon as possible."

While the youth was still questioning her, another officer approached of a very different type. He was a small, fat-faced, and rather elderly Jew, glittering with epaulette and gold teeth and thick-lensed spectacles. One glance at the woman was apparently enough for him. "Don't argue with her, Poushkoff," he ordered, sharply. "Put her with the suspects—I'll deal with her myself in a few moments."

Poushkoff saluted and then bowed slightly to Daly. "You will have to go over there for a further examination," he said, and added, not unkindly, to A.J., "Don't be alarmed. You can go with her if you like."

They walked across the square, and on the way A.J. whispered: "Don't be alarmed, as he said. We've come through tighter corners than this one, I dare say." She replied: "Yes, I know, and I'm not afraid."

The second examination, however, was brutally stringent. The Reds were determined that no White sympathizer should escape, and it was altogether a matter of indifference to them whether, in making sure of that, they slaughtered the innocent. The fat-faced Jew, who appeared to be the inquisitor-in-chief, made this offensively clear. He took the male suspects first, and after a sneering and hectoring cross-examination, condemned them one after another. He did not linger a moment over the professor of philosophy. "You are a bourgeois—that is enough," he snapped, and the man was hustled away towards a third group. When this grew sufficiently large, the men in it were arranged in line in a corner of the square and given over to the soldiery, who, no doubt, took it for granted that all were proved and convicted Whites.

Then followed a scene which was disturbing even to A.J.'s hardened nerves. The men were simply clubbed and bayoneted to death. It was all over in less than five minutes, but the cries and shrieks seemed to echo for hours.

Many of the waiting women were by that time fainting from fear and horror, but Daly was still calm. She whispered: "I am thinking of what he said—that one hasn't lived until one has faced death. Do you remember?"

The Jew adopted different tactics with the women. He wheedled; he was mock-courteous; doubtless he hoped that his method would make them implicate one another. With any who were even passably young and attractive he took outrageous liberties, which most of the victims were too terrified to resent, though a few, with ghastly eagerness, sought in them a means of propitiation. When Daly's turn came, he almost oozed politeness; he questioned her minutely about her past life, her parents, education, and so on. Then he signaled a soldier to fetch him something, and after a moment the man returned with a large book consisting of pages of pasted photographs and written notes. The Jew took it and began to scrutinize each photograph with elaborate care, comparing it with Daly. This rather nerve-destroying ordeal lasted for some time, for the photographs were numerous. At last he fixed on one, gazed at it earnestly for some time, and then suddenly barked out: "You have both been lying. You are not a peasant woman. You are the ex-Countess Alexandra Adraxine, related to the Romanoffs who met their deserts at Ekaterinburg last July. Don't bother to deny it—the photograph makes absolute proof."

226

"Nevertheless we *do* deny it!" A.J. exclaimed, and Daly echoed him.

"It is absurd," she cried, with well-acted emphasis. "We are two poor people on our way to visit our friends, and you accuse us of being people I have never even heard of!"

The Jew laughed. "I accuse you of being the person you are," he said, harshly. "Stand aside—we can't waste all night over you."

The sensation of the discovery had by this time reached the ears of the soldiers, and had also attracted the attention of a small group of officers, among whom was the youth who had conducted the earlier interrogation. He hurriedly approached the Jew and whispered something in his ear, and for several moments a muttered discussion went on between them. Meanwhile the rank and file, fresh from their slaughter of the first batch of suspects, were waiting with increasing impatience for the next. "Let's have her!" some of them were already shouting. The Jew seemed anxious to conciliate them; he said, loudly so that they might all hear him: "My dear Poushkoff, it would not be proper to treat this woman any differently from the rest. Women have betrayed our cause no less than men—especially women of high rank and position. The prisoner here may herself, if the truth were known, be responsible for the lives of hundreds of our soldiers. Are we to quail, like our predecessors, before a mere title?"

Poushkoff answered quietly: "Not at all, Bernstein—I merely suggest that the woman should not be dealt with before she is definitely proved guilty. After all, she *may* be speaking the truth, and it would be too bad if she were to lose her life merely because of a slight resemblance to one of those exceedingly bad photographs that headquarters have sent us."

"Slight resemblance, eh? And bad photographs? My dear Poushkoff, look for yourself."

He handed the book to the other, who examined it and then went on: "Well, there seems to me only a slight resemblance such as might exist, say, between myself or yourself and at least a dozen persons in this town if we took the trouble to look for them. Frankly, it isn't the sort of evidence on which I would care to condemn a dog, much less a woman. And we have this fellow's statement, also—he sounds honest."

"About as honest as she is, if you ask my opinion. We'll attend to him afterwards, all right."

"I merely suggest, Bernstein, that the matter should be deferred for further investigation."

"But, my dear boy, where's the need of it? Surely we are entitled to believe the evidence of our own eyes?"

"Photographs aren't our own eyes—that's just my point. If this woman is really the Countess, it could not be very difficult to have her identified by someone who knew her formerly. There is bound to be somebody, either at Sembirsk or Samara, who could do it."

"But not at Novarodar, eh? How convenient for her!" The soldiers began a renewed clamor for the prisoner to be surrendered, and Bernstein, with a shrug of the shoulders, exclaimed: "You see, Poushkoff, what the men are already thinking—they believe we are going to favor this woman because of her high rank."

Poushkoff replied, still very calmly: "I beg your pardon, Bernstein—I thought the point was whether she is guilty or not. If it is merely a matter of amusing the men, doubtless she will do as well as anyone else."

228

Bernstein snorted angrily. "Really, Poushkoff, you forget yourself! The woman, to my mind, is already proved guilty—guilty of having conspired against the Revolution and against the lives of the Red army."

"Quite, if you are positive of her identity. That is my point."

"Your point, eh? You change your point so often that one has an infernal job to keep up with you! No, no, my dear boy, it won't do—we've proved everything—the Countess is guilty and this woman is the Countess. There is no shadow of reason for any delay."

"I am afraid I do not agree."

"Well, then you must disagree, that is all. The responsibility, such as it is, rests with me."

"Take note, then, that I protest most strongly."

"Oh, certainly, my dear Poushkoff, certainly."

"And in any case, since she is a woman, I suggest that she should be treated mercifully."

"And not be handed over to our young rascals, you mean, eh?" He laughed. "Well, perhaps you deserve some small reward for your advocacy. Arrange the matter as you want—you were always a lady's man. But remember—the penalty is death—death to all enemies of the Revolution. You may gild the pill as much as you like, but the medicine has to be taken."

After this sententiousness Poushkoff saluted and signed to A.J. and Daly to accompany him. He led them into the town-hall through a small entrance beneath the portico. He did not speak till at length he opened the door of a basement room in which a number of soldiers were smoking and drinking tea. "Is Tamirsky here?" he asked, and an old and gray-bearded soldier detached himself from the group. Poushkoff took him out into the corridor and whispered in his ear for a few moments. Then, leading him to Daly, he began: "Do you know this woman?"

Tamirsky gave her a profound stare from head to foot and finally shook his head.

"You are prepared to swear that you have never seen her before?"

"Yes, your honor."

"And you were—let me see—a gardener on the estate of Count Adraxine before the Revolution?"

"I was."

"So that you often saw the Countess?"

"Oh, very often indeed, your honor."

"Thank you. You are sure of all this, and are ready to swear to it?"

"Certainly."

"Then come with me now." To A.J. he added: "Wait there with the soldiers till I return."

They waited, and in that atmosphere of stale tobacco-smoke and heavy personal smells, Daly's strength suddenly gave way. She collapsed and would have fallen had not A.J. caught her quickly. The soldiers were sympathetic, offering tea, as well as coats for her to rest on. A.J. began to thank them, but one of them said: "Careful, brother—don't tell us too much about yourselves."

After a quarter of an hour or so Poushkoff and Tamirsky returned together, and the former signaled to the two prisoners to follow him again. Outside in the corridor several Red guards, fully armed, were waiting. Poushkoff said: "Sentence is postponed. You are to be taken to Samara for further identification. The train leaves in an hour; these men will take you to the station." He gave an order and went away quickly.

A few minutes later, thus escorted, they were hastening through the dark streets. Scattered firing still echoed over the town, but all was fairly quiet along the road to the railway. Dawn was breaking as they passed through the waiting room; the station was crowded with soldiers, many asleep on the platforms against their packs. The line, A.J. heard, had just been repaired after the recent flood damage. A train of teplushkas, already full, lay at one of the platforms, and on to it a first-class coach, in reasonably good condition, was being shunted. As soon as this operation was complete, A.J. and Daly were put into one of the compartments, with two soldiers mounting guard outside. The inevitable happened after that; the two fugitive-prisoners, weary and limp after the prolonged strain of the day and night, fell into almost instant sleep. When they awoke it was broad daylight; snow was falling outside; the train was moving slowly over an expanse of level, dazzling white; and in the compartment, quite alone with them, was Poushkoff. He smiled slightly and resumed the reading of a book.

A.J. smiled back, but did not speak. He felt a sort of bewildered gratitude towards the young officer, but he was not on that account disposed to be incautious. The youth's steel-gray eyes, curiously attractive when he smiled, seemed both a warning and an encouragement. If there were to be conversation at all, Poushkoff, A.J. decided, should make the first move.

Several times during the next quarter of an hour Poushkoff looked at them as if expecting one or the other to speak, and at last, tired of the silence, he put down his book and asked if they were hungry.

They were, quite frantically, having eaten scarcely anything for twenty-four hours, despite the fact that their bundles, miraculously unconfiscated, were bulging with food. A.J. said "yes," and smiled; whereupon Poushkoff offered them hard, gritty biscuits and thin slices of rather sour cheese. They thanked him and ate with relish.

"We are due to reach Samara late this evening," he said, after a pause.

"A slow journey," A.J. commented.

"Yes, the line is shaky after the floods. When the train stops somewhere I may be able to get you some tea."

"It is very kind of you."

"Not at all—we are condemned to be fellow-travelers— is it not better to make things as comfortable as we can for one another?"

So they began to talk, cautiously at first, but less so after a while. There was something queerly likable about Poushkoff; both A.J. and Daly fought against it, as for their lives, but finally and utterly succumbed. Its secret lay perhaps in contrast; the youth was at once strong and gentle, winsome and severe, shy and self-assured, boyish yet prematurely old. Like most officers in the new Red army, he was scarcely out of his teens; yet his mind had a clear, mature incisiveness that was apparent even in the most ordinary exchange of polite conversation. After about ten minutes of talk that carefully avoided anything of consequence, he remarked reflectively: "The curse of this country is that we are all born liars. We lie with such simple profundity that there's nobody a man dare trust. You, for instance, don't trust me—obviously not. And I, just as naturally, don't trust you. Yet, once granting the initial untrustworthiness of both of us, we shall probably get on quite well together."

"We learn by experience how necessary it is to be cautious," said A.J.

"Oh, precisely. Don't think I'm blaming you in the least."

Then Daly, who had not so far spoken, interposed: "Still less are we blaming you, Captain Poushkoff. On the contrary, we owe you far more than we can ever repay." A.J. nodded emphatically to that.

"Not at all," Poushkoff courteously replied. "Yet even that, now you mention it, is a case in point—it could not have happened without hard lying."

Daly smiled. "On our part, Captain?"

"Well, no—I was rather thinking of Tamirsky. He lies so marvelously—it is a pure art with him. And so faithfully, too—his lies are almost more steadfast than the truth. You certainly owe your life to him, Madame."

"And why not also to you, Captain, who told him what lie to tell?"

"Oh, no, no—you must not look at it in that way. My own little lie was only a very poor and unsuccessful one compared with Tamirsky's."

"What was your lie, Captain?"

He answered, rather slowly, and with his eyes, implacable yet curiously tender, fixed intently upon her: "I said, Madame, that in my opinion the photograph bore only a slight resemblance to you. That was my lie. For the photograph, in fact, was of you beyond all question."

She laughed. "Nevertheless, don't suppose for one moment that I shall admit it."

"Of course not. Your best plan is so clearly a denial that I don't find your denial either surprising or convincing." He suddenly smiled, and as he did so the years seemed to fall away and leave him just a boy. "But really, don't let's worry ourselves. Quite frankly, I don't care in the least who you are."

233

A.J. had been listening to the conversation with growing astonishment and apprehension. There was such a charm about Poushkoff that he had been in constant dread of what Daly might be lured into saying; yet an almost equal lure had worked upon himself and had kept him from intervening. Even now he was waiting for her answer with curiosity that quite outdistanced fear. She said: "That leads up to a rather remarkable conclusion, Captain. You believed I was really the Countess, yet you made every effort to save my life."

"Yes, perhaps I did, but I don't see anything very remarkable in it."

They sat in silence for some time, while the trainwheels jog-jogged over the uneven track, across a world that was but a white desert meeting a gray and infinite horizon. A.J. was puzzled still, but less apprehensive; it was queer how the fellow's charm could melt away even deepest misgivings. More than queer—there was something uncanny in it; and he knew, too, that Daly was aware of the same uncanniness. He glanced at her, and she smiled half-inquiringly, half-reassuringly. Then she said, all at once serene: "Captain, since you do not care who I am, there is no reason why we should not all be the greatest of friends." And turning to A.J. she added: "Don't you think we might share our food with the Captain?"

A.J., after a moment's hesitation, returned her smile; in another moment one of the bundles that had been so neatly and carefully packed at the Valimoffs' cottage was being opened on that shabby but only slightly verminous compartment-seat. There was a tin of pork and beans, a tin of American mixed fruits, shortbread, chocolate, and—rarest delicacy of all—a bottle of old cognac.

As these treasures were displayed one after another, Poushkoff showed all the excitement of a well-mannered schoolboy. "But this is charming of you!" he exclaimed, rapturously, and then, with swift prudence, rushed to lock the door leading to the corridor and pull down the blinds. "It will be best for us not to be observed," he laughed, and continued: "And to think that I offered you my poor biscuits!"

"We were very grateful for them," Daly said, with a shining sweetness in her eyes.

Then began a most incredible and extraordinary picnic. Zest came over them all, as if they had been friends from the beginning of the world, as if there were no future ever to fear, as if all life held nothing but such friendship and such joyous appetite. Poushkoff's winsomeness overflowed into sheer, radiant high spirits; Daly laughed and joked with him like a carefree child; A.J. became the suddenly suave and perfect host, handing round the food as gayly as if they had all been on holiday together. It was like some strange dream that they were all, as by a miracle, dreaming at once. They shouted with laughter when Poushkoff tried to open the tin of fruit with the knife-blade and squirted juice over his tunic. They had to eat everything with their fingers and to drink the brandy out of the bottle—but how wonderful it all was, and how real compared with that unreal background of moving snowfields and flicking telegraph-poles! They did silly inconsequential things for no reason but that they wanted to do them; Poushkoff made a fantastic impromptu after-dinner speech; A.J. followed it by another; and Daly exclaimed, in the midst of everything: "Captain, I'm sure you speak French—wouldn't you like to?" And they all, in madness to be first, began gabbling away like children. The brandy passed round again, and Poushkoff made cigarettes out of the coarse army tobacco, and they puffed away furiously as they chattered. It was brilliant chatter, for the most part; Daly and Poushkoff were perfect foils for each other, and the queerest thing of all was that they talked in an intricate, intimate way that somehow needed neither questioning nor explaining on either side. A.J., not talking quite so much, was nevertheless just as happy —with a keenness, indeed, that was almost an ache of memory, for he felt he had known Poushkoff not only before but many times before. Then Poushkoff interrupted one of his own fantastic speeches to thank them both with instant, tragic simplicity. "I suppose," he said, "we shall not see one another again after we reach Samara. That is a pity. The French say—'*Faire ses adieux, c'est mourir un peu*'—but in this country it is '*mourir entièrement.*' We have all of us died a thousand deaths like that during these recent years." He seized Daly's hand and pressed it to his lips with a strange blending of gallantry and shyness. "Oh, how cruel the world is, to have taken away my life far more than it can ever take away yours. . . ." Then he suddenly broke down into uncontrollable sobbing. They were astounded, and moved beyond speech; Daly put her arm round the boy and drew his head gently against her breast. He went on sobbing, and they could not stop him; his whole body shook as if the soul were being wrenched out of it. Then, as quickly as it had begun, it was all over, and he was looking up at her, his eyes swimming in tears, and saying: "I humbly beg your pardon. I don't know what you must think of me—behaving like this. It was the brandy—I'm unused to it."

They both smiled at him, trying to mean all they could without speaking, and he took up his book and pretended to read again. A.J., for something to do, cleared away the remains of the meal and repacked the bundle, while Daly stared out of the window at the dazzling snow. A long time passed, and at length came the same calm, controlled voice that they had heard first of all in the market-place at Novarodar. "Do you know Samara?" he was asking.

"I've been through it, that's all," A.J. answered.

Poushkoff continued: "It's a fairly large town—much larger than Novarodar. As you know, our army has just taken it from the Czechs. It's full of important people—all kinds of people who were all kinds of things before the Revolution. There are bound to be many who knew Countess Adraxine personally."

Daly said, still smiling: "And no Tamirskys, eh?"

"Probably not. The perfect Tamirsky is the rarest of all creatures."

"I see. So you are warning us?"

"Well, hardly so much as that. But I am rather wondering what is going to happen to you."

"Ah, we none of us know that, do we?"

"No, but I thought you might possibly have something in mind."

She looked at A.J. inquiringly and said: "I'm afraid we just do what we can, as a rule, don't we?"

"You mean that you just take a chance if it comes along?"

"What else is there we can do?"

"Do you think you will manage it in the end—what you are trying to do?"

"With luck, perhaps."

"And you have had luck so far?"

She said: "Wonderful luck. And the most wonderful of all was to meet you."

"Do you think so?"

"I would think so even if tomorrow sees the end of us, as it may do."

Every word of speech between them seemed to have infinitely deeper and secondary meanings. He said, without emotion: "You are the most astonishing woman I have ever met. I altogether love you, as a matter of fact. I loved you from the minute I saw you last night. Am I being very foolish or impertinent?"

"No, no, I'm sure you're not."

"You mean that?"

"Absolutely."

"Ah, how perfect you are!" He stared at the pages of the book for another short interval. Then he turned to A.J. "I wonder if I might be permitted to have a little more of that excellent cognac? It would be good for me, I think—I feel a trifle faint."

A.J. unpacked the bottle for him, and Daly said, warningly: "Remember now—you said you were unused to it."

Poushkoff answered, taking a strong gulp and laughing: "I promise it won't have the same effect again." Then he leaned back on the cushions and closed his eyes. The train rattled on, more slowly than ever; snow had stopped falling; it was nearly dusk. Neither A.J. nor Daly disturbed the strange silence through which the boy appeared to sleep. Suddenly he opened his eyes, yawned vigorously, and strode over to the window. "I think I can see a church in the distance," he said, in perfectly normal tones. "That must be Tarzov—we have to change to another train there. Pick up your luggage and come out with me to the refreshment buffet—I may be able to get you some tea."

In a few moments the train ground down to an impotent standstill at a small, crowded platform of a station. It looked an odd place to have to change; there was no sign of any rail junction, or of any other train, and Tarzov, seen through the gathering dusk, had the air of a very second-rate village indeed. There was the usual throng of waiting refugees, with their usual attitude of having come nowhence and being bound nowhither; and there was the usual shouting and bell-jangling and scrambling for places. Poushkoff led them through the crowd to the refreshment buffet, which, by no means to A.J.'s surprise, was found to be closed. The boy, however, seemed not only surprised but depressed and disappointed to a quite fantastic degree—he had so wished, he said, to drink tea with them once, before they separated. "You see," he said, "the next station is Samara, only thirty versts away, and of course the authorities there have been notified about you by telephone, and there will be an escort waiting, and—oh, well, it is all going to be very difficult and complicated. Whereas here we can still be friends." He led them some distance along the platform away from the crowd to a point whence there was a view of the village—a poor view, however, owing to the misty twilight. He seemed anxious to talk to them about something—perhaps about anything. "Tarzov," he said, "is only a small place—it is on the Volga. If you go down that street over there you come to the river in about ten minutes. There is a little quay and there are timber-barges usually, at this time of the year. They take the rafts downstream during the

239

daytime, and tie up at the bank for the night. Of course the passenger-boats have been stopped since the civil war, but I believe the timber-barges sometimes take a passenger or two, if people have the money and make their own arrangements with the bargemen. Some of the bargemen are Tartars—fine old fellows from the Kirghiz country." He added, almost apologetically: "This is really a most interesting part of the world, though, of course, you don't see it at its best at this time of the year."

Suddenly, as if remembering something, he exclaimed: "Excuse me, I must go back to the train a moment—I shan't be long." He dashed away into the midst of the still scurrying crowd before they could answer, and in the twilight they soon lost sight of him.

"He looked ill," Daly said.

A.J. answered: "He drank nearly all that brandy."

"Did he? Poor boy! Do you like him?"

"Yes."

"So do I—tremendously. And he's only a boy."

It was very cold, waiting there with the wind blowing little gusts of snow into their faces.

A.J. said: "It's rather queer, having to change trains at a place like this. There doesn't seem to be any junction, and if it's only thirty versts to Samara, where else can the train be going on to?"

"Perhaps it isn't going on anywhere."

"Then why is everybody crowding to get into it?"

She clutched his arm with a sharp gesture. "Do you realize—that we could *escape—now?* It's almost dark—there's a mist—we should have a chance, surely?"

He answered, his hand tightening over her wrist: "Yes —yes—I believe you're right!" But he did not move.

240

"Yes, it's a chance—a chance!" Yet still he did not move, and all at once there came the splitting crack of a revolver-shot. It was not a sound to attract particular attention at such a place and at such a time—it would just, perhaps, make the average hearer turn his head, if he were idle enough, and wonder what it was. A.J. wondered, but his mind was grappling with that more insistent matter—*escape*. Yes, there would be a chance, and their only chance, for, as Poushkoff had told them, Samara was close, and Samara meant armed escorts and prison-cells. Yes, yes,—there was no time to lose—Poushkoff would be back any minute—they must think of themselves—they must go *now—instantly*. . . . But no—not for a minute—a little man with a ridiculously tilted fur cap was pacing up and down the platform; he would pass them in a few seconds, would reach the end, turn, pass them again, and then would come their chance. . . . Yet the man in the fur cap did not pass them. He stopped and remarked, cheerfully: "Exciting business down there, comrade," and jerked his head backward towards the crowd. "Officer just shot himself. Through the head. Deliberately—everybody saw him. Not a bad thing, perhaps, if they all did it, eh?" He laughed and passed on. A.J. stared incredulously; it was Daly who led him back to the crowd. "We must see," she said. "We must make sure." When they reached the crowd, soldiers were already carrying a body into the waiting-room; it was she again who pressed forward, edging her way in what doubtless seemed mere ghoulish curiosity. When she rejoined A.J. it was only to nod her head and take his arm. They walked slowly away. Then she began to whisper excitedly: "Dear, I'm just understanding it—that's what he *wanted* us to do—all that talk about the road to the river, and the bargemen who might take us if we offered them money— Dear, we *must* do it—think how furious he'd be if he thought we hadn't had the sense to take the chance he gave us!"

"Yes. We'll do it."

They came to the end of the platform, but did not stop and turn, like other up-and-down walkers. They hastened on through the darkness, across the tracks and sidings, in between rows of damaged box-cars, over a ditch into pale, crunching snowfields, and towards the river.

They skirted the village carefully, keeping well away from the snow-covered roofs, yet not too far from them, lest they should lose themselves in the mist. But A.J. had sound directional instinct, and despite the mist and the deep snow it was no more than a quarter of an hour before they clambered over a fence and found themselves facing a black vastness which, even before they heard the lapping of the water, reassured them. They stopped for a few seconds to listen; as well as the water, they could hear, very faintly, the lilt of voices in the distance. They walked some way along the path, their footsteps muffled in snow. Then a tiny light came into view, reflected far over the water till the mist engulfed it; the voices became plainer. Suddenly A.J. whispered: "The timber-barges—here they are!"—and they could see the great rafts of tree-trunks, snow-covered and lashed together, with the winking light of the towing barge just ahead of them. Voices were approaching as well as being approached; soon two men passed by, speaking a language that was not Russian, though it was clear from sound and gesture that one of the men was bidding farewell to the other. They both shouted out a cheerful "Good night" as they passed, and a moment later A.J. heard them stop and give each other resounding kisses on both cheeks. Then one of them returned, overtaking the two fugitives near the gang-plank that led down at a steep angle to the barge itself. They could not see his face, but he was very big and tall. He cried out a second cheerful "Good night," and was about to cross the plank when A.J. asked: "Are you the captain of this boat?"

The man seemed childishly pleased at being called "captain," and replied, in very bad Russian: "Yes, that's right."

"We were wondering if you could take us along with you?"

"Well, I might if you were to make it worth my while."

To accept too instantly would have looked suspicious, so A.J. went on: "We are only poor people, so we cannot afford very much."

"Where do you want to go to?"

"A little village called Varokslav—it is on the river, lower down."

"I don't think I know it at all."

A.J. was not surprised, for it was an invented name. "It is only very small—we would tell you when you came to it."

"But how can we settle a price if I don't know how far it is?"

To which A.J. answered: "Where is it you are bound for, Captain?"

"Saratof. We are due there in three weeks."

"Very well, I will give you twenty gold roubles to take us both to Saratof."

"Thirty, comrade."

They haggled in the usual way and finally came to terms at twenty-four. Then the bargeman, whose Russian became rapidly imperfect when he left the familiar ground of bargaining, conveyed to them with great difficulty the fact that accommodation on the barge was very poor, and that there was only one cabin, which he himself, his wife, and four children already occupied, and which the passengers would have to share. A.J. said that would be all right, and they did not mind. Then the bargeman confided to A.J. that his name was Akhiz, and A.J. returned the compliment. Having thus got over the introductions, Akhiz gave A.J. two very loud kisses as a token of their future relationship and invited both passengers to come on board immediately. It was beginning to snow again, for which A.J. was thankful, since their tracks would soon be covered. As they crossed the steep plank there came, very faintly over the white fields, the sound of a train puffing out of Tarzov station.

Akhiz was a Tartar from Astrakhan—a young, genial, magnificently strong, and excessively dirty monster, six feet five in height and correspondingly large in face and mouth. His perfectly spaced teeth glittered like gems whenever he smiled, which was fairly often. His wife, small, fat, and of the same race, was less genial, but almost more dirty, and their four children, ranging from a baby to a six-year-old, were noisy, good-looking, and full of ringworm.

The position of Akhiz in the scheme of things was simple enough. He went up and down the Volga with his timber-barge. He had been doing so for exactly twenty-six years—since, in fact, the day he had been born on just a similar barge on that same Volga. He was not a man of acute intelligence; he could handle the rafts and work the small steam-engine and strike a bargain and play intricate games with dice, but that was almost all. Above everything else, he was incurious—as incurious about his two passengers as he was about the various excitements and convolutions that had interfered with the timber trade during recent years.

A.J. and Daly settled down effortlessly to the tranquil barge-life; they had been traveling so long and so far and so cumbrously that the large, spacious existence in swollen mid-stream seemed the most perfect and enchanting rest. Even the stuffy cabin, swarming with children and fleas, did not trouble them, though there was no privacy in it, and Akhiz and his family conducted themselves at all times with completely unembarrassed freedom. They rather liked Akhiz, however, and soon found it possible to behave before him with no greater restraints than before some large and good-humored dog.

Every evening, at dusk, the barge drifted in to the bank and was moored for the night. Akhiz was aware of every current and backwater, and showed great skill in maneuvering the rafts into place. It was typical of him that he knew practically nothing of the land beyond the banks; he did not know even the names of most of the villages that were passed. With an instinct for adapting himself to circumstances without understanding them, he managed somehow or other never to be short of food, even though the near-by country was famine-stricken; fortunately, he and his family could eat almost anything—queer-looking roots and seeds that A.J. would have liked to know more about, if Akhiz had been intelligent enough to be questioned. A.J. and Daly still had ample food for themselves; at first they were afraid

of what Akhiz might deduce from their luxurious provender, but they very soon realized that it was the way of
Akhiz to notice as little as possible and never to make
any kind of deduction at all.  Once they went so far
as to share with him a tin of corned beef; he was hugely
delighted, but completely and almost disappointingly in-
different as to how they had come to possess such a rarity.

It was so restful and satisfying to be on the barge
that during their first night aboard they hardly gave
thought to the dangers that might still be ahead.  Dawn,
however, brought a more dispassionate outlook; it was
obvious then to both of them that their escape would
soon be discovered and that efforts would be made to recapture them.  A.J.'s immediate fear was of Samara,
which they must reach during the first day's journey; it
seemed to him that the authorities there were likely to
be especially vigilant and would probably suspect some
method of escape by river.  During that first day, as the
wooded bluffs passed slowly by on either side, he de-
bated in his mind whether he should take Akhiz somewhat into his confidence.  Daly favored doing so, and
A.J. accordingly broached the matter as delicately as he
knew how.  But delicacy was quite wasted on Akhiz; he
had to be told outright that his two passengers were escaping from enemies who wanted to kill them, and that
anywhere, especially at Samara and the big towns, he
might be questioned by the authorities.  They half expected Akhiz to be furious and threaten to turn them
ashore, but instead he took it all in with a comprehension
so mild and casual that they could only wonder at first
if it were comprehension at all.  "I don't think he really
understands what we've been getting at," A.J. said, but
there he certainly did Akhiz an injustice, for about an

246

hour later the huge fellow, beaming all over his face, drew them to the far end of the barge and showed them a small and inconspicuous gap which he had arranged amongst the piled tree-trunks. "If anyone comes to ask for you, my wife will say nobody here," he explained, in broken Russian. "You will go in there—see?—and I will put the logs back in their places—so. Plenty of room for you in behind there." He grinned with immense geniality and bared his arms to show them his bulging muscles. "Nobody move those logs but me," he declared proudly, and it was satisfactory to be able to believe it.

The presence of such an improvised hiding-place for use in an emergency gave them a feeling of comfort and security, and to A.J.'s further relief the barge did not even put in at Samara, owing to high dock-charges, but went on several miles below the town to a deserted and lonely reach where no stranger came on board and no suspicious inspection seemed to be taking place from either bank.

They reached Syzran on the fifth day, passing under the great steel railway bridge on which, but a few yards above them, Red sentries were keeping guard, and reaching the end of the long river-loop. The air turned colder, but there was no further snowfall, and during the day-time the sun shone with a fierceness that was quite cheerful, even though it did not lift the temperature much above freezing-point. Already round the edges of the backwaters ice had begun to form. A.J. and Daly used sometimes to choose a sheltered and sunny place among the tree-trunks from which to watch the slowly-changing panorama; it was bitterly cold in the open air, but for a time that was preferable to the fetid atmosphere of the cabin. The river was so wide that they were safe from observation, and the country, especially on the left bank, so lonely that often whole days passed without sound or sight of any human existence on land. Compared with the chaos of which their memories were full, the barge-life seemed a kind and leisurely heaven. A.J.'s normally robust health benefited a great deal from the rest and the cold, keen air; at dusk and dawn he sometimes helped Akhiz with the rafts, and was amused to give proof that his own personal strength was not so very much inferior to that of the Tartar monster.

He would, indeed, have been very happy but for re-newal of his anxiety about Daly's health; the strain of the journey seemed again to be weighing heavily on her. Yet she was very cheerful and full of optimism. They began now to talk as they had hardly dared to do before—of their possible plans after reaching safety. Denikin's out-posts, A.J. believed, could not be much more distant than a few days' journey from Saratof; it would probably be best to leave the river there and cross that final danger-zone on foot and by night. Then it seemed to occur to them both simultaneously that they would be passing through the town of Saratof, and that somewhere in it lived the ex-butler and the little princess of whom the Valimoffs had so carefully informed them. Should they take the trouble and incur all the possible extra risks that a visit might involve? A.J. decided negatively, yet from that moment they began to feel that the ex-butler and the child were really living people, not merely abstractions talked about by somebody else. They even began to imagine what the girl might be like—dark or fair, pretty or plain, well-bred or spoilt.

One cold sunny afternoon, as they sat together on the timber with no sound about them save the swish of the water and the occasional distant cry of a curlew, A.J. told her, quite suddenly and on impulse, that he had been born in England and had lived there during early youth. She was naturally astonished, and still more so when he told her the entire story of his early life and of the affairs that had led to his loss of nationality and subsequent exile. "But you are really English for all that?" she queried, and he replied that he was not sure how the technical position stood—there was little he could prove after so many years. "Perhaps I am as I feel," he said, "and that is no nationality at all."

It was curious how their life in the future, that was to be so strange and different from any life they had known together so far, seemed as much an end as a beginning. They tried not to admit it, yet the feeling was there with them both; it was so hard to think of a world that did not consist entirely of the dangers of the next hour and mile, of a life in which everything could be bought for money, in which day after day would bring peaceful, prophesiable happenings, and every night a bed and sleep. She said to him once: "Dear, what shall we do? Shall we live in Paris? Would you like to live in Paris?"

"I think I would like to live anywhere."

"Anywhere with me?"

"I meant that. I can't imagine life without you."

"Can you imagine life without all this worry and adventure?"

"Hardly—yet. I don't know."

"How long will it take—the rest of the journey—if we have luck?"

"We shall be in Saratof within a week or so. Allow another week for reaching the Whites. I suppose then we could get through to Rostov or Odessa, and there are boats from those places to Constantinople, but we might have to wait some time to get one. There would be passport formalities and all that sort of thing."

"And from Constantinople?"

"That again depends. Don't let's look too far ahead. At present I've got my mind on Saratof."

"Saratof and our little princess."

"No." He smiled. "I don't propose to have anything to do with her royal highness. And in any case she isn't *ours*."

"Nevertheless, I shall always think of her as ours, even if we never see her."

One evening in mid-November when the barge tied up near a small village, A.J. heard a few men talking to Akhiz. They were saying that the war in Europe was over and that Germany had surrendered to the French and British, but the information did not create the expected sensation. Akhiz was unaware of a European war as distinct from any other war; the world, seen from his timber-barge, seemed always full of fighting, and he was entirely uninterested in details.

They passed Volshk on the fourteenth day, but by that time the clearing horizon of the future was dimmed again, for Daly was ill. It was the cold, she confessed abjectly, and bade A.J. not to worry about her; she would be all right again when they reached a warmer climate. In former times, she said, she had never been able to endure the Russian winters; she had always gone either abroad or to the Crimea. Besides, she had possessed furs in those days—"and now," she added, half-laughing, "only Red generals dare show them." She was still very cheerful, and inclined to joke about her own weakness, but A.J. was uneasy, because he knew that the cold was not excessive for the country and the time of the year, and that there were at least five hundred miles to be traversed before they could expect warmer weather.

The trouble was that the only alternative to the open air was the atmosphere of the cabin, which was always so sickening that it was quite as much as they could do to sleep in it during the nights.

They reached Saratof on the twentieth day, in the midst of a heavy snowstorm. A.J. had been a little apprehensive of the landing, which was just as well, for it enabled him to spy out Red soldiers, suspiciously armed and eager, waiting on the quay at which the barge was to berth. He saw them out of the cabin window, and there was just time to warn Akhiz and hurry Daly and himself to the arranged refuge amongst the timber. Akhiz fulfilled his part to perfection, pulling a huge log back to cover up the entrance to the hiding-place. It was all accomplished in good time and without mishap; again A.J.'s chief fear was for Daly, who shivered in his arms with an unhappy mingling of fear and cold. A.J. whispered to reassure her; it was only a precaution, he said; the soldiers on the quay might not be in search of them at all; and in any case, there was no reason yet to be alarmed—they had come successfully through many worse crises. But Daly would not or could not be comforted; she whispered: "Oh, my darling, I'm sorry—I'm sorry—I haven't any nerve left at all—I can't help it— I'm just more terrified than I've ever been!"

They felt the barge bumping against the quayside; they heard sharp voices questioning Akhiz and the latter's slow, good-tempered answers; then they heard footsteps scampering on deck and over the piled timber. A.J. could not hear much that was said, but from the whole manner of the proceeding he guessed that a search was, after all, to be made.

About a quarter of an hour later voices came quite near to them. One said: "Well, you know, this may be all right as far as we've seen, but look at all this timber—anyone could hide amongst it."

A.J.'s arm tightened round Daly, and from her sudden stillness he thought she must be half-fainting.

Another voice said: "Yes, of course, that's true. And this fellow's been putting in for nights at all kinds of lonely places—nothing at all to stop anybody from coming aboard while he's been asleep."

Akhiz said: "Timber very heavy to move."

"She had a man with her."

Akhiz repeated: "Timber very heavy."

"Yes, you fool, you've said it once."

Then from various sounds and movements it was apparent that a few of the men were trying to move some of the logs.

Later a voice said: "Well, how *do* you move the stuff then?"

"Big crane comes along," said Akhiz.

"Well, keep a look out when you unload, that's all. I don't suppose anyone can be here, but still, as I say, keep a look out."

After which the voices and footsteps disappeared. That was during the afternoon, and Akhiz did not release his prisoners until dusk. By that time they were stiff with cramp and chilled to the bone. "Very heavy, eh?" whispered Akhiz, beaming at them, when he had pushed the log a foot or so out of place. He seemed delighted at his own share in the escapade, though still incurious as to what it was all about. The quays were quite dark; the whole town, which in daylight had looked so important and flourishing, was now no more than a light here and there and a hushed, overmastering stillness. Akhiz gave them scalding tea in his cabin; A.J. then gave Akhiz the twenty-four roubles agreed upon, plus another six for his extra services in outwitting the searchers, plus a small tin of American baked beans. Then they bade good-by to their faithful host and savior, who kissed A.J. with tremendous fervor, and even then, at that last moment, forebore to ask where they were going or what they were intending to do. Finally Akhiz went on deck to see if the quays were clear for them. There were sentries patrolling around, on the look out for pilfering, but it was not very difficult to choose a safe moment to cross the litter of railway tracks and reach one of the steep alleys leading up from the docks to the town.

When they came to the less deserted streets they were able to judge that Saratof was in a scarcely happier condition than Novarodar. The shop-windows were empty; the cafés closed and shuttered; no trams were running. It was all depressing enough, except for the fact that it was, after all, Saratof—the last important stage-point on their long journey from danger into safety. The Whites were but a few score miles away, which, after reckoning for so long in terms of hundreds of miles, seemed next to nothing at all; Denikin's army, too, might have been advancing and have made the interval even less. As he trudged over the crunching snow, A.J.'s spirits rose as he contemplated the future.

But there was a more immediate future to be decided. Refreshed and abundantly fit after the river-journey, he would have pushed on that very night, and Daly also was anxious to avoid delay. For a time they talked of reaching some village perhaps ten miles or so out of Saratof and seeking accommodation there. Villages were safer than towns; the people in them were usually more kindly, less terrified of the authorities, and less likely to be inquisitive about passports and travel-permits.

But before they reached the suburban fringe of the town this plan became suddenly impossible, for Daly was clearly on the point of collapse. It was obvious that she could not walk another mile, much less the unknown distance to the nearest village, and there was nothing for it but to contemplate the risks of seeking shelter in Saratof itself. The town was noted for its strongly Red sympathies, and A.J. did not feel happy at the prospect of spending a night in it. He tried a few near cottages, playing the part of the wandering but not quite penniless working-man who could pay a small sum for a bed for himself and his wife until the morning; but in every case he was turned away. One haggard housewife told him that nobody was allowed to take in strangers, and that if he wanted accommodation he had better apply to the Labor Bureau at the Commissariat offices of the local Soviet. When he reached Daly, whom he had left a little distance away, he found her lying on the snow-covered pavement. He picked her up; she was shivering and trying to smile, but incapable of speech and only able to stagger along with great difficulty. There remained one last resource, which he had not wished to be driven to— the address of the ex-butler. He mentioned it, and she nodded agreement. Then he called at another house and inquired the way; by good fortune it was in the same quarter of the town, quite close.

A few moments later he was tapping at the door of a small workman's cottage. An elderly white-haired man appeared, to whom he said: "Does Stapen live here?" At that the man's face took on an expression of sudden terror. "Stapen?" he exclaimed, acting very badly. "No, there is no one here of that name." Then A.J. realized the fears that might be in the man's mind, and added: "I was sent here by the Valimoffs, of Novarodar." The old man stared incredulously and, after a pause, asked them inside. He had been almost dumb with fear, and now was in the same condition with astonishment. A.J. talked a little to reassure him, while Daly sank into a chair too weak to take any part in the conversation.

In the end their identities were satisfactorily established, and the old man admitted that he was himself Stapen, the ex-butler. He was also more than willing to help them, though he had very little food and no money. His wife was out at that moment, trying to get bread. Life was terrible in Saratof, and he prayed that Denikin's army might arrive soon.

Daly recovered a little in front of the fire, and Stapen recognized her—or so he said—he had seen her in the old days in Moscow. Daly also said (but perhaps from mere politeness) that she thought she remembered him.

It was soon apparent that Stapen's mind was obsessed with some other matter which he was afraid to mention until Daly broached it first. She said: "Well, and have you the little girl with you still?" Stapen's voice dropped then to a throbbing whisper; he was evidently delighted that the strangers knew all about it, yet at the same time awestruck to be discussing it with them. He replied: "Yes, the princess is upstairs. She has been ill—she has had typhus—but she is now getting better. You would wish to see her, eh? Or no—she may be asleep—perhaps tomorrow will be better. You are going to take her with you when you go?" He turned to A.J. and added: "Ah, I knew the Valimoffs would make a good choice— how I have been longing for the day when I should hand her over to someone such as yourself!"

His sincerity and devotion were beyond suspicion, but A.J. at that moment was hardly in a mood to be appreciative. He felt, indeed, a little impatient with the fellow. Did nothing matter except the rescue of a princess? He realized again how difficult and complicated would be the escape to Denikin's lines if he and Daly were to be burdened with a small and illustrious child.

"For the present," he answered, rather coldly, "we can hardly look ahead as far as that. My wife is ill and needs rest."

Stapen bowed, controlling his excitement like a well-trained servant who allows it to be supposed that he had momentarily forgotten himself. Within a short time he had prepared a bed and Daly was being put into it. She whispered, as A.J. laid her head on the pillow: "Dear, why are you so angry with people like Stapen? You were angry with the Valimoffs, too." He answered: "I'm not really angry with them—I'm everlastingly grateful in most ways. It's just that they seem to think other things matter more than you."

"Well, don't they?"

"Possibly, but I can't be expected to agree to it."

"I don't think you care, then, for this little princess?"

"Not a bit. I hate her, even, because I see in her a possible danger to you. It's all very selfish, I know, but I can't help it. I won't even try to help it. The world is so full of misery that one can't—one daren't—open one's eyes to it all. The most to be done is to make sure of what one loves and never to let it go. All the rest must be put outside—entirely."

"Do you think Poushkoff felt like that?"

"Probably. He loved you, too."

She smiled and closed her eyes, and he went down to talk to Stapen. Her words, however, had made him rather more friendly towards the old man, who proved, on acquaintance, the pleasantest and simplest of types. His wife, who came in later in the evening after failing to secure any bread, was very different, but perhaps necessarily so in order to strike a balance with a husband of such benignity. She was a shrewd and rather embittered woman who gave A.J. but the chilliest of welcomes. A fruitless four-hour wait in a bread-queue had put her into a mood of outspokenness that her husband sought in vain to check; she almost began by saying: "Well, if Denikin's men are on the way, let them bring some food with them. For my part, I don't care whether we are governed by Reds or Whites, so long as working people can get enough to eat."

Afterwards Stapen apologized for her with stately courtesy. "She was always like that," he said. "Many's the time that my dear old master, Prince Borosil, said to me—'Stapen, you should whip her!'—and I promised I would. But, somehow, I could never bring myself to do it."

In the morning Daly seemed much better, and A.J.'s hopes began to be optimistic again. It was all, of course, a little more difficult now that they had met Stapen. The fellow assumed so completely that they intended to take the child along with them when they made their dash for safety; it was a dream he had been dreaming for months, and now it seemed about to be accomplished he could only build pretty details all around it. Would they take her to Paris? Or to Rome? Or to London? There were royalties and semi-royalties all over Europe who, it appeared, would be delighted to extend unlimited hospitality to such an exalted babe. For she was, Stapen explained, in a whisper, within measurable distance of being heir to all the Russias. The Bolsheviks had killed so many of the ex-Emperor's family and relatives—far more than anyone could estimate exactly—and the careful, systematic process of extermination was still being carried out. "That is why they are always on the watch for the princess," he added, "but so far I don't think they have the slightest idea where she is. They have her photograph, of course, but it is bound to be an old one, and she is different now, especially after her illness."

A.J. and Daly were solemnly presented to the princess that morning. She was a thin and sad little thing, wasted by fever and obviously very weak. Stapen treated her with rather absurd decorum, while his wife treated her exactly as if she had been her own child; and the princess showed unmistakable affection for them both.

But the more Stapen outlined the child's social and dynastic importance the more unwilling A.J. was to encumber himself with her. Yet it became increasingly difficult to convey this to Stapen. It was not only that A.J. did not wish to offend the fellow, but rather that no means existed by which Stapen could be brought to conceive A.J.'s point of view. "He won't realize that we have our own future to think of," A.J. told Daly. "Frankly, I'm not interested in dynastic intrigues—it doesn't matter a jot to me that the child's a princess, next in succession, and so on. All I care about in the world is getting you to safety, and I won't agree to any-thing that will lessen the chance of it."

She smiled. "That sounds very ruthless."

"I don't see why I shouldn't give first place to what matters most to me, and you have shown me what that is."

"Dear, I love to hear you say things like that, even if they aren't the right things to say."

"But they *are*—for me. Don't you feel the same?"

She said slowly: "I suppose it's natural that love at first should be a desperate, self-centered thing. And by self-centered I don't mean *your*self or *my*self—I mean *our*selves. We're so much one that I wonder if it's a sort of selfishness to think about each other as we do?"

"I haven't yet reached the stage of feeling like that."

"Oh, neither have I—it's only a silly mood I'm in. Dearest, you aren't angry with me?"

He shook his head with tender deliberation. "More than anything in the world," he whispered, "I want to get you out of this country, and I hate anything and any-body who makes a complication."

"You hate my being ill, then."

"But—you're not *very* ill? Oh, you don't mean—"

"Darling, no. I'm almost fit for anything. I wish I were of more use to you."

He gave her a look of uninterpretable affection, and they suddenly clung together in an embrace. She said at length: "I understand what you mean—we can't take the child with us and we must tell Stapen that we can't."

"Yes, and the sooner the better. I'll tell him in the morning."

But in the morning Daly was ill again, after being sick and feverish during the night. Their departure

259

looked as if it must be postponed for another day or two, and so, in the circumstances, there did not seem any particular need to present Stapen with the arranged ultimatum.

By noon the whole situation was changed utterly and for the worse, for Daly was by this time very ill indeed, and A.J., with fair experience of such matters, diagnosed typhus. It was not really astonishing, and yet, for some reason, it was a possibility that he had never even considered.

There was no doctor to attend her; there had been none for the little princess, either. There was no private doctor, in fact, in the whole town. Typhus, spread by the war and nourished by the famine, had overwhelmed Saratof to an extent that A.J. had hardly realized during his few days in the place  The hospitals were full, with patients lying on stretchers between the beds; emergency hospitals were also full, and more were being hastily built; yet still the disease raged and spread, and the death-rate had been steadily and appallingly on the increase for weeks. All the hospitals were being managed by skeleton staffs of doctors and nurses, and it had lately become so difficult to give patients proper attention that many who stayed in their homes with no professional doctoring at all had probably an equal, if not a superior, chance of recovery. Stapen evidently thought so, and urged A.J. not to try to get Daly into one of the hospitals. It would have been quite impossible, in any case, for they were state institutions and every patient entering had to pass through a sieve of official enquiries. The same reason had prevented Stapen from trying to find a hospital-bed for the princess, and now, as he comfortably explained to A.J., he was very glad of it. "The Countess will be far better here, just as the princess was," he assured him, and A.J.'s heart warmed towards the old man for showing such willingness to share the burden of this extra misfortune, though, in fact, it was Stapen's wife on whom the burden mostly fell.

A.J., fortunately, was at his best in an emergency of such a kind. He had a fine instinct for doctoring, and had acted as amateur doctor for so long and with such success during a part of his life that he felt none of that vague helplessness that afflicts the complete layman when faced with medical problems. He had also a particular knowledge of typhus itself; he had often diagnosed cases and was quite familiar with the normal course of the disease. Apart from which, he possessed the proper temperament for living through anxious moments; he was calm, quiet, soothing, and never despondent. Stapen, he soon found, was no use at all except as an amiable figurehead to surround the whole affair with an atmosphere of benignity and good will; it was his wife who did and was everything. This hard-faced, dour, and rather truculent woman soon drew from A.J. the deepest admiration; he perceived that it was she, and she alone, who had saved the child's life. And she tackled this additional job of nursing Daly with an apparent grudgingness which concealed, not so much a warm heart, as a thoroughly efficient soul. A.J. could well imagine the sort of cook she had been, and he could also well imagine the sort of butler Stapen had been.

So Saratof, which was to have been but a stage on a final dash to freedom, became instead a last prison closing them round. To A.J., sitting at the bedside, nothing remained but love. He realized now as never before how dear she was, and how utterly beyond beauty to him.

His mind glowed and throbbed with a hundred memories of her; he saw her dark eyes opening at dawn, and heard her deep tranquil laughter echoing amongst the boles of great trees; he felt again the slumberous passion that had seemed to wrap them both in unity with every little rustling leaf. From his first sight of her in the prison-cell at Khalinsk, everything had had the terrible, lovely reality of a child's fairy-tale.

A good deal of the time she was in delirium and talked ramblingly, but sometimes her mind cleared for a few moments and she would beg him to take care of himself and try not to take the disease from her. She often said: "Oh, I'm so sorry—just at the end of our journey—I do feel I've managed things badly. . . ."

He comforted her by relating how Denikin's army was advancing, thus lessening the distance between themselves and safety even while she lay in bed.

Often, in her delirium, she called his name, appealing to him to protect her from shadowy terrors, but sometimes even her delirium was calm and she would talk serenely about all kinds of things. She constantly mentioned the girl, calling her "our little princess" in the way they had joked about her during the barge-journey.

About a week after the onset of the fever she appeared to become very much better, and A.J. began to hope that the crisis was passing. She talked to him that day quite lucidly about their plans for escape; the Whites, he told her, were now only forty or fifty miles to the south, so that they might count themselves fortunate, even in the delay. Then she asked suddenly: "Where can we be married, do you think?"

He answered: "In Odessa, perhaps—or Constantinople, at any rate."

She smiled, and seemed very happy in contemplation of it. After a pause she went on to ask if he had yet told Stapen that he did not intend to take the child with them.

He answered that he hadn't, but that he would do so whenever the matter became urgent.

She said: "I suppose we can't possibly take her with us?"

"Do you want to?" he asked, and she replied: "I would like to, if we could, but of course it's for you to decide. It's you who'd have all the bother of both of us, isn't it?"

"It isn't bother I'd mind. It's danger—to you."

"Do you think there would be much danger?"

"More than I'd care to risk."

"I know. I agree. We won't have her."

"I wish we could, for your sake."

"Oh, no, it doesn't matter. I don't quite know why I'm worrying you so much about it."

"You're really keen on having her, then, if we could?"

She answered then, almost sobbing: "Terribly, darling —*terribly*. And I don't know why."

A few hours later the sudden improvement in her condition disappeared with equal suddenness, and the fever, after its respite, seemed to attack her with renewed venom. To A.J. the change was the bitterest of blows, and all the old iron rage stalked through his veins again. He could not look at the rapidly recovering child downstairs without a feeling of dislike; but for her, he worked it out, they would never have called at Stapen's house, and Daly would never have been ill. (Yet that, he knew in his heart, was far from certain; the whole district was typhus-ridden, and it was impossible to establish how and from whom contagion had been passed.)

On the tenth day he knew that the crisis was approaching; if she survived it, she would almost certainly recover. He was at her bedside hour after hour, helping in all the details of nursing; Stapen's wife and himself, though they rarely exchanged more than sharp question and answer, were grimly together in the struggle. And it was not only a struggle against disease, for every day the search for the barest essentials of food was a battle in itself. Only rarely could milk be obtained, while nourishing soups and other invalid delicacies were quite beyond possibility. The last of the food that he had brought with him from Novarodar had long since been consumed, so that now he too was relying on the acquisitive efforts of Stapen's wife. Sometimes she went out early in the morning, with the temperature far below freezing-point, and came back at dusk, after tramping many miles—with nothing. A.J. never offered her copious sympathy, as Stapen did, yet there was between them always a secret comprehension of the agonies of the day. When he looked up from Daly's flushed and twitching face it was often to see Stapen's wife gazing from the other side of the bed with queer, companionable grimness.

Once while Daly was sleeping they held a curious whispered conversation across the bed. She asked him how he intended to proceed when Daly was better, and after he had explained to her his plans, she said: "You'll find the child a nuisance—perhaps a danger, too. There's a very strict watch on all the frontiers."

"I know that."

"I wonder you bother to take her with you at all."

"Oh?" He was surprised, and waited for her to continue. She said, after a pause: "Look after your own affairs—that would be my advice, if you asked for it."

"And the child?"

"She can stay here."

"For how long?"

"For always, if necessary. I don't see that it matters whether she's here or in a king's palace, so long as she's happy. And the way the world is just now, princesses haven't much chance of happiness."

"What would your husband say to that, I wonder?"

"Oh, *him?*"

She uttered the monosyllable with such overwhelming emphasis that it was not even contemptuous.

Neither of them pursued the argument further. Yet it was strange how the problem of the child was growing in importance; hardly an hour passed now without some delirious mention of it by Daly. It seemed to be on her mind to the exclusion of all other problems. On the twelfth day she suddenly became clear-headed and told A.J. that she was going to get better. Then, with her next breath, she said: "But if I don't, you *will* take the girl with you alone, won't you?"

That word "alone"—his first glimpse into another world—sank on his heart till he could scarcely reason out an answer of any kind.

She went on: "Will you promise that—to take her with you alone—if—if I don't—"

"But you are—oh, you *are* going to get better!"

"Darling, yes, of course I am. But still, I want your promise."

He could do nothing but assent. But a moment later he said: "She would be all right, you know, left here—the Stapens would give her a good home."

265

"But she's ours—the only thing we can call ours, anyway. Darling, I'm pretending she belongs to us—I want somebody to belong to us. Do you understand?"

He nodded desperately.

"And so you *do* promise, then?"

"Yes, yes. You can trust me."

She seemed to be suddenly calmed. In a few moments she went to sleep and slept so peacefully that A.J.'s hopes surged again as he watched her. Then about midnight she woke up and touched his hand. "Dear," she whispered, "I am quite happy. It has all been so wonderful, hasn't it?" He laid his cheek against her arm, and when he looked up she had closed her eyes. She never opened them to consciousness again. She died at a few minutes to one on that morning of the fourth of December, nineteen hundred and eighteen.

A.J. took the child with him and set out from Saratof. There was a look of nothingness in his eyes and a sound of nothingness in his voice. Bitter weather had put a stop to Denikin's advance, and the fugitives who passed by along the roads were freezing as well as starving. A.J. neither feared nor hoped; he pushed on, mile after mile over the snowbound, famine-stricken country; he was an automaton merely, and when he reached the Bolshevik lines the same automatism functioned to plan the necessary details of the final adventure. But it was no adventure, after all; he crossed over without a thrill, and was soon heading for the coast.

The long journey was full of hardships, and the child, barely recovered from her earlier illness, soon ailed again. Suddenly one morning, waking up in a small-town inn where they had both slept huddled together on the floor,

A.J. knew that he was ill himself. He had scarcely strength to move, and fell in the roadway outside when he tried to resume the southward journey.

There was an American Relief detachment stationed in the town—a tiny fragment of the teeming wealth of the Far West, transferred bodily, as by some miracle, to become an object of amazement on the stricken plains of Russia. When A.J. and the child were carried into the examination shed, particulars concerning them were neatly taken down by a Harvard graduate. A.J. gave his assumed name, and when asked for an address shook his head. He was asked other questions, but he was too ill to answer in detail, even had he wished to. When, however, separate questions were asked about the child, and the latter was assumed to be his own, he made an effort to explain something. But the matter was not understood, and A.J., seeing a whole world swimming round about him in vast circles of incredibility, was barely coherent. An hour later, when he was being helped to undress, the papers in his pocket were discovered, examined, found incomprehensible, and placed efficiently in the fumigating-oven alongside his clothes and other possessions. The whole parcel of them were handed to him a month later when he left hospital.

He found then that the child had been transferred to a children's camp in the Crimea, run by the Americans with the support of their big charities, and that an attempt was being made to have some of the children adopted by families in America. He did not enquire further; he was scarcely in a mood to feel that it mattered. Later he learned that his small protégée had been among the first fortunate transhipment; she was already across the ocean.

267

PART FIVE

FROM THE GOLDEN ARROW AT
Victoria there stepped a man whom the porters, even on that plutocratic platform, singled out, attracted not so much by a leather handbag plastered with foreign hotel-labels as by a certain elusive but highly significant quietness of manner. And the voice was equally quiet. "Taxi —yes, and there are a trunk and two large suit-cases in the van. The name is Fothergill." To the driver a few moments later he said merely: "The Cecil." It was the only hotel he could remember from the London of his youth.

They gave him a lofty bedroom overlooking the dazzling semi-circle of the Embankment, and he spent the first few minutes gazing down at the trams and the electric advertisements across the river. He was a little tired after the journey, and a little thrilled by the sensation of being in London again. He changed, though not into evening clothes, and dined in the grill-room, chatting desultorily with the waiter. Then he smoked a cigar in the lounge and went up to his room rather early. In bed with a novel he heard Big Ben chime several successive quarters; then he switched out the light and tried to believe that this small, comfortable, well-carpeted, and entirely characterless hotel bedroom was somehow different from all the dozens of similar ones he had occupied in other cities.

268

In the morning he breakfasted in bed, enjoyed a long hot bath, made himself affable with the hotel-porter, and strode out into the cheerful, sunny streets. There were so many little odd jobs to do—some of which he had been saving up for a long time. He saw his lawyer, and made an appointment to see a Harley Street doctor later on in the week. He called at a firm of publishers and heard that his book "Rubber and the Rubber Industry" had crept into a second edition. The publisher asked him to dinner the following evening; he accepted. Then he bought some ties and handkerchiefs and a hat of rather more English style than the one he was wearing. By that time, as it was noon and he was in the Strand, he stepped down to Romano's Bar for a glass of sherry and exchanged a few words with the dark-haired girl who served him. He liked, when he could, to obtain the intimacy of talking to people without the bother of knowing them, and that, of course, was always more easily accomplished with one's so-called inferiors. The barmaid at Romano's was a type he liked—pretty, alert, friendly, and fundamentally virtuous. He asked her what were the best shows to see, and she gave him the names of several which he imagined he would be sure to detest exceedingly. Then she asked if this were his first visit to London, and he rather enjoyed answering: "My first for twenty-three years. I used to live here." Afterwards he lunched at Rule's in Maiden Lane—the first place he found that seemed to him very little changed since the old days. In the afternoon he took a bus to the Marble Arch and walked through the August sunshine to Hyde Park Corner and Green Park, just in time for tea at Rumpelmayer's. And after that there was nothing to do but return to the Cecil, change into dinner clothes, and begin the journey out to Surbiton.

"There is a good electric service from Waterloo," Philippa had written in her letter to him, and the sentence echoed in his mind with fatuous profundity all the time he was fixing his collar and tie in front of the bedroom mirror. It was strange to be visiting a person whom you had not seen for twenty-three years. It had been on impulse that he had written to her, and he was not sure, even now, that the impulse had been wise. She had married, of course, a second time—that was something. She had even a nineteen-year-old daughter. And, if one chanced to think of it, she had the vote—that vote for which in the past she had clamored so much. She would be forty-eight—his own age. Her letter had really told him very little except that her name was now Newburn, that she would be delighted to see him, and that there was that good electric service from Waterloo.

When he arrived at Surbiton station an hour later he declined a cab and enquired the way from a policeman. The walk through placid suburban roads gave him a chance to meditate, to savor in full the rich unusualness of the situation. He lit a cigarette, stopped a moment to watch some boys playing with a dog, kicked a few pieces of orange-peel into the gutter with an automatic instinct for tidiness; it was past seven before he found the house. It looked smaller than he had expected (for, after all, hadn't she inherited the bulk of old Jergwin's fortune?); just a detached suburban villa with sham gables and a pretentious curved pathway between the garden-gate and the porch. The maid who opened the door to his ring took his hat and coat and showed him into a drawing-room tastefully if rather depressingly furnished. He stood with his back to the firegrate and continued to wonder what she would look like.

She came in with her daughter. She was rather thin and pale and eager, and the daughter was a large-limbed, athletic-looking girl who moved about the room as if it were a hockey-pitch.

"Isn't it romantic, Ainsley, for you to have come back after all these years?"

He found himself shaking hands and being presented to the girl. "I suppose it is," he answered, smiling. Rather to his astonishment he felt perfectly calm. He began to chatter pointlessly about the journey. "Found my way quite easily—as you said, the service is very good. Didn't think I'd be here half so quickly. You must be pretty far out of town, though—twenty miles, I should guess."

"Twelve," the girl corrected.

They began to discuss Surbiton. Then the maid brought in complicated and rather sugary cocktails. They continued to discuss Surbiton. By that time he was beginning to anticipate the arrival of Mr. Newburn with almost passionate eagerness, and was rather surprised when they adjourned to the dining-room without waiting for the gentleman. "Is Mr. Newburn away?" he asked, noticing that places were only laid for three. The girl answered, with outright simplicity: "Father died two years ago."

Well, that was that, and there was nothing for it but to look sympathetic and change the subject. So, to avoid at all costs the resumption of the Surbiton discussion, he began to talk about Paris, Vienna, and other cities he had lived in during recent years. The girl said: "Mother told me you were in Russia during the Revolution. Do tell us

271

about it!" He smiled and answered: "Well, you know, there was a revolution and a lot of shooting and trouble of most kinds—I don't know that I can remember much more." She then said: "I suppose you saw Lenin and Trotsky?"—and he replied: "No, never—and neither of them. I'm rather a fraud, don't you think?"

Then Philippa chatted about various causes and enterprises she was connected with; they ranged from a hospital for crippled children and a birth-control clinic to Esperanto and Dalcroze eurhythmics. He listened tolerantly, but shook his head when she offered to show him authentic photographs of slum children suffering from rickets. "I'll willingly subscribe to them," he said, "but I never care to have my feelings harrowed after a good dinner." The girl choked with laughter. "I don't blame you," she said. "I think they're horrible photographs, and mother *will* show them to everybody." Philippa replied: "I show them because they *are* so horrible—people ought to realize the horrible things that go on in the world." He felt suddenly sorry for her then and said: "It's a splendid cause, I'm sure, and I didn't mean to make fun. You will let me send you a check, won't you?"

But he soon perceived that his compassion had been unnecessary. She was tough; she was thick-skinned; she was obviously used to all kinds of gibes. When she told him that it was her habit to stand at street-corners lecturing about birth-control, he felt that he need no longer be afraid of hurting her feelings. He was more sorry, then, for the girl; she was such an ordinary, straightforward, averagely decent girl.

They took coffee in the drawing-room, and when they were comfortably smoking, Philippa suddenly said: "My husband isn't really dead—my daughter had to tell you that because the maid was there and that is what we tell *her*. The truth is, he left me."

"Really?"

Then she launched into a detailed account of the catastrophe of her second marriage. The man had been a labor organizer, had speculated with her money and lost most of it, and had finally run off with a girl secretary. It was all rather pathetic, and also—which was worse— a trifle boring. He kept making hints about a return train, and she urged him to stay the night, but he said he couldn't. Then she asked him questions about Russia, and mentioned an informal literary circle to which she belonged and which would be so pleased if he would give a talk about his adventures in that country.

But he replied, smiling and shaking his head: "My dear Philippa, none of my Russian experiences were nearly so dreadful as the one you are suggesting."

"But didn't you escape from the Bolsheviks?"

He smiled again. "Well, you see, I heard that my brother was in Cairo, so I joined him. He'd been fighting with Allenby in Palestine—it was just after the War ended. He had a rubber estate out East and gave me a job on it."

She continued to cross-examine him, but without much success. "Anyhow," she said, as they shook hands, "now that you're intending to make a home in England, I shall simply insist on getting to know you."

But he wasn't sure that he did intend to make a home in England, he reflected a few moments later, as he sat in the corner of the railway compartment.

In his hotel bedroom that night he felt a slow and rather comfortable disappointment soaking into him. Subconsciously he knew he had been expectant over this meeting with Philippa; now he realized, not without relief, that all such expectancy had vanished. It wasn't only she who had failed him, but he who had failed himself. He didn't want to know anybody in that eager, confidential way; he had no energy for it; he would rather chat with some passing stranger whom he would never see again. It had been a mistake to go to Surbiton; perhaps it had been a mistake even to come to England.

The next morning, after he had talked to the girl in Romano's Bar about some theaters he was intending to visit, she said: "You seem to go about a lot by yourself. Haven't you any friends?"

"Not in London," he replied. "A few people the other side of the world—mostly Chinamen. That's all." He liked to see her eyebrows arch in astonishment.

"I say! Fancy being friends with Chinamen! But you must know *somebody* in London, if you used to live here?"

"A few business acquaintances, but I don't count them. Oh, and two people in Surbiton. I went to see them last night, but I don't suppose I shall go again."

"Why not? Weren't they nice to you?"

"Oh, yes. Rather nicer, perhaps, than I was to them."

"Then why—"

He laughed. "Never mind. I hardly know myself. But you can fill me up another glass of sherry and have one with me."

"Righto, and thanks, though mine's a gin, if you don't mind. . . . Well, here's luck to you, anyway."

Once he toyed with the idea of asking her out to some theater or music-hall, but he decided, on reflection and without any sort of snobbishness, that the perfection of their relationship depended on the counter between.

274

He stayed in London over a week, and on the whole he enjoyed himself. He dined at his publisher's town house and met there a man on the staff of the *Times* who promptly commissioned from him a series of articles on the future of the rubber industry. It gratified and perhaps slightly surprised him to realize that his book had become, in its own field, something of a classic.

He also went to theaters, cinemas, exhibitions; he walked in the parks; he listened to the open-air speakers near the Marble Arch; he lunched and dined in any hotel or restaurant that chanced to catch his eye; he sat in the Embankment gardens and penciled drafts of his *Times* articles; he had casual and agreeable chats with policemen and bus-conductors.

Then one morning he went to Harley Street to be examined and overhauled by a specialist. He went quite calmly and came away equally so. It was about noon, and he took a taxi back to the hotel, where he found a letter awaiting him—one he had been expecting. After reading it through he said to the bureau-clerk: "I shall be leaving tomorrow." Then he stepped out into the sunshine and walked across the Strand to Romano's Bar. The dark-haired girl placed his sherry before him with a smile. "Here again," she said. "You're becoming one of our regulars."

"Not for long, I'm afraid," he answered. "I'm off to-morrow."

"Where?"

"Ireland."

"Business?"

"In a way, yes."

"Going for long?"

"Don't know, really."

"It's queer, seems to me, the way you don't know any-body and don't seem to know even things about yourself. Fact is, I'm beginning to think you must be a queer one altogether."

He laughed. "I had a queer sort of adventure this morning, anyway. Went to the doctor's and was told I ought to give up smoking and drinking, go to bed early every night, and avoid all excitements. What would *you* do, now, if your doctor told you that about yourself?"

"I don't suppose I'd take any notice of it."

"Quite right, and I don't suppose *I* shall, either."

"Go on!" she laughed. "You don't look ill! I don't believe you went to any doctor at all—you're just having me on!"

"Honestly, I'm not. It's as true as those Chinese friends of mine."

He joked with her for a little longer and then went to lunch at Simpson's. Afterwards he returned to the hotel, wrote a few letters, and began to pack his bags in readiness for the morrow. Then he went out for a stroll; he walked up to Covent Garden Market, where there were always interesting scenes, and then westward towards Charing Cross Road, where he liked to look at the book shops. But he felt himself becoming very tired long before he reached this goal, so he turned into the familiar Maiden Lane for a drink and a rest at Rule's. But it wanted a quarter of an hour to opening time, he discovered, when he reached the closed door, and as his tiredness increased, he entered the little Catholic church almost opposite and sat down amidst the cool and grateful dusk.

He felt refreshed after a few minutes and began to walk round the church, examining the mural tablets; in doing so, without looking where he was going, he almost collided with a young priest who was also walking round. Apologies were exchanged, and conversation followed. The priest, it appeared, was not attached to the church; he was merely a sight-seer, like Fothergill himself. He was from Lancashire, he said, on a business visit to London; when he had time to spare he liked going into churches—"a sort of busman's holiday," he added, with a laugh. He was a very cheerful, friendly person, and Fothergill, who liked casual encounters with strangers, talked to him for some time in the porch of the church as they both went out. Then it suddenly occurred to both of them that there was no absolute need to cut short a conversation that had begun so promisingly; they walked down Bedford Street to the Strand, still talking, and with no very definite objective. The priest, whose name was Harington, said he was going to have a meal somewhere and take a night train back to Lancashire; Fothergill said he was also going to have dinner. Harington then said that he usually took a snack at Lyon's Corner House, near Charing Cross; Fothergill said, all right, that would do for him too. So they dined together inexpensively and rather uncomfortably, surrounded by marble and gilt and the blare of a too strident orchestra.

Yet Fothergill enjoyed it. He liked Harington. He liked Harington's type of mind—intellectual, sincere, interested in all kinds of matters outside the scope of religion, worldly to those who saw only the surface, spiritual to those who guessed deeper. He was emphatically not the kind of man to insist on rendering to God the things which were Cæsar's. During the meal Fothergill chanced to mention something about rubber-plantations, and Harington said immediately: "I say, didn't you tell me

277

your name was Fothergill? I wonder, now you're talking about rubber, whether you're the Fothergill who used to be at Kuala Simur?"

"Yes, I am."

"That's odd. It means I know quite a lot about you— Father Richmond and I are great friends—we were at Ware together."

"Really? Oh, yes, I remember him very well. Where is he now?"

"Still at Kuala Simur. He had a great opinion of you —especially after that small-pox epidemic."

"Oh, that wasn't much."

Harington laughed. "It's too conventional to say that, surely? I wish you could see some of Richmond's letters about you, anyway—he almost hero-worshiped."

"I hope not."

"He did. His great dream, I think, was to convert you some day."

"Well, he didn't come far short of doing so."

"Oh?"

"We used to argue a good deal about religion and so on—and I used to joke with him and say I should end by becoming a Catholic. At least, perhaps he thought I was joking, but all the time, in a sort of way, I meant it. Then my brother died and all the rubber estates fell to me, and I got suddenly fed up with everything and sold out. That just happened to be right at the top of the rubber boom in 'twenty-five, which is why I'm more or less a rich man now. I sold out to an Anglo-Dutch syndicate, packed up, and pottered about Europe from then till now. The syndicate, incidentally, paid me about five times what the place is worth today."

"That must have been very good for your bank account."

"Better than for my soul, perhaps, eh? To come back to that, the rather curious thing is that all the time I was at Kuala Simur I felt a sort of conversion going on—if you can call it that—I know of course that nothing really counts until you're definitely over the line. Probably if I'd had much more to do with your friend Richmond, whom I liked exceedingly, he'd have pushed me over."

"I wish that had happened."

"Oh, well, I pushed myself over a year later, so perhaps it didn't matter."

"So you are a Catholic?"

"I was received into the Church in Vienna three years ago. I'm not sure that I'm entitled to call myself a Catholic now, though. Slackness, I suppose. All very unsatisfactory from your point of view, I'm afraid."

"And from yours too, surely?"

"Well, perhaps—perhaps."

They talked on for some time, and Fothergill found it strangely and refreshingly easy to be intimate with the young man. Harington's train was due to leave at midnight, and towards nine o'clock Fothergill suggested that they should adjourn to his hotel for a drink and a smoke. They walked along the crowded Strand to the Cecil and were soon snugly in the lounge. There and then conversation developed as if all barriers had suddenly been destroyed. Fothergill said: "You know, Harington, there was one thing I never told Richmond, and that was the whole truth about my life."

"I know. He used to grumble about that in his letters to me. He said he was sure you had some mysterious and

279

grisly past which you never breathed a word about to anybody."

"Really? He guessed that? How curious!"

"Well, we priests aren't such simpletons, you know."

Fothergill laughed. "I'll bet he never guessed the sort of past it had been, though. I dare say I'd have told him if I hadn't known him so well. As a matter of fact, I knew he liked me, and I liked him to like me, and I didn't want to see my stock going down with a bump. . . . You see, I seem to have broken so many of the commandments."

"Most of us have."

"Yes, but I've gone rather the whole hog. I've killed men, for instance."

"If you walked out now into the Strand you could find hundreds of middle-aged fellows who've done that."

"Oh, the war—yes, but my affairs weren't in the war— at least, hardly. One of them was pretty cold-blooded murder. And then there are other matters, too. I never married, but once I lived with a woman."

"That, again, is nothing very unusual."

"I dare say not, but if my soul depended on it, I couldn't say I was sorry. It's the one thing in my life which I feel was fully and definitely right."

"Of course, without knowing all the circumstances—"

"If you've time, and if you think you wouldn't be bored, I'll tell you them."

"I wish you would."

"Very well." And Fothergill began at the day he left England twenty-three years before. Nearly an hour later, when he came hoarsely to an end, Harington said: "That's really a most astonishing story. But you'd better finish it for me. When you got better in that American hospital, how did you manage to establish your English identity?"

"Quite simply. I just told them who I was and they believed me. You see, I'd chattered English in delirium, and when I recovered they kept me on as an interpreter—still supposing me to be Russian, of course. Then, when they all packed up to return to America, I suddenly decided that I wanted to go with them. I'd had enough of chaos, and I felt I couldn't face any more of it. I thought it would advance my chances if they knew I was really English, though it didn't, as a matter of fact—their immigration authorities wouldn't budge. It so happened, however, that one of the American doctors had recently met my brother in Egypt, so he put me in touch with him. That's how I definitely became an Englishman again."

"Did you tell the Americans about your various adventures?"

"No. I thought it wiser not to put their credulity to such a severe trial."

Harington laughed. "Well, you must be relieved to have got it all off your chest at last."

"Yes. Relieved and rather tired, to tell you the truth."

"Not to tired to continue our talk for another half-hour or so, I hope?"

"Provided you do most of the talking."

"Oh, I'll engage to do that." Harington kept his word, and the conversation went on till it was absolutely necessary for him to leave to catch his train. Fothergill, eager despite his tiredness, accompanied him in a taxi, and their talk lasted until the moment the train began to move. "We probably shan't meet again," Fothergill said, as they shook hands, "but I shall never forget how—how *reason-*

*able* you have been. Does that sound a rather tepid word in the circumstances?"

"Not at all. Just the right one, I should like to think. Though there's no reason why we shouldn't meet some-time—you have my address—it's only a tram-ride out of Manchester."

"I hate tram-rides and I'm sure I should hate Manchester." He laughed excitedly, and was aware of the silliness of the remark. He added, more soberly: "In my old age I'm beginning to attach great value to comfort—just comfort."

"Old age, man—nonsense! You're not fifty yet!"

"One is made old, not by one's years, but by what one has lived through. That's sententious enough, surely—another sign of age." The train began to move. "I shan't forget, however. Good-by."

"I must make the most, then, of your rubber articles in the *Times*. Good-by, then." They laughed distantly at each other as the train gathered speed.

He drove back to the hotel with all his senses warmed and glowing. On what trifles everything depended—if he had not made for Rule's that evening and been those few minutes too early!

In a corner seat of a first-class compartment on the Irish Mail the next morning, he had leisure to think everything over. So much had happened the day before. But the interview with the Harley Street man hadn't surprised him; he had been suspecting something of the sort for several months, and wasn't worrying; there was no pain —at worst a sort of tiredness. He would take a few, but not all the precautions he had been recommended, and leave the rest to fate.

He opened a small attaché-case on the seat beside him

and took out letters and papers. The proofs of his first *Times* article—how well it looked—"by Ainsley Jergwin Fothergill, author of 'Rubber and the Rubber Industry' "! He seemed to be staring appreciatively at the work of another person—the hardworking, painstaking person who had spent five years in Kuala Simur. Five years of self-discipline and orderliness, with the little rubber trees all in line across the hillside to typify a certain inner domestication of his own soul. He had liked the plantation work; it had given him grooves just when most of all he had wanted grooves. To save himself he had plunged into rubber-growing with a fervor that had startled everybody, especially his brother; and the result, by an ironic twist of fortune, had come to be two things he had never known before—a status and a private income.

He turned over a few letters. One from his publisher, enclosing a check for six months' royalties and suggesting a small "popular" book in a half-crown series—something rather chatty and not too technical—could he do it? . . . It would be rather interesting to try, at any rate. . . . A letter from Philippa, hoping he would manage another visit soon—he could come any time he liked and stay as long as he liked—"both Sybil and I are looking forward so much to seeing you again."

He would never, in all probability, see either of them again.

A letter from a firm of enquiry agents in New York City, dated several months back and addressed to him in Paris: "With reference to your recent enquiry, we regret that up to the present we have found it impossible to obtain any information. We are, however, continuing to investigate, and will report to you immediately should any development occur." Another letter, some weeks later: "We are very glad to be at last able to report progress. It appears that the child was adopted by a family named Consett, of Red Springs, Colorado, middle-class people of English descent, moderately well-off. Mr. Consett died in 1927. We have had difficulty in tracing the rest of the family since then. They left Red Springs, and are believed to have gone to Philadelphia. We are continuing our enquiries." A third letter, dated three weeks back: "We are now able to inform you that Mrs. Consett and daughter crossed the Atlantic in November of last year and spent Christmas at Algiers. Our European representative, to whom we have cabled instructions, will take the matter in hand as from there." A fourth letter, from this European representative, conveyed the information that the Consetts had left Algiers with the intention of touring in France, Germany, and the United Kingdom. Pretty vague, that, but a fifth letter had narrowed it down to "England and Ireland," and a sixth letter—the one that had arrived only the day before—had stated, with admirable definiteness: "I understand that Mrs. and Miss Consett left Stratford-on-Avon on Tuesday last and crossed to Ireland. They are now believed to be staying at the Shelburne Hotel, Dublin."

He gathered the letters into a pile and took them into the dining-car with him when he went to lunch. He was on the right-hand side of the train, whence he could see the North Wales coast, blue sea and sandy shore, streaming past the window like a cinema-film. Crowds of holiday-makers, pierrot entertainers, bathers bobbing up and down in the water, a sudden jangle of goods yard, a station, a tunnel, the sea and shore again, deserted for an odd half-mile or so; then bungalows, boarding-houses, a promenade, a bandstand, bathing-huts, crowds, a jangle

284

of goods yard, a station—on, on, beyond the soup to the fish and the underdone roast beef of that very English and mediocre train-lunch.

He arrived in Dublin at seven that night, and drove straight to the Shelburne. The Consetts, he learned from the hotel-porter, had gone on to Killarney two days before. "Americans, sir. See Killarney and die—you know the kind of thing? After that, I expect they'll be rushing to kiss the Blarney Stone."

He stayed at the Shelburne for the night and caught the morning express to Killarney. The porter at the Shelburne had given him the names of some of the more likely hotels, and it was easy to drive from one to another making enquiries. At a third asking he discovered that the Consetts had left that morning for Carrigole, Co. Cork, where they were almost bound to be staying at Roone's Hotel.

There was no railway to Carrigole, so he hired a car to drive him the forty odd miles over the hills. It was a marvelous summer afternoon, just beginning to fade into the soft glow of evening; by the time he reached the top of the pass and the driver pointed out Carrigole harbor in the distance, all the world seemed melting into a rarefied purple dusk. After the metropolitan bustle of Dublin and the stage-Irishness of Killarney, this, he felt, was the real Ireland, and immediately, in a way he hardly understood, he felt kinship with it. Successive days of travel had increased his fatigue, but the calm, tranquil mountain-air was uplifting him, giving him satisfaction, almost buoyancy.

It was dark when he reached Roone's, and the yellow oil-lamps were lit in the tiled hall and under the built-out veranda. Somehow by instinct as he took his first step in that cool interior he knew that he would have to go no further, and for that reason he did not ask about the Consetts when he booked a room. All that would come later; he must give himself the pleasure of doing everything sweetly and with due proportion. "May I have dinner?" he enquired, and was directed to a room whose windows, ranging from floor to ceiling along one side, showed the still darkly glowing harbor with the mountains brooding over it as in some ancient, kindly conspiracy.

The room was fairly full, but he had a table to himself, and the dinner was good. The faces of others glowed yellow-brown in the lamplight; the night was full of talking and laughing, the bark of a dog, the hoot of cars entering the drive; yet permeating it all, in a queer way, there was silence—silence such as seemed to rise out of the very earth and sea to meet the sky.

He chatted to the waiter; it was his first visit to Carrigole, he explained, or for that matter to Ireland at all. "You seem pretty full—the height of the season, I dare say?"

"Just a little past it, sir. We get a lot of American tourists in June and July, but most of them are beginning to go back by now."

"Ah, yes. I suppose, though, a few of the people here now are Americans?"

"Oh, yes, quite a number. Most of them come on from Killarney and stay here a night or so on their way to Cork."

He did not enquire further, but that evening, after dinner, the problem became merely one of identification. For he was asked to sign the hotel-register, and as he wrote "A. J. Fothergill—London—British" he glanced up the column of names and read in plain round handwriting a few inches above—"Mrs. and Miss Consett, Philadelphia."

He lit a cigar and took coffee in the lounge and wondered who they might be among the faces that passed him by. It would be simple, of course, to enquire directly, to approach them with equal directness, to introduce himself remarkably and dramatically, to talk till midnight about the exceeding singularity of the fate that had linked, then sundered, and now linked again his life and the girl's. Yet he shrank from it; his mind was sore from drama, aching for some quieter contact, for something at first and perhaps always remote. He wanted everything to be peaceful, gradual, even if it were additionally intricate; he wanted to preserve some path of secret retreat, so that at any moment, if he grew too tired, he could escape into forgotten anonymity. Yet, on the other hand, there was some urgency in the matter that he could not avoid, for the Consetts might not be staying at Carrigole for long, and he could not undertake to follow them all over the world.

Chance came to his aid. The post arrived at Roone's rather late; he saw the bundle of letters brought in by the cyclist-postman and handed across the counter to Mrs. Roone, who began to sort them. A cluster of people gathered around, and suddenly he heard a girl's voice asking if there were anything for Mrs. Consett.

There was, and she took a letter, studying its envelope as she walked away across the tiled hall to a table under the veranda where a woman sat reading a magazine.

For a moment he did not look at either of them; all had happened so calmly and comfortably. Then he suddenly knew that his heart was beating very fast. That would never do. He *must* see them; he *must* know what they were like. He got up and strolled deliberately by, puffing at his cigar and appearing to stare through the windows at nothing. The woman was plump, cheerful, talkative, fairly attractive; but the girl was less ordinary. She was quiet, rather well-featured, with calm brown eyes that were looking at him before his dared to look at her. It was curious, he thought, that she should have stared first.

He went to bed, slept well, and was down early for breakfast. The Consetts came in later, but to a table at the other end of the room. During the meal the waiter asked him if he would care to join an excursion to visit an ancient hermitage some score miles away over the hills. "It is quite interesting, sir," he recommended, "and if you have nothing else in mind, it would make a pleasant trip."

"Are most of the others going?"

"Practically everybody, sir, except the fishing gentlemen."

"I don't want to have a lot of walking to do."

"There is hardly any—you just drive right there by car."

"All right, I dare say I'll go."

It was a chance, he realized, and perhaps a better one than many others.

Four large five-seater touring-cars were drawn up outside the hotel. The excursionists arranged themselves as they chose, usually, of course, maneuvering to be with their friends. It was natural that he should wait rather diffidently until most had taken positions, and that, as an odd man, he should be fitted into the back seat of one of the cars with two other persons. Partly by luck and partly by his own contrivance, those two compulsory fellow-passengers were the Consetts. He was at one side of the car, Mrs. Consett at the other; the girl sat in between them. The driver and a large picnic-hamper shared the seat in front.

The convoy set off at eleven o'clock through lanes full of wild flowers and spattered with sunshine from a dappled sky. The harbor, reaching out into the long narrow inlet, gleamed like a sword-blade; the hills were purple-gray and a little hazy in the distance. He passed some merely polite remark about the weather, and the girl answered him in the same key. But the woman, seizing the opportunity, began to talk. She talked in a strong, copious stream, with never-flagging zest and ever-increasing emphasis. Wasn't Ireland lovely?—had he visited Killarney?—had he been on the lake and up to the Gap of Dunloe? *They* had—a most beautiful and romantic excursion, but the flies had been a nuisance during the picnic-lunch, and the food from the hotel had been just *awful*. It was a curious thing, but the hotels over this side seemed to have no idea . . . etc., etc.

He listened, occasionally venturing some remark. He said, in response to questioning, that he had never been to America, but had traveled a little in Europe. That opened further flood-gates. He received a full and detailed account of the Consett odyssey from the very day it had begun at Philadelphia. Paris, Interlaken, the Rhine, Munich, Innsbruck, Rome, Algiers, Seville (for Easter), Biarritz, Lourdes, Chartres, Ostend, the battle-fields, London, Oxford, Cambridge, Stratford-on-Avon, Dublin . . . how much they had seen, even if how little. They had loved it all, of course, and Mrs. Consett added, across the girl, as it were: "Mary is just eighteen, you see,

289

and it is *such* an impressionable age, I think, and I *do* so want her to see the world when she is young, because later on, you know, one can never be sure of getting such chances—in America *so* many women live narrow, self-centered lives after they marry—they think they're seeing the world if they spend a week in New York. My own brothers and sisters, for instance, who live in Colorado, have *never* traveled further than Los Angeles, and even *I* never saw Europe till Mary and I landed last fall. And now, though I'm *terribly* ashamed to think of what I'd missed for so long, yet I'm just glad to know that Mary's seeing all these marvelous places at an age when everything means most—the Coliseum at Rome, for instance, and Westminster Abbey, the Shakespeares' *dear* little house, and those *quaint* little jaunting-cars they have at Killarney—have you been on them? We had a most amusing driver to take us—so amusingly Irish—I quite intended to make notes of some of his remarks when I got back to the hotel, but I was just *too* tired after the long drive, and it was *such* a beautiful drive—rather like parts of Virginia. . . ." And so on, and so on.

They reached the hermitage about noon; it was a collection of ruins on an island off the shore of a lake—the latter overshadowed by gloomy mountains and reached by a narrow, twisting road over a high pass. The island was still a place of pilgrimage, and many of the arched cells in which the hermits had lived were littered with tawdry votive offerings—beads, buttons, lead-pencils, pieces of ribbon—a quaint miscellany for the rains and winds to disintegrate. The tourists made the usual vague inspection and turned with relief to the more exciting business of finding a place for lunch. Fothergill still remained with the Consetts; indeed, rather to his private amusement, he realized that it would have been difficult to be rid of them in any case. Mrs. Consett had by that time given him the almost complete history of her family and was engaged on a minute explanation of the way in which her husband had made money out of steam-laundries. From that, as the picnic-lunch progressed, she passed on to a sententious discussion of family life in general and of the upbringing of children in particular. At this point a sudden commotion amongst the rest of the party gave the girl an excuse to move away, for which Fothergill did not blame her, though it left him rather unhappily at the mercy of Mrs. Consett. Soon, however, an opportunity arose for himself also; the men of the party began to pack up the hampers and carry them to the cars. He attached himself to their enterprise for a sufficiently reasonable time, and then strolled off on his own, deliberately oblivious of the fact that Mrs. Consett was waiting for him to resume his rôle of listener. He walked towards the lake and across the causeway to the island— a curious place, of interest to him because, with its child-like testimonies of faith, it reminded him of things he had seen in Russia. Was it too fanciful, he wondered, to imagine a spiritual kinship between the countries? He was thus reflecting when he saw the open doors of a small modern chapel built amidst a grove of trees; and inside the building, which was scarcely bigger than the room of a small house, he caught sight of the girl. She heard his footsteps and turned round, smiling slightly.

"I didn't notice this place when we first went round," he remarked, approaching.

"Neither did I. It's really so tiny, isn't it?—quite the tiniest I've ever seen. And isn't it terribly ugly?"

It was—garishly so in a style which again reminded

291

him of Russia. The comparison was so much on his mind that without any ulterior motive he added: "I've seen the same sort of thing abroad—especially in Russia. Simple people always love crude colors and too much ornament."

She seized on that one vital word. "You know Russia then?"

"Fairly well. I used to live there."

"Did you like it?"

"Very much, in some ways."

"I wish mother and I could have gone there, but I suppose it isn't really safe for tourists yet."

"I dare say it would be safe enough, but I should think it would hardly be comfortable."

"Oh, then it wouldn't do at all." She laughed in a way which Fothergill liked instantly and exceedingly—a deep fresh laugh as from some spring-like fountain of humor. "Mother hates hotels where you don't get a private bathroom next to your bedroom."

"She can't be very keen on Roone's, then."

"I don't think she is, but I just love it. I'd hate to find everything exactly like the Plaza at New York. Besides, I don't think it really matters if you miss the morning bath once now and again."

"No, I don't think it really does." And they smiled at each other, sharing their first confidence.

As they left the chapel he was surprised to see her genuflect; so she was a Catholic, then. That set him thinking of the profound reasonableness of Catholics in holding their faith in reverence while at the same time being free to call one of their churches ugly if it *were* ugly; and that, in turn, set him thinking of the reasonableness of Father

Harington, and of that long conversation in London before he left. . . .

She was saying: "What *is* your name, by the way?"

"Fothergill."

"Ours is Consett. I don't know whether you knew."

"I did, as a matter of fact. I overheard you asking for letters last night."

"Oh, did you? That must have been before you passed us on the veranda, then? I noticed you particularly because—I dare say you'll smile at this—you looked what in America we should call 'typically English.'"

"'Typically English,' eh?" And for the first time for some years he was thoroughly astonished. To be called *that,* of all things!

She said: "The quiet way, I suppose, that Englishmen have—a sort of look of being rather bored by everything, though really they're not bored at all. Perhaps I oughtn't to have said it, though—you don't look very complimented."

He smiled. "Would *you* be complimented if I were to describe you as 'typically American'?"

She paused a moment and then gave him a look of amused candor. "That's rather clever of you, because I wouldn't. And, anyhow, in my own case—" She stopped hurriedly, and he said, holding open the wicket-gate for her to pass from the island on to the causeway: "Yes, what were you about to say?"

"I was really going to say that I'm not an American at all."

"Oh?"

There was rather a long interval until she went on: "It's queer to be telling you all this after knowing you for about five minutes—I don't know what mother would think. But, as it happens, you once lived in Russia, so perhaps that's an excuse. I'm Russian."

"Indeed?"

"Yes. I came over with the refugees in 1919. That sounds a bit like coming over with the Pilgrim Fathers, doesn't it, but it's really not quite so illustrious. There were just a few hundred refugee orphans who were allowed into America before the government woke up and decided it didn't want any more of them. They were all adopted into families in various parts of the country. I was six when I came over."

"That makes you how old now?"

"Just eighteen."

"I don't suppose you remember much of your life in Russia."

"Hardly anything. Sometimes I dream of things which I think might have something to do with it. I wonder if that's possible?"

"It might be."

"Here comes mother to meet us. I think I'd better tell her how much I've told you."

The confession was made, and Mrs. Consett, after hearing all the circumstances, bestowed her magnanimous approval. It enabled her to continue the conversation with Fothergill on rather more intimate lines, and this she did all the way during the drive back to Roone's. "So curious that we should all be learning about one another so quickly, isn't it? But there, I always think that one should take all the chances one can of making friends wherever one goes—I'm sure Mary and I have already met some *charming* people during our trip—there was a most *delightful* man in the hotel at Naples—a Swiss—only a commercial traveler, I surmised—but still, who are we to be snobbish? I'm sure I never try to conceal the fact that my husband made his money out of other people's washing. But this Swiss man, as I was saying, was such a pleasant companion—he went to Pompeii with us to see those wonderful Roman ruins—and he was most helpful, too, when we wanted to buy anything in the shops. I should think he saved us quite a lot of money, for, as you know, the Italians think every American must be a millionaire, though, as a matter of fact, we're not really very well-off—we've been saving up for this trip for quite a time, haven't we, Mary?" And so on.

When they all reached Roone's again it was quite settled that they should arrange with the waiter to have a larger table, so that they could take meals together. They dined that night, the three of them, by the side of the large window, through which the harbor burned with little, dark specks on it that were the rowboats bringing the fishermen ashore by dusk. After the outdoor air and the long drive over the mountains he felt tired, yet in a way that gave him a certain rich serenity, breaking only into fitful astonishment that she should be there, that he should have found and spoken with her after so many years. But it was she herself who astonished him most of all. The lamplight touched the ivory white of her face with a glow of amber, and there were five lamps, hung on chains from the ceiling, making islands of light in the huge dark room. Her eyes were like pools that might have been in a forest, and the creamy sweep of her neck against that background reminded him of some old, brown, Vandyke painting. Contentment closed over him as he looked at her; Mrs. Consett's continual talking echoed in his ears, yet somehow was not heard; all about the room was chatter, rising to the roof and hovering there, yet to him it was no more than a murmur—as if, he thought fantastically, some monster choir at an immense distance were intoning Latin genitive plurals.

So began a week of purest holiday. The Consetts, it appeared, had no definite plans; they just stayed in one place as long as they liked, and Roone's was apparently suiting them, despite the lack of private bathrooms. The weather, too, held out in a blaze of splendor just beginning to be autumnal; every morning when Fothergill rose and saw through his window the gray-green mountains across the harbor he felt a surge of happiness that reminded him, not of his own childhood, but of some remoter and more marvelously recollected childhood of the world. Then after breakfast came plans for the day—delightful arguments in the veranda-lounge, while Mrs. Roone was packing sandwiches for them, and Roone was tapping the barometer and prophesying fine weather. It was always Mrs. Consett who seemed to make the plans, yet always Fothergill who did the real work of organizing—finding the route on roadmaps, seeing that food was sufficient, arranging terms with motor-drivers. Then they would set out under the long avenue of just fading leaves, swing down the winding hill through the village, and up the further hill to the mountains. He felt the years falling away from him as he rose into that zestful air, and when they halted for picnic-lunch at some lonely vantage-point, with the valleys like clouds beneath them, he was a child again in his enjoyment. He loved the fire-making routine—the collecting of sticks on the hillsides, with the girl but calling distance away from him, and her mother dozing in the car a hundred feet below; the finding of large stones to build a hearth; the careful watching till the kettle boiled at last. Once, tempted by a glorious sunset, they stayed late round a fire they had made at tea-time and talked till the flames seemed to bring all the darkness suddenly over their heads. As she stirred the fire to a last blaze before they left it, the girl remarked on the heat of the big stones, and he said: "If I were going to camp here for the night I should wrap one of those stones in a piece of blanket and use it instead of a hot-water bottle. That's always a good dodge if you're sleeping out."

"Have you ever slept out?"

"Oh, often."

"You seem to have done all kinds of things."

"*Many* kinds of things, perhaps."

"I wish you'd tell some of your adventures."

"I might, sometime."

Yet he continually put it off. Partly, of course, because it was always easier to do so; Mrs. Consett's chatter was a strong current that *could* be swum against, but it was far less trouble to relax and let it carry one along. And partly, too, because he felt a curious reluctance to break the tranquillity of those simple days, and what tranquillity or simplicity could remain after he had told his entire story?

He had, in fact, few chances of talking to the girl alone, and he could not, he felt, tell her the final secret—her own identity—at any other time.

One night, after dinner, someone brought a gramophone into the tiled hall and put on dance records. The girl asked him if he danced and he replied, smiling: "I'm afraid I don't—I never learned, and I'm too old now." She said: "I'll teach you, then," and as other couples were by that time moving from their seats, he replied, with sudden decision: "Will you? All right." He found it easy; she was a good pilot, and he himself had a sure sense of rhythm. "As if you were too old to learn," she whispered, reproachfully, as they drifted in amidst the lamp-lit shadows. "I don't think you're really too old for anything."

"Although I'm nearly three times your own age?"

"That doesn't matter. You don't *feel* old, do you? And if anyone saw you when you were making a fire for a picnic, they'd think you were only a boy."

"Really?"

"Yes. I was watching you this afternoon. You *were* enjoying it, weren't you?"

"Absolutely, I admit."

"So was I. I don't think I've ever got to know anybody so quickly as I have you. It seems rather an awful thing to say, but sometimes—sometimes I wish mother wasn't quite so—so *everywhere*—and *always*—she's a dear, but she does chatter terribly, doesn't she?"

"Just as well, perhaps, because I'm not much of a talker myself."

"Neither am I, yet I'd rather like to give ourselves a chance. By the way, were you once a rubber planter out in the Malay States?"

"Sumatra, it was. But how did you know?"

"Oh, mother seems to have been finding out all about you. She happened to see an article in the London *Times*, and thought it must be you, from the name and initials. Then someone else told her—some people staying here, but I think they've gone now—that you'd been a planter out there and had made heaps of money."

"It depends how much you mean by heaps."

She laughed. "Personally, I'm not very curious, but

mother seems to think you're a millionaire traveling incognito, or something of that sort."

He laughed also. "You can contradict the rumor," he assured her.

They went on dancing. They danced, in fact, with hardly a pause until nearly midnight, and when they finally rejoined Mrs. Consett he said, with eyes and cheeks glowing: "Your daughter is a most charming teacher. I hope we haven't been allowing the lesson to last too long?"

"Oh, not at all—not at all." Indeed, she seemed quite pleased.

He was tired that night when he went to bed, but it was the sort of tiredness to be expected after a day on the mountains and an evening of fox-trots. Curiously, in a way, he felt much better since he had begun the more strenuous life of Roone's; it seemed to tire him far less to scramble up a mountain in search of fuel for a picnic-fire than to take leisurely strolls along city pavements.

The girl and he had more time together during the second week; there were occasions when Mrs. Consett professed fatigue and said she would write letters in the lounge while they, if they cared, took a walk. Roone's was growing emptier; the eight months' season of slack business was approaching and the first gales of autumn had already laid bare the trees in the woods. As an offset to the general exodus of visitors, a light cruiser came to anchor in Carrigole Bay for a few days' visit. Most of the officers and men came ashore to Roone's; bluejackets swarmed into the public bar, while the hall and the long veranda terraces were filled with shouting and laughing naval officers. Every night they kept up their merriment to a late hour and most of the day a group of them hung about the counter in the hall, chatting and joking with the Roones.

One morning Fothergill and the girl made the ascent of the Baragh, a steep, cone-shaped peak that rose a thousand feet at the back of the hotel. An hour of scrambling through heather brought them to the summit, whence could be seen the roofs of Carrigole and the long bay stretching westward into the sunlit sea.

*Now,* he felt, as he sat on a rough stone with the sweep of sea and mountain all around him and the girl seated on another stone somewhat below,—*now* was just his chance. He could talk without interruption; he could begin at the beginning and tell all that was to be told.

Yet he didn't even begin to tell. Another thought came to him—that in all the world she was probably the only person he would ever meet who had ever known Daly— the sole surviving contact with all in his own life that had mattered most. And that dark passion of his, subdued for years, spilled over now in a little tender flood of affection for the girl.

Suddenly she said: "Do you remember I told you I sometimes had dreams that might have something to do with the time before I left Russia?"

He nodded.

"I had a dream of that sort last night. Too queer to be remembered, really, but the queerest part was that you were mixed up in it somehow."

"*I* was?"

"Yes. We seemed to be going somewhere all the time —just one place after another—and at night we slept out in the open and used hot stones for water-bottles." She laughed. "Isn't it curious the way everything gets mixed up in dreams?"

The chance to tell her was again full on him, yet once again he forebore. He was still wrestling with memories of those old and epic days. He said, abruptly: "Are you happy in America? What do you do there? Tell me the kind of life you have."

She looked amused. "I rather thought mother had told you everything you ever wanted to hear about our home life. As a matter of fact, we really *do* have a good time and get on splendidly together. We play a little bridge and tennis (though we're both very bad), and we just have money enough to travel now and again and go to theaters and have friends to stay with us. I shall have to earn my own living, of course, for which I'm rather glad —I think it's a mistake to do nothing but idle about and wait to be married to somebody."

"Don't you wish you'd been born rich, or high up in the world—a princess, say?"

"I wouldn't mind if I'd been born rich, though I don't suppose it would have made me any happier. And as for being a princess, when I feel romantic I sometimes try to kid myself that I *am* one—after all, nobody knows who I really am, do they?"

"I suppose not."

"Though I dare say I wouldn't really like it if I were. It must be very tiresome having to be important all the time. It would stop me from doing things like this, wouldn't it?"

"Like *this?*"

"Yes. Scrambling up a mountain with you."

He laughed—a sudden almost boyish laugh that startled the mountain silences. "Yes, you're right. You're happier as you are, no doubt."

"I *know* I am. Oh, it *has* been such fun, traveling all

over Europe ever since nearly a year ago, and the queer thing is, it all somehow seems to have been leading up to this. I mean this—here—now—just *this.*" She looked at him quickly and then stared far across the distance to the furthest horizon. "I like these mountains ever so much better than the Swiss ones, don't you? I suppose it's heresy to say so, but the Alps rather remind me of wedding-cake."

And all the time and all the way down as they descended he was thinking of something else—of gilded salons and baroque antechambers, of consulates and embassies and chancelleries, of faded uniforms and tarnished orders, of intrigues and plottings and counter-plottings, of Paris cafés where Russian émigrés passed their days on a treadmill of futile anticipation, of Riviera hotels where the very waiters were princes and expected extra tips for so being, of dark and secret assassinations, of frontiers stiff with bayonets, of men in Moscow council-rooms, ruthless, logical, and aware. That madly spinning world lay so close, and it was in his power to thrust her into the very vortex of it.

That night he took out of a sealed envelope certain curiously-marked papers. They were twelve years old; time and a fumigating oven had considerably faded them. He looked them through and then replaced them in the envelope. It was late, past midnight; the sailors had returned to their ship; even the Roones had gone to bed, and the lamps in the corridor were all out. He groped his way downstairs and found the drawing-room. There was the remains of a fire just faintly red in the grate; he knelt on the hearth-rug and fanned the embers till they glowed into flame. Then he placed the envelope on the top and watched it burn with all its contents. He waited till the last inch was turned to ashes and he could break and scatter them with the poker. Then he went back to his room and to bed.

But he did not sleep too well. If one problem had been settled, another remained; if he had not traced her in order to tell her who she was, why had he traced her at all? What need was there to stay at Roone's any longer? And so, bewitching and insidious, came again the memory of the past; she was a shadow, an echo, reminding him that he was still young, and that the Harley Street man might have made a mistake. And the idea came to him that he might tell her some day, not about her own identity, which did not matter, but about himself and Daly.

The next morning began a chaotic interlude of travel; he wired to his London lawyer and the two arranged a halfway meeting at the railway hotel at Fishguard. The dignified elderly solicitor, obviously flustered by such hectic arrangements, scratched away for an hour in a private sitting-room; then Fothergill signed; and two hotel servants acted as witnesses and were suitably rewarded. The lawyer saw his client off on the Rosslare boat and parted from him full of misgivings. "It is not for me to offer criticism, Mr. Fothergill," he said, accepting a drink in the saloon before the gangways were lowered, "but I do hope you have given all this your most careful consideration." Fothergill assured him that he had, and added: "Anyhow, I hope I'm not going to die just yet—it's only a precaution." To which the lawyer replied: "I must say I think you're looking very much better than when I saw you in London," and Fothergill answered: "My dear chap, I really don't think I ever felt better in my life. It's the Irish climate—it seems to suit me."

He was at Roone's again by the afternoon of the next

day, with Mrs. Consett immensely curious about his lightning dash to England. "Business," he told her, and she was satisfactorily impressed; her idea of the successful business man was perfectly in accord with such fantastic journeys on mysterious errands.

Back at Roone's he yielded again to the spell of magic possibility. Could he tell her about their earlier meeting when she was but a child; could he thus make fast to his own life this new and charming fragrance that might otherwise fade away?

So he perplexed himself, but that Saturday night as he saw her talking to a young naval sub-lieutenant he came to sudden decision. He saw her smiling at the pink-cheeked and handsome boy; he heard their laughter together; then they danced, and all at once, as he watched them, he felt old again and knew that he was old; and when Mrs. Consett began her usual chatter, he felt: We are a couple of old folks, watching the youngsters amuse themselves. . . .

But half an hour later she came up to him, having left her partner, and said: "Don't you want to dance tonight, Mr. Fothergill? I suppose you're tired after the journey?" And he was up in a moment, ready to whirl through the world with her, old or young.

She said, as they danced: "That was a nice boy, if he wasn't so silly."

"I thought he looked a very attractive young fellow."

"Yes—but silly. I suppose most girls like it and I'm the exception. I never could get on very well with boys of that age."

"*That* age, indeed? I wouldn't be surprised if he's half a dozen years older than you."

"Yes, I know—it's strange, isn't it? Perhaps the silliness is in me, after all."

"In you?"

"Why not? Probably I'm old for my years. I've a sort of theory that I aged a good deal before I was six and that now I'm anything between thirty and forty."

"That would put you nearer me."

"Yes, wouldn't it?"

Her calm friendly eyes were looking up at him, and he had to exert every atom of will-power to prevent himself from yielding to the call of so rich a memory. His brain reeled and eddied; he began to speak, but found his voice so grotesque and uncertain that he broke off and tried to fix himself into some kind of temporary coherence; he heard her saying: "I don't think you're dancing very well tonight—you look as if your mind's on something else all the time."

"As a matter of fact, it just is."

"Shall we stop, then? *I* don't mind. Perhaps you feel tired?"

"I never felt less tired in my life. What I'd just like now is to go out and climb the Baragh."

"Really? Do you mean it—really?"

He hadn't, at first, but he did then, suddenly. "Yes," he said.

"Well, we could, couldn't we? It's bright moonlight and we know the way. It's quite early—we should be back before the others begin clearing off to bed. I love doing odd things that most people would think quite mad."

They slipped out through the veranda and began, hatless and coatless, the steep scramble through the woods, drenched with dew, and then up the rough bowlderstrewn boreen to the summit. They climbed too swiftly and breathlessly for speech, and all the way he was dizzily making up his mind for all the things he would say when they reached the topmost ridge. He imagined himself telling her: "Dear child, you are all that means anything in my life, and I want to tell you how and why—I want you to know how I missed my way in life, over and over again, yet found in the end something that was worth it all." And other confessions equally wild and enchanting. But when he stood finally on that moonlit peak, with the sky a blue-black sea all around him, he could not think of anything to say at all. She stood so still and close to him, thrilling with rapture at the view, pointing down excitedly to the tiny, winking lights of the cruiser, and then swinging round to peer into the silver dimness of the valley on the other side. "I shall never, never forget this as long as I live," she whispered. "It's far more wonderful than in the daytime when we climbed before."

Then suddenly he realized why, or perhaps one reason why, he was not speaking. He was in pain. He felt as if a bar of white-hot steel were bending round his body and being tightened. Yet he hardly felt the pain, even though he knew it was there; it was as if the moonlight and the thoughts that swam in his mind were anesthetizing him. He opened his mouth and tried to speak, but could only hear himself gasping; and he felt, beyond the knowledge of pain, an impotent fury with his body for spoiling such a moment. He smiled a twisted smile; he had been too venturesome, too defiant; he had climbed too fast. And all at once, just then, the thought came to him: supposing I were to drop dead, up here—poor child, what a shock it would be for her, and what a lot of damned unpleasant fuss for her afterwards. . . .

"You *are* tired," she said, staring at him intently. "Shall we go down?"

He nodded slowly and hoped she did not see the tears that were filling his eyes.

They began the descent, and after a few yards she took his arm and helped him over the rough places. Half-way down he felt better; the pain was beginning to leave him. "I'm sorry," he said.

"Sorry? For what? I enjoyed it ever so much, but it tired you, I could see—we mustn't do such mad things again."

"Except that I like mad things just as much as you do."

She smiled, and he smiled back, and with her arm still linked in his he felt a marvelous happiness enveloping him, especially now that the pain was subsiding with every second.

"I'm not so bad for my age," he added. "I suppose I oughtn't to expect to be able to skip up and down mountains like an eighteen-year-old."

"Your age?" she said, quietly. "I never think of it, or of mine either. What does it matter?"

He laughed, then; he was so happy; and now that the pain had all gone he could believe it had been no more than a fit of breathlessness after the climb—a warning, no doubt, that he must avoid such strenuous risks in future. His only big regret was that he had missed the chance of telling her what had been in his mind, but it was too late now—the lights of the hotel were already glimmering through the trees. As they entered along the veranda he said: "I really *am* sorry for being such an old crock—sorry on my own account, anyway, because I'd rather wanted to have a particular talk with you about something."

307

"Had you? And you'd stage-managed it for the top of a mountain in moonlight—how thrilling! But it will do somewhere else, surely?"

He laughed. "Of course. The question is when rather than where."

"Why not tomorrow morning? We could go out on the harbor in the motor-boat—mother wouldn't come with us—she hates sailing."

"Good idea. That'll do fine."

"Directly after Mass, then. I think they'll be having it in the hotel tomorrow—I heard Roone saying something about it. That'll save the walk down to the village and we can have a longer time on the water."

"Splendid."

"And I'm so thrilled to wonder what you have to tell me."

"*Are* you?"

But later, after she had said good night and gone to bed, his mood of perplexity changed. Beyond a certain natural fatigue he felt himself no worse for the mountain adventure, but to brace himself after the strain he did what he had not often done at Roone's—he went into the bar for a night-cap. The Roones were there, with a few naval men and a fishing youth in plus-fours; they tried to get him into conversation, but he said little and stayed only for a few minutes. The fact was, he could not even *think* of anything but the talk he would have on the morrow.

Then he took his candle (Roone's was old-fashioned enough for that) and went to his room on the first floor. He would get up early, he decided, and go to Mass—his first for so long—*too* long. He saw the moon and the clear sky through the window, promising another fine

308

day. He saw the cruiser's masthead light shimmering softly over the harbor. He undressed and got into bed and closed his eyes—the whisky had made him drowsy—and suddenly, falling asleep, he felt most magnificently and boyishly certain of everything, and especially of love.

**THE END**